SECOND SITTING

Casey Jones is Entertainment Director on board the luxurious *Countess Georgina* for her trip to the Caribbean. Casey's days – and nights – are filled with an endless stream of prima-donna singers and feather-clad chorus girls. But when a guest collapses during the second sitting at table two, and later dies, Casey finds herself trying to uncover a bizarre chain of events – helped by the gorgeous Cruise Doctor, Samuel Mallory.

SECOND SITTING

A Casey Jones Cruise Ship Mystery

Stella Whitelaw

Severn House Large Print
London & New York

This first large print edition published 2009
in Great Britain and the USA by
SEVERN HOUSE PUBLISHERS LTD of
9-15 High Street, Sutton, Surrey, SM1 1DF.
First world regular print edition published 2008 by
Severn House Publishers Ltd., London and New York.

British Library Cataloguing in Publication Data

Whitelaw, Stella.
  Second sitting. -- (A Casey Jones cruise ship mystery)
  1. Cruise ships--Fiction. 2. Detective and mystery
  stories. 3. Large type books.
  I. Title II. Series
  823.9'14-dc22

  ISBN-13: 978-0-7278-7821-2

Printed and bound in Great Britain by
MPG Books Ltd, Bodmin, Cornwall.

To
Harriet and Thomas McKew
grandparents, soulmates

Acknowledgements

With gratitude and thanks to the staff of Oxted Library and Worthing Library for coming up with the answers to a stream of questions. Also to Fran Reynolds, fabulous cruise ship dancer and now a very talented choreographer and producer.

P & O staff on board and on shore were so helpful and kind to an ignorant landlubber. Any nautical errors are entirely mine.

And, of course, as always thanks to my wonderful editor, Anna Telfer, who somehow managed to fit in a wedding while editing *Second Sitting*.

Prologue

A swarm of passengers were descending the sweeping stairs for the second sitting of dinner which was about to be served in the Windsor Dining Room on E deck. They were hungry, not starvation level but peckish, and a little apprehensive. Everything was so new and unknown. The bracing sea air could do strange things to people and the Bay of Biscay had claimed a few casualties.

They had to wait until eight thirty in the evening, which was late for eating and the temptation to nibble was hard to fight. The bar peanuts always went first. But then the first sitting at six thirty was too early for many. The first sitting had been uneventful. That was about to change. And it wasn't on the menu.

Some passengers had been hovering outside the dining room for ten minutes, talking and laughing with new friends or tablemates, wearing their classy best. The women's dresses were eye-catching and superb. Tonight's suggested dress was 'smart casual'. These were expensive clothes. I could recognize a designer label accurately at fifty yards. It was a useless gift. I could spot Top Shop and Monsoon, too. I'm no snob.

7

The Windsor Dining Room was the last word in ocean-going elegance. This was good living in a sumptuous setting. Beautifully set tables with white linen, silver cutlery, china embossed with the Conway Blue Line emblem and sparkling glasses. The napkins were folded differently every evening.

This evening, the second dinner out of Southampton docks, the napkins were folded into swans. Tomorrow would be the bishop's mitre. All the immaculately garbed waiters were trained in folding. They cleared and reset the empty tables with swift efficiency. The dining-room staff had very little time between sittings. They had to work fast. It was a finely honed operation.

The trace debris of the first-sitting diners vanished. There was one riotous table still drinking coffee and eating petit fours, fudge pyramids tonight topped with grated chocolate. Graham Ward, the head waiter, was making his way over to their table. They knew the rules, his steely eyes were saying. But he had to remember that they were also good tippers.

At last the dining room was ready. They heard the maître d'hôtel's announcement over the tannoy loudspeaker. He said it twice with a definite accent. Was it French, Spanish, Portuguese? Hard to tell.

'Second sitting is now being served in the Windsor Dining Room. Bon appétit,' he said with a certain aplomb.

The passengers filtered in, some still unsure of where they were sitting. There were tables of eight for couples and unaccompanied passen-

8

gers, tables of four, and select tables à deux.

I stood by the elaborate flower arrangement on one side of the double door entrance, smiling and nodding. I was being gracious and welcoming, part of my Keep the Passengers Happy job.

'Good evening, good evening,' I said as the diners went by into the room. Some smiled back, a few answered, not a clue who I was or why I was there. They saw a tall young woman in a sleek, shimmering rose-coloured dress, her dark, streaky hair pulled back into a tight chignon with a silver clip. There was a streak of blonde from the brow. Don't ask me how it got there. A stray gene. I look like a dancer, but of course, I didn't dance any more.

A table of eight would always be my choice. How could you really want to talk to the same person, every meal, for the entire cruise? Not unless he was Johnny Depp. He'd keep you amused and feeling special, be a different person every meal. Those eyes, that mouth. Hopefully not always a pirate, though I loved the beard. George Clooney would be second choice if Depp was busy.

I hovered in the atrium, watching the late-comers sauntering in, holding out their hands for a squirt of the antiseptic spray. Everyone had to be sprayed, no matter how posh or titled they were. It was a procedure more closely adhered to than in some hospitals.

This was lull-time, halfway between my appearances. I had to go back to the Princess Lounge soon, ready to MC the second presentation of tonight's show for the first-sitting passengers who were digesting their gargantuan meal. Life was a continuing, complicated round-about aboard the MV *Countess Georgina.* I needed to keep a strict eye on the time and my watch. Minutes counted. Even seconds could be crucial.

I always tried to get to know everyone on board. Hence the hovering outside the Windsor Dining Room. I was imprinting faces. Next I would try to learn their names and cabin numbers. I had a passenger manifest, even if no one else outside the purser's office had one.

And I didn't do it for the tips. No one tips the cruise entertainment director. They barely knew I existed. I was some exotic bird who floated around in the evening in gorgeous dresses, apparently having a high old time. If only they knew the behind-the-scenes flog and slog in my cramped office.

I read the menu displayed outside the dining room. It was on a stand between the two enormous displays of fresh flowers. The florists on board were good at their job. They took on huge consignments of fresh and frozen flowers at each port of call.

The selection of dishes advertised today abolished any diet. Avocado with raspberry vinaigrette and toasted pine nuts; blended mushroom and parsley soup; lemon sole meunière; tiger prawn and monkfish curry with summer vegetable goulash and wild rice; apricot pavlova with pineapple coulis. Four different kinds of rolls. Cheese, fresh fruit, candies, coffee and speciality teas. We didn't get quite the same food in the officer's mess down on deck F. It only sounded similar. This menu read like the Booker prize.

And there were lighter options offered. Who wanted lighter options? I suppose the thin people did. We had some seriously thin people aboard. Walking clothes pegs.

I was supposed to host one of the big tables but I rarely had time. This evening I made a brief appearance, introducing myself, making the seven passengers at the table feel at home. There was only time for the avocado and the soup tonight.

'Hello. I'm Casey Jones, the entertainment director,' I said, smiling as I sat down. 'I'll join you as often as I can but evenings are a very busy time as you can imagine. All the shows to MC. Make sure everything is going along smoothly.'

There were two tables of eight either side of the main entrance. They were on the raised outer level which skirted the dining room and gave the proportions more balance. Wide cabin windows flanked the walls but at night you couldn't see out of them. Sometimes there was an occasional flash of white phosphorescence dancing on the waves. Pretty to watch, if you had one of those tables. Passengers tipped heavily for a window seat.

I heard a crash as glasses and plates went flying and looked up. This was not an unusual occurrence with new waiters still finding their sea legs. They could clear up a disaster zone in minutes, whip on a clean tablecloth, lay fresh

11

cutlery and glasses, replace spilt drinks.

But there were raised voices also, some woman was screaming. A red-faced man was running out of the dining room. I followed him quickly. He was sweating and flapping. 'We need a doctor,' he shouted to anyone.

I picked up a nearby phone and dialled the medical centre. Everyone knew the extension by heart. It was drilled into every member of the crew. We could have dialled it in our sleep. Sometimes we had to.

'Dr Mallory,' came a laconic voice.

'Windsor Dining Room,' I said. 'Medical assistance required immediately.'

'What sort of medical assistance?'

'I don't know.' Wrong answer. Compose yourself, Casey.

'You should always find out,' said Dr Mallory abruptly. 'I should like to know whether I am going to deliver a baby, resuscitate a heart attack or stop femoral bleeding.'

'I'll go and find out.' I put the phone down and hurried back into the dining room. People at nearby tables were craning and staring, talking in hushed voices.

A man was sprawled across table two, his grey-haired head in a frothy puddle of wine. At least I thought it was wine. It couldn't be blood, surely not? A strange cherry-red colour. A glass of water had gone over as well as the wine. Two of the waiters were hauling the man to his feet. He hung in their arms like a particularly well-dressed scarecrow. His white shirt front was spotted with spreading stains of crimson. A

12

woman was still screaming, her mouth a gaping ruby hole. Another older woman, was patting the man's face and his hand, her face white with concern.

'George, George,' she was murmuring. 'Hold on. Help is coming.'

'I've phoned for the doctor. Is it a heart attack, do you think?'

'Yes, I think it's a heart attack,' she said.

'Don't move him,' I said quickly. 'The doctor is coming.'

The head waiter came over to me at speed. His face was expressionless, black tie only slightly askew. 'We are moving Mr Foster to a side room. It will be better. The other diners, you understand.'

'No, you mustn't move him till the doctor gets here.'

Graham Ward drew himself up to his full height and he was an imposing man.

'Nobody dies in my dining room,' he said, sternly. 'I'm sorry, Miss Jones, but I insist. Company policy.'

There was no answer to that.

One

Southampton

MV *Countess Georgina* was without doubt, a beautiful ship. A white lady. It would be easy to fall under her spell. The clean line of the bows, rising above the quayside, white and glistening, like an ocean clipper. Every inch of her scrubbed Persil white. She was so clean, you could eat off the decks and maybe some of the passengers did after a hilarious, on-deck Caribbean party. Rum punch afloat and streamers streaming.

I was about to find out. She beckoned to me. A new world. A medium-risk disclosure as they put pompously on my last learning curve.

She was not a top-heavy floating hotel. The *Countess* was a proper ship and looked like a ship. Her funnels had the Conway Blue Line emblem. One of the last majestic liners still sailing the oceans.

I stood under the towering hull, admiring the sweep of the bows, awed by the ship's size. This was the beginning of a dream, my new ambition, and I was here now, ready to grasp all that had been offered. My second chance. Nobody wake me up, please.

'Hello, *Countess*,' I said, tugging at my pull-along suitcase. 'Let's get aboard and see if you are as splendid inside as you are outside.'

I went up the crew gangplank. All the paperwork had been checked in the terminal. Endless queues at desks. Passengers arriving with mountains of luggage. Some were taking back-to-back cruises and needed twice the amount of everything. But at last I was actually going aboard, passport intact, all the right crew cards and passes, seaman's discharge book, etc.

The crew entrance was not as elegant as where the passengers stepped on board. Their first glimpse inside was the atrium, a circular space with a fountain and a sculpted tree in silver metal, very Japanese looking. This area had the sweeping reception desk, counters for excursion sales, flower sales, chocolates. And the double doors that lead into the Windsor Dining Room. Stewards leaped forward, greeted arriving passengers, taking any hand luggage and escorting them to their cabins. Passengers didn't have to push or pull anything. Only their passports and their credit cards.

I had to find my own way. The corridors were endless, winding and twisting. I wasn't sure if I was at the front or the back of the ship, that is the bows or the stern. It all looked the same once inside. I had been given cabin number 414 on E deck.

Then I realized I was hurrying along on the wrong side of the ship. These cabins were all uneven numbers. I needed to get over to the other side, which could be port or starboard. This was something I had to learn again.

Dancers never bothered with their left or right, unless it was in a dance routine. They used different signposts. Stage right, stage left, towards those curtains, the exit door, the lights, move diagonally or in a straight line.

I came to a fairly unpretentious lobby with a pair of lift doors and went across to the opposite corridor. Nice pictures though. All prints. Even numbers. This was it. I was getting tired of dragging my suitcase. The pull-handle didn't make the case any lighter. And I had a lot of clothes for my job.

A slim young Asian steward appeared, in his trim white uniform. 'Can I help you, miss?'

'Cabin 414, please. I'm not sure if I'm going the right way.'

'Yes, miss. This way. I will take your case. Follow me.'

He took my case and I followed him. I had no idea where he was taking me. Perhaps I had mistaken my contract and I was going to be set to work in the laundry. Somehow, in a very short time, like ten minutes, I had got to learn my way about this confusing labyrinth of decks and corridors. Across a closed door was a discreet sign: 'No Entrance – Crew Accommodation'. This was a signpost I had to remember. I spotted a fire extinguisher on the opposite side, another signpost, and a Monet garden print. My brain logged on.

The steward opened the door and ushered me along another corridor, and then used his key card to open the door to cabin 414.

'This is your cabin, miss. And I am your

17

steward, Ahmed. Your other suitcase has already come aboard. I have put it inside. Please ring if you would like some more hangers.' He was about twenty, had a very shy, uncertain smile. He was not sure what kind of crew member I was going to be. I knew that some could be very demanding.

I thanked him warmly. 'Thank you for showing me the way, Ahmed. I was quite lost. Yes, I would like to have some more hangers. I've brought an awful lot of clothes. And could I have a cup of tea, please?'

'There is a tray here for your tea and coffee making,' he said politely. Ah, so stewards didn't bring a china pot of tea on a tray these days, not on this line. 'I will bring you some hangers.'

He closed the door and I was left to look around my home for the next few months. It was basic, functional, not exactly spacious. The second single bed was folded against the wall, giving extra shelf space which would be handy for putting things out on and extra floor space. There was a desktop which doubled for a dressing table with a mirror and drawers underneath. Two fitted wardrobes had hanging space and shelves. The en suite bathroom was all white, functional, clean. Set of three towels. A shower gel fitment was attached to the wall, full of some blue stuff for showering and shampooing. I had my own shampoo for my unmanageable hair.

I liked the clean look. I like anything clean and plain.

There was a porthole, double-glazed, which was almost too high up to see out of. I stood on tiptoe and stretched up, managed a glimpse of watery blue sea which seemed very near. This deck was near sea level. One deck above the Plimsoll Line, probably. No opening of this porthole, ever.

The hospitality tray was on the desktop, and underneath was a small refrigerator. I liked the bottles of mineral water already provided.

There was a knock on the door and Ahmed stood there with an armful of wire hangers. Enough for a tribe of entertainment directors. He looked like a porcupine.

'Thank you so much, Ahmed,' I said. 'You're a total star.'

'Entertainment directors always have a lot of clothes,' he said, with a glimpse of mischief as if he had seen many come and go. Entertainment directors worked on a rota basis, so many months on board, a few weeks of shore leave, then back again. Not always the same ship. The Conway Blue Line had three main cruise ships, all *Countesses*, and several smaller ships, tankers and ferries too. The line was run by a woman, Gina Conway, who had inherited the line from her grandfather.

'They do indeed,' I said. 'It goes with the job. And thank you for the bottles of mineral water. Entertainment directors also drink a lot of water.'

A first smile touched his face. He nodded and closed the door.

'Hello, Miss Jones,' I said to my reflection in the mirror. My face was pale and tired from the long, stressful journey by train to Southampton.

There had been a points failure and I had started to imagine missing the ship. It was the crewman's nightmare, arriving in time to see your ship and your contract gliding away from the quayside. My stomach had churned. But I made it.

'You are an entertainment director now, Miss Casey Jones. And you'd better not screw it up. This is your chance for a new career. Hang up your clothes and get along to your office, fast. There will be a lot of work to be done.'

The cruise entertainment director's office and the deputy's office were behind the stage of the main theatre in the Princess Lounge. It was another maze of corridors and offices, as well as the showgirls' dressing rooms and storage space for costumes and props. Scenery was stored in every odd space. It was a hectic, manic place and the heart of the entire entertainment business on the *Countess*.

'So, you are Casey Jones? The fabulous Miss Jones that we have heard so much about. Hi, I'm your deputy, Susan Brook.' My deputy was sitting behind a desk covered in paper and files, the computer screen blinking.

'Fabulous'? What did she mean by that? Who'd been talking?

Susan Brook was smiling a pleased-to-meet-you mouth but her veiled eyes were saying something quite different. I knew instantly that she thought she ought to have been promoted to my job. Conway Blue Line always wanted fresh blood. I was fresh blood, new ideas, a different

20

person. But a tired face.

Susan Brook had a face that was struggling to stay young. She was also battling against serious weight gain. Her uniform shirt buttons were straining. It was that lovely display of food upstairs in the Terrace café on Lido deck. A more or less conveyer-belt buffet, from breakfast to midnight. Few could resist it. She was not one of them.

No one was allowed to age on cruise ships, only the captain. He was permitted to be grey-bearded and grizzled. It evoked confidence in his ability to dock without bumping other ships and reach destinations on time.

'Nice to meet you, Susan,' I said, holding out my hand. 'I hope you haven't been too busy during the handover.'

She took my hand but her grasp was limp, like a fish. I tried not to drop it. Wet fish is not a favourite.

The cruise director I was replacing had left the moment the *Countess* berthed quayside that morning at Southampton. There was some family problem and he was anxious to get home. I was an emergency replacement, although ready for the position. I'd done my apprenticeship on other cruise liners.

'The usual thing. Lost cruise cards, lost luggage, lost props, costumes, music. Perfectly normal day in Southampton.'

'We'll soon sort it out,' I said cheerfully. 'Anything I can do to help?'

'You can look through these drafts for the ship's newspaper. I haven't had time.' She

21

pushed over the drafts. The newspaper was set up on land but we did the amendments, change of times, schedules, any special announcements on board.

Now I knew that the production of the ship's newspaper was the deputy's responsibility. I'd done it myself when I was a deputy. I didn't argue with her, but she needn't think I was going to do it regularly. Today I would be amiable and helpful. Tomorrow I would be a fire-spitting dragon.

I had my own Ten Commandments for cruise directors. They had gone down well at my interview with Conway Blue Line. A balance of always and never.

* Always listen sympathetically
* Always listen with patience
* Never look bored
* Never discuss politics or religion
* Never mention illness
* Never ask personal questions – even if the passenger offers answers
* Never boast – exude authority and confidence
* Always be tidy
* Always be sober
* Smile

One of the directors had asked me which was the most important commandment.

'The last one,' I'd said. 'Always smile.' Gina Conway had smiled back. She had a radiant smile. Perhaps that's why I got the job.

The next consignment of singers, dancers, cabaret turns, lecturers and craft teachers were beginning to arrive on board. Newcomers were bewildered and nervous. Old hands were unpacked and halfway to the bars already.

'Sure. Is this my desk?' I said, sitting down at the one opposite Susan.

'No, actually that's mine.' She was sitting at my desk. I nodded. I was not territorial. Not today. Tomorrow she had better move – and fast.

Entertainers had to present themselves to the entertainment director's office as soon as they boarded. It was essential that we knew they had arrived with all their bits and pieces, check what they needed to do their job and that they were allotted a cabin.

We had a real assortment on this cruise. An author who would give lectures and workshops on creative writing, an artist teaching drawing and painting, a clever needlewoman taking classes in cross-stitch, beadwork and patchwork; lots of the female passengers brought needle-work to do. There was also a lecturer on nautical history, Nelson and sea battles and warships. The passengers wanted a choice of occupations between sunbathing and eating. Deck days watching never-ending sea wake could become tedious.

Not for me. All I wanted to do was to lean over a rail and watch the waves. The sea is an endless procession of mysteries. It constantly changes colour. How deep is it? Where is it going? Where has it been? I loved the movement, was mesmerized by the waves. Call me wet.

The procession of people through my office was also never-ending. There was a changeover of entertainers as well. Many were old-timers who signed papers, checked show times, headed for their cabins and a kip before the first show. Others were full of questions, understandably nervous, awed by the size of the ship and the sheer complication of the stage shows planned. Rehearsals? When would they get time to rehearse? Although the musical shows were pre-planned on land by an independent producer, they were anxious to rehearse in a new venue.

'What happens if the stage wobbles?' asked one new and pin-thin dancer. 'You know, rough weather.'

'You counter-balance,' I said. 'You go with it. Don't worry, you'll soon learn how to do it.'

The safety checks had been completed, clearance granted and the captain made his departure broadcast over the loudspeaker. I could hear the anchor being winched up. It rattled a lot, a horrendous noise if you had a cabin near the anchor. They would soon be throwing off the heavy ropes – lines as they were called – that kept the *Countess* secured to the quayside.

There was a moment when I found I could escape to go on deck and catch a last glimpse of Southampton docks as we sailed away. All those tall cranes leaning into the sky like fingers. Cruise ships and cargo ships berthed in other docks. A brass band was playing farewell on shore. No streamers from ship to shore these days, like in films. All that papery debris in the water was deemed an environmental nuisance.

24

But not the champagne. That was circulating.

The *Countess* was already twenty yards from the quayside, gliding slowly, powerful engines throbbing. Passengers leaned over the rail, waving farewell to family and friends who crowded the viewing balcony of the terminal.

The ship was passing through Southampton water and there was the huge Esso Oil terminal at Fawley on the bank. Calshot Spit, Thorn Channel and Brambles Bank ... the names tumbled out of my memory. At last we passed between the great forts and into the Solent.

My last cruise as deputy had been on a different line. This was my first on the Conway Blue Line. I liked them. I thought I would do well with this growing group. And the MV *Countess Georgina* was the most beautiful ship I had ever seen. I was her slave instantly. I was sure she had a soul, somewhere in the depths.

The sky was beginning to darken. This was England, dammit, and we had these absurd clock changes. Soon it would be evening, when it needn't be evening. Why couldn't we go along with the rest of the world? I couldn't stay on deck much longer. I wanted to see the Isle of Wight and the ruined Carisbrooke Castle, but I had to go back to the office. Muster drill soon, showing passengers how to put on their life-jackets. I had to be present. Part of the job.

A man joined me at the deck rail, not standing too near. I didn't know if he was a passenger or crew, very casual. No uniform. In the half light I only caught a glimpse of him. What I saw was startling. He was tall, dark and amazingly good-

25

looking. The cruise cliché. He must be a single passenger on the make, looking for a rich widow.

'Strangely beautiful, isn't it?' he said. His voice was deep and right for his looks. He was staring ahead, more intent on the view than me.

'Yes, I love it. There's something about sailing away, seeing the land grow smaller and smaller, leaving everything behind.'

'Where is everyone? They are missing all this.' This area of the deck was deserted.

'Everyone is eating or drinking or changing clothes. Maybe even reading the muster drill instructions. And that would be a first. They should be up here looking at our last glimpse of English shores for nearly four weeks.'

'You are right but, of course, food and clothes come first on a cruise.' He sounded cynical. 'No, maybe drink comes first.'

'Not always. Lots of people are hooked on the sea and seeing new places.'

'But some only want to go home looking like brown leather.' He sounded tired, too. Perhaps he'd had a long journey, or little sleep last night. I couldn't see if he had a tan. All I could see was a sharp profile, long straight nose, firm chin and a mass of smooth dark hair. Then I caught a glint of gold. He was wearing rimmed spectacles. I'd know him again.

I moved away, reluctantly. I liked the proximity of a really gorgeous man, however briefly. It felt good. He smelt good. Like a benevolence from the gods.

'Well, I have to go. Things to do,' I said.

'You're a show dancer?' he asked, turning towards me, seeing me for the first time.

'No, but close, quite close. Five out of ten for trying.'

'I'm not even trying. It's a brand of calculated small talk. I always suggest to a lone woman that she is a dancer or an actress. Then she is immensely flattered and I get the warmth of her smiles.'

'Well, I'm not in the least flattered. And I'm not smiling.' No sign of a smile. Rule one overboard already.

'I can see that. You have a singularly cool look, Miss...? Is the look permanent?'

'Miss Jones. And, yes, it's permanent.'

'I shall remember to keep my distance.'

I shivered. It wasn't the light southerly wind or the darkening sky. It was something more ominous. My first evening aboard the *Countess* and I had managed to alienate the best-looking man on ship. Still, this was nothing unusual with attractive men. I had a reputation for maintaining iceberg coolness even in the Caribbean.

Global warming didn't stand a chance.

Two

At Sea

It had been a long, leisurely day at sea and the passengers of the MV *Countess Georgina* had taken full advantage of the glorious sunshine, sunbathing from after breakfast till dressing for dinner. They lay in rows on the loungers, turning to burn, like oiled sprats on a spit. I rarely sunbathe. I never have the time nor the inclination to bare myself, and know that with my pale skin, I'd be first in the queue at tomorrow's surgery with burns the size of saucers.

'What an absolutely glorious day, Miss Jones,' said Mrs Fairweather, a regular cruiser, who already knew many of the crew and staff by name. 'I kept telling everyone that as soon as we got through the Bay of Biscay, we'd hit the sunshine. And wasn't I right?'

'You were right, as always,' I said, smiling. She was a nice woman, a widow, spending her late husband's insurance. And why not? On board ship, she was well looked after, found plenty to do during the day and could make new friends. I knew that some of the passengers made fun of her and called her the Weather Forecast but she was harmless and never caused

28

any trouble. Not like some of them.

There were a few troublemakers. They seemed determined to pile up enough grumbles to warrant a refund when they got home. They grumbled about everything: lifts breaking down, lights not working, loos not flushing, not being able to sleep because of the noise. Some complaints were genuine, but most of them were fixed immediately.

I'd had complaints already about passengers reserving theatre seats and deck loungers. The open-air Terrace Café on the Lido deck had been quite empty this morning. No problem finding a window seat for my sliced melon and croissant. I wouldn't even look at a Danish pastry. The Bay of Biscay had been relatively calm, although there were quite a few passengers missing yesterday. Now we were sailing along the coast of Portugal. A beautiful day, light and airy, with fine and clear skies.

'Are you coming to the first showing of this evening's entertainment?' I asked Mrs Fairweather. 'It's a great show, all the Sinatra songs, a take-off of the Rat Pack.'

'Oh, I shall love that. Frank Sinatra was one of my favourites. That man could really sing. Well, I'd better go and change or I shall miss my favourite seat.'

There was always a rush for the front row of seats in the Princess Lounge. In fact, they were fought over in a genteel, silver-handbags-at-the-ready sort of way. All the seats in the theatre were comfortable and everyone had a good view, but that front row was magnetic. Everyone

29

wanted to sit right up close to the stage, especially the men. But I suppose they wanted to get a good eyeful of the scantily dressed showgirls. And we did have some gorgeous dancing girls.

They lived on mineral water and three lettuce leaves a day. I once saw a dancer eating a grape. The job demanded thin bodies. Their costumes were mainly sequins sewn on to a net base and loads of feathers and a single extra ounce would ruin the look. How they stayed upright on their heels when the ship was rolling, I never knew. And their headdresses must weigh a kilo or two. I had enough trouble going on stage every night, and my heels were mostly kitten heels. I'm tall enough already. But I could take my shoes off in the wings and pad about barefooted. Bonus for my feet.

The shows were professionally produced and choreographed on land, then transferred to cruise ships. Then the dancers had to adapt what they had learned ashore to a tilting stage. They worked hard, afternoon rehearsals for every show.

One thing Head Office never told you was how many times you would have to change your clothes during the day. There was a different uniform for every function, from best full dress with smart jacket and hat, to casual skirt and shirt, to lifeboat drill shirt and trousers gear, from cocktail wear to full evening dress according to the dress code. I could shower and change in ten minutes and that included making a cup of tea in my cabin. I made it myself while I pranced around in a towel. I do prance when no one is looking at me. On deck, I am brisk and efficient, always elegant and a lady.

Being elegant and a lady is sometimes a little difficult to remember. As an only daughter with three older brothers, I had to be a tomboy to survive the male-dominated jungle. It was not something I told anyone. Would anyone be impressed that I could swing on a rope across a tumbling river or abseil down a cliff in a gale?

My first task of this evening was to MC the first performance of the Rat Pack stage show. As usual, I would go on stage, introduce the performers, encourage applause and then go on again at the end, to thank the performers and encourage the applause again.

In between shows, my routine was to rush down to the officer's mess on deck F and grab something to eat. Tonight I might have time for the starter, Nicoise salad: tuna, egg, French beans, tomatoes, potatoes, anchovies and olives. It came in a portion the size of a pin cushion. It would just about keep me going.

Then I repeated the performance for the second showing of the stage show, with another run for coffee and maybe some ice cream. They made wonderful ginger ice cream on board but it was hard to get any. By then the dancing would have started in three different venues and I had to circulate and talk and make sure everyone was having a good time. My remit did not include the cinema which was where I would rather be. I am an old-soak film addict and could sit through a special film several times, like reading the same book over and over again because of the pleasure. Don't ask me how many times I've seen *Neverland* or *Braveheart*. Did it matter?

The cinema was the lecture theatre during the day for port lectures and specialist lectures. Our author was here, twice a day, with her enthusiastic group of would-be writers. There was always a lot of laughter coming from the theatre as I went by. Sometimes I slipped in at the back to check on how her lectures were going and how many passengers attended. There was an average of seventy – pretty good for literature. After the author came the lecturer in maritime history, spruce in a navy blazer and flannels. He used slides to illustrate his talks.

I stepped into a strapless turquoise silk dress, three-quarter length so I had to wear matching turquoise strappy sandals. They hurt. My hair was pulled back into its usual tight chignon and fixed with a silver clasp. Make-up was applied with the speed of light as learned in my dancing days. Then I took the back way to the Princess Lounge, cutting it fine, as usual. Though it was called a lounge, it was the main theatre with a stage and circular dance floor with tiered armchair seating.

'I thought you weren't going to make it,' said Trevor, the stage manager. 'I was just about to go on in your place.'

'In that old T-shirt?' I said, smoothing my hair. 'You'd have been a riot.'

The resident band were playing the introductory music. On the final roll of drums, I stepped on to the stage into the spotlight.

It always alarmed me, those first few seconds,

blinded by the brilliant lights, and the rows and rows of six hundred expectant faces. They wanted the best and they were paying a lot for the best. They got me for a few minutes. They looked me up and down, marked my dress out of ten, tried to price the shoes. I'd bought them in Los Angeles during a brief port of call. They were Patrick Cox, T-bar heels. Rather expensive but worth it.

'Good evening, ladies and gentlemen,' I said. 'Have you had a wonderful day? Hasn't it been brilliant? Sunshine at last and that choppy Bay of Biscay behind us. Now, we have a spectacular show for you tonight, one packed with songs that you all know and singers who know how to sing them. Please welcome the Countess Show Company in tonight's spectacular!'

It was acting really. I acted the part of being the MC. Hopefully I remembered all the right names, which changed with every cruise, and said the right things. The audience clapped and I raised my arms in welcome as the dancers raced on in swirls of perfume and deodorant, skimpy black shorts, top hats and brief silver crop tops. They went effortlessly into their dance routine. They had been rehearsing all afternoon on a floor that might move.

The show had started. It could take care of itself now, unless there was a calamity. I took the service lift down to deck F and hurried through the myriad of passages, some storing stacks of unwanted passenger suitcases, crates of supplies, cables snaking the floor, admin offices on either side. I passed the canteen where the crew ate. As usual it was busy and noisy. The crew took no notice of my glamorous appearance. They saw me every day. It was nothing new to them.

The officers' mess was down another narrow passageway. It was fairly empty at this time of the evening. Everyone was working. The dancers and stage show artistes had the first hour in which to eat their lettuce and rocket. The second hour slot was for lecturers, the ballroom dancing teachers and the art team. The third hour was for officers. I rushed in and out whenever I could. No one noticed or cared.

It had two long tables, correctly set with white clothes, silver cutlery and glasses. The food was set out buffet style, each dish in a keep-warm container. Some had been keeping warm for hours, since it first left the kitchens. The baked salmon fillets looked like shrunken shrimps.

I went to the cold buffet. Salad again. But at least it was fresh and I could make up the mixture as I wished. Cold salmon gave me plenty of Omega 3.

An officer was sitting alone at the far end of the table. He looked as if he did not want to be disturbed, a journal propped up on the cruet in front of him. Even without registering the red tabs on his shoulders, I knew who he was. It was that attractive man. We had met on the rail, steaming out of Southampton.

'I will only disturb your meal for one moment, Dr Mallory,' I said, not putting down my plate of salad. 'But I'd like to know how Mr Foster is. You remember, the passenger who was taken ill

34

at table two.'

'Mr Foster is having a nice, long rest,' said Dr Mallory, hardly pausing. 'He is at present in a freezer, awaiting shipment home. Didn't you know? I thought the crew knew everything. He was dead on arrival, as they say.'

'Have you done a post-mortem?' I asked. I was shocked. I didn't know he had died.

'Not my job.'

'What did he die of?'

'Heart attack. Didn't feel a thing. Out in a flash. The way to go.'

I didn't like the way he was talking, without any feeling for Mr Foster or his family. Besides I remembered that puddle of red froth on the table. I didn't know that a heart attack was preceded by a haemorrhage. There might be a book in the ship's library, though they usually kept anything vaguely scary off the passengers' reading list.

'Don't you have to log a death? If you're sure of the cause of death?'

'Of course. I log everything. I am sure, Miss Whoever-you-are. It was a heart attack. His heart had stopped beating. We gave him heart compression and artificial respiration, but it was too late. We'll keep him cold until we get back to the UK. It's normal procedure.'

'But Mr Foster could be flown home?'

'Yes, but it's very expensive and a lot of paper-work. I never recommend it. Mrs Foster was agreeable to the current arrangement. She said her husband had been looking forward to this cruise so he might as well stay on board.'

It was not funny. I suppressed a shiver. Death at sea was not an unusual occurrence. Quite a lot of passengers were elderly and a death or two was natural. But the passengers didn't like it. Nor did the crew. The ship was like a village with everyone getting to know everyone else. And everyone gossiped. Every little item of news was passed round the dining tables and bars.

'So, who are you?' he asked, looking up from the page. 'When you are at home and not wearing yards of turquoise and killer heels.'

His eyes were a clear, granite grey. They glinted with the sharpness of steel behind his spectacles. He had lashes, long and dark, sweeping a tanned skin. His nose was strong-boned but the right shape for a man, and his mouth was curved, soft and generous. Dr Samuel Mallory was, without doubt, the best-looking man on the ship. And I knew he was lithe and tall. He had stood beside me at the rail, watching the last of England's coastline disappear.

No wonder the queue outside the medical centre was so long every morning. Every matron on board would pay for five minutes of Dr Mallory's time. They'd pay extra for a smile. And I knew he flirted. Word had got around. I'd been warned. I'd seen him chatting up the ladies, several times.

'I'm Casey Jones,' I said, taking a deep breath. 'I joined the *Countess* as Cruise Director at Southampton. I'm in charge of entertainment. I introduce all the shows in the evening, make sure there's enough going on to keep the passen-

36

gers occupied during the day. Hence the fancy dress. I have to look the part.'

'You look very nice. Casey Jones? That's an unusual name. Isn't it a boy's name?'

Dr Mallory didn't sound all that interested. Perhaps he didn't flirt with crew, only with female paying passengers. Fair enough. I was only talking to him in a professional capacity.

'It actually stands for KC. My initials,' I said. 'I was christened Katherine Cordelia by my parents to make up for having a plain surname. But no one could manage such a mouthful and have always used my initials instead.'

'KC,' he murmured. 'Fair enough.'

Dr Mallory had gone back to his pamphlet. I could see it was a medical journal. I hoped he was keeping current with new knowledge. It wasn't all sea sickness pills and twisted ankles on board ship. There were some serious injuries but then he would know that. Passengers were often flown home for treatment.

'Nice to meet you,' he added, with a brief nod. He went back to his journal and his home-made apple pie and cream. I was dismissed, me and my salad.

Later that night I went up on deck, to take a last look at the star-studded night sky and the night sea. We were travelling at a rate of knots. I didn't know how many, but fast. You could tell by the flurry of white on the wake that the ship was moving fast. The captain often made up time at night. Soon we would be passing Cape St Vincent at the south western tip of Portugal, then making for the Gibraltar Strait. In the earliest shipping days, sailors stopped and turned back at the Gibraltar Strait. They believed the earth was flat and this was where they would fall off.

A lot of passengers were tucking into sandwiches, savouries and cakes at the midnight buffet. Maybe they thought the same. They were stocking up in case we fell off.

Three

At Sea

All the passengers were looking forward to the captain's cocktail party that evening. That is, all the female passengers were keen, maybe not the men. Though they made an effort. Some even wore kilts or medals pinned to tuxedo lapels.

It was the first big party of the cruise. The women's clothes were fabulous, gold and silver, brocades and silk, sequins galore. I'd seen it all before. And of course, yards and yards of black. Any colour stood out. A flame of crimson, a shocking yellow, a pure white, Alexander Mc-Queen, Versace, Celine, Calvin Klein. The hairdressing salon had been busy all afternoon.

I wore my special Versace dress. It was vintage, bought for a song and a half from a little shop tucked away behind Harrods. It always made me feel good, the shades of lilac and pink, fading to white, three layers of chiffon, floating from a tightly folded bodice and tiny straps. The sandals were see-through straps on impossible heels. I could barely walk in them.

I was checking invitation cards as the line of passengers were introduced to Captain Nicolas. As always, there was a first-sitting party and a second-sitting party. Some passengers aimed to come to both. Usual excuses, left invitation in cabin, lost it overboard, my wife's got it. My memory was good. I let them know they'd been spotted, in the nicest way, of course.

Stewards circulated with drinks trays and stewardesses brought round the canapés, little smoked salmon rolls, black caviar on toast, shrimp vol-au-vents. They tasted cold. Most of the officers attended one or other of the parties. Some had to work, keep the ship going, make sure she was heading in the right direction. Palma tomorrow. We would soon be crossing the Greenwich Meridian.

I caught a glimpse of those red shoulder tabs. The handsome doctor was talking and laughing with a group of admiring women. He was being his most charming, looked devastating in his full dress uniform. I wondered if he had had his teeth veneered. They were very white, film-starry, especially when the lights in the Princess Lounge were seductively dimmed. It wasn't even dark outside yet.

Captain Nicolas had his photograph taken with every passenger. He was good at it. His smile was genuine. The line took a long time to disperse through the lounge. Half the drinking time had gone already.

'Miss Jones,' said Captain Nicolas in a break. 'Don't you want your photograph taken with me? Your first cruise on the *Countess*. Something to show the grandchildren in the future.'

'My grandchildren will love it,' I said, same joking tone.

'How about I join you?' said Dr Mallory, suddenly appearing at my side. 'We can't waste that fabulous dress and those eyes. Let's make it a threesome. Beauty and two beasts.'

'I can only count one beast,' I said.

The camera girl snapped us before I could say anything more. I thanked the captain, ignored the doctor, and moved on. The doctor was so smooth, it was a wonder he didn't slide and glide across the floor. The chiffon swirled round my legs like a sea of mist. Mrs Foster was at the party, swathed in gold and black velvet. She'd had her hair and nails done at the beauty salon. She was certainly making an effort to join in some of the cruise activities. But her face was taut.

'Does it help to come and talk to people?' I said to her.

She nodded. 'It's what George would have wanted me to do, after paying all that money. His hard-earned money. He wouldn't have wanted me to mope in our stateroom, all by myself. I'll try to do my grieving when I get home.'

'That sounds very sensible. What did your husband do?'

'He was an art dealer. He knew a lot about the art trade.'

'That sounds very interesting. Did he have a look at our collection of art that is for sale on board in the art gallery?'

She nodded, with a suppressed noise. 'Yes, he did but it's not quite his scene. Mostly reproductions and prints. But I guess it sells well. We call them wall furnishings. You know, just filling up a space, like wallpaper.'

I knew exactly what Mrs Foster meant. But the art auctions were very popular and so was the free champagne served at them.

'Palma tomorrow. Lots of sightseeing and shopping, but you may not feel like going ashore. Have you been there before?'

'A long time ago,' she said. 'It was on our first cruise. We had a very modest cabin then. It was inside on some lower deck with bunk beds. George took the upper berth and kept falling out of his bed.'

I laughed and her face lightened. That's what Mrs Foster needed. Lots of good memories to hang on to. Laughter.

'They need a lot of practice. There's an excellent film on tonight, if you don't feel like watching the stage show.'

She nodded. 'Thank you, but not really. I may just sit and listen to the pianist in the lounge. He plays such lovely music.'

'Yes, he does. We'll talk again, Mrs Foster,' I said, knowing I must circulate. It was my job.

'Perhaps you'd like to come and have a drink in my stateroom one evening? I know you're very busy, Miss Jones. You always seem to be rushing somewhere.'

'I'd like that very much. We'll make it a sea day. You'll be tired after a day in port if you go ashore. Now, if you'll excuse me, Mrs Foster...'

I hoped she had booked some excursions. Sometimes I was roped in to be a tour escort if they were short of volunteers. Crew enjoyed doing this because they got a free trip. There was always a registered local guide so being an escort was mostly counting heads and keeping the stragglers together.

It was easy to talk to people at parties. And there were lots of parties on board. The POSH club always had a party, and any other groups travelling together. Mostly Rotarians and Masonic clubs.

I usually made a beeline for someone standing on their own, or a couple who seemed a little out of it. Some passengers, especially those on their first ever cruise, found this kind of socializing difficult. By the end of the first week, they would be chatting to everyone.

'So our lovely Entertainments Director is hard at work, shepherding her nervous lambs, and patting their little woollen trotters.' The deep voice was easy to recognize. I didn't know why he was wasting valuable networking time talking to me. Perhaps I amused him or made him feel more secure.

'No need to be sarcastic,' I said, keeping my voice down. 'There are many shy and nervous people on board who need encouragement to mix. Maybe you'll never find them queueing outside your surgery. But I assure you, I can spot them. And by the way, trotters are part of pigs.'

'Have you seen them at the midnight buffet? Still eating.'

'Food is addictive. It's the famine syndrome.'

'Famine, is that what you call it? Let me know when we are down to the last roll and butter.'

'Have you decided anything more about Mr Foster's death? I told you about the cherry-red blood on the tablecloth, didn't I?'

'Yes, you did,' said Samuel Mallory sharply. 'And I'd be obliged if you would keep your nose out of medical matters. Mr Foster died of a heart attack and that's the end of the matter.'

'The tablecloth was whipped away,' I went on. 'But there might have been traces of blood on his shirt or skin.'

'Don't tell me my job and I won't tell you how to do yours. Though I am surprised you are not in dress uniform. Isn't it de rigueur at these formal things?'

He was right. I felt my cheeks redden. Careless, Casey. He was right. I should have worn the long black skirt, white blouse with bow tie, and cropped gold-braided dress jacket. There was just time to change before the next cocktail party. I'd forgotten.

Only I didn't have time to change then. I noticed a young woman holding on to the edge of the bar. She looked very pale and shaky and I don't think it was the drink. The stewards are not over-generous with glasses of champagne or going round with refills. You'd be lucky if you got a second one. A third was an unheard of indulgence.

'Are you all right?' I said, going over to her.

43

'Do you need some air? It's a bit stuffy in here.'

She clutched my arm. Her long red nails went into my flesh. She was about twenty-eight or -nine, beautifully dressed in slim ivory satin, long flowing blonde hair, diamonds sparkling in her ears. She was lovely.

'Help me, help me,' she whispered.

She was starting to hyperventilate, breathing fast. And she was sweating, her forehead beaded with moisture. It was a panic attack. Time to get her out of here before she fainted.

'What's your name?'

'Amanda.'

'Come along, Amanda. You need some fresh air.'

I took her outside the Princess Lounge. My elementary first-aid knowledge immediately keyholed a brown paper bag. But the *Countess* rarely carried available supplies of brown paper bags. I dashed into the ladies' cloakroom and grabbed a small sanitary bag. It would have to do.

We took the lift to the Lido deck. Meanwhile I helped Amanda breathe into the bag, so that she was eventually breathing carbon dioxide and not gulping extra oxygen. We leaned over the rail, watching the distant lights of other ships moving in the growing darkness. Her breathing calmed. She was still clutching me.

'Do you feel well enough to talk?' I asked. 'There's no one about up here. No one will hear.'

Amanda was taking deep breaths now but steadily. She patted her face with a tissue and

44

then looked at me. She had wonderfully startling blue eyes. Very photogenic. Perhaps she was a model.

'Two years ago my fiancé was killed in a motorway rage incident. You may have read about it in the newspapers. It was all over the front pages, especially the tabloids,' she said. '"Driver Stabbed by Maniac" – those were the headlines.'

'I may have done,' I murmured.

'He was knifed by this mad man, right in front of me. It was quite awful. Giles died in my arms, on the hard shoulder. And no need for it at all. We'd done nothing wrong. We were simply driving the wrong sort of car. Giles had an Aston Martin but he'd worked hard for it. He was entitled to drive a good car. He'd paid for it.'

'Wasn't he caught? This road rage maniac?'

'No, never. He just disappeared. Straight down to the nearest ferry, I expect, and then holed up somewhere in France for months.'

She was starting to cry now, reliving those past moments. 'Do you think you are in any danger?'

'I don't think so because I was in the car when it happened. My face was plastered over the newspapers the next day but I was younger and dark then, and I'm blonde now.'

'Could you manage to come back to the party?' I knew it was asking a lot. 'It would help.'

'Yes, I'll do that.'

But it was too late. They were clearing up the party. Passengers had gone to dinner, suitably fuelled for a lovely meal. Amanda and I walked

45

to the dining room.

'Where's your table?'

'I'm on a table with my mother. We're travelling together.'

'Amanda, I'm going to leave you now. Relax and have a nice meal with your mother. Go see the show or the film.'

'Thank you, thank you so much for helping me.' It was the first time she'd let go of my arm. 'I really appreciate it.'

I fast changed to formal uniform in my cabin, gulped some water and was back in the Princess Lounge for the second cocktail party. It was like knitting fog as I circulated, talking and laughing, exchanging superficial information.

Some passengers came to both cocktail parties. I spotted Nigel Garten. He was hard to miss with that big build and shock of reddish hair. He seemed harmless.

'Nice to see you again,' I said, letting him know that I'd spotted him.

'Sorry,' he said with a grin, knowing he'd been recognized. 'It's those cavier canapés. I can't resist them. And the lovely ladies, of course. Can you arrange some introductions?'

'Not my job.'

'What a pity.'

'Don't miss the cathedral at Palma,' I said. 'It's spectacular. And do look at all the living statues in the grounds around it.'

'Living statues?'

'Yes, living statues. They are real people, sprayed in gold or silver paint, keeping so still it's difficult to see them breathe. Mostly

46

students, I suspect. Sometimes they move slightly, beckon to a child, who jumps a mile high. It's electrifying.'

Dr Samuel Mallory was at my elbow. He was drinking orange juice. 'So you took my advice?' he said, nodding towards the long dark skirt.

'Don't you have an evening surgery?' I asked.

'My surgery nurse is taking it. She'll call me if she needs assistance. I was more interested in sussing out our passengers. I've spotted two high blood pressures already, several alcoholics and a severe case of depression.'

'And I have a passenger who had a panic attack because she saw her fiancé murdered,' I said. 'What do you prescribe for that?'

'An early night and a bottle of vodka.'

It took me a moment to fillet my thoughts and find the right response.

'I don't think I have ever met a man so callous and unsympathetic. You're supposed to be a doctor, a caring member of the medical profession. It's not just about prescribing antibiotics and painkillers and overcharging for a sprained ankle. This young woman is traumatized.'

'Why do you think I'm working on a cruise ship?' he said sardonically. 'I need rest and recuperation, like every other member of the medical profession. Two years in Manchester's A & E had me on my knees and groaning for sleep. You should try working twenty-four-hour shifts, dealing non-stop with rowdy drunks, drug overdoses and fatal car accidents scraped off the road. You'd soon learn.'

He turned away and all I got was a glimpse of

47

his straight back, the broad shoulders and a shock of dark hair. For a second I wanted to call him back and apologize, but the moment passed. He had been so rude to me.

I hurried down to the Windsor Dining Room and found my new friend, Graham Ward, the head waiter, waiting around until he had a free moment. He had so many problems to sort out in a very short time. Complaints, queries, requests. It was an endless procession of passenger problems. And I had brought him another.

'I wonder if you could help me. I'm trying to locate a passenger called Amanda, who's travelling with her mother. Second sitting, I think.'

He had a camera memory for names. I don't know how he managed to remember them so quickly.

'Mrs Banesto and Amanda, table forty-two.'

'Thank you. You're a star.'

He grinned. 'I know. And I twinkle at night.'

Four

Palma

There were a few moments of peace on deck, very late that night. I leaned over the rail, watching the spray on the waves, glad that the days of piracy at sea were long gone. Or were they? Pirates used to capture ships to order, because of their valuable cargoes. I suppose it does still happen today. We were certainly carrying a valuable cargo and they were people.

The ship was a floating prison, a luxurious prison for the passengers, slightly more claustrophobic for crew and staff on the lower decks. But soon we would be able to get off, wander the streets of Palma, delve down little side streets, get lost in its medieval past.

'So here you are,' said a voice I was beginning to know. 'I have come to apologize so don't push me overboard yet. I can swim but not in this wake.'

'You don't need to apologize,' I said stiffly. 'You were right. I was in the wrong outfit. Never compete with the passengers.'

'Casey Jones, you have the biggest chip on your shoulder, I have ever seen. Shall I get it surgically removed for you? No charge, I assure you.'

I relaxed an inch. Dr Mallory could be so charming. Now he was working that charm on me. Well, it wouldn't work, buster. I was charm proof.

'It's been that kind of day. The DJ who's supposed to do the afternoon bingo didn't turn up. Heavy party the previous night, I gather. So I did bingo this afternoon. I'd almost forgotten the calls. There were talks to cover, complaints to sort out, two cocktail parties, then I had this girl who had a panic attack because she's traumatized by seeing her fiancé knifed in a road rage attack. I had her to calm down. I had shows to introduce because my deputy, Susan Brook, had period pains and couldn't go on. I've been rushing about like a demented hamster.'

'A tired and demented hamster is almost fascinating,' he said, as if he understood. Writing out a few prescriptions twice a day must be so tiring. But he looked dishevelled, his bow tie undone and hanging loose.

'And now I've found a dead bird on deck, not a seagull, but a land bird.' I was near sobbing. 'It flew into the superstructure and got killed.'

'No sense of direction. Where's the bird now?' he asked.

'I put it on the deck, over there,' I said, pointing to the stack of secured deckchairs. Every night they were strapped down in case of gales, high seas, the odd roll.

Samuel picked the bird up, a grey feathery thing, quite tenderly. 'Its neck is broken. A pigeon, I think. Shows we're near land. So it was quick, Casey. Instant and painless.'

50

'But so unnecessary,' I said.

Samuel Mallory nodded. 'I agree, but then so many deaths in this world are unnecessary and we can't weep for all of them. Shall we consign him to the waves or do you want a proper funeral, flag draped over a shoebox, a hymn or two?'

'No,' I said, shaking my head. 'Back to the waves.'

'Together, then,' he said.

'Amen.'

We threw the bird into the waves and watched as the sea sucked him up and he disappeared. I was tired. I needed some sleep. This had been a long day. Dr Mallory walked me back to my cabin. I don't know how he knew the number or deck. He opened my door for me and put the card into the light slot.

'Sleep well, Casey,' he said. 'I don't want to see you outside my surgery tomorrow, hung over.'

'Good night,' I said, already half asleep.

Palma was gorgeous. The vast port was bathed in sunlight. Ships lined at berths in every direction, cargo, cruise, gin-floaters. White hotels rimmed the harbour, their balconies cascading with flowers. And the great soaring Gothic cathedral dominated the skyline. It lifted every heart. Passengers crowded the decks, excited by their first port of call. Some even skipped breakfast to be first off the ship, took the packets of biscuits from their cabin trays.

I had morning chores, mostly paperwork. The

51

passengers were never aware of the paperwork associated with my job. Then I could go ashore. I changed into a navy sundress, factor thirty-five sunscreen, hat and sunglasses. The *Countess* was berthed at a distance from the old town and there was a shuttle bus waiting on land. The docks seemed to have grown since my last visit. There would be a few hours to wander around Palma. It was a necessary port of call for fuel and water before we began the long sea trip to the Caribbean. And somewhere that the passengers could stretch their legs on land and do some shopping. Days at sea could seem endless, and we didn't want boredom setting in.

The shuttle bus took us along the coast road, a long way from the new docks, and deposited us on the front below the cathedral. Passengers gasped as they alighted from the air-conditioned bus. Heat rose from the stone slab pavements. You could fry an egg on them. Everyone hurried towards the shade of the shops and the streets inland. I nearly drank all of my bottle of water. Caution, Casey. Rule one of survival: always save some water. The heat was stifling.

The hatless were rushing to the shops to buy hats.

But then the body accommodated and the bus party began walking towards the cathedral. I was not part of the group, but I kept them in sight. This time was my own. I was off duty, but still around, as you might say.

I loved the cathedral. It was huge, Gothic and cool with enormous stained-glass rose-windows at each end which blazed with colour. Nowadays you had to pay to go in. But once it was free and worshippers could wander at will, stopping to pray at some small chapel or read a medieval tombstone. The mummified remains of King Jaime II were very popular. Commercialism had stepped in since. You had to buy tickets for everything. There was an adjacent museum which was choked with interesting artefacts, at a price.

So I toured the gardens and precincts. The living statues were a wonder to watch. Gold, silver, bronze, brass, they graced the gardens and walkways. Grecian, medieval, Roman gladiators, bronco cowboys, mermaids, monks and fairies. They were a delight. No matter how long you stared, you could not see a movement. It was a wonder that they ever breathed. I suppose they had trained themselves to do shallow, controlled breathing. It must be pretty tiring, standing so still in the heat.

The old town of Palma nestled close to the skirts of the soaring cathedral. The houses were solidly built in narrow winding streets, many with balconies and interior patios. I loved catching an intimate glimpse of how people lived.

By midday the heat was climbing. I was staying out of the sun, sipping *trinaranjus*, a mixture of orange and lemon juice, at a street café under an umbrella. I was surprised at the number of passengers not wearing hats. Dr Mallory would have a lot of sunstroke and heat exhaustion patients on his hands this evening. Most of them cabin visits. Sunstroke is pretty serious.

I spotted Amanda Banesto strolling with a

blonde young man who was in jeans and a T-shirt. At least she was wearing a big shady hat and huge sunglasses, but there was no mistaking the mane of blonde hair and lovely figure. There were long queues for the returning shuttle buses and nowhere to wait out of the sun. People wanted to get back to the coolness and cleanness of the ship. The litter-strewn streets of Palma had been a shock after days aboard the immaculate *Countess*. Wait till they saw Acapulco.

At last I got aboard a shuttle bus after standing back to let the paying sufferers return to the ship first. They needed to cool down and fast. The best cure for too much sun is a cool shower.

'Come on, Miss Jones, we've seen you waiting. You'll fry if you stand out there much longer.' It was Nigel Garten, the enthusiastic cocktail party goer. 'There's a spare seat over here.'

'Thank you, Mr Garten,' I said. 'I was beginning to feel like a fried egg.'

'Pass the tomato sauce,' he said, grinning. I spotted the loneliness in his eyes although he hid it well.

He was obviously looking forward to the buffet lunch laid out in the Terrace Café. It would be salad for me with some cold salmon, maybe a few prawns. Then a fruit salad, maybe a yogurt and back to the office. There was some problem with one of the entertainers whose entire collection of props was lost midships. The box had come on board at Southampton but since then had gone astray. It couldn't have gone far, though she was a big ship.

'I can't go on without them,' he had stormed in

54

my office, his face redder than his striped shirt. He was billed as Merlin the Magician, real name Reg Hawkins. But he was good. I'd seen his act on another ship and was amazed at the illusions he managed at such close range to his audience. 'You know I need all this stuff. And the box. It's my disappearing box trick.'

'Don't worry, Reg. I quite understand your concern,' I said. 'No props, no tricks. We're going to scour the ship, search every nautical inch. Your first show is tomorrow evening, so there's still time.'

'But I need a rehearsal in the afternoon,' he fumed. 'Lights, music, sound.'

'Of course, don't worry. I'll get out my divining rods. Fingers crossed.'

'Everything crossed,' he growled. He was quite a difficult entertainer, somewhat temperamental, although I could understand his frustration in this situation. But he seemed more distraught than usual. Perhaps it was the heat.

The passengers put their empty luggage into store during the cruise. No room for empty cases in cabins. Somehow Merlin's props box must have got mixed up with them during the general mêlée of moving everything. The whole mountain of luggage would have to be searched. I had a word with the head steward. Karim was from Goa, had been working cruise ships since a boy. He understood the urgency and promised a thorough systematic search.

'Yes, Miss Jones. We will find the magic box.'

'It's clearly marked Merlin.'

'Merlin, like the bird.'

'Well, not quite, but it doesn't matter.' It did cross my mind that Merlin, aka Reg, might have forgotten to bring his props. He was known for being absent-minded, and seemed particularly distracted on this cruise. Why wait till now to report the loss of his box? I wouldn't put it past him to blame us for the loss of essential illusions. It was up to me to protect the company, keep our entertainers happy and our passengers entertained. All at the same time.

Passengers were arriving back on ship in droves, falling into the dining room for the set tea, the Terrace Café, the bars. All that remained ashore were those touring the island on excursion coaches. I had once been to Deya, near where Chopin had lived with the writer, George Elliot. It was a high-up, magical place on the edge of a sheer drop. A place of lost love and passion.

I was on deck watching the coaches arrive back, disgorging tired people who were only too glad to climb up the gangway, show their cruise cards, have their purchases checked through the x-ray machines. Already the *Countess* seemed like home to them. I understood that feeling. She was safe, she was clean, and everyone spoke English.

Dr Mallory was hurrying down the gangway, medical bag in hand. A passenger had slipped, getting off the high step of the coach. The woman was crumpled on the quayside, in pain, momentarily engulfed by a crowd of do-gooders. But Dr Mallory dispersed them with a few words. A wheelchair appeared and she was taken aboard, straight to the ship's hospital, where an x-ray would determine her injury.

'Nice to see you in action,' I said, as he came up the gangway.

'Glad you appreciate my dedication. No swanning ashore for me.'

'I was merely taking care of passengers who had no hats, no sunscreen, no water and making sure they got back safely.'

'I'm sure they appreciate your concern. How about I see you in the Galaxy Lounge at six? You deserve a drink after all that dedication.'

'Don't count on it. I may be busy.'

I couldn't count on it. Karim came to me, quite disturbed. He didn't know what to do. They had found a metal box marked Merlin, stored in the wrong place, no reason why. And they were unhappy about it.

'We'll find Merlin and get him to check that it is his box,' I said. 'Thank you for finding it. You've done well. There's no need for you to worry. I'll see to it from here on.'

'Thank you, Miss Jones. My stewards are worried that they will get into trouble. It is not where they put it. Someone had moved it.'

'Tell them not to worry. I'll sort it out.'

But Reg Hawkins was nowhere to be found. The announcement went over the tannoy several times although I know that it's difficult to hear, and near impossible in some parts of the ship. He was probably catching up on some sleep in his cabin. I phoned his cabin but there was no answer. The last passengers came aboard and were checked. No strays.

The ship was making ready to leave. A few well-wishers were waving from the quay as the heavy lines were tossed into the sea. How agreeable to have friends who lived in Palma. The *Countess* inched her way from the island of Majorca with hardly any movement, gliding on the water, the control of the engines so light and sure. I loved watching a receding shoreline, everything getting smaller and smaller, no larger than a dot, then disappearing into a haze. But not today. I had to find Reg Hawkins and give him the good news about his box. There was time to change into working gear, straight navy skirt and white shirt, Conway Blue Line scarf. I was on duty again.

Reg was still not answering the phone in his cabin. He was not in any of the bars and no one had seen him talking to passengers or other entertainers. It was a big ship and it was easy to miss people as they walked about, so many corridors and staircases and decks.

There was a last minute dancing rehearsal on stage in the Princess Lounge. One of the dancers was unwell and a routine had to be altered. The original choreographer was back in London, so the company were having to work it out for themselves. Most of the dancers and the shows were cast and rehearsed in London, and came on board as a package. The guest entertainers and star performers did the cruise circuits, changing ships like changing trains.

'Has anyone seen Merlin the Magician?' I asked around. No one had.

I was beginning to worry. He was due to

perform in tomorrow's show and still needed rehearsal time, though that was mainly to arrange lighting effects and music and check the sound. If we still couldn't find him, there'd be a gap in the programme that needed filling. I wondered which of my artistes could be persuaded to do an extra turn. They were usually helpful and obliging. Occasionally I had a prima donna. There was one due to join us at Barbados. Heaven help me when Estelle Grayson arrived plus two dozen stage costumes.

Merlin's box of tricks had been delivered backstage and I made a mental note to thank the stewards involved. It was a large black metal box which contained the props for his illusions and doubled on stage for the disappearing act. Usually the smallest of the girl dancers was happy to 'volunteer' for this trick.

There was something about the box that made me look at it again. Something was wrong. It normally came on board with sturdy straps holding it fast both ways. But both straps were missing. The lock was hanging loose.

I didn't want to open the box. Something told me not to touch it. I needed a witness, support, someone to hold my hand.

Someone like Richard Norton, our ex-Marines security officer, the man in charge of security on board the *Countess*. He was the nearest we had to a policeman.

He answered the phone immediately as if he had been waiting for my call. I told him that the box looked funny.

'Don't touch it,' he said. 'I'll be with you in

five minutes.'

I went back into my office and made myself some coffee. I needed it, black and strong. I checked my emails but my heart wasn't in it and none of them got answers, not yet. My brain wasn't functioning.

The security officer arrived. He was always in a well-pressed khaki uniform. It made him look different from crew officers and other personnel. At six feet three inches with a severe crew cut, he already looked a lot different.

'I'm sorry to bother you, but I've a funny feeling...'

'Women's intuition? At least they found his box of tricks. Reg Hawkins was spitting blood last night because it was lost. Stand back. I'll open it.'

Richard Norton prised open the heavy lid and it fell back, jolting the whole contraption. He glanced inside and drew away hastily. He looked at me, pushing me away with his arm, closing the lid.

'And he's still spitting blood,' he said.

Five

At Sea

Word spread round the ship like wildfire. And it wasn't only because Merlin the Magician was a popular entertainer. It was because he had been sitting on table two, second sitting. For two people to die on the same table was a little unnerving. I kept smiling. We did not want an anxiety disorder spreading

We had already disembarked the pilot once through the breakwater, so there was no question of turning back. The formalities were now the responsibility of the ship. The lovely *Countess* was not a jinxed ship. Nothing had happened on board on other cruises. It was table two, second sitting, that was jinxed. An elderly couple asked to be moved. They weren't taking any chances with their anniversary cruise. I had a feeling Graham Ward was going to get other requests.

It seemed an age ago since we were happily berthed at Palma, hot but content. Lunch was a vague memory. No one would explain to me how Reg Hawkins had died. Richard Norton had immediately secured the area and the night's show was cancelled.

The dancers reacted with the usual mixture of

theatricals. Some had hysterics, some felt sick, others went and had a drink in a bar. But everyone was talking about him. Rumours spread like melting butter on a hot plate.

Instead the classical pianist gave a concert in the Galaxy Lounge, Greig and Gershwin which suited all tastes. The music sounded glorious, piano notes tinkling like heavenly drops of sound. I was sorry I could only look in, spread my smile around but not stay for long. The pianist was in the cabin next to mine, so I'd met him briefly walking along the corridor. I was making statements and writing reports and showing my face in all the bars, reassuring passengers that all was being taken care of in every department.

More rumours began circulating. It was a heart attack. Another heart attack? But how did he get inside his own box of tricks? Was he checking the contents and fell in? Somewhat unlikely. He was knifed, said a rumour. Blood everywhere.

I would have liked to talk to Dr Mallory if he was in a talking mood. But he had a hospital full of patients. The passenger who tripped down the step from the coach had broken her ankle. There were several sprains from slips on board, and a number of sunstroke patients. One severe case of sunburn. A bald-headed passenger who went ashore without a hat. There were warnings in all our literature and regularly on the cabin television, but some people think they have divine and heavenly protection from the sun's rays.

I went to see the woman passenger who now sported half a leg in plaster. She was adamant that she did not want to be flown home.

'No way,' she said, with a distinct North American drawl. 'I'm on this cruise and I'm staying. I like it here. I'll get around in a wheelchair. There are the lifts to everywhere and plenty of ramps over the doorsteps on to the decks. It would be nice to cash in on the sympathy vote.'

'That's the spirit, Mrs Laurent,' I said. 'I'll find a rota of stewards who will help you get around, particularly to meals. You don't want to develop huge arm muscles, propelling yourself. And Excursion Sales are offering you some free excursions if you feel well enough to take them. They'll make doubly sure you get on and off safely, and that the wheelchair is stored on the coach.'

'Well, that's very nice,' said Mrs Laurent. 'I'd like that. I don't want to miss out on everything. As it is, I can hardly sunbathe and only get one leg brown.'

'You could always even things up with a fake tan when you get home,' I said. 'They are surprisingly good these days.'

'Thank you so much for coming to see me, Casey,' she said. She was a bobbed platinum blonde, mid-fifties, a racy looking lady, lots of glittery jewellery. 'It's good not to be forgotten. And don't worry, I'm not going to sue Conway. It was my own fault. I wasn't looking where I was going.'

I made a note to visit Mrs Laurent again and soon.

And that was a reassurance. Passengers sued

for anything if they could get away with it. We had one passenger who sued over a fly in her soup. I swear she brought it aboard and dunked it in the crème de celery herself.

We were now heading into the Atlantic. There was a long stretch of sea days ahead. Passengers got grumpy with boredom. So we laid on a programme of activities that made the mind spin. We had ballroom dancing, aerobics, deck quoits, mini golf, port lectures, history lectures, creative writing for the would-be authors, bingo, trivia quiz, a cooking demonstration by the chief chef, how to make cocktails by the barman, how to carve ice by an iceman.

The ship's newspaper, *Countess Today*, gave a full itinerary. It took half an hour to read it. Some passengers put it straight into the bin and then complained if they missed a film or a show.

Cocktail shaking was always popular. The barman made sure everyone got a generous sample before lunch. His Fuzzy Naval was a dream and his Peach Schnapps and orange juice was simply sensational. No shortage of volunteers for the tasting session.

I had not seen Dr Mallory all day. Passengers kept asking me questions that I couldn't answer. I wanted to be kept informed. I sent him an email via the office computer. It was quicker than trying to look for him.

'Dr M,' I emailed. 'Kindly keep me informed re Reg Hawkins. I have a dozen questions a day to answer. KC Jones.'

Answer: 'Dear Casey. Say heart attack. SM.'

This was not good enough. I didn't have time

to beard him in his den. All the entertainment had had to be rescheduled. Happily everyone on board was co-operative.

We were ploughing through endless dark-blue, white-tipped waves. Some shipping passed on the horizon. This was the dolphin watch, too early for the whale watch. Passengers leaned over the rails for hours, video cameras cradled at the ready. I would do the same, but then I was sea-witched. I loved the sea, the water and the waves, the endless blue. It was my medication, my soul, my dream.

'Casey Jones,' Samuel said, taking a rail spot near mine. 'How are you coping? We didn't expect this, did we? So early on in the cruise.'

'Where is Reg Hawkins now?'

'Refrigerated alongside Mr Foster. Fortunately we have plenty of space. This is a very big ship below decks. We do nothing until we get back to Southampton when we hand him over to the authorities. I'm not qualified to do more than the most preliminary post-mortem. As far as I could see, it was a heart attack.'

'So, what else did you find? How long had he been in the box?'

'I found nothing. Not long, I think. A few un-explained scratches.'

'And who put him there?'

'I don't know. I'm not a detective. He didn't have a label attached to him, giving that infor-mation. I'm a plain, ordinary bedside doctor.'

'Haven't you made any enquiries? Where was the box found for a start? I'd be asking questions all over the ship. The whole business is shrouded in mystery,' I said, almost angrily.

'You solve it then. You're the expert. It's only coincidental, circumstantial,' said Samuel Mallory, dismissing the whole affair. 'Don't worry about it.'

'Two heart attacks on the same table? It's not possible. Passengers are asking to be moved.'

'I don't blame them. I wouldn't sit there either.' Samuel Mallory was not joking. He looked perfectly serious. 'Are you all right? You look a bit fraught.'

'Of course, I'm fraught. It is not exactly the perfect beginning to a cruise but it happens. It'll get better from now. We've the Caribbean ahead of us. And before then, Maderia. Everyone loves the Caribbean, all those sun-drenched beaches and waving palm trees. We've lots of Americans on board, determined to enjoy themselves.'

'Would you like a drink at a beach café? A swim on a deserted beach in the moonlight?'

'No way. What about all those other women you have been chatting up? The swarm of blondes. Surely they come first in the seduction stakes?'

'Let me know if you change your mind. It isn't as if I have to book a patch of sand.'

'I haven't made up my mind.'

'So I thought. Lack of feedback or confidence. I have pills for it. Now, if you'll excuse me, I also have patients to attend to.'

'And I have passengers. Don't let me delay you.'

I took the lift down to the Galaxy Lounge where a small group of musicians were playing dance music for the dance class. They were the officially elderly dancing ladies, pin-thin bodies, stretched tanned skin, their partners even older and less energetic. They were using the dance floor as their practice ground, twirling and shuffling to the beat of the music. The women's clothes were flamboyant and gorgeous. They looked like tropical birds, still managing to walk in impossible heels. The traditional crossbar helped.

'You haven't lost your enthusiasm for dancing?' I asked a couple who were taking a breather at a table. Mineral water on the table. No overspending here.

'Never,' they said, almost in unison. 'It's what keeps us young and fit. We love dancing.'

I rarely had time to dance, sometimes on the last night, but even then there was masses of paperwork to catch up on, sales forms to be signed, before everyone disembarked. And the arrival of the next batch in the pipeline.

It wasn't easy to dance on a floor that occasionally tilted. A few unscheduled lurches caught them unawares and several couples gave up, preferring the terra firma of an upholstered seat.

The bravehearts were jiving to Glenn Miller. You could see they had learned to jive at post-Second-World-War canteen dances. They were reliving their youth. They had so much energy.

'We met at a dance,' said the same couple, still in unison. 'We danced to this very tune. "In The Mood", it's called.'

Nostalgia tugged at them and they couldn't

resist the music or the memories. They got up and began quite a spirited jive, considering their combined age, with complicated steps and turns. The floor filled up again as the music reminded the couples of flirtations and romances of long ago.

A tall, elegant woman stood beside me. She was not a gaudy bird of paradise but more of a dove, her silvery grey lace dress the last word in high fashion, but I couldn't put a known label on it.

'I once met a gorgeous American GI dancing to this tune,' she said. 'The GIs always had such wonderful manners, and of course they had chocolates and nylon stockings which were practically unobtainable in England.'

'So did you become a GI bride?' I asked, more as a joke than being personal.

'I often wished I had,' she said with a smile. 'It might have been more fun than living in Pinner and working in London. I had a choice. Work in London or work in Paris. And I picked the wrong city, out of misplaced loyalty. I stayed in England. This was after the war, of course.'

'So when did you meet the GI?'

'I don't remember the year. I escaped from France before the war ended. A little disorientated. War does that to you.'

Escaped from France? I hoped this interesting woman was going to tell me more but she spotted some friends across the dance floor and went to join them. I noticed she had a slight limp and sat down quite quickly. She was not intending to dance. A stewardess came over and took her

68

order. The woman looked in my direction and with a slight, very French inclination, offered me a drink. But I shook my head with a smile and a 'no thank you'.

The ballroom tutors, Tony and Janet, were doing the rounds, dancing with wallflowers of both sexes. They worked non-stop on the cruises and ran a dance school in Surrey. Classes every sea day, practices, and they always turned up at the evening dances to encourage their sail-alone pupils to find partners.

'Bet you've got your hands full,' said Janet. She was a neat, dark-haired woman, always wearing pretty pastel clothes. 'You've got that gap to fill. What a headache for you. Will they fly someone out to Maderia? Pick the ship up there?'

'Head Office are working on it. Not easy at such short notice. But we need someone for the long sea leg to the Caribbean. And we don't pick up Estelle Grayson till Barbados.'

'Oh Lord, not that woman? I didn't realize the prima donna was joining us again. I shall keep out of her way. She's always trying to get me to choreograph her numbers. She can't dance and never will. Wishful thinking. She has three legs and one of those is short.'

I had to grin. It was such a good description of the temperamental singer. Careful, Casey. Don't say anything which might get back to Estelle. I needed a fresh pair of kid gloves every day she was on board.

'She'll want a seat in the Windsor Dining Room straight away, at the best table with lots of

69

admiring passengers to buy her CDs.'

'Well, there's plenty of room on table two, second sitting,' I said. 'No problem there. I can arrange that immediately.'

It was not the kindest of thoughts.

Six

Maderia

The magical island of Madeira was appearing on the horizon as a smudge. I remembered the first time I had visited the island as a young girl. It had been a different place then, embroiled in politics, with posters and slogans plastered over every wall in the capital of Funchal. The wild fennel place. I'd been frightened by the feeling of violence.

It had all changed since then and was back to being an island of flowers, jacaranda trees and bougainvillea, open markets and canal walks. I knew the passengers were going to love the ancient rainforests, green gorges and sparkling waterfalls cooling the air, though maybe not the three rivers struggling through the centre of the town. There were handsome old palaces and fortresses from different eras along the front, with fine Portuguese architecture, not far from the quayside, many now museums or army headquarters or government buildings.

And they were going to have an evening in port which was always enjoyable. To eat at a local restaurant for a change or wander along the sea front promenade or the palm-tree lined avenues, enjoying the lights, the stalls and the balmy warm late-night air, blown from North Africa. *Countess* would not be leaving till midnight. Getting everyone back on board would be a headache. They might linger over a glass or two and lose track of time.

Especially if they went in search of the famous Madeira wine, a dark brown fortified wine. There were dozens of wine-tasting shops in Funchal. Madeira came in four main types – all very potent – a dry wine, Verdelho, Bual and Malmsey, all dessert wines. Malmsey had been the favourite in past centuries. History was in that drink.

The *Countess* had entered the harbour of Funchal early that morning and swung 180 degrees before mooring starboard side to the quay. The temperature was seventy degrees Fahrenheit or twenty-one degrees Celsius.

I stood at the quayside as passengers alighted from the gangway and reminded them of the departure time. There was a board with the last time for boarding chalked on it but many walked past, not looking, more excited by a new place to explore and keen to go shopping. Many never got further than the nearest café or the statue of Henry the Navigator. The overlooking Parque de Sante Catarina was another favourite place and not far to walk. It had a good view of the harbour

71

and the town. A yacht once owned by the Beatles was now a floating restaurant.

I was swamped in paperwork, as usual, so it was some time before I could go ashore. No time to go to the lush sub-tropical interior, or nearby Camara de Lobos, the fishing village where Winston Churchill liked to paint. Although I knew that there was still squalor in the narrow streets.

Madeira had been cleaned up. The flowers on sale in the markets were something special. I wanted to buy huge armfuls of intoxicating colour. I took a taxi up to the Jardim Botânico in Caminho do Meio, and was swept away by the flowers and the astounding views, especially the spectacular viaduct soaring over the steep valley. I could stay there forever. I was far too late for the early morning fish market or the flower market. Though I wanted some flowers.

'So, you like flowers?' It was Dr Samuel Mallory, leaning over the rail beside me that separated us from a steep drop on to the twisting road below.

'My mother loved flowers. She grew them. It's inherited.'

'Is she still alive?'

'Sadly, no. She has died. I miss her.' He did not pursue the subject.

'Have you seen the tropical bird garden, those primeval parrots, or the garden with all the orchids? Apparently 3,000 different varieties. A Madeiran speciality.'

'There isn't time to see everything.'

'So shall I buy you a plant instead?'

'No, thank you. I'm not sure I can take a plant on board. Isn't there some regulation?'

'I know you can't take a plant into the States. So how about tonight? What are you doing? We've all that extra time in port. Fancy a walk around the quayside, maybe a coffee or a glass of Madeira?' he asked.

Samuel was in a black T-shirt and white jeans, sneakers, wrap-around sunglasses. He looked like any other tourist except for the cool, handsome, chiselled jaw. I was not that impressed by his good looks. Not like some of the women passengers who crowded round him the moment he appeared on deck.

'I'll see if I'm free,' I said. 'It'll be a busy night, getting everyone back on board. I can see myself doing a sweep of the bars.'

'Then it makes sense if we do it together,' said Samuel. 'How about that we meet at eight o'clock, have a coffee and a walk, and then set to work. Two officers working together should have the required authority to get passengers turning back to the ship. What do you think?'

'Put like that, it sounds good,' I said, wondering what I had let myself in for. I didn't fancy wandering around the harbour of Funchal with this attractive man late at night. He might be difficult to handle. There were no guide books for dealing with men who knew they had everything and thought they were the answer to every maiden's token prayer. Caution, Casey. Stay alert. Don't wear anything that looks like a come-on. No cleavage or clinging skirt.

That's how I came to meet Samuel wearing

73

navy slacks, matelot striped shirt, and low-heeled navy sandals, hair loose. He had changed into chinos, a linen jacket and open-necked white shirt. His eyes swept over me.

'Very ... er, masculine,' he said eventually.

'It's the pseudo-authoritarian look,' I said. 'It's about getting people back on board, not about enjoying myself.'

'I hope that I'll be able to change that,' he said, taking my arm to guide me through the throng of evening strollers along the front. 'A hard-working lady like you deserves a few treats.'

I noticed that he didn't describe me as beautiful, or lovely or elegant. Hard-working was how he saw me. It was a small stab in the back. I tried not to let it hurt.

The line of sea-front stalls were fun. Lots of passengers were spending their last Portuguese escudos on knick-knacks and fripperies. The stalls sold everything from food to souvenirs, exquisite embroidery, painted tiles, local produce and flowers. The big cruise ships in the harbour meant lots of money changing hands.

Samuel went up to a stall that sold hair ornaments of all sorts, shapes and designs. He cast an experienced eye over the assortment and pounced on a circle of exotic white flowers sewn on to some stretchy stuff.

'Perfect,' he said. He bought it and before I knew what was happening, he had pulled back my straggling hair and threaded on the circlet of flowers. I could hardly fight him off. 'A touch of glamour,' he added.

'Very nice. Thank you,' I said ungraciously. I

knew it was perfect but I wasn't going to tell him so. The flowers were over the top but took away the severity of my navy outfit. My step lightened. I couldn't stop my feet wanting to dance. And there was music coming from a nearby café.

Samuel noticed the change in my mood and steered me towards the old-style Café Apolo in the street running down from the cathedral. 'Coffee or wine?' he asked.

I'd forgotten 'Caution, Casey'. 'Wine, please. White with ice.'

'Ice in wine?' he raised one of those dark eyebrows. Did he know how suave he looked? 'That's new for me. Do I detect a puritan streak?'

'That's for me not to say and for you to find out,' I said. This was not an entirely original response. I'd read it somewhere and liked it. This was one smooth baby. For a moment I could forget all the shipboard problems and the two bodies in freezer compartments down in the depths. I wondered if Mrs Foster had come ashore or whether she had stayed on board, listening to Cole Porter and Gershwin.

Samuel ordered in hesitant Portuguese. 'I've ordered you a white port on the rocks,' he said. 'Something different for you to try.'

'Does it have a floral overtone?' He was too bossy for words. My hair, now my drink. What else was he going to change?

I saw Mrs Laurent being wheeled along by an older man in a blazer. She was wearing a long floaty mauve dress to hide the plaster. He looked very attentive, listening to her every word. He had a captive companion who might be a first for a long time. There were a lot of lonely people on board.

'Nice lady,' said Samuel, nodding towards the departing wheelchair. 'She had a tricky break but she made no fuss. Pops a few painkillers and is getting on with the cruise. Some of my patients ... you wouldn't believe it. They expect a Harley Street consultation for a headache.'

'It takes all sorts,' I said vaguely. 'But they don't allow wheelchairs into the casino, so she can't gamble.' I wasn't going to gossip about the passengers. I didn't trust this man half an inch. But the port was lovely and it made me smile at him. The extra coldness gave it a bite.

'You should smile more often,' he said. 'It lights up your face.'

'I smile all day long,' I said. 'Give my muscles some time off. I'm off duty now.'

'I hear they are departing table two, second sitting, in droves,' he said. He was drinking some ice-cold local beer. 'It's down to four now. No one wants to sit there. They are spreading stories about the table being jinxed.'

'The waiters won't like it. They'll lose their tips. The magician's box ... I suppose it has been put safely into storage somewhere?' I was digging.

'Sure. It's evidence, apparently.'

'I'm not so sure,' I said. 'I've been thinking about Merlin's act. He did those illusions right under the nose of the audience. Very clever. He did it by distracting their attention with something totally irrelevant. I think the box is totally irrelevant. I think we are being distracted.'

'Now there's a clever girl,' said Samuel, grinning.

'Hard working and now clever? That's two compliments in one evening. I'll have to chalk it up. Will I be able to stand it?'

'Just you wait. You might like the third even more.' He was laughing at me, understanding my sarcasm, going along with it. He'd earned half a point. 'And you may be right. I couldn't see the point of the box. Unless he didn't die of a heart attack and wasn't meant to be found for quite a time.'

'So what about the cherry-red blood?'

'How do you know there was cherry-red blood?'

'I was there. I saw it. Remember, when Mr Foster collapsed?'

'And what exactly do you know about cherry-red blood? Tell me, like you've read some books or are a failed medical student.'

'Neither. But it's a sign of cyanide poisoning, isn't it?'

'Exactly. Whereas with a straightforward heart attack the blood is usually a dark purple.'

I shivered. I didn't want to talk about this death any more. 'But where would anyone get cyanide? You can't buy it in any shop. Surely we don't have it on board.'

'It's used in photography and some jewellery work. It can also be extracted from laurel leaves and some seeds. That's why it has a bitter-almond smell.'

'Who got near enough to smell anything?'

Samuel leaned across the table. He touched my hand. It was fleeting but like an electric shock. 'Shall we talk about something different, Casey? This is an evening for the living, not for dying.'

He was right. The night was balmy, a beautiful sickle moon, the harbour full of lights. And the music. My life has always been full of music. Now I had to live without it.

I spotted Amanda Banesto, looking gorgeous in something straight from L'Eclaireur, Paris. It must have taken weeks to sew on all those shimmering beads. She was strolling with the same young man I had seen with her in Palma.

'Do you know those two?' I asked, forgetting that I wasn't going to gossip. Perhaps this was my night for forgetting. I had a lot to forget.

'Yes,' he said, clamping down. 'She has some trouble sleeping. Don't ask me anything else about Ms Banesto. Patient confidentiality.'

'I'm not surprised if she witnessed her fiancé being knifed. I'd have trouble sleeping.'

I'd finished my drink. A second would not be a good idea. Samuel understood and didn't offer. We got up and started to wander, meandering through the crowds.

Nigel Garten spotted the two of us. 'Hey,' he said with a grin. 'Isn't this called internal crew fraternization? Is it allowed?'

'Purely professional,' I said. 'Mr Garten...' I was calling him back. 'Aren't you on table two, second sitting? I'm glad to see that it doesn't worry you.'

'No way, Miss Jones. I'm not superstitious.

Both heart attacks, weren't they? I'm as strong as an ox. Why don't you join us? There's a couple of empty places now. It would be nice to have a pretty face on our table.'

'I may well do that, but you know what my evenings are like. Hardly time for a bite. Maybe my deputy will stand in at a show and I'll join you.'

'That would be real nice.'

He was overweight but pleasant with it. He had a cheerful open face, was the kind of man who didn't make snide remarks, no put-downs, always outgoing, even if he did go to a lot of parties. I wondered about his background. Was he divorced, separated, widowed, single? I didn't know.

'You've an admirer,' said Samuel as we started touring the bars. 'He seems very nice. Could do with losing a few pounds but people forget to eat less as they age.'

'He is nice but lonely. A lot of lonely people come on cruises.'

'And it's not only the passengers. Crew as well. Crew are lonely too. They are separated from their families for months on end. They sign contracts. But they need the money to send home.'

'I know. You don't have to tell me. I know how long the stewards work before they can go home. My steward has a wife and two baby girls. He's shown me their photos. He sends money home to support them.'

'So where is your home, tell me, Miss Jones?'

'West Sussex, on the coast. And how about

79

you, Dr Mallory, such a handsome man of many charms?'

'It's Irish charm. Haven't you detected the accent? I've been working on it for years. It is not trusted in some parts of the world.'

'I'm so sorry. I trust you, sort of, I think. Don't let me down. I've a feeling we are going to need each other on this cruise. In a purely professional way, of course,' I added hastily. I didn't know why I was suddenly serious.

'That may be very true, Miss Jones. Look, I know that we didn't get on very well, at the start. But I like you. And it's not just Madeira moonglow. We need each other. You're clever, and don't get me wrong, you are also quite beautiful in a remote way, a face to launch a thousand ships. One look at you and I'm floating, and that's not good.'

I didn't know what to say. Dr Mallory was staring at me, those light grey eyes so intent. I was thrown. It was time to move on. I looked at my watch. One hour before departure. The *Countess* was primed to leave soon. Time to round up the late-nighters still in the bars.

'So forget launching ships. Shall we get going?' I said, a real smile touching my face. 'You and me, Dr Mallory. The last round-up. It'll be fun. Hand in hand, like the Sundance Kids. Let's get going.'

'Hey, I need a kiss. I can't ever get going on round-ups without a kiss.'

No soft lights. But he kissed me. Not quite sure where, on the cheek, but it was enough to get us both going. We went out to round-up the late-comers. The chivvying was light-hearted but they got the message. Except for one passenger who was sitting in a café right on the front, drinking beer, watching the *Countess* making her preparations to leave.

He was dragged on board by an eagle-eyed crew member when the electronic cruise-card check at the top of the gangway didn't tally. The man apologized profusely, said it was such a lovely evening, he had quite forgotten he was on the ship.

Seven

At Sea

We were heading for the Caribbean now at an average speed of twenty knots and the days at sea were getting hotter. Passengers lay in rows on the deck, determined to toast themselves to a crisp. The sea breeze was deceptive and they did not realize how the temperature was climbing.

The stewardesses did a roaring trade in serving cold drinks while managing to stay looking cool and trim. There were two small swimming pools and a Jacuzzi, all packed with bodies. I never swam in a ship's pool. Four strokes and you bumped your head on the opposite side. I preferred to wait for a beach and sand, and maybe make friends with a shark or two.

I rarely went out on deck till after four o'clock. My morning run round the promenade deck was early before breakfast. The air was cool then, but already warming up. Three times round was slightly under a mile. I made sure I staggered at least a mile even though I totted up a good few miles touring the decks each day on my usual rounds.

Our first port of call in the Caribbean was Barbados where we would be picking up Estelle Grayson, the soprano. I'd met her on other cruises. Her career was hopping between cruise ships with her solo act. Her touched-up photo was already displayed prominently in our entertainers' showcase.

Estelle was glamorous, with any lines or wrinkles that dared to appear quickly Botoxed out, her dark hair lustrous and piled high. Once on board, she demanded a daily appointment at the beauty salon. Never thought of washing her own hair between shows. Extensions are tricky to wash. She queened it around the bars, cadging drinks from admirers. Strictly against company rules but she took little notice. I knew I would have to warn her. And she would make a beeline for our gorgeous doctor. Maybe I ought to warn him too.

I came across the lady in grey lace whom I could now put a name to. She was Madame Maria de Leger. Every time I saw her she was at a deck table, scribbling away in a notebook.

'I'm writing my life story,' she told me. 'I went to one of the writing lectures about putting your life story on paper, and have got completely

82

carried away. I can't stop writing. I've got to get it all down before I forget everything. It is taking over my life. Of course, I shall go ashore at all our ports of call, but it's wonderful to have something real to do on board, apart from eating and drinking.'

'I expect you've had a really interesting life.'

'Can you believe I was parachuted into France during the war?' she laughed. 'Wait until you read my story. I must think of a good title. That writing lecturer said a good title was really important. It's your selling point.'

'Maybe I'll think of a few for you. *Ready, Steady, Jump*? *Ripcord Rebel*?' I suggested. Madame de Leger was not wearing lace today, but a cool looking linen pastel apple-green safari suit with lots of pearl-buttoned pockets. She had superb taste.

'I need all the help I can get. I like *Ripcord Rebel*. I suppose I was a bit of a rebel, for my time,' she said, offering me a drink. 'But it was wartime and people did strange things, found new strengths.'

I refused the drink again, politely, lightly, and moved on. There was an art auction this afternoon and I had to make sure everything was ready in the Princess Lounge. The crime scene tapes were down and we were back to normal, or near normality.

Tonight's entertainers were rehearsing and the lounge was closed to passengers as the dancers tried to remember what they had already forgotten. The music sounded good. It was an Abba orientated show, all their popular songs. We had some good singers aboard. Estelle would have to look to her laurels. She could easily be out-classed.

Samuel appeared at my side. He was in his medical whites and strangely had an after-six shadow on his chin. His beard was very dark. It was a groovy, Brad Pitt look. I liked it. Dishevel-led I go for. It must be something from way back.

'You look as if you have been up all night,' I said.

'I have. Two coffees please,' he waved at a stewardess. She obeyed instantly, still smiling. 'Mrs Foster. She took an overdose, Temazepam and a handful of aspirins. It shows you should never judge outward appearances. She seemed to be well-balanced and coping with life. But she wasn't. A steward found her in her stateroom this morning, couldn't rouse her, sent for me. I've been walking her for hours. She's coming round properly now.'

'Oh dear, I'm so sorry. Maybe it was acciden-tal. She could have forgotten she had already taken her sleeping pills. Temazepan's a sleeping pill, isn't it? I meant to go and see her,' I said, appalled. 'She was on my list.'

'You and your lists. Don't blame yourself. Listen, Casey, do what your heart says to do now. Forget making lists and follow your heart. It's always too late tomorrow.'

The stewardess arrived with the coffees in double-quick time. She glowed with happiness. She obviously adored the doctor. I thought about his words as I stirred my coffee. He was right.

It's always too late tomorrow. I looked at him with renewed interest. He had never struck me as profound before.

'Do the crew ever come to see you?' I asked without thinking.

'They do. But I don't charge them.'

'I'm crew,' I added without thinking.

'You can come any time. I'd always make a space for you. Feel free, Miss Jones. Bring me all your problems.' He was smiling, and it was a sweet smile despite the dark stubble. 'It may be a long and thorough consultation.'

'You need some sleep,' I said.

'I know,' he said. 'But I get very lonely in bed. Have you any suggestions?'

'How about a teddy bear? The shop has some gorgeous ones.'

'I was thinking of something a little softer and warmer than a teddy bear. Besides I'm allergic to acrylic.'

Samuel was laughing at me, again. But this time I didn't mind. 'I'll draw up a list for you,' I said. 'There is probably a queue of female passengers, softer and warmer, ready and eager to share your lonely bed.'

'You disappoint me, Miss Jones. I was hoping for a more personal suggestion. But I guess you have your work to do and I have mine.'

I finished my coffee and stood up. 'Time for forty winks now, Dr Mallory. I'm glad Mrs Foster is all right. Let me know when I can visit her.'

'I'm more interested in when you can visit me.'

85

The auction area of the Princess Lounge was full. The gallery staff had arranged their works of art, mostly contemporary prints of mediocre value, on easels for viewing. Quite a selection of tastefully naked ladies and colourful rural scenes. A lot of fishing boats and poinsettias on display. The prints were all very pleasant, but as Mrs Foster had said, they were wallpaper art. Not a Monet among them.

Tamara Fitzgibbons, the manager, and her assistant, were greeting their customers with flutes of sparkling champagne and tiny canapés, a mere mouthful of something savoury. It was halfway between lunch and supper so there might be a temporary gap to fill.

The gallery staff were both very glossy: hair, nails, cheeks, lips. They used a ton of gloss a day. It was a wonder they didn't slip on deck.

It was a painless way to buy a painting. They bubble-wrapped it for you and shipped it to your home, took care of any tax payable. Many of the passengers would never think of going into an art gallery in normal circumstances. This was something to do. Filling a window of time, as they say these days. And it made them feel that they knew something about art, that they knew the names, recognized a painter's work. They felt like collectors when in fact they weren't.

'Everything all right?' I asked Tamara. She was so institutionalized by cruising that she acted as if she was one of the passengers. Tamara was contracted to be on board for months on end, sailing over endless wastes of water, depths of 5,200 metres as now, simply to sell her firm's paintings. She barely knew where she was.

'Like a dream,' she said, flashing a veneered smile. 'We've had so many bids already. And of course the lucky draw attracts a lot of attention.'

They gave away one painting each auction. Punters collected a ticket as they arrived through the doors. I tried to move on. They gave away the same print every cruise. They had a cupboard full of them, stored at the stern of the ship. I'd seen the door open once or twice, when they had been moving stock around. It was stacked with rack upon rack of paintings, like eggs.

'Excellent,' I said, which meant nothing.

'Would you like some champagne?'

'No, thank you. It's too early for me. Glad it's all going well. Let me know if you need anything.'

'Another pair of hands?' she said archly. As if they did much work the rest of the day. Some people have a strange idea of their capacity for work. Make two sales, do a little dusting and they are exhausted and have to put their feet up with a scented icepack on their eyes.

I had other work to do. I faxed ahead, making sure Estelle Grayson would be met at Barbados airport by our port agent and driven to the quayside to board the ship. I checked that her cabin was ready. I checked that there would be flowers in the cabin to welcome her. The other entertainers didn't get the same treatment, no way. But then the other entertainers were not so awkward.

And she would want a place in the Windsor

Dining Room straight away, no slumming it down on deck F in the officers' mess for her. Well, I knew of a very pleasant table where there was plenty of room.

I met Richard Norton, the security officer, on his way to the bridge. He looked concerned. I knew better than to try to get information out of him. But he seemed pleased to have someone to offload his worries on to.

'Big trouble?'

'You've said it, big trouble.' He pursed his lips, clamping down on a sigh. 'It's all these late films you watch in the cinema.'

'They are an education,' I agreed, shaking my head. 'We should censor them. We could so easily be corrupted.'

'How about I come along with you, one evening? Make sure you are watching the right stuff.' He was looking down at me from his six-foot-three bulk.

I was thrown. I had this oceanic reputation for being cool. It followed me from ship to ship and no man had a pickaxe handy for the ice. Being an ice maiden suited me. I never wanted any on-board complications. No romancing the officers even though their smart uniforms and tanned legs were enough to send palpitations through the entire female passenger list.

Richard Norton was nice looking in a cuddly-bear crossed with ex-Marine way. He was big, burly, somewhat overweight, with crisply cut greying hair, cleft chin. I couldn't see the colour of his eyes. He was too far up to see.

'I'd really like that,' I heard myself answering.

What was I saying? I went to the cinema on my own. I like being on my own. It was my way of chilling out in the darkness, in a cocoon of fantasy. My time with the stars. 'But don't expect any holding hands in the romantic bits.'

'As if I would?' he said grinning, walking away.

The art auction was going well. I was on the verge of leaving it when Samuel Mallory appeared at my side again. He looked even worse for wear.

'What's the matter?' I said. 'You look awful.'

'I need some sleep,' he said. He was blinking hard to keep his eyes open.

'So why are you here and not in your cabin?'

'I wanted to tell you that there are medical tests to measure blood and urine levels of cyanide. Tissue levels can also be measured but it rapidly clears from the body. So I took samples of blood and urine and tissue from both of the victims of sudden death. It's not something I normally do.' He looked drawn and exhausted. There were shadows under his eyes.

'Cyanide? Do you mean that Mr Foster's death was from cyanide poisoning? That bright red skin? The cherry-red blood on the tablecloth? For heaven's sake, how would anyone get cyanide on board ship?'

'It's used in the fumigation of ships.'

'No way. It isn't possible,' I said. 'It's the poison of crime novels. Agatha Christie, she wrote one, and there are others.'

'Casey, I'm only telling you this so that you

89

will be careful. They were not normal deaths. I've said nothing before because I don't want there to be a major panic on-board ship. You know how rumours travel. I'm not sure about Reg Hawkins. Could be death from natural causes.'

'Are you trying to tell me something?'

Samuel took me aside with a gesture that was almost paternal, although the touch was light and impersonal. We walked down one of the inside decks, past the Bond Street shopping gallery, the Internet Study, the library. He was always taller than me but now he seemed bowed with exhaustion. None of the usual suave charm. He was like any overworked GP in a downtown area.

I didn't know where he was taking me. Nor did I care. My afternoon time was running out. Very soon I would be back in my office, checking arrangements, before changing for the evening's entertainment. He was leaving me short of time as it was.

'Is this important?' I asked.

'Yes,' he said. 'It is important. If you want to stay alive.'

This was too melodramatic for words. I shook my head, wishing he would go away and put his head down.

'Have you been along here recently?' he went on.

'No. Why should I?'

'This is the corridor where they display crew photographs and then on the opposite wall are all the photographs of the entertainment staff.'

'So what? I know that. Rows of photographs. No one looks at them.'

'I think you should look at them now,' said Samuel.

The corridor was opposite one of the double flights of stairs, lifts central and cloakrooms at either end, a few sofas and tables for discreet conversation. And as always, beautiful displays of flowers.

Strangely the temperature seemed to have dropped. Yet it was still early evening and we were nearing the Caribbean. The air was humid outside on deck. Samuel had his hand lightly on my arm.

'Don't be afraid,' he said. 'I'm with you.'

I stood in front of the crew photograph display. Everyone was smiling and smartly uniformed. The names were printed under their photograph. Dr Samuel Mallory was one of them. He looked, as always, incredibly handsome. It was a wonder he wasn't signed up for the next James Bond.

The next display was of the entertainment team including the dancers, choreographer, stars, musicians, lighting operator, sound engineer, stage manager. At the top was my photograph, taken quite recently. A studio photograph, poised, in my Conway Blue Line uniform. Dark hair pulled back, the blonde streak visible. A smile, as always, on my lips.

A chill ran down my spine. I swallowed a gasp. Samuel's hand tightened on my arm.

'Don't be afraid,' he said again. 'Breath deeply.'

The photograph had been slashed, twice. Two

91

knife cuts, right across my face. They were deep and vicious cuts.

'They don't hurt a bit,' I said, my voice trembling.

Eight

At Sea

I'm not usually found propping up any bar but Samuel propelled me to the nearest and almost deserted bar, and ordered a double brandy and soda. I was shaking. For once I was not checking the time, nor greeting faces or exchanging smiles. I was taking myself off duty.

'Drink up,' ordered the doctor.

My hand was shaking so much he had to help me. The brandy went down my throat like firewater, making me cough.

'Are you all right?' said Mrs Laurent, looking concerned, being wheeled past on one of her circuits. 'Can I get you some water?'

'Thank you,' said Samuel. 'Miss Jones will be all right in a moment. She has had a slight shock. I'll take care of her.'

'Always in the right place at the right time,' she said, smiling. 'You are the perfect doctor.'

'Who would do that?' I choked, wiping my chin with a tissue. 'And why? Why would they do that?'

'I don't know, Casey,' he said. 'Perhaps it's a warning. Perhaps you have been making too many enquiries. Getting too close to something.'

'But I haven't done anything,' I protested. 'Just getting on with my everyday job, seeing that all the entertainment runs smoothly. What enquiries? I haven't made any enquiries. At least, I don't think I have.'

'Perhaps you've been seen talking to the wrong people, me or Richard Norton.'

'We were talking about unsuitable films at the cinema,' I wailed. 'Hardly photo-slashing material.'

'Maybe they have seen you talking to me. We've discussed the recent deaths, several times. Someone may have overheard us. Or maybe it's a warning to me, to keep off, to mind my own business.'

'But surely they would slash your photograph, if that was the case?'

'Yes, I suppose so.' He was deep in thought. A pencil-thin woman in a see-through black and gold caftan waved from across the bar but he didn't see her. Her smile dropped, annoyed.

I knew what the slashing could mean. The threat was aimed at me if he didn't lay off his enquiries. They didn't know that I meant nothing at all to him. Perhaps they were relying on some aspect of old-fashioned chivalry, thought that we were an item, but I had yet to notice much itemizing going around.

'So what enquiries have you been making?' I asked, actually enjoying the high alcohol-factor of the brandy now. It was not my normal drink.

This one had a definite wow-factor.

'Nothing much. But I took samples of blood and urine and tissue from both of the dead men and did some tests, as I told you. Also hair strands. Medical tests can measure the levels of cyanide but it rapidly clears from the body. I thought I ought to have a few samples, just in case.'

'Cyanide? You really think Mr Foster died from cyanide poisoning?' This was such a shock. I hope it merited another double brandy. 'But how could anyone get hold of cyanide these days? It's not exactly an over-the-counter rat poison. How does it work?'

'From the inside. It blocks the body's ability to absorb oxygen, that's why the skin is red and the blood is still red. It's full of oxygen.'

'But it looks like a heart attack to an outsider?'

'That's right, gasping, clutching the heart, collapsing. Classic heart-attack symptoms. It's also used for executions in prisons. They used it in the gas chambers.'

I shuddered. 'Perhaps these were mob executions.'

'It's around in solvents and plastics. A cyanide solution is used in photography and jewellery and the fumigation of ships. They stun fish with it in the Caribbean in the coral reefs. It's even present in some old nail varnish removers. There's plenty around if you know where to look for it.'

'So we are looking for a member of the crew with an interest in fishing and photography, who makes jewellery as a hobby?'

'Some sort of mixture like that. Does it fit any-one?'

'And someone who has a key to the photo displays in the lobby. The photos are behind a glass frame and the key is kept in my office. Only my staff know that it is there. No graffiti, or drawing moustaches and cartoon spectacles on photos allowed on this ship.'

Samuel peered at me. It was the first time I had clearly seen his eyes. They were grey, the clearest grey, steel-like, cobalt and silvery. And he had lashes that were positively lethal. They shouldn't be allowed on a man.

'But what about Reg Hawkins. Surely not the same?'

'I'm not sure about him yet. You're looking better, Casey. Not so washed out any more. The colour is coming back into your cheeks,' he said.

'Not cherry-red, I hope?'

'No, thank goodness. I don't want to see that again on this cruise. You didn't need to tell me about the blood. It was written on their faces. They both had cherry-red skin. Did you know that they tried to poison the Russian, Rasputin, with cyanide?'

'I don't want to know,' I said.

'But it didn't work because they fed it to him in sweet pastries and Madeira wine. Sugar is a natural antidote.'

'I'll remember to keep taking the sugar,' I said.

'I think another double brandy would do you more good,' said the perfect doctor, waving to the barman. 'Have you a photograph to replace that one?'

'How about leaving it in the display case? To show that person that I don't give a fig? That I'm not scared?' I wasn't scared after two double brandies. I could face anyone. Fisticuffs at dawn, on the quoits deck.

'Yes, leave it. If you replace it, the same could happen again. But you could then have a watch placed in the lobby. We could fix up a CCTV camera, catch them in the act.'

'But they might be expecting a camera, hear about it, see it being fixed, that is if they were a member of the crew. Nothing is sacrosanct. Word goes round faster than an epidemic of food poisoning.'

'Don't mention food poisoning. It is the medical department's nightmare. Pray for antiseptic sprays that work and everyone washing their hands after going to the loo. It ought to be printed on their tickets.'

The conversation was slipping. I could see that Dr Mallory was tiring. He'd been tired to start with, but he was now on the verge of nodding off.

'Time for bed, doctor,' I said firmly. 'Thank you for looking after me. Go back to your cabin and put your head down on your pillow. You look all in. You need some serious sleep.'

'Are you coming with me?' he asked, suddenly all sleepy and sexy, but not really meaning it, no energy for physical activity. He was teasing, a sort of last resource of energy dredged up before he collapsed on the bar.

'You go dream about it,' I said, guiding him towards the lift. I had no idea to which deck he should be heading. I didn't know then, that he was among the elite, with a cabin on the bridge, near the captain's quarters. The posh part. 'No Admittance' signs on all the stairways that led to the bridge.

'Goodnight, sweet Ophelia,' he said, saluting me.

'No drowning allowed on this ship,' I said, pushing him into the lift.

The evening's programme was somewhat up the creek but no one seemed to notice. There were several hiccups. The shows went on, the quiz, the films. There was music everywhere. The ship was afloat with music. I wondered if I was completely redundant.

'We need you urgently.' It was Susan on her phone. 'The DJ hasn't turned up in the Galaxy Lounge. Everyone is waiting there for the late-night disco dancing to start. Have you got time to do it, Casey?'

'Sure,' I said. 'I know how to turn a turntable.' I didn't ask why Susan wasn't doing it. Maybe she had already gone to bed in her baby-doll PJs with her hair in rollers.

This confidence was sheer exaggeration. I was hoping there would be some passenger with an ambition to be a DJ who might take pity on me and help out. I rushed to my cabin, threw on a disco-like shimmering purple tunic top and trousers, clipped up my hair, bits sticking out like a hedgehog. I was back in the Galaxy Lounge in less than two minutes. Sheer genius.

'Here we go, folks,' I said into the loudspeaker, only slightly out of breath. I took a quick look at the record label. '"Nutbush City Limits". We want to see all of you on the floor. Not exactly on the floor, but dancing on the floor. You know what I mean.'

Good start.

As the music echoed into the lounge, beat pounding, song raucous, the dancers were on the floor in seconds, gyrating in circles. I really wanted to put my head down and go to sleep. Those brandies on an empty stomach were not helping.

A stewardess, bless her, came to the DJ's booth with an enquiring smile. It was late for her, too. 'Would you like anything, Miss Jones?'

'I really need a long, cold drink,' I said. 'And something to eat. Anything will do.'

'No problem,' she said, with an enigmatic smile, gliding away.

Sometime later she came back with a glass of orange juice with ice and a plate of tiny, crustless sandwiches, left over from the midnight buffet. 'Sorry,' she said, shrugging, 'all I could do.'

'You're a star. Thank you.' I needed to line my empty stomach.

She went away, to twinkle somewhere on deck, where lovers hung over the rails and made promises into the swiftly flowing foam.

The absent DJ had left a pile of sorted records so I didn't have to make any decisions. I made a mental note to check this man's record. He'd missed a bingo session too. Two black marks. I got a little bored with the selection and slipped in a few requests of my own, George Michael's

'Careless Whisper' and SpyroGyra's 'Morning Dance'.

'Don't you ever sleep?' asked an amused, gravelly voice. I'd seen him around on the decks. He was a forty-something American, travelling on his own, who read a lot, stayed on the fringe of the marshmallow matrons.

'No one sleeps on this ship,' I said. 'It's forbidden. Far too much going on. Sleep and you miss a film, a lecture, a meal, a show.'

'I'd sure like to miss a few meals,' he said. 'No willpower.'

He wasn't dancing. I'd noticed him before sitting right at the back of the lounge, always a book and a drink on his table.

'I see you aren't dancing. There are lots of ladies here who would love a dance,' I said. 'Why don't you ask one of them?'

'I'm waiting for my dream woman,' he said. He half-smiled as if hoping his enigmatic statement would not be taken too seriously. He had a crooked eye tooth.

'Sorry, we don't have any of those on board,' I said flippantly.

'Sometimes dreams are more fun than real life,' he said. 'Miss Jones,' he added, inclining his head. He went back to his seat and opened the book. It was a hardback, looked heavy going. I was sorry he had left the booth. He sounded an interesting person to talk to. Maybe I'd see him in Barbados.

When I played the same dance number twice running, without noticing, I decided to pack it in. It was two a.m. and I was almost too tired for my traditional night deck stroll. Yet it was my special time to myself, for letting my hair down, allowing the night air to cool my skin, watching the fast flow of sea as the *Countess Georgina* ate up the nautical miles. Time when I assured myself that all was well on-board, and sweet sleep was ahead.

But as I strolled the empty decks, some still wet from their nightly hosing and mop down, I knew that not all was well. Two men had died in mysterious circumstances and someone hated me enough to slash my photograph. Something was wrong.

I was being watched. I had that sudden, shocking spine-tingling feeling run through me. My hand clutched the rail to steady myself. I could feel eyes boring into my body, surrounding me with fear. The spray flew back into my face and I blinked, feeling confused and dizzy, strangely rooted to the deck.

I couldn't move.

Panic rolled over me. What was happening? I'd been well enough to walk up the stairs and on to the Lido deck. Sleepy yes, but suddenly I was no longer in control. My body was weighted, felt as heavy as an anchor.

One word came into my brain. Sandwiches. I had only eaten two of them, not liking their strong meat content. Had something been put into them? Had they been tampered with? Not enough to kill me, but something to paralyze my nerves or my muscles? My paranoid imagination was into overdrive.

I had to get help but my feet were not obeying

the smallest of my instructions. And someone was watching me. I tried to move my head but a stiffness was invading my neck, numbing it, tingling and icy. Waves of sleep rolled over me, and I clung to the railing, trying to keep myself upright.

This couldn't be happening to me. I wouldn't allow it. I tried to call out for help but there was no voice inside my throat. My vocal cords were mute. If I could reach my phone, maybe I could call someone for help. Where was my phone? My hands wouldn't go into my pockets. They floundered about like fish in the moonlight.

The sky was so beautiful, all those diamond-bright stars twinkling in the velvety hemisphere, and this was happening beneath them. But then everything happened under their watchful eyes. They saw everything. Every war, every explosion, every disaster, man-made or natural. Every death.

'Casey? Miss Jones? Are you all right?'

Richard Norton was walking towards me, his body all wavering about like a mirror at a fun fair, and strangely, tall as he was, I thought I could see two of him, one beside the other.

I tried to say his name but all that came out was a strangled grunt.

Nine

Barbados

Dr Samuel Mallory was none too pleased to be called from his bed in the early hours of the morning. Richard Norton had carried me to my cabin as I was incapable of walking. I don't remember much about being carried.

'Sleeping pills,' said Samuel, putting away his stethoscope. 'Double vision, sleepiness and mental confusion? Did you take some sleeping pills and then go up on deck?'

My voice was coming back, sleepily, slurred. They had been walking me around to keep me awake. But I desperately wanted to put my head down and sleep.

'No sleeping pills,' I murmured. 'I don't take them.'

'Wake up, Casey. Don't go to sleep. Wake up, talk to me.'

'Don't wanna talk. I'm tired enough, running that disco, and it's late. I don't need ... a sleeping pill...'

'Come on, think. What did you have to eat or drink?' He didn't sound at all sympathetic. He'd left his bedside manner in his cabin.

'I had orange juice and s-sandwiches in the

Galaxy Lounge. I didn't finish them.'

'Any alcohol?'

'I was drinking orange juice. But you bought me ... two brandies.'

'Sufficient time lapse, I think. I made sure there was a lot of soda.'

'I don't know ... anything.'

'I'll get the juice tested. And I'll take a blood sample to find out exactly which type of benzodiazepine was used. Probably Mogadon or Dalinane. The effects come on in about half an hour. Or it could have been a barbiturate, Nembutal is another short-acting one.' He jabbed a syringe into my arm and helped himself to some blood. No 'please' or 'may I'? 'Try to keep awake, Casey. We don't know how much they gave you.'

'But I'm so tired. I wanna go to sleep. Please let me have some sleep,' I moaned. 'Who gave me what? What do you mean? Let me sleep.'

'Sorry, not yet. We'll see what they pumped into you and the percentage still in your blood. Drink lots of water. When the level becomes non-threatening, then you can sleep it off.'

'I'll keep her awake,' said Richard Norton, to the rescue. 'I'll read her a manual on fire safety on board ship.'

'Count yourself lucky,' said Dr Mallory, closing his bag with a snap. 'You could have fallen overboard. And no one would have known.'

'There was someone there ... watching me.'

'Hallucination.'

'It's not an overdose, is it?' I asked, still slurring my words.

'No. You'd be in a coma by now if you'd over-dosed. You'll live to compère another spectacular show. I'll do these tests, then I'd like to get some beauty sleep. And I need it more than you do.'

If I hadn't felt so woozy, I'd have rated that as a second-grade compliment. As he left, Richard poured some more water down me. Then he slipped a cardigan over my shoulders and pro-pelled me towards the door. He seemed to be enjoying it. He was very much like a big, cuddly bear.

'I think three times round the Promenade Deck in the fresh air would be a splendid idea. If anyone sees us, they'll think we're lovers, too much in love to say goodnight. That's a song,' he explained wryly. 'But I guess you're too young to know it.'

'I think I know it,' I said, still struggling, bare-ly able to keep my eyes open. My eyelids weighed a ton. 'A duet.'

'Come on. Let's hit the deck. Three circuits on the trot.'

'That's a whole mile,' I said, shaking my head as the air hit my face like a wet flannel. It was tinged with salt. 'I can't walk a mile. I can't trot.'

But I did, leaning heavily on Richard, making my feet work, pushing them forward. It took ages, staggering about. Richard was big enough and bulky enough to support me and keep me in some sort of line, otherwise I'd have been bash-ing into rails and stacked deckchairs and deck equipment. The sides of the ship were going in and out, the deck wavering.

Richard took a call on his mobile. We stood in the shelter of a windbreak. The dawn was beginning to tinge the sky with streaks of rose madder, peeking from the horizon like a timid nymph.

'Norton here. Yes, she's still walking. Reckon she's really worn out by now. Her legs are definitely shorter. Can we give her a break? Good, that's great. I'll tell her that the levels are not lethal. Twenty minutes more and she can go to bed, if she's coherent and lucid.'

'I heard that,' I said, yawning hugely. 'I am coherent and lucid. What do you want me to do to prove it? Say my nine times table?'

'How about something a little less mathematical and more in keeping with the dawn? Do you know any suitable poems?'

'I know a few poems but I can't recollect any at the moment. I can remember the words of some songs.'

'Songs will do,' he said. 'Sing to me and then I'll take you back to your cabin.'

That's how I came to be walking round the Promenade Deck as the dawn rose in all its splendour, singing Cole Porter and Gershwin and Hoagy Carmichael in a suspiciously groggy voice. It took a long time to live down. Word got around the ship about the perambulating singer at dawn. Even Captain Nicolas started humming every time he saw me.

Barbados loomed on the horizon in all its Caribbean glory. The palm-fringed beaches stretched in all directions. A diamond necklace of beachfront hotels dazzled with their white walls and balconies and sprawling bougainvillaea, hibiscus and oleander. Little England they called Barbados but the climate was far from the UK norm. Today was a blistering summer temperature tempered by the trade winds.

The *Countess* was too big to weigh anchor along the bustling waterfront of Bridgetown and instead she was docked in the new dock area. It was a typical frenetic dockyard, beset with restrictions on movement, and there were lines of coaches waiting to take passengers on island tours, and shuttles for those only wanting to go into Bridgetown to shop, gawp and wander.

Passengers were warned not to walk around the dock area on their own. It was strictly restricted admittance. Things had changed since my last visit. You caught the shuttle bus or stayed on-board. I hoped the passengers would take notice of these restrictions. Bailing someone out of the police station immediately before departure was no fun and pretty fraught.

I still felt a little woozy but I had slept off the worst of the drug. Several cups of black coffee had woken me up enough to dress and get to the office. The weekly departmental meeting was fixed for this morning. It was a good time when the bustle of the ship keyed down and most of the passengers went ashore. A few stayed on-board, liking the quietness of the ship to themselves. No stampede to find a free lounger.

The two deaths were recorded and Richard Norton said he was making the necessary enquiries. Dr Mallory made his report, no epidemics. The other departments brought up a few issues. Entertainments (me) said Ray Roeder, the Eighties pop star, was a last minute replacement booking. He would be joining us in a few days. But Estelle Grayson was due to arrive today. There was a general groan. Every department on ship would feel her mighty personality.

Estelle Grayson arrived, late. She had been somewhat put out that the port agent's vehicle was a minivan and not a limousine. The fact that it was a sensible mode of transport for all her baggage, plus the replacement dancer, and the new comedian, had quite escaped her.

'I don't travel on a bus, you know,' she said immediately as I greeted her on-board. 'I expect something better than a bus.'

'There were three of you, Miss Grayson,' I said. 'And all the baggage. It would have been a bit of a crush in a car. Anyway, you're here now, safely, and I'm very happy to welcome you aboard the *Countess Georgina*.'

I smiled at them. The skinny-thin dancer looked as if she was about to drop with the heat. The comedian was white-faced, having been flying for twenty-four hours. He'd travelled from South Africa, after leaving another cruise ship. Estelle Grayson was the freshest of the bunch and yet she was making the most fuss.

'I hope I've got the same cabin,' she said. 'And the same steward. He knows exactly what I want.'

'It is the same cabin,' I assured her. 'But not the same steward. Your usual steward has gone on leave. Some family matter.'

'Oh no, that's impossible. I can't have some strange steward. I shall be completely thrown. Everything will be diabolical.'

'He's a very good steward. One of our best. He's been taken off stateroom duty, just so that he can help you settle in. You'll find him exceptional.' This was a complete fabrication, made up on the spur of the moment, to placate Ms Grayson. All our stewards were good. But she seemed to swallow it and started dabbing her brow with a lace-trimmed handkerchief.

'Show me to my cabin then, Miss ... er?'

'Jones. Casey Jones. I'm the new Entertainment Director.'

'Oh, so you're new, are you? No wonder I got a minivan.'

She sailed away, following a flotilla of stewards with her hand luggage. She had more make-up cases than our entire troupe of dancers.

Both the comedian and the dancer had been waiting patiently. The comedian was an old hand at this and nothing worried him. He threw me a sympathetic smile.

'Well done, Casey girl,' he said. 'Got anything for me to sign? Then, if you don't mind, I'd like a kip. My head will be out before it touches the pillow.'

'Lovely to have you on board again,' I said. I'd looked him up on our computer files. He was a regular. 'I know you'll be as brilliant as ever. I won't miss one of your shows.'

'Got a few new jokes,' he promised.

'I'll look forward to them.'

I took the young dancer to meet the troupe. She was obviously timid and nervous despite the trendy Top Shop and Monsoon clothes. Her luminous make-up was melting down her face. 'Is it always as hot as this?' she asked, fanning herself with her crew card. 'I can't stand it.'

'Don't worry, you'll get used to the heat. It is the Caribbean, after all. And the ship is air-conditioned everywhere so you'll be comfortable enough on-board.'

Susan was eyeing me from the other desk as I completed the paperwork attached to the newcomers. She was as pasty faced as always, a roll of fat over the belt of her jeans. I don't think she ever went out on deck, whereas I was collecting a dusky honeyed skin without any sunbathing.

'You recovered from your little fracas?' she asked, off-hand, flicking through a new manual that had arrived. Someone had to read it.

'What little fracas?' I asked. 'I don't know what you're talking about.'

'Out on the deck, after the disco. Singing and larking about. I heard there was some trouble,' she said, looking all innocent and unworldly. 'I hope everything is all right?'

'Heavens yes, no trouble,' I said, keying in replies to some urgent emails without looking at her. Emails might be fast and efficient but they always needed answering. You could put a letter in an in-tray and forget about it. 'Merely a very pleasant stroll around the deck in excellent company. Pleasant company is always a bonus, don't you agree?'

'Nice company, of course. But I heard you were in trouble. Someone spiked your drink.'

'Then you heard wrong,' I said with a laugh. 'Do I look as if someone spiked my drink?' This was a bluff. How is someone supposed to look? Hollow-faced and red-eyed?

'No, you're looking very smart,' she said sulkily. 'But then you always do.'

I didn't get much time ashore in Barbados. Estelle Grayson suddenly found a dozen things which were not to her liking. Her rehearsal times, one of her cases was missing, the flowers were giving her hay fever, she had jet lag, the pianist didn't know how to transpose keys, some sheet music was lost.

I went ashore on the last shuttle bus into Bridgetown. The sight of the fields of sugar cane, the hills and dales, the limousines and donkey carts, the peaceful and unhurried ways, were an instant tonic. Agriculture was still the main occupation of the island but tourism was fast catching up. The Bajans lived in their colourful wooden houses that clustered along the roadside, women sitting on the front balconies, making ready the vegetables to cook for that evening meal. There would be fresh fish from the sea to bake.

There was only time to wander around the waterfront of Bridgetown and down Broad Street, the main shopping street, and then along the Careenage to where boats and schooners are repainted and refurbished. A statue of Admiral Lord Nelson still stood in Trafalgar Square, a slightly smaller version than his London abode. He'd saved their sugar profits in the nineteenth century and this was their thank you. The air was full of steel bands playing and the cries of street hawkers.

I strolled over the many bridges of this inlet, before turning to catch the last shuttle bus back to the ship. It was very full. Many of the passengers had left it to the last minute to return. I squeezed up on a seat to allow an extra person on-board. We could not afford to leave anyone behind.

But anyone who missed the last shuttle could always get a taxi. The drivers knew this and stood around expectantly. No hassle about fares when the *Countess* was waiting to depart.

'I'm glad to see you looking so well,' said Samuel Mallory, pushing himself on to the seat beside me. He was too close. I could feel the heat from his thigh against mine. We were both hot.

'I needed the sleep,' I said, reminding him. I had not seen him since that episode. No follow-up call. 'It did me the world of good.'

'Your orange juice had been doctored,' he said, then realized what he'd said. 'Not by me, your doctor. What I mean is there were traces of barbiturate. Fragments in the glass which had not dissolved. Fortunately, not enough to kill you. But you could have passed out on deck and fallen overboard. It would only have needed a little push. If someone was there for the push.'

'And I thought someone was watching me. I had this awful feeling.' I shuddered, recalling the uncanny sense of eyes. 'Someone was there. Even though I was half asleep and feeling all woozy, I knew I was being watched.'

'Fortunately Norton found you. So all is well.'

'Don't you understand now why I am so suspicious about the second-sitting deaths? They are not normal. It's not a coincidence,' I said, keeping my voice down. We were surrounded and hemmed in by hot and untidy passengers who were knee-high with shopping. I didn't want to start any rumours.

'We'll see when we get back to Southampton,' said Samuel complacently, waving to a middle-aged, glossy, tanned woman sitting further along the bus. One of his on-ship admirers. She wore big tortoiseshell sunglasses on top of her blonde hair, which looked so pretentious, so tacky. 'It'll all be sorted out then.'

'It might be too late,' I said.

He squeezed my hand. 'But at least you're all right now. The show must go on and all that jazz.'

'I hope so,' I said, removing my hand. 'Estelle Grayson arrived today. The soprano from Hades. By now Captain Nicolas will be in receipt of her numerous complaints. He will, no doubt, have to invite her to cocktails in his cabin before she can possibly go on.'

Samuel chuckled. 'You stay very cool and calm. I like that. I don't like women who panic.'

'I can do panic,' I said.

The shuttle bus was groaning with its extra load, easing out of the square, negotiating traffic. Bridgetown's shopkeepers were waving to us.

112

They were so friendly. Perhaps the passengers had spent an awful lot of money. I hoped so. I hadn't spent anything, not even a penny. Skinflint.

'So the divine diva is throwing her weight about, is she?' Samuel went on, his eyes on the scenery. He seemed to take a real interest in new places. His dark hair was dented smooth where he had been wearing a straw trilby and his clothes were creased. It was the first time I had ever seen him looking crumpled.

'And it's some weight. Didn't you hear the ship creak as she stepped aboard? She thinks she's on stage all the time. Life is one endless theatre. Don't stop applauding.'

'And have you found her a place in the Windsor Dining Room? I'm sure she won't want to eat in the officers' mess, down among the luggage and the stores.'

'Oh yes, I've found her a table,' I said. I could barely conceal my smile. 'Can you guess where?'

'Table two?'

I nodded. 'Second sitting. She'll love it. Won't she?'

Ten

At Sea

It was a miracle that everyone was eventually aboard before sailing time. I patrolled the decks, listening to the listed announcements of passengers unaccounted for by the computer. It was pretty scary. But the plastic cruise cards were not infallible. Sometimes they didn't register on the scanner. A blip, a speck of dust, a drop of sweat could render a card magically non-existent.

They were casting off the lines that held the ship to the dockside. The heavy ropes splashed into the water and were winched aboard. A few people waved from the shore, but not many. Cruise ships were two a penny in Barbados. A pilot was guiding the *Countess* between all the shipping and a tug was needed to swing her stern to port. She set course to pass through the breakwaters.

Some of the smaller craft, especially holiday yachts, came far too close, just to have a look at such a beautiful ship. Or perhaps they wanted us to look at them. They did own their boats. Or most of them did.

I took a last farewell of the coral island and went downstairs to my office. I knew there

114

would be plenty of work waiting there, then hopefully a freshly caught red snapper on the supper menu tonight.

'Miss Jones? Where have you been? I've been looking for you everywhere.' The voice was in full throttle.

It was Estelle Grayson. She was robed in a multi-coloured silk tent, hair piled beehive-style spiked with huge sunglasses, make-up flawless, face set into a list of complaints.

'Hello, Miss Grayson,' I said, putting on a smile that didn't quite stretch to my eyes. But I was too happy to care much. Samuel had been amusing company on the bus journey and I was still floating on the fun of it all. He had charm in a bucket load.

'Where were you when I needed you?' she demanded.

'What did you need me for?' I asked. Rule 99: always respond with another question. A useful ruse in difficult situations. The politicians do it all the time.

'The pianist is hopeless. He doesn't play the right tempo. He can't transpose keys. I cannot work with him. I refuse to work with him.'

'So, shall I go give him some lessons?' I said. I hoped it sounded like a joke. I really didn't care. I knew that such a cavalier attitude could lose me my job, but this woman was hopelessly difficult. The ship wouldn't sink without her. The cruise wouldn't falter mid-Atlantic, winch down the lifeboats and abandon ship. Maybe a few passengers would complain ... so give them a rebate.

'You are not due for a first billing night spot until tomorrow evening,' I went on. 'There is plenty of time for us to meet and discuss the show. I know that your repertoire requires the support of a pianist. We have several aboard, all excellent pianists. If you can't work with any of them, then we will arrange to fly you home from the next available airport. No problem, Miss Grayson.'

It was an ultimatum. And the sooner, the better. She could take it how she pleased. I had several entertainers who'd be happy to have an extra spot. The passengers would barely notice a change of name. Who looked at the photographs in the frame anyway?

'I'm not standing for this,' she said, going rather pink.

'Then perhaps you'd better sit down. Think about it. After all, you are a professional.'

She looked shocked. No one had ever stood up to her outrageous demands before. She had always got her own way. I let her recover, poured out a glass of water and set it on the desk.

Estelle composed her face before answering. She was going through the options.

'He's just not what I expected,' she floundered.

'Perhaps you are not what he expected either,' I said.

She swallowed this. Obviously no other cruise directors had ever spoken to her so openly. It was not easy. If she broke her contract and went home, then I would have to answer for the consequences to Head Office. But if the pianist, who played the ivories for hours and hours in dif-

116

ferent venues, the lobbies, the bars, the stage, also threw a wobbly, he would have to be replaced. Passengers liked their live music.

I know which one I would prefer to listen to. We didn't use wallpaper music on-board.

'Perhaps he's not used to your high standard of production,' I said, pouring on some oil. 'Some of your songs are very difficult.'

'Perhaps we could go over the numbers again,' she said between her teeth. She didn't want to lose her fee. If she objected to the pianist, then she might forfeit the payment. The kill-fee might be peanuts.

'That's a good idea,' I said. 'Let's arrange a suitable time.'

She had calmed down a few degrees but I could see she was seething inside. She was a boiling cauldron of fury. Her hands were clenching and unclenching. She needed a doctor, a couple of calming Prozac or something. Dr Mallory would hardly regard it as an emergency if I called him.

'That's fine, then,' I said. 'How about six o'clock? When everyone is eating or getting ready to eat. The Princess Lounge will be all yours. You can rehearse to your heart's content.'

'Miss Jones? Are you busy?' It was one of the uniformed young women from the purser's office. She looked a bit flustered and out of place. 'Do you have a minute?'

'What is it? I'm with Miss Grayson.'

'There's a slight problem with security.'

'OK, I'll be along as soon as I can.'

'Something else that you have got wrong?'

said Estelle nastily.

'No, I don't think so. Maybe your passport is out of date. Perhaps you put the wrong date of birth on it, by mistake, of course,' I said, laughing as if it was another joke. 'If you'll excuse me. Miss Brook will see you out.'

I left my office before I chucked my screen at her and ruined that perfect hairdo. It would be quite easy to do. It was rarely that I longed for some sort of physical release but this woman was the pits. Perhaps I should go on deck and chuck a few quoits overboard.

Susan threw a look of despair at me. She didn't want to be landed with Estelle Grayson for even five minutes. She would be flattened in minutes. I sent her an encouraging smile.

'Miss Brook has my complete confidence,' I said. 'She will arrange the new rehearsal time. Come back to me with any further problems.'

I hurried to the purser's department, down amidships. Screens were humming. The computers recorded data about every passenger. It was all on screen. Even down to their last bar order of cokes.

'So?' I asked. 'I'm here. Casey Jones. What's the matter?'

Richard Norton was in his office. There were two stewards with him, looking grey and gaunt despite their naturally light-brown Asian skin. I knew the name of one of them. It was Karim, the head steward, and a younger man.

'This is Karim, the head steward. He has reported bad news. The suite of Mrs Foster has been turned over, burgled, ransacked, however

118

you choose to put it. I've had a quick look round the stateroom and will return again shortly, but I thought you should know, Miss Jones.'

'Yes,' I said. 'I'm really sorry. How is Mrs Foster taking this?'

'Quite badly.'

'I'll go and see her immediately. Was anything stolen?'

'She doesn't really know. That's partly the problem. Her jewellery is still there. But she has no idea what her late husband might have had with him. The safe was forced open.'

The younger steward was still shaken. He thought he might lose his job. I felt really sorry for him. 'It's not your fault,' I said. 'You can't keep an eye on every stateroom and still do your work. Please don't feel responsible. You can't be watching for twenty-four hours of the day.'

Karim gave me a ghost of a smile. 'Her steward saw no one,' he said. 'Coming or going, any time. Mrs Foster found the stateroom in this mess. He called me immediately.'

'That was the right thing to do. You reported the break-in and for that we thank you.'

'Miss Jones, he is also worried about his job. He has a family. They are dependent on him.' The young man still said nothing, eyes down-cast, leaving it all to Karim.

'Don't worry, Karim. No one will lose their jobs. Please assure them, Mr Norton. It's not their fault. I'll go and see Mrs Foster.'

'Thank you. I'll need to take a statement from Karim and Ali just for the record. Please tell Mrs Foster that I'll be calling on her later, when she

119

is more composed, so that she can also make a statement.'

'Mr Norton, I have much work to do. All the bathrooms, putting clean towels. May I come back in half an hour?' Ali spoke up for the first time.

Richard Norton let the young man go. He knew nothing except what he had seen when he went into the stateroom to refill the minibar and take a supply of fresh ice. The entire suite had been turned over. Every drawer and cupboard and shelf was tipped on to the floor.

'Come back when you have finished your duties.'

'So, another twist in the tale,' I said, when they had gone. 'Two deaths, an overdose and the ransacked stateroom. Does it hang together?'

'You've forgotten a spiked drink and walking the deck.'

I flushed a little. I couldn't remember much about walking the deck. I hoped I hadn't said or done anything I might regret. But Richard Norton was a decent man. He might not remind me.

'Have the right people been informed?'

'The captain, of course. Southampton CID. Dr Mallory. We can't make an international incident out of it. So far it is confined to the ship. We have to deal with it ourselves. Unless, of course, anything else significant happens.'

'I hope not. My diva is making enough trouble.'

'Warn her that she could be bumped off. It seems this is a very dangerous cruise.'

I laughed. I didn't take it seriously, nor would

she. But I might use it as a threat. 'I'll go and see Mrs Foster and help her sort things out.'

Richard nodded. 'I thought you would. She'd trust you. I know it's not easy having a strange person hanging up your dresses or folding your undies.'

'You have trouble, do you, hanging up your dresses?'

'Always.' He hid a grin, wrote something in a folder and closed it. 'See you around, Miss Jones.'

'You can reckon on it. I can't get off until the next port of call.'

'And that is off the coast of Venezuela.'

'The Isla Margarita and a chance for a swim. It has a beautiful beach within walking distance of the ship. I love going there.'

'I know it. But it's somewhat shallow unless you walk a long way out,' said Richard. 'Maybe I'll see you on the beach.'

Swimming was so good for my ankle. Two casts of plastering, one casually indifferent and one good, had rendered my ankle prone to pain and stiffness. The physiotherapist had recommended swimming to strengthen the muscles. But I hadn't needed telling. I'd learned to swim at a young age, mostly a survival tactic when being chucked in the deep end by a brother or brothers. Testing whether I'd sink or swim was their routine holiday occupation.

My brothers had dispersed all over the world so there was no chance of the duckings any more, but the instinct to swim to safety was inherent. It was another reason I liked a beach and not the pool.

I left a message at the medical centre, telling Samuel Mallory what had happened and suggesting that a courtesy visit to Mrs Foster after that evening's surgery might be appropriate. If he bit my head off, then I had another one.

Mrs Foster had one of the best suites on the upper deck, not far from where they were preparing for this evening's sail-away party on deck. It had a private balcony, a spacious sitting room, a magnificent king-sized bed and a marble bathroom with bath and jacuzzi. I knew there was also a separate shower and two vanity hand basins. There was also a mirrored dressing room lined with cupboards. The sitting room had everything one could need: a long sofa, coffee table, writing desk, fridge, television, video, radio, private safe, telephone. Bliss.

It would have made a very nice, self-contained flat for me. I could have lived in it quite comfortably. Mrs Foster opened the door an inch to my ringing the bell.

'It's Casey Jones, Mrs Foster. May I come in?'

The sitting room was in chaos. Everything had been tipped on to the floors and cupboards and shelves were open and empty. Mrs Foster had been sitting on the edge of the sofa, drinking some tea. Ali had had the sense to make her a pot of tea and had cleared a space on the coffee table for the tray.

'Come in, Miss Jones. I'm afraid we are in an awful mess. Look at it. I don't know what to do or where to start.' She was trembling and near to tears.

'It looks awful, I know. What a mess. But I'll help you tidy up.'

'I really want to go home, you know. George dying so suddenly and now all this. I don't think I can stand much more.'

'That's very understandable, Mrs Foster, and something we can talk about. The company can fly you home from any port. It all depends on who will be at your home, to look after you.'

'Well, there's no one actually. We don't have any children. We have an excellent housekeeper, but I gave her the time off to go visit her son in America. I certainly wouldn't expect her to come back to look after me.'

'Let's talk about it more later. Meanwhile, I'll make a fresh pot of tea and we'll start putting everything away. It won't take long with two pairs of hands. And please tell me if you think anything is missing. There must have been a reason for this. It doesn't make sense.'

'No, it doesn't make sense,' Mrs Foster repeated. 'None of my jewellery has gone. It's still all in its box in the safe. Not that I have much. George always said he preferred art to decorations.'

It seemed to help Mrs Foster, to be immersed in a physical task. She told me where to hang things, and folded her own clothes. The intruder seemed to have given Mr Foster's clothes a thorough going-over. Pockets were turned inside out, sleeves pulled through, even the trees in his shoes had been removed. I noticed that the hem of his outdoor coat had been ripped open but I didn't mention it. Sometimes people kept things

123

in linings.

The drawers from the writing desk had been turned upside down, every shred of paper turned over. And all the books on the shelf above had been turfed out and flipped through, pages crumpled. I started restacking the books.

'Did your husband bring a briefcase on board with him? Some men find them useful for passports and tickets and things, even when they're not working.'

'Oh yes, he brought his briefcase. He wouldn't be separated from it. Worse than any woman and her handbag.'

'So where is it now?' I asked.

She straightened up from folding a pile of cotton tops. They were once so colourful and fresh, but now they were creased and crumpled. I held out a laundry bag and she put them all in, nodding, adding a pile of her undies.

'Yes, everything needs washing and ironing,' she said. 'I'd throw them away, but then I'd be left with only what I'm wearing...'

'What about your husband's briefcase?'

'I don't know where it is.'

'Shall we have a good search?'

She wandered about, looking behind the sofa, under the bed. 'I don't know where he kept it. It was of no interest to me. He carried it on when we boarded at Southampton and put it somewhere.'

The stateroom was looking more shipshape now. I would ask Ali, her steward, to come in, thoroughly clean and vacuum everywhere, get the florist to deliver some flowers.

'Mrs Foster, I think you should have someone stay with you tonight. I'll arrange for one of the nurses from the medical centre to keep you company.'

'Oh no, that won't be necessary. I'll be all right.'

'I think Dr Mallory will insist. He's coming to see you as soon as this evening's surgery is over.'

'That's nice. He's such a lovely man,' she said. 'So attentive.'

'And such a good doctor,' I added, crossing my fingers.

I was beginning to see a glimmer of light. The only missing item was Mr Foster's briefcase. But Mrs Foster couldn't give me much of a description of it.

'Black leather, all black,' she said. 'An ordinary briefcase, you know. Oh, but it had one of those digital locks with secret numbers. I don't know what numbers George used. Birthdays, I expect.'

'Let me know if it turns up,' I said, writing my mobile number on a pad of paper. 'Or give me a call if you want some company.'

'You're very kind, Miss Jones. Thank you.'

I leaned on the door of the suite as I closed it. What had I promised? I was going to have to be in about three places at once this evening. I could see my red snapper slithering down someone else's throat for supper. I wouldn't have time to eat. Perhaps the seagulls would throw me some leftovers.

Eleven

At Sea

There was a farewell sail-away party in full swing on the Lido deck. Full swing means a lot of noise. It was farewell to Barbados, so a steel band was playing and the calypso dancers were stunning in their colourful costumes.

The stewardesses were plying the passengers with trays of rum punch. It looked as if they were offered for free but they weren't. Passengers had to sign for them, but by then the evening breeze was cooling and they were feeling good with the world and what was another fiver anyway?

I would rather be leaning over a rail and watching the receding shore line and scanning the horizon for the string of tiny islands called the Grenadines. How I would love to go island hopping in a private yacht. One of the tiniest islands, Mayreau, is only two square miles with about a hundred people living on it. There are no roads, a small salt pond and a cluster of buildings that they called a resort. Give me a hut on a beach plus a kettle and a book.

The five uninhabited islands are the Tobago Cays where enthusiasts go diving and snorkelling, not my favourite pursuits. I would die underwater. There was once an island called Prune Island but the name was unpopular so now it's called Palm Island. It was a mere speck on my imagination. No big ships have a port of call there, more's the pity. I'd like to see what happened if we put some of our passengers ashore on an island where there were no shops, no cafés, no bars and if they wanted a drink, they would have to hack open a coconut.

That would be something to write home about. Pass me a postcard.

'So, how has the rest of your day been?' Our dishy doctor leaned on the rail beside me, still in his whites. Funny, how he always seemed to find me leaning on a rail, often at this particular spot. It didn't have my name on it.

'Do you want the full version or bullet points?'

'Bullet points.'

'Stateroom ransacked. Mrs Foster's suite. Estelle Grayson re-arranging the entire entertainment programme to suit herself.'

'I can add another bullet. Susan Brook, your deputy, is down with a raging migraine. I've suggested it might be an allergy to a four-lettered word.'

'Which four-lettered word? There are several in use.'

'Food or work.'

I had to laugh. She could be allergic to both. I felt sorry for her. It was no fun being overweight and not having the willpower to do something about it. Or maybe it was her metabolism. I knew someone once who only needed ninety calories a day to survive. How do you live with lettuce for every meal?

'Did you have freshly caught red snapper for supper?' I asked.

'I haven't had any supper.'

'Nor have I.'

'Then I suggest we meet at eleven at the midnight buffet? They might make us a red snapper pizza.'

'OK. I'll be wearing my famine face.'

'I'll try to wear something rather less intimidating.'

Then he had gone. I was due elsewhere. I had both shows to MC, and the disco to spin. Thank goodness, the trivia quiz was in good hands. And the concert pianist in the Galaxy was reliable. There was just time to change.

I ran down to my cabin, mentally assessing which outfit to throw on. It had to be very Barbados, nothing too debutante. I went for my long white silk jersey, rope-detailed dress, with matching wrap. The Louboutin heels hurt but I had to wear them. I was already counting down to when I could take them off. If it came to the corn crunch, I'd change into jewelled flip-flops.

The two deaths receded into the balmy night. How could anything so awful happen on such an idyllic cruise? This was like a floating village, somewhere in the Cotswolds. We were all together. We knew each other. Nothing awful could happen in such contented rural surroundings.

It was about ten o'clock when I felt the wind freshening. When you work on ships, you get

that feeling. The *Countess* was hug¸
the right stabilizers, she could outride
And being an older ship, she had a de¸
which usually meant a smooth ride. S¸
she needed a tug to negotiate a tight be¸
her strong, plated hull could take the ᴡ
well.

The stewards were moving round the d¸
quickly, securing all the stacks of deckchairs ᴀ
netting the pools. I could see foam-crested waᴠ
hurrying by, the sea darker and more ominou¸
than earlier. Some of the waves were menacing,
rearing like wild horses.

There was an announcement from the bridge.
It was Captain Nicolas at his most calming. He
spoke as if he were merely announcing a change
of port of call.

'Good evening, everyone. I hope you are having a very pleasant evening. We are currently
running into some inclement weather and
passengers are advised not to go out on deck. We
may be able to navigate round this squall. Meanwhile, enjoy your evening.'

He called it a squall. Anything not tied down
was already scuttling along the decks and being
blown overboard. I pulled my wrap round my
shoulders. Most of the doors leading on to the
decks were now secured with 'Not In Use' signs
slung across the handles or 'No Admittance'
boards by the ramp or step.

And still there were passengers trying to get on
to the decks with their video cameras to take
pictures of the rising seas.

'Excuse me, sir,' I said to one idiot, slung with

meras. 'It really is too dangerous for you to go
ut on deck.'

'It's Hurricane Dora,' he said, eyes bright with
excitement. 'I've got to get some shots of this to
take home. They'll never believe me.'

'You won't be going home if you go out on
deck,' I said. 'And Captain Nicolas is not likely
to stop the ship to fish you out of the water.'

A sudden lurch of the ship underlined my
words. A wave washed over the deck, drenching
everything, spraying the windows. Some of the
excitement faded from his eyes.

'I suggest you take your pictures from the
safety of a lounge,' I said.

I held on to the handrails to negotiate my way
round the ship. It was my job now to reassure
people that all was well. Hurricane Dora had
been on the news that morning but she must
have changed course. The *Countess* was heading
straight into her. Stewards were fastening extra
roped handrails so that passengers could cross
open spaces and the lobbies between corridors.

A sudden crash of glass announced the closure
of one bar area. It was time to bring out the
plastic glasses and put the real ones away. Somehow the bands played on in the various dance
venues, very *Titanic*, though the dancers had
given up. How to negotiate a lurching floor was
not included in the ballroom classes.

The second showing of this evening's spectacular theatrical presentation was cancelled. It
was a stroll down memory lane, that is, a full-
scale Music Hall, but even our best dancers
couldn't stroll far in this difficult weather.

Time to take off my shoes. Heels were a hazard in rough weather. I started checking D deck, port and starboard. No one was playing bridge. The art gallery was a mess. A lot of the paintings had fallen off the walls and those on easels had collapsed on to the floor. Tamara was in tears, mascara running, trying to stack up her wares into some order.

'I'll get some stewards to come and help you,' I said, on to my mobile immediately. 'Quite a few won't have anything to do this evening.'

'Thank you,' she said tearfully. 'I can't manage on my own.'

'Where's your assistant?'

'Gone to her cabin, feeling sick.'

The Internet Study was awash with paper, instruction books, flying mouse mats and swinging mouses. No one was taking charge. The man who operated the facility seemed to have disappeared. I was not surprised.

I didn't have to worry about Bond Street, the retail shop that had entrance doors on both sides of the deck. They had closed for business and the manager and his staff were rushing around putting loose stock into cupboards and drawers. He gave me a brief wave, no time for more.

Casino Royale had closed its table games, only the fruit machines could keep going in any weather. And dedicated passengers were glued to the fruit machines – in any weather. Fortunately the books in the library were all behind locked glass doors, but the jigsaw on the felt covered table was no more. Its pieces had flown to all points of the compass.

I phoned the housekeeping department and asked for extra female staff to check the ladies' loos on each deck. This was often where accidents happened, nothing much to hold on to, tiled floors, wash basins, confined space.

'Don't forget keys,' I said. 'No fun to fall inside a locked cubicle.'

'We'll see to it, Miss Jones.'

Even I was decidedly unsteady, weaving instead of walking as if I'd had more than a couple too many. This was one heck of a storm. The noise was horrendous, the wind howling through the ship like a banshee. I think the noise scared people more than the actual movement. There were a lot of scared faces.

'Heavens, I'm not sure that I like this at all,' said Maria de Leger, the lady who was writing her memoirs. She was sitting, ramrod straight, in an armchair in the Galaxy Lounge, anchoring her half-full tumbler of whisky on the table. Its contents were sloshing from side to side.

'Are you sure you want to stay here?' I asked. 'It's getting pretty rough. Shall I help you back to your cabin?'

'No, there's a film I want to see. It starts in twenty minutes.'

'I'll find someone to escort you to the cinema.'

'Thank you, but I'm quite all right. I've stayed upright in rougher weather than this.' In a brief lull she took a quick sip of her drink. The timing was perfect.

'I don't think I could sit through any film in this,' I said.

'It's a very good film,' she said. *'Moulin*

132

Rouge. It'll be me and the operator then. I love the music.'

The American was sitting alone, as always, with a drink and a book. The storm didn't seem to worry him. Perhaps he came from a coastal town in the States, maybe Virginia, that was used to hurricanes all year round. Or he had a naval background. Yes, that was it. He was ex-US Navy.

He nodded to me. 'Wind Force Twelve, ma'am?'

'Maybe. Something like that,' I said. It was not advisable for passengers to know wind speeds, particularly when it was well over seventy-five miles an hour. A hurricane could reach 150 miles an hour. I didn't want to know either. I could feel the vibrations of the powerful engines, thrusting through the huge waves. The bridge is manned at all times and I guessed Captain Nicolas and other senior officers would be on watch. I didn't care if I died.

'You take care,' he said, returning to his book after a glance at my bare feet. How could he read in this weather? It looked like a pretty hefty tome, maybe legal or *War and Peace*.

Many of the passengers were having an early night, watching television in the comfort and safety of their cabins. The lounges and bars were deserted. The lecture theatre was midships and felt less turbulence. A few stalwarts, including Maria de Leger, were waiting for the film to start.

I caught glimpses of the hurricane through the windows, glad they were reinforced double thickness and good protection from the fury of the wind. The spray was like hailstones battering the glass. No crew were on deck now. If anything broke loose, then it went into the Caribbean Sea, lost forever.

For once there was nothing for me to do. I made double sure that no one was in agony anywhere, clutching a broken ankle. The lift took me to the Terrace Café where the midnight buffet was usually laid out, but it had shut. Very sensible. The pitching was worse here, high up at the top of the ship, near the funnel casing. My pizza with Samuel Mallory was definitely off.

I was leaving the area when Samuel lurched out of the lift. He grabbed my arm to steady himself. He was still in his whites, a stethoscope slung round his neck on duty.

'Are we the only ones still wide awake?' he asked.

'I think so. Though I hope those manning the bridge are even wider awake.'

'Pretty rough, isn't it? Do you still fancy a pizza?'

'It's too much to ask anyone to do,' I said. 'Let's take a rain check.'

'Nonsense,' he said, propelling me back into the waiting lift. 'The medical centre is fully equipped. We can microwave our own pizza. And as we are overflowing with patients, I'll be able to keep an eye on them as we eat.'

'Is this ethical, eating while on duty?'

'Do they want their doctor to starve? Both wards and the side rooms are full. I've even had to put a patient in the operating theatre as we are

134

so short of space. You could read them bedtime stories while I heat up our supper.'

'I'm sure this is breaking some company rule,' I said as the lift took us down to the medical centre in the depths of the ship. It was clearly signed for walking wounded and surgery times. I'd been there before but it always surprised me because it was like stepping into another world with consulting rooms, X-ray rooms, an operating theatre, two wards and private side rooms.

It looked like a very modern private hospital somewhere out in the country, except that there were no windows. No one wanted to watch a shark swimming by.

Samuel took me into his private office. It looked as if a bomb had hit it. His paperwork was in chaos. But he had anchored most of it to his desk with large conch shells. I wondered which beach they had come from.

'Sit down, if you can find a chair.' He opened the corner refrigerator and took out a bottle of rosé. He opened it with surgical expertise and poured out two glasses. He slid one across to me. It tasted good. Rosé was exceptional.

'I'll put the pizza in the microwave after I've made a quick round. Two of my passengers need to go home as soon as we are in calmer waters. The air ambulance service are sending a helicopter.'

'Breaks?'

'Hips. Very painful. They need hospital treatment as soon as possible. There are a couple of broken wrists, one cut and concussion, and some nasty sprains. I hope you like three cheeses and

135

anchovy?'

'Sounds fine. Are you sure there isn't something I could do to help?'

'One of the women is anxious about her daughter. I can't let her wander about the ship with her arm in a sling. She's safer here. We've phoned their cabin several times but the daughter isn't answering.'

'Perhaps she's swallowed a couple of stiff brandies and gone to sleep. Would you like me to have a word with her?'

'Please. She's in the first side room. Her name is Banesto.'

Samuel was weary, running a hand through his hair. He'd been working non-stop for hours.

I nodded. 'I know her, or rather I know the daughter, Amanda.'

'Thanks, Casey. I'll put the pizza in later...'

I had a few more sips of rosé and followed Samuel out into the corridor. All was quiet except for the creaking of the internal timbers. I tried not to think of how far down in the water we were now. It was better not to ask how deep. Better not to think about submarines and the crush of water against the hull.

We never did get that pizza. The night was too busy with accidents. Heaven knows what happened to it in the end. Perhaps Samuel ate it in the middle of the night and finished up the wine. He probably kipped out on a consulting couch, staying near his patients.

Mrs Banesto had broken her wrist getting out of the shower. She seemed calmer once I said I would go and look for Amanda. I had no idea how I was going to find her. I could hardly knock on the door of every unattached bachelor. There was that blonde young man, whoever he was.

'Do you know of any friends she might be with?' I asked.

'She has so many friends. She's such a lovely girl.'

'Absolutely beautiful,' I agreed. 'I'm sure she is probably staying with some friends. Much nicer to have company on a night like this. Does she have any special male friends?'

'No, I don't think so. Her fiancé was killed, you know. She hasn't got over losing him yet.'

'I'll go and find her,' I said. 'And ring down to Dr Mallory with any news.'

'Thank you so much, Miss Jones,' said Mrs Banesto. 'It would put my mind at rest.' Her face was wan and her make-up had long worn off. She looked like a mother now, and not a fashion plate. 'I'll try to get some sleep and hope this wind dies down soon.'

'We're getting through it,' I said hopefully. 'It'll be a lovely day tomorrow.'

'Let's hope so.'

I spent a useless hour trying to find Amanda Banesto. No one had seen her or who she had been with earlier in the now deserted bars or lounges. We could hardly make a public announcement over the loudspeakers and wake up everyone who had managed to get to sleep.

Before giving up and going to my cabin, I thought I'd make a last call on Mrs Foster and make sure she was all right. I checked that there were still lights on in her suite and rang the bell.

A tall tousled blonde beauty in slinky white jeans opened the door. She smiled, recognizing me. And I recognized her.

'Hi,' she said. 'Come in.'

'Good heavens, I've been looking for you, Amanda,' I began. 'I've been looking for you everywhere. Your mother is worried stiff. She's in the medical centre, deck F.'

'Heavens, I thought she'd be fast asleep by now. What's the matter?'

'She's broken her wrist, but she's being taken care of. All she is worried about is you. She doesn't know where you are. Could you phone her? Put her mind at rest. I'll give you the number.'

'And this is the last place she'd expect to find me,' said Amanda Banesto, going into the sitting room to the phone. Mrs Foster was on the sofa, wrapped in a towelling robe, her feet in slippers. She looked happier than she had that afternoon.

'Hello, Mrs Foster,' I said. 'Are you all right?'

'Oh yes, I'm fine now that Amanda is here, keeping me company. She's my niece, you see. Her mother and I are sisters. Sad thing is, we haven't spoken for years...'

Twelve

At Sea

I had thought that after working on cruise ships for several years, nothing could surprise me. But this did surprise me. I had to stop my mouth falling open. Sisters travelling separately on the same ship and not speaking? Whatever had happened in the past between them must have been something catastrophic. Surely it couldn't be a motive for murder?

But I did persuade Amanda to phone her mother in the medical centre and say she was all right for the night. It was not my business where she spent the night or with whom. I'm sure Mrs Foster was appreciating some company during this bad weather.

And I was not supposed to get involved with passengers. Here I was up to my neck in them. I felt like a bundle of knitting that had got into a twist, with a lot of dropped stitches and pattern errors.

We were in the eye of the storm now, a central zone where it's calmer, but we might have another rough patch before morning. This was the best time to get some sleep. Sleep? When had I last slept, or eaten, or anything? The rosé wine was the last thing I could remember going down my throat. I hoped Dr Mallory had at last got his handsome head down on a couch.

I wondered where Hurricane Dora was sweeping her devastation, lifting tin roofs, felling palm trees, overturning cars and buses. These Caribbean islands might be idyllic but they could be wrecked by one storm. And it took months to put things right for the tourists. Years even. And ruined lives and businesses were harder to repair.

The *Countess Georgina* rode the mountainous, hissing waves, the wind hurling past with horrendous howls and moans. It's a wonder anyone slept. I tried to close my eyes and ears to the noise. The cabin rocked. I held on to the sides of my bed, terrified that I would fall out.

The sea was still choppy first thing the next morning, but we'd travelled through the path of the hurricane. The sky was fresh and blue as if it had been tumbled in a launderette with fabric softener. Officers were on deck assessing damage and reporting back to the engineers' department. The *Countess* had weathered the storm well. It appeared to be the passengers who had suffered the most.

Only the hardy appeared for breakfast in the Terrace Café. I was hungry and piled a bowl with grapefruit, melon, pineapple and grapes. I also helped myself to a warm roll, sliced cheese and marmalade. Very Welsh. Quite a feast for me.

'So you're hungry, too,' said Samuel, sitting down opposite me. His tray was laden with a

140

cooked breakfast, cereal, toast and fruit. I pointed at the Danish pastry.

'What's that? All those calories, fat and sugar,' I said.

'Fancy some cold pizza instead?'

'How are your patients?'

'Remarkably cheerful. Most of them will be returning to their cabins now that it's calmer, except the head wound. I want to keep an eye on him. And two are being flown home today once the helicopter arrives.' He had been up most of the night and was wearing a fetching Brad Pitt after-six shadow, and his eyes were red-rimmed with weariness.

'Such a sad way to end a holiday. I always feel so sorry for them. I discovered something interesting last night. Mrs Banesto, your broken wrist patient, and Mrs Foster, widow of the late Mr Foster, are sisters. But they are not on speaking terms and haven't been for years.'

'It happens,' said Samuel, munching through his cereal. 'Any ideas?'

'Well, there might be a connection. It all depends on why they are not on speaking terms. I know of a pair of sisters who quarrelled over a pint of milk and never spoke to each other again for the rest of their lives.'

'Sad.'

'It happens,' I repeated.

'Perhaps the gorgeous Amanda will spill the beans,' he said, starting on his eggs and bacon, hash browns and mushrooms. The man was hungry. He took my roll to mop up the egg yolk.

'Do you know the gorgeous Amanda?'

141

'Who doesn't know Amanda?'

'Then who is the young blond man she's always seen around with?'

'No idea, could be any of a dozen attentive admirers. Such a brilliant description, Casey. Knew who you meant immediately.'

I gave up on that tack. 'And Mrs Foster's suite was ransacked yesterday. Very unpleasant. As far as we know nothing was stolen but Mr Foster's briefcase seems to be missing.'

'Ah, *The Case of the Missing Briefcase* by Agatha Christie. Very good book. Have you read it?'

'You're making that up. She didn't write one with that title.'

'Are you sure?' His eyes were twinkling. 'I should check in the library or on Google. You may get the entire mystery cleared up in a flash.'

'I don't think you are taking any of this seriously and yet you have two bodies in freezers who shouldn't be there. They should be enjoying this cruise and having a wonderful holiday.'

Samuel was savouring the crisp rashers of bacon. 'You're right, Casey. It's that damned protective shell. You have to grow one in A & E or you wouldn't survive the horrors. I won't even tell you about them nor mention anything. But the sights are not pretty, and the traumas are devastating. That's why I'm here. I need to recover some peace of mind, some joy of life.'

'And you like the sea?' The sea was part of my life. I had seawater in my blood. I could watch the sea for hours, never tiring of the endless blue.

'I love the sea. My dad had a boat. I've been sailing since I was old enough to take a tiller. We went out every weekend, any weather.'

'So if the *Countess* goes off course, you'll be able to navigate?'

'I know my stars,' Samuel said, getting up to fetch some fresh coffee. 'Do you want a cup?'

'Thank you. Black, please.'

The drinks counter was busy and Samuel had to wait in the queue. It gave me a chance to look at him when he was not aware. He was outstandingly attractive even when dishevelled. Two female passengers immediately latched on to him, talking animatedly. He was as charming as ever to them, bending to listen politely, although I could see the weariness in his shoulders.

'Dolphins,' the cry went up from somewhere. 'Dolphins!'

Everyone rushed to port then over to starboard, not knowing where they were. It was a wonder the ship didn't tilt like in *Pirates of the Caribbean 3*. I saw a pair of big silvery fish leaping out of the water, so elegant and so playful. They were putting on a show for the passengers, enjoying themselves and the sport. They kept us company for a few miles and then fell behind. As I watched them, it broke my heart that so many of them died in fishermen's nets.

Samuel turned and looked at me as if reading my thoughts. He knew and smiled hesitantly. There was nothing we could do individually about saving dolphins. It was out of our control. He came back with two brimming cups of coffee.

'Did you see them?'

'So beautiful...'

He nodded. 'Part of the universe, the great cosmic plan. We are all specks of dust. Count it as a special gift that they came and entertained us, a huge white floating container. A tin box. They are so small in comparison yet they chose to swim alongside and say hello. They recognize people as living humans.'

'It was amazing.'

'What do they think of us?'

I shook my head. 'Heaven knows. A sort of harmless monster gliding by, quite unable to leap or dive. Perhaps they feel sorry for us.'

Samuel grinned. 'That's it, they felt sorry for us. A big, floating hotel encased in steel.'

Time for me to go before he stole any more of my breakfast. The dolphins were my bonus. They would stay in my mind as I went down to the office behind the Princess Lounge stage and immersed myself in the day's routine. Work had to go on. I wondered what Estelle had dreamed up for me overnight. She was probably going to complain about the hurricane. Captain Nicolas should have taken a different route?

Call it a nightmare. Estelle must have sat up all night compiling a dossier of complaints. Susan Brook got up as I came into the office. She looked distraught.

'I'm not staying if she comes in. I've had her on the phone three times already, asking where you were.'

'Watching the dolphins.'

'Don't tell her that. She'll complain to Head

Office.'

Susan swallowed but sent me a look of pure hostility. I don't think she had been on deck for days. Her skin was sallow. Somehow I had to get some air into those lungs. Perhaps Samuel could be the bait. I'd have to talk him into it, twist his arm. Call it admin therapy.

'Did you hear about the stowaway?' Susan produced her trump card. She wasn't called my deputy for nothing.

I stopped mid-email. 'No, really? Where did they find him?'

'It's a her, a female. She was in a lifeboat and had been living there for days on scraps she had managed to steal from trays left outside the Terrace Café. But the hurricane frightened the life out of her and she was found clinging to some super-structure, crying her eyes out.'

'And where is she now?'

'Locked in an empty cabin, I should image, twiddling her thumbs.'

I made a mental note to talk to Richard Norton. A stowaway had to have a reason to stow away. And a woman. That was unusual. It was usually men who needed a ticket to ride or a job.

I started a bullet list. It was my way of sorting out my head:

* Mr Foster collapses and dies
* Reg Hawkins dies inside his magic box
* Sleeping pill in my drink
* Mrs Foster's suite ransacked
* Mrs Foster and Mrs Banesto are sisters
* Stowaway found in lifeboat

I wondered if anything was connected and began to draw connecting lines. The stowaway might know Reg Hawkins. The person who ransacked Mrs Foster's suite might have put the sleeping pill in my drink. Mr Foster's briefcase might be in the lifeboat.

My connecting lines began to look like a spider's web. The possibilities were endless and confusing. This was no way to run a ship's entertainments department. I was not paid to solve crimes. I needed more coffee. Pass the honey for my throat.

Estelle Grayson needed more than coffee. She needed serious therapy, a pay rise, several new dresses and some magic slimming pills. Apparently the Lothario lounge pianist was impossible. He insisted on playing at the right tempo. The luggage that was still missing held all her stage costumes. Her cabin was noisy and she could hear the disco pounding all night.

'I don't expect to be treated like this,' she said, overflowing on to my visitor's chair. She was wearing a caftan of rainbow-challenging bright colours. I reached for my sunglasses. 'I want my cabin changed and my luggage found.'

'We are still searching for your piece of luggage. I wonder if you could describe it again and tell me what identifying label it had on it,' I said.

'It's a large navy pull-along case. Label? I don't know what label it had on it. What a ridiculous thing to ask. Am I supposed to remember labels?'

'It would help. Most passengers label their luggage with ship and cruise number and cabin number if they know it.' My patience was beginning to run out.

'I'm not a passenger. I'm a star entertainer.'

'And a really brilliant singer,' I soft-soaped. 'We are lucky to have you aboard. And you are lucky that you were spared entertaining throughout Hurricane Dora. Tonight is your big night, and things had better be sorted. Don't you have any other outfits to wear?'

'I always wear my red on my first night. It's a theatrical superstition, you know, or perhaps you don't know, never having been on the stage yourself,' said Estelle, drawing on some more lipstick. 'I have to feel right. I can't go on wearing the wrong dress.'

'I'm sure you are professional enough to be able to do your numbers in some other costume,' I said. She was exhausting me. 'I'm sure you will be just as mesmerizing in say midnight blue or white.'

She shuddered. 'I never wear white. Not with my skin.'

'Have you got another favourite with you?'

'I have got a spectacular gold lamé...'

'Gold sounds wonderful,' I gushed. 'With your hair and your amazing complexion. Pure porcelain. Like Royal Worcester.'

I didn't have a clue what I was talking about. It was absolute gibberish. Somehow I had to get her out of my office before I threw something at her. Susan was looking at me with something close to admiration. A first from that quarter.

'Thank you, Casey,' Estelle said, gathering up her folds. 'I can see you really appreciate an entertainer's problems. It's a gift, of course.' She shot a disparaging look at Susan. 'I'll go and try on the gold, see how it looks, maybe change a few numbers.'

'Wonderful,' I said. 'It's going to be a brilliant show. I can hardly wait.' I couldn't wait to get it over. 'I'll be there tonight to make sure everything works smoothly.'

'If you could talk to that pianist...'

'I will indeed. Anything to help you, Estelle.'

She graced me with a crimson gilded smile and glided out of the office. It was some moments before I even had the energy to collapse.

Susan did a slow handclap. 'How did you manage that?' she asked.

'Divine guidance,' I said.

I wondered if Richard Norton would tell me anything about the stowaway. He was a busy man and already had enough to deal with. He wouldn't welcome interference. Yet he always seemed to have time for me which was generous. Perhaps I reminded him of someone in his past.

I got him on the phone. It seemed better that pestering him in his office, getting in the way.

'Hi, it's Casey Jones. Are you all right? Survive the hurricane?'

'Slept through worse,' he boasted. 'Is this a social call or do you want to get information out of me?'

'It's a social call,' I smiled. I could smile down

148

a phone. 'I thought about an early drink tonight, a little late supper together in a quiet spot, some midnight singing and cosy dancing on the deck.'

'OK, you can quit all that, Casey. What do you want to know?' He sounded amused.

'The missing briefcase. Has it been found? And who is this stowaway? Does she have a name and a history?'

'Don't want to know much, do you? And why should I tell you? Are you now part of the security department?'

'No, but I'm very useful. You know I will pass on to you any information that comes my way. And I keep my eyes and ears open at all times. I am one of most well-informed people on this ship.'

'I'm impressed,' said Richard. He was a really nice person. He could have shot me down in flames and cut the cords to my parachute. 'How about a coffee in the Terrace Café in ten minutes?'

'It's a date,' I said, putting down the phone.

'You dating Richard Norton now?' said Susan. 'What about the dishy doctor who's always hanging around you?'

'He's all yours,' I said warmly. 'Why don't you give Dr Mallory a ring, Susan? I know he wanted to talk to you about something, but I've forgotten what it was. Why don't you suggest meeting him for a drink, say Lido Bar? He'd love that. It's one of his favourites.'

'Should I really?' There was a spark of interest in her leaden features. Her voice was without any resonance or vibrancy. 'Shall I call him?'

'Why not? He's a really charming person and he would enjoy your company. Give him a call.'

Samuel Mallory would crucify me. I had to get to him first, prime him, call in a few favours. Beneath that suave exterior and flirtatious manner, he had a compassionate heart. Though whether that kind heart extended to Susan Brook, I was not sure. But his attention might help Susan.

I ran up on deck. I was in my morning tropical gear, cut-off white trousers, Conway Line shirt and scarf. Passengers were emerging, relieved that the hurricane was over, anxious to share experiences. They had so many tales to tell. There was a lot of laughter, now that it was all over.

'So you survived?' I said to Maria de Leger.

'I've survived worse,' she said. 'The Baltic can be horrendous.'

'The other ankle is OK?' I said to Mrs Laurent in her wheelchair.

'I went to bed with a large glass of brandy and a good book,' she said. 'I don't know which I finished first.'

There was a special curry buffet on deck for lunch. Appetites were recovering and there were already a group of passengers hovering for the ritual opening of the on-deck buffet. Stewards were hurrying forward with steaming cauldrons of different curries, saffron rice and side dishes. It was going to be a banquet.

I spotted Richard Norton in the Terrace Café and hurried to join him. I knew I was late. He had two cups of coffee on the table and had kindly kept mine hot with the saucer on top.

'Waylaid, as usual,' he said.

'I have to exchange a few words. People like to talk.'

'Part of the job. I understand.'

'The stowaway,' I said. 'Who is she? Have you found out?'

'Do you really want to know?' Richard said, pursing his lips as if the coffee was too hot. 'It complicates everything. She's someone with a scary reason for being aboard. You won't like it.'

'Tell me.'

Thirteen

At Sea

The helicopter was landing on the pad at the stern of the ship. Some of the passengers peering out of the hi-tech gym were curious but they were kept at a safe distance. The two patients were brought up in the lift and carried carefully on stretchers to the waiting aircraft. Dr Mallory was in attendance, his white coat flapping.

I watched from a lower deck as the helicopter took off and wheeled overhead, her rotor blades causing a huge draught. Several straw hats took a dive into the ocean. I hoped a mermaid found them for Sunday wear.

I'd had a word with the pianist allotted to

Estelle Grayson, and he said he didn't know what she was griping about. Their last rehearsal had been amicable and her songs easy to accompany.

'No problem,' he said. 'The pieces are standard. The show will be great.'

His name was Joe Dornoch, a regular on cruise ships for his ability to play show standards for hours on end. He had once, several decades ago, been a very good-looking man but even now he spruced up debonair in a dinner jacket and black tie. He could play any request. His mind was an encyclopaedia of tunes, past and present. Hum a few bars to him, and he was there, fingers picking out the tune.

'Don't you worry, Casey, I'll make sure that Estelle sounds good.'

I wasn't quite sure what he meant by that. If she hit a dud note, he'd do what? Change key, add a few chords or a jingle?

'Thanks, Joe,' I said, 'I was hoping I could rely on you. We need a good show tonight after last night's cancellation.'

'It'll be ... the tops.'

'The Eiffel Tower?' I sang.

'You're the tops,' he went on.

'Call it Micro Power.'

'You ought to be on that stage,' said Joe. 'You sing good.'

'I used to dance.'

'I thought so. You move like a dancer.'

No good thinking about those halcyon days, those flying-through-the-sky days. I nodded my thanks and moved on. There was a lot to do.

The two airlifted casualties had left behind travelling companions so there was no need to get their cabins packed up. I'd hate to have some strange stewardess packing my things, tut-tutting about the state of knicker elastic, sniffing out-of-date mascara and free samples of night cream.

Once on dry land, they would be air-ambu-lanced to a hospital near their home. They'd be back in the UK by the afternoon. I hoped their insurance covered everything.

We were on course for the Isla Margarita, off the shore of Venezuela. I'd been there before and liked the informality. I hoped there would be a steel band playing to welcome us and dancing in the cafés. There was always a huge quayside market of local goods for souvenirs, fun to look at on the way to the nearby beaches.

The curve of beaches were in sight from the ship. No getting lost en route. Head straight for the white sand with a beach towel, suntan lotion and a bottle of water. There were several beach cafés that sold a quenching Margarita, the local drink with a kick, very acceptable on a hot day.

A huge American cruise ship was ahead of us, twice the size of the *Countess*. I could barely count the towering decks. She would not be able to berth alongside the quay but had to anchor at sea and disembark all her passengers ashore by tender. It would be an ongoing headache for the crew. It was getting such a large number of people back on board that was the headache. No one wanted to leave the soft white sands and clear blue seas till the last moment.

'So how is my favourite Entertainment Director?' said Dr Mallory, coming alongside, crisp in tailored white shorts and open-necked white T-shirt. I tried not to look at his long brown legs and the drift of dark hair on his brown arms.

'Frazzled. Are you off duty?'

'Yes, for an hour or so. Decided to get in some much needed tennis practice at the nets. A bit of exercise.'

'Good for you. Wish I had the time.'

'We could fit in a game of deck quoits later?'

'More my style. I can't wait.'

I was glad to see him looking rested. Samuel had rapid recuperative powers. No doubt stemming from his days and nights in A & E in Manchester. It must have been horrendous. I'd witnessed a few minor car accidents and they had been bad enough. My stomach was not hardened.

'So your patients were airlifted OK?'

'Both relieved to be going home to the arms of the NHS or BUPA. Conway Blue Line are pretty good in such circumstances. They often make an irresistible offer for another cruise. They don't want to lose any passengers.'

'So they won't lose out completely?'

'Their cruise is on hold. There could be another on the way.'

'Have you heard about this stowaway?' I asked.

'News travels fast.'

'What do you know about her?'

'She is eighteen years old, red haired, a dropout student, and at present resident in the medical centre, with a female guard, suffering multiple cuts and bruises, sunburn and severe malnutrition.'

I didn't know what to say. He knew more than me. And I'd been the one trying to get information out of Richard Norton. He'd clammed up on me.

'And who is she?'

'Her name is Rosanna Hawkins. She's the daughter of Reg Hawkins, at present residing in one of my freezers. She was looking for her father after receiving a threatening phone call at their home in Bermondsey. She caught the train to Southampton and somehow got aboard. Don't ask me how. These things are a mystery. I thought security was tight.'

I thought of my bullet list. This was another curious item to add.

'Can I speak to her?'

'Of course. She's not in prison, merely under security. Come along down.'

'Have you told her about her father?'

'Sorry ... no. It didn't seem the right time.'

'Do you want me to tell her?'

Samuel looked at me, his grey eyes piercing me like lasers. I couldn't fathom the expression. Then he leaned forward and put his hand over mine. His skin was warm and firm. It was like a caress. I did not know where to look.

'Could you. Casey? I'm not very good at breaking bad news. Too brusque and unfeeling. We've seen it all too often.'

'I'll go and see her. I'll tell her. Sorry, but I need a favour in return.'

155

He groaned. 'Oh God, not Estelle Grayson? Please, Casey, have mercy on a poor, lowly medical practitioner. I'm vulnerable and low in stamina. I couldn't cope with her or her tantrums.'

I had to laugh. 'No, it's my deputy, Susan Brook. She needs some fresh air and diet guidance. She might take it from you, being that you are so handsome and drop-dead gorgeous, etc. Say you'll take her dancing if she loses a stone.'

'How can I resist the way you put it, the way you massage my ego?' Samuel was laughing at me now and I liked that. It was a nice feeling. He knew I was taking the mickey and he didn't mind. The doctor went up a few notches on my scale.

'So will you do it, please? For me? Susan needs help before she becomes a large plate of semolina pudding.'

'Anything for you, Miss Casey Jones. But we still haven't had that last dance on the Lido deck. I'm looking forward to it.'

'There's still time,' I said, sliding away.

It was late before I went down to the medical centre. A dancer had sprained her ankle and was limping about the deck on crutches, surrounded by male sympathy. The DJ had gone AWOL again, and I was looking into his credentials. Estelle Grayson's last piece of luggage was found stacked on the dock at Southampton without a label. I contained my words of wisdom. The luggage could stay there.

The red dress had had it. Estelle would have to wear the gold one. It would be diplomatic to keep the whereabouts of her red dress under wraps until after the show. The news might be too much for her delicate temperament.

On my way I met the Windsor Dining Room head waiter, Graham Ward. 'How's the morale of table two, second sitting?' I asked.

'Very low,' he said. 'No one will sit there for long. Word has got round that the table is jinxed. Two deaths is two too many.'

'I could come between shows and join them for a course or two. It might improve things. What do you think?'

'Good idea, Miss Jones. It's worth a try. Show them that you're not scared. I'll make sure that a place is laid for you. And would you like some wine?'

'No, thank you. I'll need my wits about me at all times.'

'We all do. The rumours are rife.'

I stopped in my tracks and swung round. 'Rumours? What rumours, Mr Ward? Am I working in the wrong department?'

'We hear a lot as we go around serving meals. They don't call us Big Ears for nothing. We say nothing but we listen. You would be fascinated.' He was teasing me. Was this Casey Jones Tease Day?

'Fascinate me then,' I suggested, leaning on his desk. 'I've got five minutes.'

'It'll only take sixty seconds,' he said with a grin. 'Both men were murdered apparently. There's a hit list. Several more are going to be bumped off before the cruise is finished. A gang on board is blackmailing female casino winners.

The *Countess* is going to be hijacked by asylum seekers going through the Panama Canal. There's a stash of gold bullion hidden on the ship and oh, yes, someone has smuggled a parrot into their cabin and keeps it in the wardrobe.'

'Is that all? Just a routine cruise then. Nothing special happening.'

'Thought you'd like to know. If you'll excuse me, I have a few kitchen crimes to solve before the first sitting. Someone has been putting garlic in the soup.'

'I thought garlic was a staple of most soups.'

'Not when it's chocolate soup.' He grinned.

He was still teasing. I hurried off. There was time to visit the stowaway before changing into some glad rags before Estelle's show. I must remember not to outshine her in the gold department. Something restrained was obvious. Dungarees or a sequinned boiler suit might suit the occasion.

A few passengers were waiting in the medical centre for the evening surgery. Anyone with a serious injury or illness was seen immediately but if it was indigestion or a splinter, they had to wait. I asked the nurse receptionist where I could find Rosanna Hawkins. The nurse was new. I didn't know her name.

'She's in the isolation unit with a member of crew. She's weak and has some bad sunburn on her face and arms. At the end of the corridor, last door on your right.'

'Many thanks. Dr Mallory said I could speak to her for a few minutes.'

'I'm sure the officer will be glad of a ten-minute break. It's pretty boring sitting in there with someone who won't talk.'

It was going to take more than a few minutes to break the news of her father's death. And there was no easy way. I'd done it before, several times, when there was a death in the family of an entertainer. The news always came through first to the Entertainments Department.

I was not exactly trained for this aspect of my work but it all came back to what feels right at the moment. I hoped that instinct and bereavement training would come to my rescue now. I paused outside the last door on the right and took a deep breath. She needed all my help and care.

Inside the small isolation room were two separate beds. One was neatly made with a white cotton coverlet and unoccupied. The coverlet of the other was thrown back, sheet rumpled and the bed unoccupied. A chair lay overturned.

The room was empty. Call this an escaped stowaway.

Fourteen

At Sea

It wasn't my fault Rosanna Hawkins had escaped. No one could blame me yet I felt responsible. My conscience followed me around like a grey shadow. Perhaps I was the jinx. I escaped from the medical centre as fast as I could take a lift and sped on winged heels to my cabin. I threw myself down in an armchair and took deep, steadying breaths. Time had disappeared.

My watch told me I had exactly seven minutes in which to shower and change. My dancing days came to my rescue. I knew how to move and do several things at once, like brush my hair and clean my teeth at the same time.

I threw off my clothes and stood under the cooling shower, letting it flow over my body. My unruly hair was not a problem. Stretch it back, pin it and forget about the blonde streak. But what to wear that would not outshine the diva? My clothes were index-linked in my head. Something understated, no cleavage, no slits.

I went on stage in the Princess Lounge to introduce Estelle Grayson. The slim silvery-grey hand-printed dress was so understated as to be lost against the scenery. My hair was pulled back into a silver clip as usual. My high-heeled sandals were held on with painful, cutting straps. The only bright thing about me was rosy lipstick and the flush of exertion.

Estelle Grayson walked on stage, a glittering cantillation of gold lamé. We ought to have supplied sunglasses. She sang a range of standards well, the audience in the palm of her plump hand. The only number which flopped was 'Big Spender'. A little out of her size or league. Joe Dornoch was the perfect accompanist. I couldn't understand why she had complained about him.

Elsewhere the hunt was on. Somewhere on ship was a lost-cannon female stowaway. Every member of the crew was alerted. But the search had to be conducted without panicking the passengers. There was a security meeting held in Richard Norton's office. It was a squash, not an inch to spare. I perched on a filing cabinet. And this was between shows. Was I ever supposed to eat? I tried to suppress my rumbling stomach for politeness' sake. Not a peanut in sight.

'Rosanna Hawkins is not in the best of health,' said Dr Mallory, giving a medical report. 'She has severe sunburn due, I think, to when there was a lifeboat drill and she had to leave cover and sit in the sun unprotected for several hours. She has red hair and a white skin. Malnutrition, of course. She's been living on scraps, left on trays on the deck outside the Terrace Café. She spent most of Hurricane Dora being thrown about in the lifeboat, hence the cuts and bruises.'

'So this young woman is not very well?' asked Richard Norton.

'I think she has taken cover, like a wounded animal.'

'Is she dangerous?'

Samuel Mallory considered his answer. 'I don't think so. She is confused and upset, still wearing a hospital nightshirt. The unmistakable Conway Line blue and white. I never managed to find out why she had stowed away on the boat, apart from some garbled story of a mysterious threatening message received at their home in Bermondsey. Her mental state is difficult to assess.'

'What happened to the crew member left in charge of the stowaway?' someone asked. 'She was supposed to keep the girl in custody.'

'Unfortunately the female crew member was caught short and took a break. It was enough time for Rosanna Hawkins to disappear,' said Richard Norton, not looking pleased. What had happened to locking doors, etc? I bet that female crew member was keeping a low profile.

'If anyone finds her, how should we proceed?' I asked. It was bound to be me. I had that sort of luck. A premonition. She was probably hiding in my cabin, trying on my dresses, using my factor thirty-five.

'Keep her quiet, keep talking to her. Phone Dr Mallory or myself,' said Richard. 'Do not involve any passenger, even if you think you are at risk.'

'Risk? What do you mean, at risk?'

'You've mentioned risk twice.'

There was no answer to that question. No one said anything. Richard Norton would not meet

162

my eyes. Samuel Mallory came alongside as the meeting broke up and helped me down from the filing cabinet.

'Some scalpel blades are missing from the medical centre,' he said. 'Norton won't say anything because it could be dangerous. She may have taken them.'

'But you don't know...'

'No, we don't really know. By the way, I'm having a drink with your delightfully plump deputy, Susan Brook, this evening in the Lido Bar.'

'Good for you,' I said. 'Thank you, doctor. Put her on a diet.'

'I thought you'd be pleased.'

'I'm overjoyed. It's a step in the right direction. Now, if you'll excuse me, I have work to do.'

I didn't know why I was suddenly so grumpy. I'd asked him to take Susan under his wing to help her confidence, but now it seemed I didn't like it when he did. The waves went from side to side in my head, sort of uncoordinated and clumsy. I needed some air.

He caught my arm and made me wheel round. I faced this devastating man, ducking the stare from his laser eyes. 'Have I done something wrong?' he asked. 'Is this a problem?'

'Sorry,' I said, struggling. 'No, you are being very kind and helpful to even get Susan up on deck and out into the fresh air. I'm grateful. I just...' I didn't know how to finish my sentence. I didn't understand myself. 'I didn't expect it to happen so soon.'

He touched my chin. It was a touch of infinite lightness, like a feather. 'I take that as a good sign, Casey,' he said and walked away.

On a ship as big as the *Countess* there were a thousand places to hide. There were more than a few empty cabins. Stores were kept everywhere. There was a honeycomb of offices. And below decks, there were vast areas. She might have gone back to the lifeboats. I didn't even know what she looked like, apart from the red hair and sunburn.

A report came through from the gym area on the top deck within the funnel casing of the ship. A bag had been stolen. It contained clothes and a cruise card. Ah, if Rosanna Hawkins had managed to get hold of a cruise card, then she could function on board ship for a short time. The cruise card was immediately cancelled by the purser's office, but even before then it was used twice in a bar and once in Bond Street shop on clothes. She'd treated herself to the day's cocktail, a Margarita Special, and bought jeans, T-shirt and a *Countess* sweatshirt at the shop. Everyone wore *Countess* sweatshirts.

She wasn't that ill. Now she would look like everyone else.

Rosanna would merge with the passengers wearing the same clothes and whatever else was in the gym bag. Red hair, that's all we really could go on and the burns. But she could tuck her hair up inside a baseball cap and no one would know. But why was she on board and what would she do when she discovered she couldn't find her father, Reg Hawkins?

Bait. The way to get her to come out of hiding was to string up some bait.

It would not be ethical to publicise a magic show in the Princess Lounge theatre when the magician was dead. But supposing we offered lessons in magic or a lecture about famous illusions? Would that draw her out of the woodwork?

There was no one to run this by, only myself. I didn't want to approach Head Office. They had enough problems. I slipped into the library and hunted the shelves for any books on magic and illusions. Who could I ask to give the lecture? I wouldn't have the faintest idea how to write a lecture from all this information and then deliver it in an entertaining way.

It would take me weeks. I was thinking hours.

The author lecturer was always surrounded by her throng of would-be writers wanting to talk or get her guidance on a piece of writing they were working on. It didn't seem fair to ask her to take on any more. The other lecturers said they had no spare time, not their style, etc.

Dr Mallory and Richard Norton were out of the question, both far too busy. And it had to be someone that Rosanna didn't know. Someone she would not suspect.

The perfect person fell into my lap, or almost. I gave her a radiant smile.

'I'm going to go and get my hair done,' Susan said, hesitantly, tripping over some cables. 'Is that all right? You don't need me.'

'Sure,' I said, with words of sweetness and light. 'Here's a couple of books for you to look at under the dryer. As we don't have a magician any more, I thought a one-off talk about magic and illusions might fill a gap. Do you feel like doing it? You could read it from the lectern. You don't have to learn it by heart. Just mark the passages and do a bit of ad-libbing in between. It could be fun.'

'Oh yes, wow,' she said, taking the books. 'I'd love to do that. A lecture. When do you think would be a suitable time?'

'How about after lunch? We could still get an announcement on cabin television and tannoy the event.'

Susan flushed with pleasure. Perhaps all she needed was more praise and more responsibility. 'I could wear my new turquoise trouser suit,' she offered.

'Sounds perfect,' I said. 'Off you go and get your hair done. I'll take your calls.'

Fool. Why did I feel I had to do this for everyone? They could catch their own stowaway. I phoned Richard Norton and told him about the bait. He thought it was a great idea. He said he would sit in the projectionist's box at the back, out of sight, but ready to assist if needed.

'We need a sort of code,' he said. 'So that you can alert me if she turns up.'

'Maybe you could alert me since you wouldn't tell me what she looks like.'

'We'll think of something.'

'How about using our mobiles?'

'Quick one there, Casey,' he chuckled. 'Right on the ball.'

There was a little time left till the *Countess*

166

would dock at Isla Margarita tomorrow. Rosanna might take it into her head to skip ship there. Not a good choice since it was a small remote island off the coast of Venezuela. Unless she planned to stay there for a good while. She could always teach English to local children.

I made sure I could go to Susan's lecture. I'd also arranged for there to be slides to illustrate her talk. It might be quite good. It might be the start of an alternative career for Susan.

I changed out of my Conway uniform and put on a cotton dress. I wanted to merge and slip into the back of the lecture theatre once it had started. I asked Joe Dornoch to introduce Susan and make some suitably complimentary remarks. He agreed. He was such an agreeable person.

The lecture theatre was quite full. It was too hot out on the decks and passengers were seeking air-conditioned entertainment. When I was watching a film, late at night in the same place, I had to wrap my shoulders in a pashmina.

Joe introduced Susan Brook with professional ease. He knew what he was doing. Susan smiled broadly, half hidden by the lectern. Her hair looked good. At least it was clean and shining.

She rattled through the information I had given her, stopping for the slides to be shown on the screen. I had slipped into the back of the theatre, as I often did to evaluate a lecturer, keeping my head down. Sometimes we got a dud.

Susan was doing OK. She even raised a few laughs. Joe had slipped out of the back door so maybe she wasn't getting a thank you. If nothing happened, then I would do it.

But it wasn't going to be that easy.

I felt a tension rising. Someone in the third row was making comments, talking over the lecture. No one likes a disruptive audience.

I slid down and eased myself along the curved wall of the theatre, pretending I was a late arrival looking for a seat. There was a woman in the third row, hair in a baseball cap, wearing a *Countess* sweatshirt. She was gripping the sides of her seat.

'Where's Merlin the Magician?' she suddenly shouted. 'Why isn't he giving this talk? He knows all about illusions.'

We'd got her. This must be Rosanna Hawkins. No one else would be aware of the non-appearance of our magician.

Susan continued, as I knew she would. She had brick-wall mentality. I'd noticed this in the office. Total oblivion sometimes.

I dialled Richard on my mobile and spoke very quietly. 'Third row, four seats in, baseball cap.'

'Roger,' he said.

'Richard,' I said.

How would the audience react if there was a sudden flurry of activity and one of the audience was carted off in custody? This had to be handled with care. Richard was all too aware of this and his men were simply stationed at the doors. There were only two exits to the lecture theatre, one at the back right, one at the front left.

Wherever Miss Hawkins went, I would be close behind. I sat myself into an empty seat two rows behind, never taking my eyes off her.

'That's one of Merlin's illusions,' she shouted.

'Quite right,' said Susan smoothly. 'One of Merlin the Magician's famous illusions and he has been a regular performer on the *Countess* for many years.'

'Where is he now?' she went on but was shushed by other members of the audience who wanted to hear the lecture. 'That's what I want to know.'

Not long now. It was nearing afternoon teatime. Scones with jam and cream were my favourite snack if I had missed lunch. No wonder some of my waistbands had trouble meeting. I was not ready yet for the elastic waist.

Susan was winding up and waffling. This was a fraction on the boring side. She had deserted the written text and was using her own minimal knowledge of the subject, but the passengers were patient and polite, knowing that tea was imminent.

There was an outburst of clapping when Susan took a breath. It was not the end of her rig-marole, but the passengers decided that it was the end. They wanted their fabulous tea. I stood up quickly and blocked the third row, only allowing a couple of innocents to proceed out. She could not escape me.

As Rosanna came face to face, I smiled pleasantly.

'Hello, Rosanna Hawkins?' I said. 'How are you?'

She looked at me, panic-stricken, eyes wide, face skinless red. No mistake in identity. I'd found my quarry. I put my hand on her arm, not in a threatening way but simply so that she knew

I had spotted her.

What happened then was all so fast that afterwards I had trouble remembering anything. She brought her other hand down on my arm, bone-hard fist side, like a karate blow. Pain shot through me. She'd broken my arm.

I fell against the wall, clutching my arm. The pain was a red swarm across my eyes. Rosanna ran out of the lecture theatre, past the security guards who were not sure who they were looking for. Where she ran to, no one knew.

Dr Samuel Mallory found me sitting on the floor of the lecture theatre, now weirdly empty, still clutching my arm.

'Dear God, Casey, what have you done now? Let me look at it. Don't move. Fold your arm back, against your shoulder. Hold it up there under the elbow. You need this X-rayed immediately.'

'I'm sorry but I cannot pay for an X-ray.'

'Have this one on me.'

Fifteen

At Sea

'Can you wiggle your fingers?' Samuel asked.
I did some digital wiggling.
'Nothing's broken. But we'll do an X-ray to make sure. She's probably bruised the bone. It was a hefty whack.'
Dr Mallory's administrations were professional and efficient. Neither arm nor wrist were broken but a bruise the size of an orange was appearing and it hurt. He suggested a wrist support for a couple of days and some painkillers. I became an interesting invalid on deck.
The passengers were curious. Most of them assumed that Hurricane Dora was to blame and I was thrown against some bulwark during my arduous duties. Time spans seem to have a way of getting mixed up on ship. People forget the date and days of the week quite easily, one merging into another. I often do the same. It's not easy to remember what day it is.
Passengers at the lecture who had witnessed the incident put around various lurid rumours. I had been attacked by a drunk, a deranged female, a jealous wife.
Rosanna Hawkins disappeared into the panel-

171

ling again. She had obviously found herself a good hiding place. One with all mod cons this time. She couldn't leave the ship at Isla Margarita without presenting a cruise card at the gangway, and the stolen one had been cancelled. But we needed to find her first.

Susan Brook was on a high after her lecturing debut and was researching new topics on Google instead of doing her work. Head Office were sending out a replacement entertainer who would be joining the ship at Curacao, an island in the Netherlands Antilles. He would be with us for the last half of the cruise, all the way back to Southampton, so he would earn his keep with several performances.

'I did very well, didn't I?' said Susan. 'They were so appreciative. People keep stopping me and asking me how do I know so much about magic.'

'And you told them that you were reading from a book,' I said.

'I told them it's in the family. My dad used to do card tricks.'

'How about a talk on card tricks, then?' I suggested, trying to type an email on my keyboard with one hand. Capital letters were awkward. I took my wrist out of the support. It didn't hurt too much.

'I don't really know enough,' she said, unaware that I was ribbing her.

'Day in port tomorrow so we can take some time off. Would you like to go ashore in the afternoon for a couple of hours? There's a lovely beach quite close to the quayside. Miles of shallow water first so you have to wade out for a swim.'

'I'm not too keen on swimming,' she said, not looking up. Ah, the swimsuit phobia. Baring all in public. She would be hesitant in a size eighteen swimsuit. An island fringed with deserted beaches would be more her style of heaven.

'Find yourself a spot on deck,' I said. 'You'll have the ship to yourself.'

'I'll research my next talk,' she said. What had I started? I kept my mouth shut. There would be the right time to gently squash her career move.

I hoped Richard Norton would keep me informed of any new developments, maybe out of politeness. I was not part of the security team but I was a victim of the circumstances. A twice-times victim. I'd forgotten the sleeping pills. So who dosed me with sleeping pills? Now that couldn't have been Rosanna – or could it? We didn't know she was on the ship but she was already bunked up in lifeboat twelve. But why me? I was hardly any sort of a threat to her.

I tried to make a list in my head of why I was a threat but could think of nothing much except that I had witnessed the collapse of Mr Foster at table two. What had I seen? Did they think I had seen something incriminating? I couldn't re-member. It had all happened so fast. We didn't have CCTV cameras in the dining room. Who wanted grainy pictures of folk slurping their soup?

I had emailed Head Office a couple of days back about the DJ who wasn't doing his job. I asked them to give me more information about his background and why we had employed him to come on to the *Countess*. He must have had good references or an outstanding CV.

A reply flashed on to my screen and I clicked into the body of the email. It was an eye-opener. They had done a lot of digging. He had signed a contract with Conway Blue Line as Darin Jack. But now it seemed that no such person as Darin Jack existed. His passport was false and the references invented. They suggested that he should be sent back to England immediately.

Darin Jack equals DJ. No one had spotted that. It could be funny if it wasn't so serious. Ha, ha. So who was this person? I would have to inform Richard. I was such a coward, I sent him a copy of the email instead and hoped he would pick it up fast. He would start to think that trouble rolled my hair and I was best kept at a distance.

'Has La Diva been thumping you?' It was Joe Dornoch on his way to the Lido deck to top up his tan. He looked a trim fifty in white shorts and white rugby shirt. I didn't look at his legs.

'Not yet. I've been practising my first aid.'

'My advice is to duck,' he grinned, swinging a towel.

'The show was good.'

'I told you it would be.'

He made me feel a lot better though he was not my type. I didn't think I had a type. My past history was a messy blank of student dating that came to nothing. What had happened to all those men? No engagements, no affairs, no matrimonial baggage. One could hardly count a shattering teenage crush on Andre Dupois, my ballet teacher. He had been my perfect man for years. Though very tight jeans on men still worry me.

There was a lull and time for a quick cuppa on deck outside the Terrace Café. My favourite table was free where I could watch the tumbling white wake of the ship. It was mesmerizing to see the thrashing water, cascading and spreading behind us. I almost forgot to take a painkiller.

'You really have been in the wars,' said Madame de Leger, stopping by the table. She was wearing a slim shift the muted colours of a kingfisher, perfect for an older woman. 'I didn't know being Entertainment Director was such a dangerous job.'

'It's kept very quiet,' I said.

'I was sitting behind when she went for you. I was somewhat concerned because she wouldn't keep quiet during the talk. It must have been distracting for Miss Brook.'

'Could you catch what the woman was saying?'

'Something about her father inventing something and people trying to steal it. Nothing really relevant. I suppose she had been out in the sun for too long. She did look rather red-faced. Is she all right?'

'Oh, yes,' I said. 'She's fine now, very sorry, of course. Full of apologies. Some kind of accidental reflex action.'

Maria de Leger gave me a quizzical look. 'Is that what it's called now?'

She wasn't fooled. There was nothing else I could say. I went on stirring my tea and she

175

drifted away.

The late afternoon sun was enough to make me feel dozy. I loved the warmth on my skin. My eyelids felt heavy, so heavy that I missed what happened next.

There was a sudden, urgent shout from below. Then another, even louder. A woman screamed, her voice piercing the air.

'Man overboard! Man overboard!'

People rushed to the rails, scattering cups, plates, trays. The crew were faster, trained to respond immediately. Several lifebelts were tossed into the sea from a lower deck. I saw one being immediately swept away on the wake, but then dragged back to the ship's side by the rope attachment.

It was a choppy sea. We were going through some strong cross-current and the waves were larger than they had been earlier. I heard the engines stop and the big ship slowed down. She couldn't stop immediately. We might be in water too deep to anchor. It was strange not to be moving.

Starboard was packing with crowds of gawping onlookers. I could see a man struggling in the water, waves swamping him, a lifebelt out of reach. He looked so small and helpless.

A gasp went up as he went under, totally immersed by a huge wave. A stout man turned to me angrily.

'Can't you do something?' he shouted. 'Can't you see he's drowning?'

'The crew are trained in rescue work,' I said. 'They will be throwing down an inflatable dinghy any moment now.'

'Well, they'd better get on with it,' he growled, 'or it'll be too late.' He stomped off to complain to someone else.

I could hear the squeaking and creaking of a dinghy being rapidly winched down into the sea. Two crew members in lifejackets were perched on it, ready to swim to the drowning man as soon as it touched the water. They would haul him aboard. They'd practised many times with a volunteer crew member acting as a casualty.

It was a tense drama. I saw the man being swept further out to sea. He was tiring, his arms flailing, not looking good. There was no time to launch a tender. The dinghy had to reach him.

'Do we know who it is?' Samuel asked. He'd appeared at my side, bag and defibrillator case in his arms.

'No, don't know.'

'How did he get in the water?'

'Don't know. I never saw it happen. I suppose he fell from the Promenade Deck.'

'The railings are chest high. They are for leaning on, not falling over. Did he climb over?'

'Don't know. I wasn't there.'

'You don't know much, do you? I'd better get down to a lower deck. He's taking in a lot of water. I may have to pump him out.'

He hurried away. He had a man's life to save. If they were in time.

The dinghy had reached the man despite the choppy waves and he was being hauled aboard. He looked unconscious. He lay inert, his clothes like a bundle of wet washing. He was being put in the recovery position so that water could run out of his mouth. His hair was plastered against his head. It was a colour I recognized.

The dinghy was brought rapidly on board and the man lifted on deck. The area had already been cordoned off. He didn't need an audience.

I found I was trembling. This couldn't be happening. I'd never seen anyone go overboard before. Death was not unknown on cruise ships because of the higher proportion of elderly passengers. We seemed to have had more than the normal number of fatalities this cruise, but then I didn't think they had been normal.

It was too late. The man, Nigel Garten, the happy-go-lucky party-goer, never regained consciousness. Dr Mallory spent twenty minutes trying to resuscitate him, using the defibrillator before he gave up and noted time of death. He was examining his head. There was no apparent reason for Mr Garten to have gone overboard. No one had seen him being pushed or climbing the rails. There didn't seem to be witnesses anywhere. The deck had been deserted.

The fall could hardly have been accidental. Unless he had climbed up to get a better view of something, or someone. Dolphins? It didn't seem right to die for dolphins.

'He was such a nice man,' passengers were saying. 'Life and soul of the party. Always had a ready joke. Great company at the table.'

I didn't dare ask.

I didn't have to ask. My spine chilled. The

word went round. Mr Garten had recently been sitting at table two, second sitting. He was the third to die.

Samuel Mallory was quiet that evening. He was depressed because he had not been able to save the man. There was nothing I could do or say to lift the atmosphere. We sat in a quiet bar, drinking white wine. A band was playing somewhere but few were dancing.

One of the trips tomorrow was an island tour and it meant an early start on the coaches. A special early breakfast was being laid on.

'That new receptionist of yours,' I began. 'Didn't she see Rosanna Hawkins leave the isolation unit? She would have had to pass the desk on her way out. There's only one way out, isn't there?'

'What new receptionist?' Samuel was preoccupied, putting his thoughts on hold. 'I don't know what you are talking about.'

'When I came down to see Rosanna. There was a new nurse at the reception desk. She was working on some reports.'

Samuel looked straight at me, eyes as usual boring into mine.

'Why didn't you tell me this before?' he asked.

'Tell you what?'

'About a new receptionist.'

'I didn't think it was important. You may recall that a lot was happening. Rosanna Hawkins had escaped and a crew member was locked in the loo.'

'I don't have a new nurse,' he said coldly. 'My

179

team is the same as the last cruise. That was probably Rosanna Hawkins sitting at the desk and you walked right past her.'

Sixteen

Isla Margarita

By now we knew that Rosanna had gathered a minimal wardrobe. A nurse's uniform, sweat-shirt, jeans and hospital nightie. We needed to make an inch by inch search of the entire ship to find her. By we, I did not mean me. It was every other member of the crew.

They were not looking for the missing DJ. Cruise card records showed he had gone ashore early at Barbados and returned before the ship sailed. But he had not been seen since nor was his cabin occupied. It was probable that he had found a way to slip ashore again during one of the frequent deliveries of fresh produce that arrived via a door in the hull, quayside level. Perhaps he had been working himself a free passage to the Caribbean, without doing any work. It has been known, only too often.

Perhaps the two might have been linked. Brother/sister. Husband/wife. Another theory down the plughole? Darin and Rosanna? It was doubtful.

Early morning was fresh and bright. The fittest

of us were doing a quick circuit of the Promenade Deck to get the blood circulating. The
Countess was already berthed at the deep water
port of El Guamache on the western part of the
island. The frantic activity ashore was riveting to
watch. Dozens of thatch-roofed stalls were being
set up and stretched as far as the beach cafés,
selling souvenirs that were locally made and a
lot that weren't. The Isla Margarita, only twenty-
five miles off the coast of Venezuela, was once
well known for its pearl fishing, but the oyster
beds had been overexploited. So no genuine
pearl bargains around.

It was one of the best places for shopping
because practically everything was duty-free. It
didn't have the chic and sophisticated shops of
Palma, but villagers from miles around con-
verged when a cruise ship was due in port, laden
with home-made jewellery and clothes and ornaments.

A group of musicians were playing Spanish
music and a couple of lithe youngsters were
twirling and whirling about in rhythm to the
beat. Pretty early in the day for a dance band.
The coaches were beginning to arrive, parking
along the front, their Conway Blue Line labels
prominent in the driver's windows. The tours
would take in the national park with lagoons,
mangroves and flamingos, the large town of
Porlamar, the castle at Pampatar, lunch out at a
fish restaurant and finally a fine beach for swimming.

They would return exhausted. I didn't know
what the interior roads would be like. Many of

these all-day tours sounded fine in the tours brochure but the poor roads were often killing. Margarita had 3,000-feet twin hills rising on the horizon and any hairpin roads might be scary. I was glad I hadn't volunteered to guide. I wanted to crash out on a beach and forget everything. Especially Dr Samuel Mallory. I wanted to forget him totally before he became imprinted on my mind.

Tony and Janet, the ballroom dancing teachers, had volunteered to guide and were waiting by their coaches. I don't know where they got the energy. I waved my amazement and they fanned back, miming 'hot' and 'exhausted'. Already the temperature was rising. The stones on the quayside were beginning to bake. The distant blue of the water lapping the white sand was enticing.

The work of the Entertainment Director's office still had to go on and we dispatched it in double quick time. I ignored Estelle Grayson's complaint that her cabin was too hot and sent an air-conditioning engineer round to see her. She had probably turned the dial the wrong way. She sat up half the night inventing complaints. Conway ought to offer an inter-departmental prize for her most outrageous complaint.

I went back to my cabin to change into a swimsuit and beach clothes. Ahmed was outside with his laden trolley of towels and sheets, still working, the never-ending cleaning and housekeeping of his allotted cabins.

'Are you getting some time ashore today?' I asked.

'No, Miss Jones. Not this today. But next port,

182

yes. We are going ashore at Willemstad. They say it is very nice.'

'Very Dutch and very colourful. There's a floating market, selling fish from boats.' Did he know about the stowaway? Such items of news would fly round the crew and the stewards. 'Tell me, Ahmed. Would you say there were plenty of hiding places on the *Countess* for a stowaway?'

'Oh yes, Miss Jones. Many, many curious hiding places. Many cupboards and storage units. Some of the panelled walls have doors in them that no one notices.'

'I bet they don't, Ahmed. Thank you. Sorry to have delayed you.'

'That is no problem, Miss Jones. Have a nice day.'

I changed into a cerise swimsuit, flowered sarong and long-sleeved shirt. The five minute walk to La Caracola beach took twenty minutes. The vendors were persistent and their goods a mass of colourful bargains. I bought two stretchy bracelets made of painted seeds for less than a dollar. It made me feel mean to give them so little but the woman and her daughter seemed pleased.

A drink of local Margarita went down well despite the plastic glass. I think it was made with a dark rum topped with loads of juice then decorated with sliced fruit. The open air bar was doing fantastic trade. The American cruise ship was anchored out at sea and the passengers had come ashore in droves on launches. It was a huge white ship. She made the *Countess* look like a midget. Her name was *Princess of the*

Ocean or something similarly vast.

'Hi,' I said to several Americans. 'Are you having a good time?'

'Sure, fantastic island. The best.'

Already the always-spruce American crew were trying to persuade their unruly and widespread pack of passengers to start returning to ship in good time. They were patrolling the beaches with loudspeakers.

'Each launch only holds forty passengers, so start making your way back now, folks,' they bellowed.

Folk had no intention of making their way back when there was all this lovely white sand to sunbathe on. They probably had minimal space on the ship. They turned a deaf ear to the announcements, rolled over and applied lashings more suntan lotion.

I walked along the first beach and passed the second smaller one. There were tiny beaches further on, only big enough for two or three people. I might get one to myself. The problem with walking too far was timing the return. It would be easy to fall asleep on the beach and then have to race back. Calamity Casey. Again?

One small bay had another cruise couple staking their pitch. I vaguely knew them by sight but recognized the cabin issue Conway Blue beach towels. They smiled, recognizing me.

'Hi,' I said. 'Do you mind if I join you on this beach?'

'No, not all. Feel free. Glad you are having a few hours off.'

'And please give me a nudge if I fall asleep.'

184

'Likewise. We certainly don't want to miss the ship sailing. It would be too awful.'

Reassured that I had back-up, I stripped off and waded through the shallow water. The water was cool as I pushed against the wavelets, splashing against my knees, then thighs. It was clear and I could see the sand on the sea bed. The couple were specks on the beach before it was deep enough to swim. I swam a few yards, then turned on my back to enjoy the sensation of floating, my eyes closed against the dazzling sparkle of the sun.

This was bliss. This was why I worked on the *Countess.*

It was heavenly. All the shipboard problems vanished. People had died in largely unexplained circumstances. We had a roaming stowaway. Something funny was going on even if no one believed me. But now, I felt as if I was a million miles away and it was a delicious feeling. Hardly real at all.

I swam for some distance. There was never any pain in water. The ankle discomfort disappeared as if the accident had never happened. But it had happened. A sudden searing pain that sent me hopping into career oblivion.

The show had stopped, but only long enough for stage hands to cart me off on an improvised stretcher. My understudy was in the wings. She went on smoothly, taking up the routine as if nothing had happened.

Those first few weeks had been traumatic. No one at the hospital seemed to understand that dancing was my life, my career. They thought

I'd get over it, get a job in Top Shop. Thank you, folks.

'Pretty girl like you,' said one doctor. 'Soon get another job.'

'I appreciate your concern,' I'd said, barely able to hide my frustration.

No one had been sympathetic. Even my parents had thought it par for the course. Dancing had been a ridiculous choice with all those A levels under my belt.

'Get a proper job now,' said my dad.

'Penny for them,' said a voice I recognized but could not see against the bright sun. 'You're miles away.'

'I was wondering if all doctors are insensitive, boorish and sometimes downright cruel.' I flipped over on to my front and swam around a bit.

Samuel was treading water. He seemed to have swum along from one of the large, closer beaches. 'It goes with the territory,' he said, flicking wet hair out of his eyes. 'We have to be caked in shellac. Several layers.'

'It shows.' I made sure I didn't look at his glistening brown shoulders, but it wasn't easy. He was only a few feet away from me and I was acutely aware of his naked skin, so close. My cerise swimsuit was a sleek and modest affair, not a couple or three of strategic triangles and some string. 'I was remembering when I injured my ankle and had to give up dancing. The medical profession were so unsympathetic.'

'Some of us are immune to personal trauma. Sorry.'

His watch was waterproof. Droplets fell off his

arm as he squinted at the dial. He had dark hairs on his forearm. They were so near and touchable.

'Time to get back,' he said. He fell into the water and began a fast crawl towards the quay-side, his arms slicing through the waves. Show-off. He'd be on board before I was. I had miles of heavy shallows to wade through. The couple on the beach were waving at me. I waved back to show that I understood. As I neared, I could see that they were packing up their goods, moving around quite quickly. I didn't like the look of that. I must have floated for longer than I thought.

Time for minor panic. I began to splash hurriedly through the shallows. The couple were leaving the tiny bay, waving good bye. I still had a way to go. I ran through the last gobbling wavelets, grabbed my sarong, sandals and shirt. It was hard going, trying to run on soft sand. The beaches were almost deserted. Everyone had gone. The bars were closing.

Time for major panic. I didn't have a watch. I flew across the sand, glad to be able to see the *Countess* in the distance, still berthed. She was waiting for me, I felt sure. There must still be time. I'd only be a few minutes late. One of the last on board. Someone had to be last.

The steps up from the beach were formed out of rocks. Normally this was OK. But some idiot had decided to wash their feet at the top of the steps and throw the rest of the water down the steps. Thank you, buster.

I fell on the slippery rock. I felt my bad ankle

go under. The strap to my sandal broke. I heard the snap although my head was full of birdsong and waves.

It seemed like a replay of that other occasion although now I had only myself to rely on. No commiserating troupe of dancers, no choreographer wailing, no producer tearing his hair.

Somehow I crawled up the steps. There was no way of repairing my sandal. I would have to go barefooted. And the pain. It hurt like hell. I grabbed a floating plastic bag and wrapped it tightly round my ankle, knotting the ends together. Good-bye glamour.

The vendors were all packing up and the market area was a throng of carts and cars. It was painful walking on hot stones but I hobbled as fast as I could, shutting my mind to the heat. There was no clear passage. The *Countess* was still at her berth but I could hear the band playing 'Sailing, we are sailing'. A bad sign. And the flag-wavers were out. A group of nationals on front of the dock, waving their flags. Very friendly and all that, but as far as I was concerned, an even worse sign. They only waved at the last moment.

Sweat was pouring off my forehead. As I broke through the last of the busy vendors, my worst fears were tossed back in my face. They were throwing down the lines. The gangways had all been hoisted and the ship was leaving. The *Countess* was barely a foot of water away from the quayside and I could have jumped it. But to where? There was no convenient open doorway or rope.

I stood riveted, heart thumping.

The ship's hull was closed shut and made fast. I could hardly jump to nowhere. I stood on the quayside, beside the flag wavers, in despair as my beautiful white lady left without me. Just that extra swim, that extra float, those moments talking with Samuel. They were my downfall. I could blame him.

My career was in shatters. No one would employ me again. How would I get home? All my documents were on board in my grab bag. I was doomed to months of fruitless embassy enquiries, moneyless, living like a bum. Maybe get a job washing up in a bar. And my ankle was really painful.

They were real tears. Casey Jones, this was a monumental cock-up. How are you going to get yourself out of this one?

Samuel was leaning over a rail on the Promenade Deck, mid-deck. I could always recognize that head, that dark hair, but I couldn't make out what he was saying. Maybe just goodbye, goodbye. He'd be glad to see the back of me.

I couldn't wave. I stood like a dejected beanpole with nothing to lean on. The ship was inching away from me, the gap widening, water swirling round her bows.

The music was driving me crazy. I couldn't hear what Samuel was saying. I hurried, limping along the quayside as the ship began to ease out to sea.

'Pilot,' Samuel was yelling. 'Pi-lot's boat.'

'What?' I yelled back.

'Pi-lot.'

189

Then I understood. There was a pilot on board, who would have to be taken off by a small launch coming alongside. My own monumental stupidity came home to thump me squarely between the eyes. Most departure times are six p.m. sharp. Isla Margarita had been scheduled for five p.m., something to do with tides or another ship coming in.

The *Countess* was backing off the berth before swinging into the Canal de Margarita and heading easterly along the southern shores of the island. The canal was a narrow stretch of water between Isla Margarita and another island, called Coche, to starboard. There were a lot of fishing boats in this canal.

I ran to the harbour master's office in the dockside buildings. Since I had no identification on me, apart from my crew cruise card, the official in charge was dubious of my story.

'But who am you?' he asked, viewing my card as if it was contaminated. 'How do I know if you not passenger?'

'I'm not a passenger. I'm a member of the crew.'

He could not believe that a crew member could be so stupid as to miss the ship. 'You do not look like crew.'

My damp swimsuit and sarong were far from a slick uniform. And the plastic bag wrapped round my foot. 'I came ashore for a swim,' I said. 'Please put me on the pilot's launch to get back to the ship.'

'Impossible. Not allowed, unauthorized person.'

'*Por favor*, ring the medical centre on the ship and ask for Dr Samuel Mallory, the ship's doctor.' I gave him the direct line number.

'*Si,*' he said, light dawning. 'You very sick passenger?'

'Yes, very sick passenger.'

Whatever Dr Mallory said eventually convinced the official. He did a lot of nodding. Then he made another call, asking for permission for the transfer.

'You will wear lifejacket and jump,' he said. 'Boat no wait. One, two, jump.'

I would have agreed to anything. 'One, two, jump,' I repeated, nodding.

I was helped down into the launch and it began the short journey to reach the *Countess*. She was ahead of us, already on course. The pilot's job was over.

The transfer was, as always, this amazing split-second timing. I had watched it many times. The launch slowed alongside, the pilot appeared at a water-level door, and as nonchalantly as stepping on to an escalator, stepped across the waves and on to the small bobbing deck.

Now, I had to do the same, in the opposite direction. The time had come. *Omigod.*

Seventeen

At Sea

There was an audience of several hundred passengers hanging over the rails, watching my inelegant late arrival on the *Countess*. They were armed with camcorders and cameras. Word had gone round. This was live entertainment, no rehearsal.

My hair was caked with salt and sand, the sarong clinging to my legs, wearing one sandal and a plastic bag. And on top of my wet swimsuit I was strapped into a cumbersome lifejacket. I was the last word in cruise line elegance.

I had one card in my favour. A tomboy childhood had me climbing in and out of trees before I could even tie my shoelaces. Surely I could time a single leap?

The pilot's launch neared the ship. The *Countess* looked bigger than ever from below and the doorway in her hull, so small and distant. The pilot was already waiting as the ship was now clear of land and rocks and his job over. He waited until the deck of the launch was level with the doorway and stepped over. He was short and jaunty, a peaked cap set on thick grey hair.

A lurch of waves sent the launch bobbing back out of reach. The helmsman put the launch into reverse and backed it closer to the towering hull of the *Countess*.

'I will help you,' the pilot said, reassuringly. What a nice man. He put his hand under my elbow. 'When I say, go now, *señorita*. You go. Trust me.'

I was terrified despite all the tree climbing. This was totally different. Vast, dark-blue choppy sea below, huge ship above. I could be crushed to death. My fear showed in my eyes. I felt sick, scared witless.

'You will be safe,' he said, patting my arm. 'Go now.'

I leaped.

Two sturdy seamen caught me by the arms and hauled me aboard. I fell against them with relief. The rubber floor of the *Countess* felt firm and solid despite the movement. One of them was stripping off the lifejacket and, casually leaning out, at the right moment handed it back to the pilot.

'Thank you, thank you, *gracias*,' I called out, still shaking. Politeness surfaced. Everything else was blurred.

A cheer went up from passengers on the upper decks, ragged but enthusiastic. The show was over. They could go and get changed for dinner now.

'*Adios*,' the harbour crew waved, grinning. They'd have a tale to tell tonight in the local bars. '*Adios*.'

'*Adios*,' I waved. '*Gracias*.'

I was way down in the depths, among all the food storage areas. Thousands of tons of vegetables, crates and crates of beer and wine, millions of eggs. The statistics were always awesome. Dr Samuel Mallory was sauntering towards me. He couldn't keep the smug grin off his face.

'Well, well, how's my sick passenger?' he asked, tapping his forehead.

'Is that what you told him?' I was furious.

'So it worked, didn't it?'

I started marching along the narrow corridor. There must be a way out, some stairs or a service lift. I had to find a bathroom soon and it wasn't only to wash my hair.

'Wrong way,' he said. 'Follow me.'

It was humbling, having to follow the damned man but I suppose he had helped to get me back on-board. I should be grateful but I wasn't particularly.

'Thank you,' I said, gathering a shred of dignity in my damp clothes. 'I need a bathroom.'

'No problem, lady. I know of a nice private one you can use.'

I was past caring where he took me. Up in a service lift, along a corridor, out on deck for some metres, then inside and along another corridor. He unlocked the door to a cabin. 'Feel free,' he said, indicating the bathroom.

It was his cabin. Dark wood panelling, large bunk bed, shelves of books everywhere, desk, a real window. Not a lot of space.

I was looking at jars of aftershave, hair cream, razors on the counter, a navy towelling robe behind the bathroom door. I didn't trawl through his possessions. I was too pleased to be in a proper bathroom to care where I was.

'Have a shower if you want,' he called out. 'I'm making you a hot drink.'

'Wonderful,' I said, swamped with relief. I could have cried.

I was standing under a warm shower, floppy shower curtain closed, when the door opened and a cup of tea arrived on the counter beside the wash basin. It looked and smelt marvellous.

'Sugar in the saucer,' he said. 'One paracetamol tablet in foil bubble. I noticed that your sandal is broken and you're limping. Have you got any cuts on your foot?'

'A few,' I said. 'It was rough going.'

'I'll take a look at them when you come out. Can't be too careful.'

'I haven't any clothes.'

I heard a sort of resigned exasperation. 'I have seen a naked woman before, Casey, though I admit it was a long time ago in my student days. Put on the robe from behind the door.'

When I came out, I was feeling clean and much better. I needed to change and fast unless Susan had decided to deputize for me at the first show. She would seize the opportunity. It was a tribute to the legendary Neil Diamond tonight.

Samuel pulled a couple of armchairs towards the desk. 'Put your foot up,' he said. He had a bottle of antiseptic and some cotton wool. He poked at my cuts and grazes. Soon he was putting on plasters without asking if I was allergic to the adhesive.

195

'You'll live,' he said, moving my foot off the chair. 'Would you like some more tea?'

'Thank you, but no, I have to go. It was lovely.'

'Do you know where you are?'

'On the bridge. Hallowed ground.'

He nodded. 'Superior accommodation, as you see. Return the robe when convenient, please. I'm rather fond of it.'

'Sorry to have wasted so much of your time,' I said, rising to go and tightening the robe belt.

'Not at all. In fact, it was quite productive. While I was waiting to cheer on your arrival, I found one lost hospital nightie hanging over a hot-air vent. Wash day probably.'

'So she's still on board?'

'Down in the depths, it seems.'

'We'll never find her.'

'Do we want to?'

'There's no answer to that.'

That was a point. We had no real idea if she could cast any light on the death of her father. She might not even know that her father had died. But she might give us some clues as to why.

I gathered up his towelling robe and departed. I could find my way back, peeping into the Princess Lounge as I passed. Susan had taken over as MC for the first show and was parading around the stage in an emerald green outfit that made her look like a parrot. I shrank back from the darkened doorway to the theatre and hurried down to my cabin.

It was basic. It was short on space. But I was

196

glad to see the familiarity. My hair was drying nicely. My foot didn't hurt so much. I needed to wear something gorgeous to lift my morale. Something really stunning. I put on a sequin-trimmed white tunic top and camisole with matching flared trousers, silver hip belt and glittering flip-flops. All from M & S. No over-draft needed for this outfit.

This was my recently jumped-on-board from the pilot's boat, laid-back heroic look. Under-stated, of course. I tied up my unruly hair with the seed bracelets I had bought from the market vendors. It worked in a weird way.

Circulating that evening was easy. Everyone wanted to know what had happened. Had I fallen asleep? Had I swum too far? I kept near to the truth but word went round that I had found an injured dog on the slippery rock steps and had to get it back to the grateful owner. How a dog came into the scenario, I had no idea.

Table two, second sitting, was half empty. I took a spare place and everyone seemed pleased to see me, greeting me with enthusiasm. There were several unaccompanied women and a new couple who disliked their former table compan-ions and had asked to be moved anywhere.

'The jinx is only on men, you see,' one spritely widow confided. 'Would you like some wine, dear? This is a very refreshing white. The wine steward recommended it.'

'Lovely,' I said. 'Thank you. I need refresh-ing.'

The food, of course, was out of this world and served with class. Goodbye Officers' Mess. I had some superb seafood concoction served in a tiny shell-shaped dish, floating in melting goat's cheese. The soup was parsnip and orange with coriander which was out of this world for taste buds. I demolished a slice of pheasant breast with mangetout and then I had to be going. Time to sign off Neil Diamond before the parrot burst her dress.

There was a short, sharp explosion. I shot to the floor and crouched there, quivering, among the table legs and dropped napkins.

'Are you all right, dear?' The old ladies peered down. 'It was one of the party balloons bursting. You know, somebody's birthday. It's always somebody's birthday every night.'

The waiters were already singing 'Happy Birthday to You' not far away, standing grouped round the victim's table.

I nodded and scrambled back into my chair. 'Just practising,' I said. 'To see how fast I could hit the floor.'

'Oh, what fun,' they said. 'We'll all do it next time.'

I was beginning to like these old ladies. They were wonderful. My sort of people. I finished off the pheasant, dabbed my mouth and stood up. 'I have to go,' I said. 'Back to work.'

'Do come again, dear,' they chorused, all smiles. 'We love having you. Wonderful about the dog. You deserve a medal.'

Don't prick me when you pin it on, please.

I was hurrying to the Princess Lounge theatre when I caught sight of Dr Mallory in his immaculate evening gear. He was looking so good, my heart stopped. I had to take a second breath. I suppose he knew it.

'How's the dying dog?' he asked.

'How's the very sick passenger?' I snapped back.

'Improving. You've cleaned up neat,' he said, an experienced eye sweeping over my white outfit. I refused to add a smile.

'It was the aftershave,' I said.

'Meet you in the Galaxy bar after the last show? I hear the music is going to be particularly good tonight.'

'I may join the queue of lonely females at your side, but on the other hand, I may not.'

'I'll save you a place at the head.'

It was as well that I turned up at the theatre in time to whip up the applause for the show. Susan had taken a turn for the worse, no doubt brought on by bilious dress, and was soaking her forehead with wet tissues. I swept on stage and was surprised to be greeted with enthusiastic clapping. Heroic leap or dying dog?

'Hasn't this been a fabulous show?' I said. 'Let's show our appreciation for the legendary Neil Diamond and our great Countess Show Company.'

Everybody clapped fervently. 'Now there's lots happening this evening,' I went on, using the hand mike. 'The popular quiz night upstairs, a good film on at the cinema. It may be your lucky night at the casino or perhaps you'll be on deck to watch the stars as the *Countess* steams through the Caribbean on her way to Curaçao in the Dutch Antilles. Whatever you decide to do, have a wonderful evening.'

The audience trooped out good-humouredly to seek further pleasures. The stewardesses descended on the tables to clear up before the dance band and the ballroom dancers arrived. It was a never-ending programme of entertainment and events. No one was allowed to be bored.

'Ah, Casey, I've been looking for you all day.' It was Estelle. I could recognize that voice three decks off. 'The flowers in my cabin have died. They didn't last long. They must have been on their last legs.'

'I assure you they were fresh,' I said. 'Perhaps you had the heating on too high?'

'No way. I've been frozen for days.'

For frozen, read fiddling with the dials, not knowing what she was doing.

'I'll ask the florist to replace your flowers,' I said.

'Thank you. I think I deserve fresh flowers every day,' she added, sweeping away on the arm of a bemused, white-haired eighty-year-old in an ancient dinner jacket. I hoped he could afford her. It wasn't my job to protect passengers from predators.

I made my rounds of the bars and lounges, fending off any doggy-type questions or jokes. There were a few woof-woofs from a merry group of revellers at a bar. My day was nearly over. I was dead tired. But I would say good-night to Samuel and thank him for treating the cuts on my foot. And, I suppose, saving my dignity with the offer of his bathroom.

He was surrounded by a throng of colourful

butterflies. They swarmed on the honey of his looks. Even he looked a fraction disconcerted by all the attention. He caught sight of me between a bare bronzed shoulder and a heaving bosom, and came straight over, murmuring apologies.

'Thank goodness, a saintly vision in white. Save me, save me from the ravaging mob. I am being eaten alive and smothered by seven different perfumes. Give me air.'

'I thought you liked all the attention,' I said. 'You can't help being so handsome and popular.'

'I enjoyed talking to women,' he admitted. 'But preferably, one or two at a time. This was mob violence. I swear if you had not arrived, they would have been tearing my clothes off.'

'Don't exaggerate. I came to thank you for fixing my foot and to say goodnight. It doesn't hurt so much now.'

'How about a glass of wine before you turn in?'

I shook my head. 'Too tired. I want to sleep.'

'How about some star gazing? The fresh air will help you sleep.'

Those light grey eyes were compelling. He was weaving his magic on me. I would certainly not be taken in by his charm or join the harem. I was a tough, career woman, immune to handsome men.

'A few minutes then,' I said.

We went up on deck and walked around. Cordoned-off areas were being washed and hosed down. Work never stopped. The crew looked at me and grinned. It would be all round the lower decks in twenty minutes that I was walking

201

alone with the gorgeous doctor. I smiled sweetly.

'Don't think that I have brought you up here for a romantic dalliance,' said Samuel, as we leaned against a rail watching the phosphorescence on the dark waves and the swift passage of the ship. She always made up time at night. She was like a greyhound let off her leash at nightfall, leaping forward.

'No dalliance? I am disappointed. There was I, pinning my hopes on a little dalliance.'

'I want to talk to you without anyone overhearing.'

'This gets more and more intriguing. I sense a Jane Austen-type proposal coming on. Down on your knees, sir.'

'Stop talking nonsense, Casey. The man overboard? Remember him?'

I sobered immediately. 'Of course, I remember him. The jovial Nigel Garten. How could I forget?'

'He didn't drown. He was hit on the head before he entered the water. A pretty nasty abrasion, something quite large and heavy. He was murdered. The third murder?'

All the magic of the darkened sky seemed to vanish. A chill wind suddenly whipped round my shoulders. Banshees of drowned people were rising from the depths. I heard a hundred screaming voices, crying out to be saved. I loved the sea, I loved the endless waves and the glorious blue colours, but they held a hidden sorrow in their depths beyond my ability to ignore.

Samuel turned my head towards his shoulder

and patted my hair awkwardly. He wasn't used to patting grieving women.

'Don't cry, Casey,' he said. 'This is real life. This is how it happens.'

Eighteen

At Sea

The missing DJ mystified me. I didn't feel like drawing a line under his name and putting the matter away to moulder in a file. There were too many weird things going on and he was one of them.

I hurried down deck and got the keys to Darin Jack's cabin. It had not been cleared since it would not be needed for a replacement DJ. Hardly worth flying anyone out to spin a few discs. I'd found volunteers to run the late-night disco. We were halfway through the cruise, almost on our way back to Southampton. There were a few more ports of call and the Panama Canal.

The cabin was a typical male mess. Give or take a few exceptions. Dr Samuel Mallory didn't live in a chaos of dirty underwear and towels, crushed cans, crumpled crisp packs, chocolate bars. The doctor's cabin was more the chaos of disturbed sleep, overwork, monumental paper-work.

I didn't really know why I was there or what I was looking for. Maybe I was looking for his cruise papers or a crew card. But it was more than that. I put on some protective gloves and began sweeping everything into a bin bag, regardless. They say there is trace evidence on everything. There's a book called *Every Contact Leaves a Trace*. If he was connected to any of the three mysterious deaths, then let CSI find it.

There was nothing in the way of personal documents. No passport or money or keys. He'd taken those with him. He'd left a few clothes behind but they were cheap and nasty. They got bundled into a different bag.

The cabin had been cleared now and looked better for the clean out. I'd suggest to Richard Norton that it was locked up and not cleaned until Southampton police had seen it and given their permission. If he was a hunted man, then there might be some piece of evidence around that none of us understood or could recognize.

I was just leaving when I remembered the orange lifejacket which normally hung inside the wardrobe. It had looked a bit protruding and out of line. They usually fitted tidily against the wall. I am of a tidy nature.

Funny thing, I knew what I would find before even moving the lifejacket. It was George Foster's briefcase.

Richard Norton took the briefcase off me with gloved hands. He put it in another bag. I gave him the other bin bags. He was collecting bags fast.

'I suppose I should say "what a clever girl" and "thank you",' he said, somewhat reluctantly. I was doing his job. He was security, dammit.

'You don't have to. It was just a hunch. As soon as we found out about his fake CV, I reckoned something was fishy. Thank goodness he's got off the ship.'

I wished I'd taken a look in the briefcase, a rummage around, but it was too late now. Whatever George Foster kept in there that was valuable to Darin Jack would have gone now. The lock had been broken.

'If he has got off. He could still be on board. We have no proof that he left at Barbados. We only know that he hasn't been seen *since* Barbados. Two totally different things.'

I could not disguise a tiny shiver. I didn't like the thought of this Darin Jack roaming the ship, unknown and unseen. We had too many vulnerable people on board. And Rosanna? Where on sea was she now? Half mad and crazed with sunstroke and hunger. Mrs Foster and her sister, Mrs Banesto, not talking. Three bodies in the medical centre, one with a head wound. I was beginning to think serving in Top Shop would have been a less stressful career.

'Hey, Casey. How's your ankle? How's your arm? Have I left out any current ailment?' It was Dr Mallory walking past with a voluptuous dark beauty in a backless white sundress that clung everywhere, mostly in front. I hadn't seen her before. He was entirely off duty.

'Only current ailment connected to meeting with pain-in-exterior medical staff. Everything else healing in a satisfactory way,' I said. 'Thank you for your efficient care. Kindly send me a bill.'

'On the house,' he said with a mock salute. The dark beauty flashed me a smile of triumph. She could have him. I was not in the queue.

'What it is to have such fatal charm,' said Richard, wryly, watching them out of sight. 'No good-looks fairy at my christening.'

'But you're a lovely person,' I said warmly. 'Kind and generous and considerate. That goes a long way. It's not all about George Clooney, drop-dead gorgeous looks.'

'Isn't it?'

'No. A woman sees a man and at first she takes in how he looks. That's natural. You know, handsome, good-looking, nice enough. Then she forgets all about how he looks and it's more about what kind of man he is. How often do you see a gorgeous woman with a bald-headed, paunchy geezer? It's because he's nice, he's fun and he's good company, not how he looks.'

It was a long speech for me. Richard looked a few degrees relieved, peering down from his lofty six foot three. 'So there's hope for me, yet?' he asked.

This was skating on ice. Did he mean me or womankind in general? Careful, Casey. It was time for me to move on. I could not get involved.

'Lots of hope. See you soon,' I said, squeezing his arm. 'We've a truckload of evidence.'

'Casey, it's important that you back off now. Go organize your shows, your entertainers, lectures. Leave all this to me,' he urged.

'I don't understand. I thought I was being help-ful.'

'Yes, you are, but it's all getting too compli-cated and too nasty. Remember the magician's missing box? All I'm going to say is that we found some ultrasound equipment in Merlin's magic box.'

'What do you mean, ultrasound equipment?'

'It's a means of detecting what is below layers of paint. They can find out what is under the top layer of a painting.' He looked as if he had said too much. I pretended not to be interested, but I was fascinated.

'So what?' I said casually. 'What's under-neath? A lot of mistaken brush strokes?'

He clammed up. It was obvious he was not going to tell me. But I knew someone who would. Little Miss Auctioneer in Person. Tamara Fitzgibbons. The font of all knowledge in the art world.

I thought I would at least tell Mrs Foster that her husband's briefcase had been found and that the security officer had it. She might be relieved to know of its whereabouts. I went to her suite.

She had been curled up on the sofa, reading a book. Crime, I noticed, from the title. She look-ed at ease and welcomed me into the stateroom, offered me a drink but I declined.

'It was very kind of you to think of me during Hurricane Dora,' she said. 'It was a bit alarming and being on a high deck, we got the brunt of the wind. But I was all right with young Amanda with me. I only see her on very rare occasions.'

'I saw Amanda today and she seemed a bit

upset.' I was snooping, plain nosey. 'Quite sharp, in fact.'

'I think she got it in the neck from her mother for coming to see me,' said Mrs Foster, a bit distantly. 'Quite unnecessarily. The girl is a free spirit. She can see who she likes. But then her mother is like that. Wants to own everybody.'

I wanted to say something, but I couldn't. It was not my place.

Mrs Foster shut her mouth firmly. She was not going to say any more. It was the wrong moment to try and find out why the two sisters were locked in a silent war. My curiosity would have to wait.

'I thought you might like to know that your husband's briefcase has been found,' I said. 'It was in an unoccupied cabin.' That was partly true. 'The security officer has it at the moment. I'm sure he will return it to you when he has finished his investigations.'

She seemed about to ask me something, then changed her mind.

'I'm so glad it's been found,' she said, nodding. She poured herself some mineral water. 'I thought someone might have thrown it overboard. Was there anything inside it?'

'I'm sorry, I don't know. Did you think that there might be?'

'I'm not really sure. Travel documents perhaps. Our passports and currency are in the safe.'

'Very wise. By the way, Dr Mallory is wanting to know if your husband was on any kind of medication for his heart trouble.'

'Yes, he was. Something to slow the heartbeat down, I think. I'm not sure. He took them every day. I'll show you the prescription.'

She went into the bedroom and came back with the normal plastic container which Boots dispense. It had a Boots label with current date and Mr Foster's name printed on it. She shook the container. 'There's still some left...'

'Would you mind if Dr Mallory had these now?' I asked. 'It's just a formality.'

'They are no good to me,' she said.

'Did he take anything else?'

'He took a vitamin supplement. B5 or B12 or something. You can buy them from any health food shop. I'll get them for you.'

They were a well-known brand. Their content was mostly vitamin B5, B12, and some trace minerals, magnesium and niacin.

'Dr Mallory might like to see them but I doubt if they would be of any help. He had a heart attack. It was his time.'

Mrs Foster did seem remarkably composed for a woman who had recently lost her husband. Perhaps the reality had not hit her yet. Cruising is like being in another world, remote from real life. The truth would hit her when she got home and she suddenly realized that George was no longer there.

'Thank you,' I said. 'I'll leave you to your book. Is it any good?'

'Very intriguing thriller,' she said. 'And funny. A good author.'

I left Mrs Foster with her intriguing thriller and hurried to the art gallery. They often closed early and then opened again in the evening when passengers were strolling around and might drop by for a look at the pictures.

There was no one in the gallery which was strange. Pictures of all shapes and sizes hung on the walls and others were propped on easels. Piles of highly illustrated brochures lay on small tables, along with the obligatory floral display. Everything was very tasteful. I looked at the price tags on the paintings. The prices were not exorbitant, but then they were mainly reproductions and prints. There were a few originals, mostly the 'white and blue oil paint laid on with a knife' school of art.

'Hello,' I called out. 'Anyone around?'

I picked up a brochure and flicked through it. Nice enough exotic pictures of Capri, Naples and Sorrento. A bit touristy. But then our passengers were tourists and if that's they wanted for a souvenir, why not buy a picture to hang in the hallway?

There was a small pen and ink print of an Egyptian cat, staring enigmatically into the distance. I liked it but I didn't like it enough to buy it. My salary was going straight into my savings pot. I was saving up for a home, somewhere along the coast, where I could watch the sea all day long. My favourite occupation.

'Hello again. Anyone here?'

This was very unusual. The girls were usually careful never to leave the gallery unattended. They were a suspicious lot. Their stock was valuable. Walking off with a print would be somewhat difficult to disguise. A framed painting was not something easily wrapped in a beach towel and casually walked along a deck.

Suddenly the lights went out. There were shutters which sealed the entrance to the gallery. They came down with a clattering and a clang. I ran to the entrance and banged on the grill.

'Hey, don't shut up. I'm in here.'

I rattled the shutters. I had no idea how they worked, whether manually or automatic. For all I knew, the gallery manager could have activated them by remote control. I knocked into an easel and sent a painting flying.

'Hell's bells.'

This was not funny. I had a million things to do and being locked in a darkened art gallery was not one of them. There was a phone on the sales desk. I checked her name, Tamara Fitzgibbons. I knew she wouldn't be a plain Jane. The answer phone in her cabin took up the call.

'This is Casey Jones, Entertainment Director. Please open the gallery immediately,' I said. I wasn't going to explain that I was locked in or why I was there.

I waited about ten minutes. I righted the painting, hoping it wasn't scratched or damaged. No gaping hole. I didn't want to involve Richard Norton, especially since the warning that morning, when he had told me to keep out of the investigation. Susan was not an option. It would have to be the ship's Lothario, if he was not otherwise engaged with current dark beauty.

He answered the phone. 'Dr Mallory.'

'Are you busy?' I asked.

'Never too busy for you, Casey. How can I

211

help? Twisted the other ankle?'

'I'm locked in the art gallery. I can't find Tamara Fitzgibbons. Would you phone some electrical engineer who knows how to open the shutters? Could you please contact the first officer and ask? He's bound to be a buddy of yours.'

'I guess I could do that for a buddy of mine.' He was laughing. 'Would you like me to pass you a sandwich through the bars? I've a few stale biscuits you can have.'

'I don't want anything except to get out. I feel so stupid, locked in here and I particularly don't want anyone to know, so please don't broadcast it over the loudspeaker system as a news flash.'

'Operation rescue in motion. Stand by the phone, Casey, and keep calm. What's the extension number?'

'I'm always calm,' I said gritting my teeth as I gave him the number.

It seemed like hours but it wasn't. I didn't calm down but cursed myself for stupid blundering. It was none of my business. Why couldn't I content myself with placating Estelle Grayson and standing in for the bingo caller? The ship's resident comedian had already added my adventures to his repertoire, quipping last night about the cruise director who missed the cruise and had to be hauled aboard like a sack of cauliflowers.

'The chef is adding the cheese sauce tonight,' he'd said. His jokes were pretty awful. Several passengers had complained about his corny act. A comedian was difficult to pitch. Sometimes passengers were broadminded and laughed at anything. Another cruise and they would want a more sophisticated routine.

The phone rang. 'Hello,' I said.

It was Samuel. 'Go to the back of the art gallery and open a cupboard door marked Private. You'll find the key in the top desk drawer. Don't ring off.'

I did as I was told. Found the key and opened the cupboard door. It held stationery supplies, wrapping materials and some crates. It also had some bottles of flat champagne.

'OK,' I said. 'Cupboard door open.'

'Go through the cupboard and you will find another door at the back, bolted and locked. The same key will open this door. Lock the first door behind you and proceed to freedom.'

'How did you find this out?' I asked, barely able to contain my embarrassment. I was so annoyed with myself.

'Ship's maps. Fascinating stuff.' He rang off.

He was irritatingly right. The back door of the cupboard opened on to a little used corridor that was a short cut for staff between two areas. I locked it behind me, knowing I would have to return the key to Tamara Fitzgibbons with some explanation. But now I was only too glad to be somewhere that I almost recognized.

I went through some heavy curtains, clearly marked No Admittance, and knew exactly where I was. In minutes I was back in my office. We learn something new every day.

Susan looked up. She'd been to the beauty salon again and had her hair done into a topknot with stiff ringlets. She was wearing an unflattering halter-necked red dress that highlighted her blotchy skin. Her feet were squeezed into pointy shoes that looked far too small.

'Another date?'

She smirked. 'Dr Mallory seems quite smitten,' she said. 'I'm meeting him again for a drink up at the Lido Bar.'

'Good for you,' I said. 'Make the most of it. He might take you on an evening of dancing. He loves dancing.'

I knew Susan couldn't dance in those shoes.

Nineteen

Curaçao

I didn't tell anyone what I had found in the sales desk as I waited to be rescued.

It was between me and a body in the freezer. It was an invoice. Nigel Garten had bought a painting to be shipped home, only a few hours before he died. It was called *Sunset Over Amalfi* and cost him £175 plus shipping, handling and insurance. His painting was waiting to be crated before being shipped home.

It was really sad. Although Nigel Garten had gatecrashed parties I felt sure it was not for the free drinks. He was lonely. He needed to meet people. Given time and opportunity, I would have introduced him to someone. Maybe Mrs

Laurent, the passenger with a broken ankle, might have suited him. She was good company and easy to get along with. She would have laughed at all his jokes.

I went into low-profile mode for a fast round of the bars and venues, but made sure of an early night, and awoke to bright sunlight.

Curaçao. I loved this island and Willemstad, the capital. It was half Caribbean, half Amsterdam, with delightful Dutch-style architecture. All candy-coloured colonial buildings with the distinctive gabled roofs. They were mainly merchant town houses, going back to the seventeenth and eighteenth centuries. My spirits rose as the city loomed in the distance, a brisk ten-minute walk from the docks.

The swinging Queen Emma Bridge that crossed over to Willemstad was closed due to maintenance and repairs. But there was a free ferry going backwards and forwards to the Handelskade embankment. A pleasant change not to be charged. Step on and step off. Buy a drink, go for a stroll, find the floating fish market. Some of the fish were still gasping. Have your photo taken with your supper.

Many of the houses were graded now and in 1997 Willemstad joined the UNESCO heritage list. And not a moment too soon. Developers could have ruined the whole of this colourful city.

And the islanders had a language of their own but I was too lazy to learn much. It was Papiamentu, a blend of Dutch and African dialects. *Bon bini* was welcome, *danki* was thank you and

215

Mi stimabo was I love you. That was as far as I'd got. All everyday useful phrases. *Ayo* was goodbye.

Early this morning we'd taken the pilot on board and were making the final approach to Curaçao's new cruise berth, the Mega Pier. The port was used a lot by oil tankers as there was a refinery close by which exported to the US and Europe.

It was a pretty windy island, sitting right in the flow of the trade winds, usually a force four, northeasterly. There'd be a few hats blown off today. But no hurricanes. Curaçao escapes most of the big blows.

There was going to be a Sailaway Art Auction in the late afternoon. It would be a good time to slip in to talk to Tamara. I'd already returned the key. I'd put it in an envelope with a note saying it was found by accident. She could make what she liked of that.

A new entertainer was joining the *Countess* here. Ray Roeder, a big name from the Eighties. He was a fading pop star but still a name to draw audiences with his string of hits. Estelle's nose would be put severely out of joint.

He arrived in the agent's car straight from Hato International Airport, instantly recognizable despite the greying floppy hair and roadmap of lines on his tanned face. He was the easiest person to get on with. No demands, no fuss, totally professional.

'I need to get my head down for a couple of hours,' he said. 'Never can sleep on planes.'

'Would you like something light sent to your

216

cabin?' I asked.

He shook his head. 'No, thank you. I feel as if I've already had four breakfasts. But I will take a quick look round Willemstad if there is time this afternoon. I've never been here before. All those colourful houses are fun.'

'Apparently there was a governor who got migraines looking at sparkling white buildings so all the houses were repainted in pastel colours,' I told him. 'In the Scharlooweg area there's a house called the Wedding Cake. It's spectacular.'

'I'll make a point of looking for it and buy some of their famous orange liqueur.'

'The Blue Curaçao.' I wondered if he was a drinker and if I would have to watch him. I hoped not. He was so pleasant. His first solo show was tomorrow night. Plenty of time for a rehearsal and a run through.

Ray Roeder disappeared to sleep off his jet lag in his cabin. He only had one piece of luggage. He travelled light.

Estelle was on to me in a flash. 'Was that Ray Roeder I saw coming on-board?' she asked.

'Yes, terrific isn't it? A great favourite. He'll go down well.'

'He's going down the drain if you ask me. Hasn't had a hit for years.'

'But everyone loves his old hits. They'll be happy enough to hear them all again.'

Estelle sniffed, flapping her eyelashes. 'Perhaps he'd like to do a double act with me. We could put something together. I could help him.'

I doubted it. Ray Roeder would not want to be

upstaged, outsung and manipulated by madam. She'd make sure that his gravelly voice was drowned and that the songs were unsuitable for his style of delivery.

'I'm sure he's got plenty of material but you could ask. No harm in asking.'

'I'll ask him at dinner tonight. I expect he'll be on my table. There's room for another man.'

I didn't tell her that he'd requested to eat in the Grill. He preferred to eat very late, a habit from the old days. And on his own. He was a loner, steak and chips every night.

It was a gorgeous afternoon when I went ashore. A colourful group stood on the quay, welcoming our passengers to their island, a melting pot of so many nationalities and a history of the slave trade. I wanted to find the Internet Wilhelmina Plein in the Punda district and cruise Google. The Internet Study on board ship was too public. Someone might be watching.

I took the free ferry and then wandered through the town. A blue sign pointed to the first floor of a big old house that had been converted into shops and offices. The staircase was wide with an iron balustrade, a relic from the days when it was a home. The internet room was lined with computers and I didn't have to wait long. It was a modest cost, one hour for four florins. The ceiling was ornate with lotus flowers and Roman figures, once a beautiful sitting room. So sad to see it downgraded.

Missing paintings. There were an awful lot of missing paintings. Pictures went AWOL every day of the week either through criminal activity or because of an anonymous bidder at an auction. I began scribbling notes. Name of painting, artist, size was important, date, medium used, how long missing ... I had enough material to write a feature if I had time to write a feature.

I kept finding the same title coming up over and over again. It was a lost Cézanne. A small painting, only eighteen inches by twelve inches, a watercolour called *L'Orange de Mer*, which had been mostly in private hands since it was painted between 1902 to 1906. It was last handled by an art gallery in Bond Street, London called Fine Art.

It was sheer chance that I had a few minutes of time left and Googled Fine Art, Bond Street in London. There was a lot of information and a list of directors. One name was familiar: Mr George Foster. Our late Mr Foster? Surely it could be no other.

I came out into the sunshine, blinking, head buzzing. The pavements were thronged with shoppers walking past the café tables. Lots of passengers were sitting in the shade, drinking coffee or a cold drink. People smiled and waved.

'Miss Jones, come and have an iced coffee. It's delicious.' It was Maria de Leger and Mrs Fairweather. They had struck up a friendship although they were rather an unlikely couple. One slim and elegant and worldly, the other a rather dowdy matron from the depths of Shropshire.

'Now that would be very nice. It is unbelievably hot,' I said, taking the vacant chair at their table. A cool wind was blowing the umbrella shade. Maria de Leger waved over a waiter and ordered three more iced coffees.

'*Bedankt*,' she said. She could speak Dutch. '*Hoeveel*?'

'Maria can speak four languages,' said Mrs Fairweather proudly. 'Isn't that amazing? French, German, Dutch and English. The war, you know.'

'I remember you saying you were you in France during the war,' I prompted.

'Only for a while, not for long. It was a difficult time.' She was not going to say much. She was more interested in the people walking by, making comments.

'Were you working for the Resistance?' I put in.

'Now that's a leading question.'

'I'm sorry. I know so little about the war. It's always amazing to meet someone who lived through it.'

'It was not amazing at the time. It was quite dreadful and frightening.'

'What if you were caught?'

'Oh, we had ways and means, you know,' she said, her mouth clamping firmly. 'Let's talk about something more cheerful.'

'Sorry.'

No, I didn't know about ways and means. But I was beginning to think there was more to this charming lady than we would ever discover.

Mrs Fairweather decided to change the subject. 'I love this town. It's so picturesque. I could

220

stay here forever.'

'So could I,' said Maria. 'All the shops and restaurants. It's a wonderful island. It would be perfect for a longer holiday.'

'Thirty-five beaches,' I said. 'All those coral reefs.'

'No snorkelling for us,' they laughed. 'We are well past wearing masks.'

'Perhaps they have glass-bottomed boats.'

'Dozens of them.'

We moved on separately when we had finished our drinks. I felt it was acceptable to have a drink on shore with a passenger, but not on board ship. We had some unwritten rules, no fraternizing, no flirting, no sponging.

The ferry back was refreshing and breezy. I leaned over the rail as if I had never seen water before. I was always leaning on rails, it was my natural position. Then began a brisk walk back to the ship through a square of market stalls. Sun-dresses, sunhats, sarongs, shirts and sandals. 'You buy, missy,' they called out, sensing the departure of the ship and moneyed passengers.

But missy wasn't buying anything, nor was she going to miss the departure time. I saw Mrs Foster ahead of me, pulling along a new suitcase. This seemed a bit strange. Why would she want an extra suitcase? Passengers who bought a lot of souvenirs often bought an extra suitcase halfway through a trip. But Mrs Foster was hardly a shopaholic.

After our cruise cards were checked quayside, I helped Mrs Foster pull the case up the gangway. Not easy, even empty. Then it went through the scanner on-board without any trouble.

'Thank you so much,' she said. 'I can manage from here.'

Tamara was in a state of near panic before her Sailaway Auction. I had heard she was a bit temperamental. She was immaculately made-up, very TV presenter in the making, classy clothes and face, checking the champagne flutes on the trays, the canapé offerings. I suppose if she did not make her sales target for the cruise, she would be demoted, sent back to some sales room in Newcastle.

'Everybody always wants to know everything,' she fumed. 'As if they couldn't read. I've written a Frequently Asked Questions handout, yet they still ask the same questions. Can we have it framed? Do we pay extra for the framing? How is the bidding handled? What is the manifest or the reserve price? They drive me mad, these people.'

'You'll cope,' I said. 'You're very professional.'

'Why are you here?' she asked, putting out more brochures.

'Just to make sure everything is all right,' I said vaguely. 'And to check on the purchase made by Nigel Garten. The sadly, late Nigel Garten.' She didn't ask me how I knew he had bought a picture.

She paused for a second. 'Yes, very sad. He was a nice man. However, there's no problem about his painting. Mrs Foster has offered to buy it off us and put it in her husband's gallery in

London. It does save us a lot of paperwork, Mr Garten being dead. We would have had to approach his estate for payment. It's such a rigmarole, probate and everything. He won't want the painting now.'

'No, I guess he won't want it now,' I echoed. 'I'm glad that's all sorted out. No problems then?'

'Unless you've got ten minutes to spare?' Tamara looked desperate. 'My assistant hasn't turned up. She went ashore and has mis-timed her return. Could you circulate with the champagne? Is it too much to ask?'

'Sure. I'm great at circulating with champagne.' Not my job, but anything to oblige. It's all part of smiling. I took one of the trays.

That's how I happened to be there when Mrs Foster arrived and started bidding for all sorts of limited editions and reproductions, engravings and lithographs. She was buying like she was high on meths. I felt that she needed steering towards a cup of tea. Then I noticed that everything she bought was small. A size of only, say, eighteen inches by twelve.

'Are you opening a new gallery?' I asked, coming alongside with a tray of champagne.

'These are all the paintings that George was interested in. He left a list. I'm only following his orders. I've no idea why. He thought that most of these paintings were really of little value.'

'Wallpaper paintings.' He left a list. Perhaps this was what the intruder had been looking for. A simple list. A piece of paper.

223

'That's right. Just something to put on the wall.'

I missed the sail-away music on deck which was a bit of a nuisance. We were way out at sea before I got a chance to go on deck and talk to people. I checked that Ray Roeder was back on board after his walkaround. Safe and sound. He'd even been to see Trevor, the stage manager, and checked a few points. Truly professional.

That evening I wore a party dress dripping with romance. It was a short black tulle and sequin dress with black patent high-heeled and ankle-tied sandals. I didn't care. I needed a load of confidence. I looked stunning and there were a few gasps as I came on stage.

Ray Roeder was sitting at the side of the audience, well back, and even he clapped. This was another of Estelle's solo performances. She was wearing the celebrated red dress which had caught up with us. She directed most of her songs towards Ray. It was a wonder she didn't go and sit on his knee. He was professional enough not to worry and joined in all the applause with enthusiasm.

But when she came back on stage to take a second encore, he had gone. It was neatly done, a fast exit. He'd probably gone up to the Grill for a late supper.

All the shows over, I sat in on a film about the Windmill Theatre. I'd seen it before but like a good book, I could always see a classic film again. I wrapped a pashmina round my shoulders as the cinema was air-conditioned and it was chilly.

'How's my baby?' a voice whispered in my ear. I knew that voice. I knew who was sitting beside me in the darkened cinema without even looking.

'Don't talk,' I said. 'This is a special scene.'

'Anything newly broken or bruised or strained? Do you need an X-ray, bandaging, a poultice perhaps?'

'Please be quiet.'

But I was pleased that he was there, leaning towards me as if he cared enough to ask, even in the middle of a good film. I could smell something really nice, an expensive aftershave. It wafted over me and I drank in the freshness and masculinity.

'This is a scary bit,' he hissed.

'I'm not scared. I've seen it before.'

'Shall I hold your hand, just in case?'

The man had such a nerve but he made me smile. I needed smiles. I needed him but he was never going to know. He was my fantasy man. Someone to dream about. Nothing to do with real life.

Twenty

Panama Canal

Mrs Foster had bought about sixteen pieces of art. She wanted them hung in her stateroom, not packed and delivered to her home. So she would need that extra suitcase when we reached Southampton. It seemed irrational behaviour.

I cornered Tamara after the auction. She had calmed down now. Maybe she had reached her target sales and there was a big bonus in her bank account for buying more Jimmy Choo shoes.

'What do you know about ultrasound scanning?' I asked, fairly off hand.

'That's all clever stuff,' she said, fiddling with her calculator but ready to show off her knowledge. 'It's a sensor which sees beneath a painting to what is underneath, measuring a map of deviations. Lots of painters were so poor that they had to re-use a canvas. But if paint layers are thicker than those specified, it could mean deliberate over-painting. This can be criminal. Hiding a stolen painting. Why do you ask? It's pretty rare these days. Sometimes what is underneath is more valuable than what's been sloshed over the top.'

I didn't think her bosses would care for her use of the word sloshed. But they were not here, and she had sipped a lot of free champagne to lubricate her vocal cords and her sales technique.

So Reg Hawkins had brought on board the ultrasound equipment in his box of tricks. And had probably been paid to do so. But he had been murdered for his trouble. So who murdered him and why? Maybe it was a big mistake, an accident.

I kept thinking of that missing Paul Cézanne. Supposing it or some other lost painting had been painted over and someone knew about it. Mr Foster, for instance, being a director of Fine Art, a Bond Street gallery, and he found out that somehow it was aboard the *Countess,* smuggled in among the huge offering of reproductions and prints, ready to be offloaded to a special client along the way, all seemingly above board. So he booked a stateroom for himself and his wife and came cruising. But he had an ulterior motive that no one else knew about. Except one other person.

It was out of my league. I was a cruise director not a private investigator. I had enough problems. There was not enough paper for one of my bullet lists.

The next day was a day at sea, watching the crested waves, hoping for a shoal of dolphins. We spotted another cruise ship on the horizon, a great white whale, bigger than the *Countess.* I wasn't sure if we were programmed to wave. The day was all about lolling on deck in flimsy clothes and eating dressed up.

Ray Roeder's evening shows went brilliantly. The audience loved all his old hits, seeing the man in the flesh, reliving their youth, then they could talk to him, buy his CDs. He took time afterwards, signing CDs, talking to fans, and it must have worn him out. He looked pale and drained. Eventually I took him away and let him escape from his admirers.

'Thank you, thank you,' he said. 'I gotta eat. I need a drink.'

I took him up top to the Grill, where he had booked a table, made sure that he had a bottle of wine and some decent food. I only intended to stay for a few moments, to make sure he was settled and not being pestered.

'Thanks, Casey,' he said. 'I was on my last legs.'

'Both your shows were wonderful,' I said. 'I know how much energy goes into a show.'

'And you would know. Didn't I once see you as a dancer?'

'I doubt it,' I said, my mouth dry. 'I wasn't that famous.'

'But promising,' he insisted. 'Didn't you break a metatarsal in the middle of a jazz ballet? I saw it. I was there.'

I couldn't believe it. No one had been there. No one remembered.

'You were actually there? That's amazing. I didn't think anyone was there or saw it happen.' It was all a fuzzy dream to me now, the stuff of nightmares.

'I saw it and I heard it. My hearing is acute and

I was sitting near the front. I heard it snap.'

I had to sit down at his table. The snap was still in my brain. I couldn't move. No one registered when it happened but Ray Roeder remembered. He had been there. It was like a valediction, someone knowing that it really had happened. It was not an invention of a disappointed dancer.

'You can understand, then, can't you, how I felt? Or how I still feel.'

He poured out a glass of white wine and pushed it towards me. 'I can understand. I know how you felt and still feel. But you are still in show business on board ship and what you do here is important. You make things happen for the passengers and the entertainers. Sad about the dancing, sweetheart, but fate decided otherwise. You have to accept fate.'

If he wasn't quite a bit older than me, I would have fallen for him, headlong, hook, line and fishing weight, there and then. I drank the chilled wine and waited until his order arrived, then I rose and left him tucking into a medium rare steak and chips. The colour had come back to his face. He looked normal again.

Tomorrow was the Panama Canal. Everyone would be on deck all day, looking for alligators basking on the shores. I did not like alligators. Their huge, gaping mouths and smeary eyes ... not happy creatures at all.

The Panama Canal is one of those engineering miracles. This bright idea of cutting through land and slicing through hills so that ships had a short cut from one ocean to another. From the Caribbean to the Pacific Ocean or vice versa. It

229

was excavated through one of the narrowest areas of the Republic of Panama. It was wide enough to take simultaneous transit of ships through the cut, in both directions, and was forty miles long. The locks were a little more tricky.

The passengers hung over the rails to watch the water levels elevate the ship twenty-six metres above sea level. At some point, the lower lounges were so dark, being tight against dock walls, barely a foot away, that the interior lights had to go on. It was eerie, being so close to the dock brick wall, looking through our windows to gloomy darkness, as if we had descended to another world.

'This is really creepy,' said Amanda Banesto, peering through the lounge window at the dock walls. 'We are so close. We could almost touch them.'

Although most vessels use their own propulsion through the Panama Canal, the *Countess* was assisted when passing through the locks by electric locomotives using cables to align and tow the ship.

Every ship had to pay a toll rate per net ton or displacement ton. I had no idea how much Conway paid for their ships. I only knew that the average was $47,000. And we probably paid in advance so that we could reserve a transit slot. Cruises didn't have the time to wait in a queue. We had an itinerary to keep to.

There was a commentator on board giving information about the canal but it was hard to hear what he said. He was drowned by the noise of the engines. There was a party atmosphere and drinks were being served on deck. No one wanted to go inside to a bar in case they missed something. One of those snapping creatures.

I had been through the canal several times so I was not glued to the rails on alligator watch. But I was always amused by the fact that in 1928 a certain mad Richard Halliburton paid thirty-six cents in tolls to swim the canal. It took him ten days and he didn't get eaten. Sheer luck.

'So how is life behind the scenes?' Samuel asked, joining me on the rails. It seemed days since I had seen him although I had returned his robe.

'Going well,' I said. 'No new disasters, as yet. Estelle seems to have calmed down. Ray Roeder was terrific last night. Mrs Foster has bought a lot of paintings.'

'Ray Roeder was good. I caught the end of his show. You looked like a dream on wheels even if your shoes hurt. By the way, I think Estelle has other things on her mind. The pianist, Joe Dornoch, was in surgery today, asking for a private prescription for a certain erectile enhancement drug. Of course, it's not something we stock but this looks serious.'

'Really?' I had to laugh. Sometimes the young have trouble in accepting a mature romance. 'Estelle Grayson and Joe Dornoch? I don't believe it.'

'Haven't you noticed? They are never apart. Glued together like Siamese twins. Always rehearsing, using some discreet and forgotten piano at odd times. Love at fourth or fifth sight.'

This was news and could explain the recently

231

diminishing complaints. I hadn't noticed. But if it was so, then I was really glad. Cruising was the place for romance to blossom even if others were totally missed out in the rush.

'Maybe a little romance will hone down the sharp edges,' I said. 'Good for her. Joe is a nice man.'

'How about your sharp edges? Do they need honing down?'

'Certainly not,' I said sharply. 'My hormones are intact.'

I knew Samuel was laughing at me but I didn't care too much. I was building up a barrier against his charm. Don't look into his twinkling eyes.

'Let me know when you need a little TLC.'

'I'd prefer a prescription.'

I continued my circuit of the Promenade Deck. My morning mile had been interrupted by phone calls and I was making up for it now. The stern was fairly empty as the view was restricted by steps down to the crew's recreation area. But someone was tucked up into a deckchair in a corner, a towel over her face.

She was still there when I made my third circuit, had hardly moved. It was the woman's stillness that alerted me, and her disinterest in the tropical forest scenery that we were passing through.

I waited until I was out of sight and out of hearing, then took out my mobile phone.

'Hello,' I said. 'I'd like you to come and meet someone on the Promenade Deck. Right now, please. Have you got a moment?'

'Where are you?'

I told him exactly where I would be waiting. The lifeboats were all numbered and I would be waiting below number five. A deckchair had been dragged to the rails, and it was pleasant to sit there with my feet up, watching the verdant green banks of dense tropical forest. An alligator slid down a bank into the water with barely a splash. I was also keeping an eye on the woman sitting so still.

'So why are you being so mysterious?' asked Richard Norton, strolling up. 'I hope you aren't wasting my time.'

'I hope so too. I could be wrong, of course...'

We went towards the deckchair at the stern, talking casually in low voices about nothing at all. The figure was still sitting there, towel over her face.

'Hello,' I said, stopping by the chair. 'I'm Casey Jones. I've been wondering if you are feeling all right? Would you like some assistance? A drink of water perhaps? Or a cup of tea?'

I lifted the towel gently, holding my breath. It would be disastrous if I was wrong. If the woman was a reclusive passenger, recovering from a hectic night.

But I wasn't wrong. The girl's face was blistered and a mass of sores, her lips cracked. She couldn't speak. She looked quite ill, her pale eyes shadowed and hunted. Her red hair was lank and tangled, her clothes crumpled.

'Miss Hawkins? Rosanna Hawkins? Why don't you come along with me? I think you could do with a cup of tea, a good meal, a bath and change of clothes, and some medication for your poor face. Don't you think that would be a good idea?'

'Don't worry, no one will hurt you,' said Richard Norton, helping her quite firmly to rise from the chair. He looked bigger than ever. He wasn't going to let her escape again. 'Come with us. You need some medical care.'

'Please, please, I want to talk to my father,' she croaked.

Rosanna Hawkins seemed relieved to have been found. She had been living in an airless dry-food store cupboard down in the depths of the ship, sleeping on the floor, little to eat or drink. She was once again taken to the medical centre for sunburn treatment, a bath and given a sedative. After several cups of tea, scrambled egg and ice cream, she was soon sound asleep. A female crew member was sitting with her.

'Well done for spotting Rosanna,' said Richard. 'That was smart.'

'It was the towel over her face.'

'Quite a giveaway.'

'It wasn't a towel from a cabin. It was the kind the waiters use when serving very hot dishes. She'd probably nicked it from somewhere.'

'I'll come and talk to her when she wakes up. They have strict instructions to keep an eye on her and not to leave her for one second. Absolutely no excuses this time,' he said.

'And just in time,' said Dr Mallory. 'That face was a mess. First-degree burns. We've cleaned

234

her up and made her a little more comfortable. She should sleep for quite a few hours till the painkillers wear off.'

'Has anyone told her about her father?' I asked.

'No, it would be better to leave it until she wakes up. She'll be more able to take the shock. I'll tell her. I think she trusts me now.'

'And perhaps I'll be able to find out more about why she stowed away in the first place,' said Richard. 'I want a lot of answers. She is still in custody.'

'And she is still my patient. I'd like to be there when you question her,' said Samuel firmly. 'Would that be all right?'

'Of course,' said Richard. 'I'd like your support.'

No one asked me to be present. And I was the one who found her. The two men had forgotten all about me and were talking about something quite different as they left the medical centre. It was pretty typical. I wanted to know what was happening. I also wanted to know why she had stowed away. But on the other hand, I didn't want to be involved. It got me into too much trouble.

Three strange deaths, a break-in, an overdose, a stowaway. It wasn't your normal five-star luxury cruise. And that wasn't even counting Hurricane Dora.

Twenty-One

At Sea

Table two, second sitting, had an extra diner that evening. Amanda Banesto had decided to join her aunt and it was obvious that this cheered Mrs Foster no end. For once she was smiling and enjoying the meal. She bought wine for everyone at the table, signing the chit without looking at the total. I was not needed as an extra body – sorry, extra diner.

This might be an opportunity to talk to Mrs Banesto, so I went over to her table. She did not seem too dismayed to be on her own.

'Hello, Mrs Banesto, may I join you as you are on your own? How's your wrist?'

'It's a nuisance but not so painful. We take mobility so much for granted, don't we?' she said. 'It's a fiddle doing up a bra, or washing one's hair but Amanda helps me. I shall be really glad when the plaster comes off. Please join me, and do call me Helen.'

'Thank you. What a blessing to have Amanda with you,' I said.

'Yes, it is. But I'm glad she's having dinner with her aunt this evening. I don't want her to feel she's tied to an invalid, having to cut up food.'

'Then you don't mind that she's with Mrs Foster this evening?'

'No, not now. I did mind when she first started going to Joan's stateroom, nose slightly put out of joint. But this wrist thing has made me realize how much I need my daughter and there's an old saying: If you want to keep your children, then you have to let them go. It's very true.'

My parents had had to let me go. I had won a scholarship to the London School of Ballet. They were both against it at first. Dancing was not a proper job. It was all right as a hobby, something to fill the evenings after work.

'It's a very wise saying. Did you know Mrs Foster was going to be on this cruise?'

'No, it was a complete surprise. I expect you've gathered that we have been estranged for years.' She sighed. 'It was very silly and a long time ago. It happened one Christmas, the season of goodwill and all that. And I suppose it was George's fault, rest his soul. Now that George is dead, it's all very unnecessary.'

I didn't probe although I was curious to know the truth. These things often come out by themselves. It might be a long wait but on the other hand, Helen Banesto was thawing.

'Did you go to the show tonight?'

'No, I didn't go. I'm not fond of the Old Time Music Hall songs. Not my cup of tea, flag waving and singing and all that. I shall catch the late film and then go to bed.'

'Good idea,' I smiled. 'It's a great film. A Johnny Depp. The story of J.M. Barrie, when he wrote *Peter Pan*.'

'Depp is such a good actor. He reinvents himself with every part. So clever and always with such charm and odd-ball humour.'

I was surprised that she seemed to know so much. She caught the expression on my face.

'I used to be on the stage myself,' she said. 'RADA and then touring with a small repertory company. But I was only a struggling third-rate actress and never really made the grade to the West End, much to my disappointment and Joan's delight.'

'Joan?'

'My sister, Joan. Mrs Foster. She was always jealous of everything that I did. And I was very glamorous in those days. The blonde hair, the sooty black lashes, the lot. I don't bother so much these days.'

But I could still see the remains of a youthful beauty in her velvety brown eyes and generously curved mouth. And Amanda was gorgeous. She got it from her mother. Those genes at work.

'You're still very good-looking,' I said, wondering why she had let her hair go a dull brassy grey colour. And it was badly cut, as if she had chopped at it with nail scissors. 'Why don't you treat yourself to some pampering at our beauty salon? Have your hair done. It would save you the effort.'

'Looks are not worth having,' she went on as if I hadn't spoken. 'They have brought me nothing but trouble. My husband was a handsome Italian actor. He fell for my glamour. When the novelty of an actress wife wore off, he went in search of pastures new, younger and richer. I was always having to leave home at some unearthly hour for filming.'

'But you still do some work, don't you?' My memory cells were clicking in. I'd always thought her face and voice were familiar, but couldn't place where or when. Why did I think bathrooms?

Helen Banesto nodded. 'Whenever they want some dowdy-looking housewife in an advert, they phone my agent. At present I'm seen cleaning a family bathroom, looking stressed and distraught at the mess left by teenage children and slobby husband. Then along comes some wonder cleaner and does the work for me.'

'And very well you do it,' I said with a smile. 'I remember now. Acting the part, that is, not cleaning the bathroom.'

'That's how I can afford to treat Amanda and myself to a cruise now and again. I'm cleaning an Aga next month, if they can write the wrist into the script.'

'How about you pretending in the ad that you'd broken your wrist in order to get out of doing the cleaning? Then teenage children and slobby husband would have to do it for you?'

She laughed. 'That's good. I'll send them an email. They might go for it.' Then she sobered. 'It was such a shame about George. I am still fond of him.'

'So you knew him well?' The words slid out as an afterthought.

'Very well, indeed. We were sweethearts and engaged for a time. He thought it was really up-market to be seen at art shows and exhibitions with a glamorous young actress on his arm. And I enjoyed his company and his serious interest in art. He also paid for a lot of meals and sometimes, as you can imagine, I was out of work and quite hungry.'

I saw a look of pain cross her face. It could have been memories or her wrist. Then she pulled herself together as the waiter came and took our orders. I noticed that she chose dishes that she could spoon or fork up. Broccoli and stilton soup and a mushroom risotto.

'It was for the best. He would have hated me going away touring round the country in rep and I wasn't ready to give up my career. I still had high hopes of becoming a star. Then Joan appeared on the scene and George was a sitting target. She's always been more intelligent than me and she could talk about art. Before you could say Paul Cézanne, they were engaged, looking at houses and mortgages, booking a wedding and reception. They had the decency not to ask me to be a bridesmaid.'

'So Joan stole your fiancé?' I said. 'From under your nose.'

'More or less, although our engagement had been teetering on the rocks for a while. I think George was relieved to be marrying the more sensible of the two sisters.'

'So that's why you and Joan haven't been talking for all these years.'

'No, it wasn't only that. I accepted that I had lost George. Something else happened. It was the first Christmas in their new home, everywhere brand new, spotless and redecorated, Joan

240

and George being the good host and hostess. I was invited along although to tell the truth, I didn't want to see them actually living together. It still hurt.'

'What happened?'

The soup arrived. It smelt delicious. I'd chosen the same to make it easy for Helen.

'Joan cooked a very nice Christmas dinner and we had all the trimmings. They made me feel welcome although I was still uncomfortable. We opened presents and had lots of coffee and strange liqueurs they'd bought on their honeymoon abroad. I think it was the liqueurs that did it.'

I held my breath. I had an inkling of what was coming. It often happened at Christmas parties.

'Joan went upstairs to change into a different dress for the evening. George caught me in the hallway and started kissing me under the mistletoe. He was feeling very affectionate and, I think, somewhat guilty that he had treated me so badly. Well, I let him kiss me. It was Christmas after all.'

'And Joan came downstairs and found the two of you in the hall?'

'Absolutely. She was furious, accusing me of dreadful things. We both said things we didn't mean. There was the most awful scene and I fled the house, out into the dark and the cold. I don't remember how I got home. And she's never spoken to me since. And I've never spoken to her. Not a word.'

'Maybe it's time to make it up,' I said. 'After all, it was Christmas a long time ago and there are always a lot of boozy kisses around at Christmas. They don't mean anything.'

'That's what I think now, especially as George has died. She's had him all these years, all to herself, living the good life. It's no good living in the past. The past is over and done with. Though I've had to work hard to keep Amanda and myself while Joan has had it cosy.'

'I think you had a rough time,' I said. 'But you do have the most lovely daughter.'

'Yes, Amanda is a great girl and her modelling work is growing. But it hasn't been easy for her either, seeing her fiancé killed. The police have never found him, you know.'

I left Helen Banesto accepting a refill coffee and some coconut confection. The perk of second sitting was that there was not the same rush to get up and leave at the end of the meal.

Joan Foster and Amanda were leaving the dining room. They were still talking and Mrs Foster had taken Amanda's arm. She did not look as well as she had an hour ago. Perhaps eating in full view of everyone in the Windsor Dining Room had been a strain. And at the same table where her husband had died.

'There's a very good film this evening,' I said. 'Starring Johnny Depp in Neverland. He plays James Barrie, the author who wrote *Peter Pan*. It's a fascinating story about how a writer's mind works.'

'That sounds good,' said Amanda. 'Why don't you come with me, auntie?'

'I'm a bit tired,' said Mrs Foster. 'I might have an early night.'

242

'It's too early to go to bed. Come and see the film. It'll take your mind off things. If you don't like it, you can always get up and leave.'

I left Amanda trying to persuade her aunt. Well, it might work. You never know who you are sitting next to in the dark. I was just in time to sign off the second showing of that evening's Music Hall show.

'Cutting it fine again,' said Trevor, as I swept past him and on to the stage. He thrust a Union Jack flag into my hand. All the audience were flag waving, too, and singing 'Land of Hope and Glory', I think it was, or was it 'Jerusalem'? Something stirring. I nearly knew the words. But I know how to stand on stage and make my mouth fake almost knowing the words.

The cast were exhausted. They came off perspiring and gasping for water. They had so many changes of costume and wigs, many of them weighty and voluminous. Their dressing room was cramped, packed with rails of clothes, no room to change in a hurry or for modesty.

'Well done. Great show,' I said, but they were too weary to even listen. I was left standing alone, suddenly very alone. Where had everyone gone? I had the busiest job, meeting dozens of people every day, always talking, sorting problems and making things work. But now I was completely alone.

'Good morning, heartache,' I said to myself. It was nearly midnight. The bewitching hour.

When it was all over, I was always on my own. Everyone went their own way, forgot the young woman who had chatted to them for a few

243

minutes. They probably thought she had a busy social life, partied every night. Ahmed, my steward, knew better. Sometimes he left a snack in my cabin, carefully wrapped in cling film, in case I hadn't had time to eat.

When we were homeward bound and making tracks for cold and rainy Southampton, it would probably be a thermos of soup.

We were heading for Huatulco, a tiny manmade coastal resort that was perfect for shopping and swimming. It was so compact, one could walk everywhere in town and then sit on a fine white beach. It was ideal for swimming. And traffic was banned to the back of the town. A sensible idea. All towns should ban the traffic.

I went up on deck for my last walk around, shaking off the day, breathing in the pure, still warm air, unclipping my hair and letting it blow around my neck. The silver-topped waves were thrashing against the side of the ship as she put on speed through the night. It was a magical sight to lift the heart.

'Penny for them, Casey?'

'I was thinking how beautiful it is out here at night, the sea, the velvety sky and all those twinkling stars. And we have three passengers who will never see this sight again. It's so very sad.'

'Maybe there are seas and oceans, waves and stars, on the other side.'

'The other side? What do you mean?'

Samuel rested on the rail, alongside me, gazing down into the depths of the sea. 'We don't really know, do we? I've seen death so many times,

244

and heard of near-death experiences. Patients tell you about things they could not possibly know. Sometimes strange things happen and then I don't know what to believe.'

He was talking to me from his heart, but I didn't want to push him. I wanted his thoughts to come voluntarily so that I could learn more about him, strip away a few of those superficial layers, find the real man beneath all the charm.

But Samuel was having none of it. 'No more gloomy talk, Casey. We ought to be making the most of this romantic moment. Supposing I were to put my arm around your waist, would you object?'

He was grinning at me, eyes full of mischief.

'I should think the two crewmen swabbing the far end of the deck would be highly amused. Perhaps we could put on a little late-night revue for them? You dance so well. We might manage a sedate samba or cha-cha without falling over.'

'I think I could manage a sedate cha-cha as long as you don't expect me to do those fancy twirly bits.'

'No twirly bits.'

He started humming *Tea for Two*, an almost unrecognizable tune but it was the right rhythm. This was more a touching-hands dance, rather than holding-on-tight dance. This suited me. I did not want Samuel holding me tight for any reason. Even the briefest touch of the palm of his hand was electric enough.

It was a few moments of uncomplicated pleasure, enhanced by the magical night sky and the seductive sound of the waves. When we finished

245

with an elaborate flourish, there was the sound of muted clapping from the far end of the deck.

'I'll walk you back to your cabin,' said Samuel. 'In case you get waylaid by an inebriated passenger desirous of your company into the small hours.'

'Thank you,' I said. 'I shall feel very safe in your company.' A touch of sarcasm goes a long way on occasion.

I thought about telling him of Joan and Helen but did not want to spoil the tranquil mood. It could wait. But I suddenly thought that on-board was yet another passenger with a motive. Helen could have been waiting for years for this opportunity.

'Would you like me more if I was just called Sam?' he asked as we walked the endless corridors.

'What a ridiculous question.'

'Sam sounds more streetwise.'

'But there are no streets on board the *Countess*.'

'I'd forgotten that.'

Twenty-Two

Huatulco, Mexico

By early morning we were entering the Gulf of Tehuantepec and took on the local pilot. The coastline was the edge of the Oaxaca Mountain range. This was an area that had a lot of localized storms with funnel winds. But today it was mainly calm.

Huatulco was a man-made resort along a spectacular coastline of nine bays and thirty-six beaches. They had built on four of the bays and everything was geared to sailing and swimming and water sports. The marina was thriving, almost surrounded by brick-paved walkways with yachts and sailing boats flying the flags of all nationalities.

Playa Santa Cruz was in sight of the new pier where the *Countess* was berthed, not far to walk. It was named after a wooden cross that was found when the Spanish landed a long time ago.

'They tried to destroy the cross.' I was talking to Mrs Fairweather on deck, watching passengers disembark. 'They chopped it up, set fire to it, hauled it into the sea. But still it survived and so it's thought that it has divine powers.'

'So what's happened to the cross now?'

'It was made into four smaller crosses. There's a delightful open-sided church right on the beach just over there. The breeze blows straight through, from one side to the other. It's next door to a café and bar and you can sit in the church listening to a pianist playing Sinatra.'

'Sounds a delightful combination. Sinatra and God.'

It was getting very hot, climbing up into the eighties. The sun was high in a cloudless blue sky. I hoped everyone had their factor thirty-five, a sunhat and a bottle of water. We'd been at sea for long enough and still there were passengers who never learned the basic sun protection.

I saw Estelle Grayson going ashore with Joe Dornoch. She was wearing a striped turquoise and pink caftan and an enormous straw hat with matching ribbons. He was slim and debonair as always, white slacks, open-necked shirt and panama hat, almost a dancing Fred Astaire. They didn't look as if they were going swimming, probably making for one of the many bars or seafood restaurants.

If I'd had time, I'd have gone to one of the wildlife reserves to see the lush, canopied jungles and all the amazing birds, pelicans, humming birds, hawks and herons, or on a sea trip to see the reef fishes and coral plates, dolphins, sea rays and turtles. There was so much wildlife along this coast. I'd be lucky if I got a quick swim in the azure sea. The last time I'd swum here, I'd lost a tiny silver ring on the beach. I wondered if I would find it on this visit. Perhaps someone else had found it or a mermaid was wearing it. I had a thing about mermaids. I checked my toes for webbing.

Samuel Mallory was already going ashore. He looked as if he was going sailing, bag of gear, jeans and dark T-shirt, peaked cap, sunglasses. He looked up and waved. I waved back, glad to see that he was on his own. I didn't want to think of him enjoying Huatulco surrounded by a bevy of near-naked beach beauties.

Then I saw her running. She was panting as she hurried down the gangway to the pier. It was Susan Brook, my deputy, laden with bags and gear, baseball cap, flat sneakers and enough snacks to feed an army. Samuel was waiting for her on the pier, staring into the water. He took some of the bags from her and she thanked him effusively. Her voice floated up. They began walking towards the marina. Perhaps he had hired a boat for the day.

I hoped they would remember departure was timed for 6 p.m. I'd checked it three times already. No repeat of Isla Margarita for me. If I ever got ashore. If I ever finished the paperwork in my office. I was starting to regret that I'd given Susan the time off. I thought she'd be in the beauty salon all day.

The routine paperwork took longer than usual. My brain was too busy delving through the facts I was collecting about the Fosters. Why had Joan Foster bought all those mediocre prints? And why had Darin Jack been on-board? It couldn't be a coincidence, simply the means of a free trip to Barbados. He had to have another reason. And why had Rosanna stowed away?

249

I phoned Richard Norton. 'Can I take Rosanna Hawkins on deck for twenty minutes? I know that she is in custody but even UK prisoners are allowed to walk outside in a yard every day. I won't let her jump ship.'

'She won't be able to. We've put a tag on her. It's a bit similar to the kind they put on clothes to stop shoplifters. It'll go off if she tries to pass the security at the head of the gangway.'

'Brilliant. Then I can take her for a walk round the Promenade Deck? That's all I shall have time for.'

'Thanks. The officer will be glad of a break.'

Rosanna was still in the medical centre. It was easier to keep an eye on her there, but she might have to be moved if there was a rush of patients this evening. Passengers often came back from trips with injuries.

She was looking much better. The rest and meals and treatment for her sunburn had made a difference. Samuel had told her about her father's death and she had taken it with resignation.

'He was so scared of something,' she'd said. 'I knew something would happen.'

'Hello, Rosanna. How are you? I thought you might like a walk on deck, a breath of fresh air. Richard Norton says it's OK,' I said. 'This part of the Mexican coast is beautiful. Lovely mountains. They're called the Southern Sierra Madre.'

'Yes, I'd like to see them,' she said. 'Will I be all right in the sun?'

'I've brought a hat for you. It's one of mine. And some sunglasses.'

250

She flashed an uncertain smile at me. 'H-how kind, Miss Jones,' she said. 'Thank you. I'll be glad to get out of this cabin. These four walls.'

They had found her some loose cotton trousers and a T-shirt. The tag was on the hem of the trousers. She seemed very uncertain as I took her up in the lift to the Promenade Deck. One side was in the shade and both ends of the ship were shaded. She was very wary of the sun now.

'It's very hot, isn't it?' she said, flinching.

'In the eighties and climbing.'

'I'm glad I'm not out there,' she added, nodding towards the beach. 'It looks scorching.'

'There'll be some burnt feet tonight,' I said. 'I'm very sorry about your father. It must have been a shock for you. But I'm sure it was an accident.'

'I dunno. I knew something would happen to him,' she wailed. 'I warned him not to come.'

'Why did you think something would happen to him?'

She seemed to want to talk or I would not have asked. 'It was all the phone calls that upset him. Someone kept phoning him, threatening him. I haven't got a job at the moment. I'm out of work, unemployed, so I'm at home, keeping house for Dad and me.'

'And your mother?'

'No Mum now. She went off with someone when I was small and Dad looked after me. Now I look after him when he's at home, between shows and cruises, only fair. But not any more ... I don't know what I'm going to do.'

She stopped walking and I let her wipe her

eyes on a tissue. 'These calls?' I prompted.

'Always the same voice, saying he'd better do it or there would be trouble. It wasn't nice. I got quite frightened. No good going to the police, they wouldn't listen to someone like me.'

'So why did you stow away on the *Countess?*'

'To warn him. Dad had already left the night before to join the ship at Southampton. He always goes early because of making sure all his gear gets safely on board. Then this bloke phones again and says if Dad doesn't do what they ask, they'd torch our flat. Now, I know it's not much, not posh, but it's all we've got. And there's all of Dad's magic stuff stored in it. Some of it really valuable.'

'I'm sure. I've seen many of your dad's shows. He's a great magician.' We kept using the present tense. Neither of us could accept the past tense. 'He always has the audience guessing and yet he's working right up close to them. It's amazing.'

'Timing, you know,' said Rosanna, nodding, her voice warming. 'He's started teaching me, you know. So I can go along with him. That disappearing box is a real con. Got so many compartments. The locking is diabolical.'

'Do you know how it all works?'

'Sure. Well, nearly all of it. You have to be ever so quick. And thin and supple. And not breathe a lot.' There was a glimmer of a smile. We were doing the shady side of the ship now and she was walking with more confidence. The glorious fresh air seemed to be doing her some good.

'Could it have been an accident?' I asked.

'I dunno. Maybe.'

There were small sailing boats leaving the marina every minute. I wondered which one Samuel was skippering with Susan as his galley slave. I hoped she wouldn't get hit on the head with a boom. You had to move quick on these small boats.

We did three circuits of the Promenade Deck before I reluctantly said that I had work to do. Rosanna seemed to have enjoyed her breath of sunshine and freedom, and the sight of the sparkling sea.

'Thank you, thank you ever so much. It's nice to do something normal.'

'It's been a pleasure.'

'Can we have a walk again?' she asked, tentatively. 'Like tomorrow? I need to get out and I won't be any trouble, I promise. It's easy to talk to you. Makes a change from those posh officers who don't say much.'

'Of course, and I'm sure it'll be OK. Tell me, what do you think you'll do when you get home?'

'If we've still got a home,' she said bitterly. 'They might have burned it down by now, for all I know. Rotten lot.'

'Richard Norton can make some enquiries for you. Give me the address. We'll find out. We can email Scotland Yard and get it checked.'

Rosanna seemed relieved that something could be done. I wrote down the Bermondsey address. If Reg Hawkins had not been able to do what this person wanted him to do, then the threat might have been carried out. And Reg Hawkins was dead. So he couldn't tell us.

Rosanna thanked me again as I handed her over. She gave me back the sunhat and sunglasses. 'Don't forget me down here, will you?'

'I won't,' I promised. 'I'll see you tomorrow for another walk.'

It didn't take long to explain to Richard Norton and give him the address. Then I was free, free, free. I raced down the gangway and walked quickly to the welcoming beach of Playa Santa Cruz. Mrs Fairweather and Maria de Leger were in the beach church, listening to soul jazz. They smiled and waved. Ray Roeder was hanging over the piano in the bar next door, singing Sinatra. I wished I could have stayed to listen but I had my swimsuit on under a sundress, my towel in a bag with a bottle of water and another of factor thirty-five.

It might not be for long but a swim in the sea was worth any amount of inconvenience. It was clear and blue and deep almost immediately. My silver ring was here somewhere. Perhaps my toes were touching it now as I skimmed the sand at the bottom. I turned on my front and began to swim lazy strokes.

The swim was pure joy. Clear, clean water. They are not allowed to dump waste black water into the sea at Huatulco. It has three water treatment plants. I turned on to my back and floated, arms moving wide, closing my eyes to the bright sunlight. The *Countess* was so close, moored alongside the pier. I could see her white shape. She was like a motherly white hen, watching all her baby chicks frolicking in the sea.

He was there, treading water beside me, before I realized who it was. How come he could always find me in the sea? It wasn't as if I had red hair. It was darkish, unruly with that blonde streak at the front. A quirk of nature, nothing out of a bottle.

'So the intrepid explorer is home from the seas. What are you doing here?' I asked, rolling over on to my front and doing an inelegant doggy-paddle. 'How did the sailing go? Did you find a deserted island for your packed lunch?'

'It was fine until we hit a bit of a wind. Nothing too rough, I assure you. But Susan was feeling a bit under the weather so we turned back. Still it was a good sail, very bracing. Spectacular coastline.'

'Is Susan all right?'

'She's gone to lie down.'

'Very sensible.'

'That's what I thought. So I decided to make sure you caught the ship this time and didn't have to jump on-board from the pilot's launch. Though you could do with the practice.'

'How very kind. You have such a thoughtful nature.'

We were both laughing by now and began to swim back to the shore. It was so easy being with him. He was so generous with laughter. He was the toast of all the ladies on board, and yet he'd come looking for me. It was difficult to understand when sometimes I was not very nice to him. Perhaps I wasn't a threat.

We clambered up the steep bit of the beach, the

hot sand burning the soles of our feet. We jumped on to towels which took away some of the discomfort, dried ourselves of a sort and struggled half wet into clothes. But the sun was drying us by the minute. My hair looked like a backcombed haystack.

We strolled back towards the ship with plenty of time to stop at a beach bar for a long, cool local drink called Mezcal. It was close to a tequila and pretty potent. Lots of passengers, returning from tours, spotted the pair of us, smiled and waved. They liked seeing me with the handsome doctor in tow. I started telling Samuel about Joan and Helen's chequered past, and my talk with Rosanna.

'It's a complicated puzzle,' said Samuel. 'But I think you are getting somewhere. At least, motive-wise. You can't solve everything. There are officials for that, at Southampton. And they will be only too glad to hear anything that you have to say that might shed light.'

Then he stopped by the red-brick open-sided church on the beach and a fleeting look of worry crossed his face. There was a whiff of sweet scent from the bunches of lilies on the altar. A couple in black were on their knees in front of the altar. He took hold of my arm.

'Seriously, Casey. You ought to write all this down on your computer, just in case, and put a copy on a floppy disc which you'll give to me. Will you do that? Promise? This evening? And watch your back.'

'That sounds ominous. What do you mean, watch my back?'

'You know too much, and if something dicey is going on, then you are in danger. Tell no one anything, talk to no one except me and Richard Norton. You can't trust a soul. On-board is someone who wouldn't hesitate to shut you up.'

I felt a chill despite the heat of the afternoon. He was right. I knew too much. I had made too many enquiries, talked to too many people. And one of those people might think I now knew too much.

And I was eating at table two tonight, second sitting. Not a good omen. No one had proved it was only men. Suddenly I didn't feel so hungry.

Twenty-Three

At Sea

A new couple from Manchester had moved on to table two, second sitting, having had a disagreement with another couple on their previous table for four, first sitting. They had not heard of the jinx. They soon would. The two sittings rarely mixed.

So I was not morally obliged to join them this evening to make up numbers. I could go have a midnight sandwich. Susan was indisposed so I was MC for Estelle Grayson's second show in the Princess Lounge. Remember to dress down.

Rule One: do not outshine star.

I was already heartily sick of everything in my wardrobe. I decided to wear a long saffron chiffon print dress by Anna Sui, which did nothing for me. Muted, washed-out colours, though I did like the curved neckline and little sleeves.

Estelle Grayson sang like a rich dream, her voice pounding through the old ballads, her hands not straying far from her accompanist's shoulders. He seemed to be just as besotted, gazing at her with rapt eyes. I've nothing against romance third or fourth time around. There's hope for us all.

The passengers loved it. They were watching a real live love affair on stage as well as listening to it. Estelle and Joe deserved a bonus. If it lasted. Cruise romances rarely survived on shore. It must be the British weather or the mail system.

Between shows I went back to my office and started a new document file on my computer. I saved it as Possible Evidence. I began typing, putting down all the information that I had gathered, all my thoughts, my list of possible suspects. The document grew and grew. There was a twisted mass of fact and fiction. It would need an expert to work it out.

It helped to write it all down. Sorted my head.

* George Foster, art dealer, died aged fifty-nine. Suspects: Joan Foster because she had suspicions that her husband still loved her sister, Helen. Maybe she wanted this mystery painting for herself. All that

money. She might think she deserved a big pay-off, a comfortable pension.

* Helen Banesto: revenge for disappointment on being dumped for sister.

* Reg Hawkins, died aged forty-seven: he was being blackmailed by someone. Who?

* Nigel Garten, died aged forty-three: he was competition for valuable painting.

* Amanda Banesto: revenge for mother's hard life on own. Still grieving for fiancé killed by road rage killer.

* DJ: to find valuable painting, etc.

* AOP: any other person. There were a dozen possibilities. George Foster had lived on the edge of a shady world.

I nearly missed the end of the second showing, being so engrossed in typing up my thoughts. I remembered to save, then closed down the computer and flew backstage. Fortunately Trevor was not there with his usual caustic comment.

It was easy to sign Estelle and Joe off to a rapturous wave of applause.

'Well done, well done,' I said in the wings as they came off and paused for a kiss before sweeping on again for a second round.

'Did I look all right?' said Estelle. She was swathed in a creation of electric emerald green satin encrusted with sequins and diamante. She looked like a walking Christmas tree. But her face was radiant so I guessed no one looked too closely at the dress. If Boots could bottle the look, they'd make a fortune. Estelle could endorse their next anti-ageing product.

'Perfect,' I said. 'And you sang like a dream.'

They swept on again for a third round of applause. But people were beginning to leave. There was a limit to milking. They came off, arms linked around each other, seeking the nearest secluded bar to whisper sweet nothings before Joe resumed an hour or so of playing show tunes at the grand piano in one of the lounges. No doubt Estelle would get an armchair near the front, so she could sing along under her breath.

I was too tired to go back to my office apart from a swift visit to make sure it was locked. Susan had not appeared all evening, still recovering from her bout of sea sickness.

All the bars and lounges were busy. The passengers had thoroughly enjoyed Huatulco, whether they had gone on a catamaran trip, bird watching or simply lazed about on the beach. No big churches or monuments to look at, no history to swot up, no guided tours, a day to chill out and relax. Chill out was not exactly the right phrase. It had been a scorcher. I'd seen some red faces and red shoulders coming aboard. Dr Mallory's evening surgery would be busy.

Maria de Leger was sitting on her own, scribbling in her notebook, a glass of brandy on the table. She looked up and smiled. I hadn't spoken to her since Curaçao. It was such a big ship and easy to lose people along all the decks and corridors.

'Hello, Miss Jones. Come and sit down. I've done enough writing for the day. My eyes are giving out. They tire so easily.'

'You seem to have covered a lot of ground,' I said, sitting at her table in the Galaxy Lounge. The notebook was full of writing. She was holding the pages together with an elastic band.

'Well, I've lived a very long time. It's not easy to condense a busy life. But it's been fun remembering things. The more I write, then the more I seem to remember. Funny how it all comes back to you.'

'What's the earliest memory you have?' I asked. This was a fairly safe bet.

'Cherry blossom floating down in the air on a summery breeze. I was leaning out of an upstairs window and watching the drift of petals falling from a tree in the garden. I thought it was snow and told my mother it was snowing but of course it wasn't. I must have been about two years old.' She stopped suddenly. 'Why aren't you upstairs on the Lido deck for the Carnival party? Dancing under the stars with your latest admirer.'

'I may go along later, in time for the streamer finale. I usually get roped in to take photos of passengers festooned with streamers. One has to be careful as there can be rather a lot of random dunking of crew in the pool.'

'And you don't want to get that pretty dress dunked in the pool.'

'Somewhat embarrassing.'

Mrs Leger smiled knowingly. 'Everyone enjoys the embarrassment of others,' she said. 'Wet or dry. I remember once getting very wet indeed, for days on end, in fact. It was in France.'

'Wet for days? How horrid. Where was this? And when?'

261

'I was hiding in a ditch. It hadn't stopped raining for days. I was soaked to the skin and cold and dead tired. I only had a hunk of stale baguette and even that was wet. But I ate it because I was hungry.'

'You were in France? Was this during the war?'

Maria nodded. 'I never say much about it to anyone because it was all so long ago. People don't want to listen to war stories any more. And it wasn't something heroic like piloting Lancaster bombers or flying Spitfires in the Battle of Britain. I was a mere messenger on a bicycle, mainly because I could speak French fluently. My mother was French.'

'So you were working for the French Resistance?' I had to ask her. All along I had thought there was something special about Maria de Leger. Special and different.

'I was barely seventeen but they needed ordinary people like me. I looked French, I spoke French, could merge into village life. But I had a bike and knew the roads and could get from one town to another fairly quickly.'

'And you survived. Thank goodness for that.'

'Only just,' she said, her face darkening. 'I spent four years in a forced labour camp, working morning till night, living on bread and thin soup in an unheated hut with twenty other women. Many of the women died of disease.'

'How awful,' I murmured inadequately.

'The Germans found me, you see, because some gallant British officer stole my bike. We were both hiding in an empty farmhouse and this soldier was trying to get to Dunkirk, where they'd heard many ships were coming to take them off the beaches. When I was asleep, he made off with my bike. I would have got away otherwise.'

She started sipping her brandy slowly as if the memories were too painful. 'I've traced him. He's still alive apparently, in his nineties now, living in England with his son and daughter-in-law. I lost four years of my life. The Germans didn't put me in a concentration camp because they weren't able to prove anything and I was French by birth.' She pulled up her sleeve. 'Look, here's my number. It won't wash off.'

It was a shock seeing the numbers tattooed on her arm. She always wore long sleeves. The numbers were roughly tattooed but still clear.

'I'm so sorry to hear this,' I said. The words were inadequate. What else could I say? 'You were very brave. I can only hope that after the war you were able to live a better life.'

'It wasn't easy. I had to work very hard. Eventually I went to Paris and became part of the fashion world. For many years, I had my own small fashion house. We made mostly bags, gloves, scarves and belts. I sold it several years ago and came to England. This is one of my scarves.'

It was the most beautiful gossamer scarf, an iridescent rainbow of blue and silver with shots of coral. The edges were hand-stitched scalloping, a work of art.

'It's quite heavenly, beautifully made,' I said. 'You did well.'

'So did the officer who stole my bike. He survived the war, started an art gallery in Bond Street and became very rich and even titled. No forced labour camp for him or his family.'

I was getting the awful feeling that I had another name to add to my list in the Possible Evidence file. Hatred stored up for over sixty years. The revenge motive was overwhelmingly strong although how this elderly lady could ever murder anyone was beyond me. But possibly she had been trained when she worked for the underground resistance movement. She said she was only a messenger but that could mean anything in those dangerous days.

There was a book in the ship's library written by one of the French underground heroines after the war. I'd read it. It said that all underground workers were given a cyanide suicide pill, to be taken if they were being forced to give away important information to the Germans. If they were being tortured beyond endurance. Maybe Maria had kept her pill all these years.

But how could she possibly have administered it? She was seated in the same sitting but at a table for six far across the dining room. She could hardly have dropped it into his soup.

The website on the Internet at Curaçao had given me more than George Foster's name on the list of directors at the Bond Street gallery. The chairman was Sir Arthur Foster, MC, his father, survivor of the evacuation of Allied troops from the beaches of Dunkirk in June 1940. Was it the same man? Did he ever remember that he had stolen a young girl's bike so that he could survive?

'You look tired, my dear,' said Maria, shutting her notebook and putting the cap on her pen. She used a fountain pen, not a biro. 'Would you like a drink?'

'No, thank you. I'd better go up to the Lido deck for the streamer finale and take a few extra beach towels in case anyone is being thrown in the pool.'

'Make sure you don't get thrown in and ruin that pretty dress.'

'They wouldn't dare.'

The party was in full swing. Anyone could hear the belting music from a long way off. There was a conga line of dancers twisting round the pool and the outer deck, dancers in sarongs and flip-flops, garlands of paper flowers draped round their necks. Stewardesses were being pulled into the dance line.

Someone grabbed my waist and before I knew it I was hanging on to someone else, trying to keep up. It wasn't dancing. It was an untidy, shambling, riotously undisciplined and chaotic parody of a South American dance but everyone was enjoying it.

There was a shout as hundreds of streamers were hurled into the air from the balconies above and the whole deck area was a mass of coloured paper, fluttering in the wind, swamping the dancers and the band and getting into everywhere. The balconies were festooned with streamers creating a wildly psychedelic canopy above, waving in the coloured lights, changing the ship into a magical fairyland.

A bundle of long streamers were being wrapped round me and I stood there, laughing. I couldn't move. I knew who it was. He was wildly dishevelled and very unlike his usual immaculate self, with streamers twisted round his neck and in his hair.

'Aha, me beauty, so I've got you in my power at last,' he said in a pirate Jack Sparrow voice. 'Don't you scream now or I'll make you walk the plank.'

Samuel had pinned my arms to my sides and was making me dance like a wooden top. The music was so loud, I couldn't tell what it was. I had only to exert my arms a bit and I could break all the streamers but somehow I didn't want to. It was easier just to boogie around with Samuel, pretending it was dancing.

'So where have you been all evening?' he asked loudly. 'I looked everywhere for you.'

'Liar. You didn't look at all or you would have seen me talking to Maria de Leger in the Galaxy Lounge. You've been up here dancing all evening. That's why you look such a mess.'

'Dancing is great exercise,' he said, stripping the streamers off me, picking paper out of my hair. 'Does you the world of good. Gets the blood pumping.'

'If that's how you want to keep fit,' I said. 'Pumping blood.'

'I'm sorry. I forgot about your foot.'

'It's not hurting. I wanted to see you anyway.'

He caught my arm and took me over to his

266

table which was covered in empty bottles and glasses and streamers. He was searching for a clean glass. 'Now, that's what I really like to hear. You wanted to see me. Let's find you a drink.'

'I've started a file. I'm putting everything down, recording everything I know for the police. And I've found another suspect, someone no one would ever think of. And she has a very strong motive.'

'Good girl, here's a clean glass. Would you like some of this wine? Might be a bit warm.' He was testing it.

'Are you listening to me? I said, I've started a file called Possible Evidence and found a new suspect.'

'I heard you, Ms Sherlock Holmes, a new suspect. But I don't want to talk about suspects on a lovely night like this. I'd rather be dancing with you under the stars. Drink up. The night is young. Just you and me and the moonlight.'

'You do talk a lot of rubbish,' I said. 'You, me and the moonlight and about three hundred other people.'

'But I only have eyes for you, dear,' he sang. He was laughing at me again. What could I do about a man who was always laughing at me? Join in perhaps?

There was a crash of glass as a stewardess stumbled as she was coming towards me and her tray went flying. Glasses flew everywhere. A gasp went up as bare arms and legs were showered with drink. I felt something wet on my face and put my hand up.

I'd been hit. A glass had hit me.

'Don't touch it,' said Samuel, sharply, catching hold of my hand. 'That's not wine. It's blood. Someone threw a glass straight at your face.'

Twenty-Four

Acapulco

It was gorgeous. Acapulco is always the high spot of any Caribbean cruise for me. I keep expecting to bump into what's left of the Rat Pack or Sinatra himself, a jaunty white panama hat shielding his bald spot from the sun.

But of course only his voice lives on in an echo. And he wouldn't like Acapulco very much any more. It has changed. It has grown out of recognition yet the setting against the majestic Sierra Madre mountains is still stunning.

It's probably the most celebrity studded beach in the world. The rich and the famous flock there to stay in the luxury hotels that stretch to the eastern end of the bay, tall white skyscrapers in striking modernistic designs. The Mexican fishing village is only a sandy memory though there are still fishing boats drawn up at the end of the beach nearest the old quarter. Some of them have been abandoned for years and their wooden hulls are slowly decaying on the sand.

I was sporting two interesting butterfly strips

on my cheek. Dr Mallory had searched the wound for glass, probing carefully while wearing special magnifying lenses.

'Someone threw that glass at you,' he said angrily. 'I saw it happen.'

'No way. It flew off the tray when the stewardess slipped. The deck was very slippery with all the paper streamers and splashes from the pool. It was an accident.'

'Accident, my foot. She dropped the tray, yes, but the glass came straight for you, over her shoulder. Whoever tripped her, was right behind, with a glass aimed straight at you.'

'Did you see them? Who was it?'

'They disappeared into the crowd.'

I laughed nervously. 'I don't believe it. You're making this up. You're trying to scare me.'

He dropped the probe into a tray. 'No fragments, thank goodness. It's not deep enough for stitches. But I will put a couple of butterfly strips on it, to hold the edges together. It should heal nicely.'

I wanted to ask if I would be scarred but knew he'd only give me a sarcastic answer. What did it matter anyway? I could do wonders with make-up.

'I'm coming with you to your cabin,' he went on. 'No objections, Casey, please. Purely as a security measure, to make sure no one is lurking in the shower. We don't want a replay of *Psycho*. Then I want you to lock your door and not open it to anyone, even if they say they are me or Richard Norton.'

'Now you are being melodramatic,' I said,

wondering if I could stand up. My knees had gone weak and wobbly. 'Who would possibly say they were you?'

'Someone who wanted to get into your cabin.'

'But I wouldn't let anyone into my cabin, especially not if they said they were you.' It was a joke but he was not amused.

'But if Captain Nicolas was standing outside, you'd let him in, wouldn't you?'

'Of course. He's the captain.'

'But how would you know it was him? Can you recall his voice?'

It was true. I'd met Captain Nicolas frequently, spoken to him lots of times, could vaguely remember his voice, a touch of the north. But that was all. If someone announces from the other side of a door that they are the captain, then you assume that they are.

'I understand,' I said. 'But do you really think I am in that much danger?'

'I think someone is trying to scare you off. You're making them nervous and nervous people do foolish things. If only you had not got yourself involved in all this business. You're in charge of entertainment, shows and lectures. There's nothing in your contract about being a private investigator.'

'But it does say that I should be committed to the welfare of passengers. And I am committed to their welfare, even to the dead ones.'

His face relaxed. 'You have a wonderful way of putting it, Casey. I hope the occupants of my freezer appreciate your concern.'

'Is Rosanna all right?'

'Singing your praises. You are the saint of deck-walking as far as she is concerned. It helped her to feel some normality, that she might have a new life ahead, once she is cleared at Southampton.'

'Will she be cleared?'

'I don't know. I'm a doctor, not a policeman.'

Samuel walked me to my cabin and opened it with the card. It was embarrassing because I had left the inside in a mess. Clothes and undies thrown everywhere. Make-up and toiletries in disarray. It had been a quick change.

He searched every inch which took about one fluid minute. He even opened the wardrobes, moved dresses about and looked under the bed. He checked the window fastening.

'Heavens, no Latin lover lurking?' I said. 'I am disappointed. I told him on the dot of midnight. He's never late.'

'Go to bed, Casey, and lock your door.'

So I slept through our approach to Acapulco but the membrane between dreams and sleep was uneasy. I went up on deck early to take in the sparkling scene. There were several big cruise ships anchored in the bay. The *Countess* was small enough to berth quayside. Already the taxi drivers were gathering to pounce on passengers. 'Two dollars to the market, signorita?'

My face didn't look too bad. It hadn't swollen. I didn't cover the butterfly strips with make-up, wary of infection. Better to leave it untouched. A big hat and sunglasses was all the disguise I needed.

Susan eventually dragged herself into the

office. She looked wan and depressed, not the vibrant deputy that I wanted to leave in charge. It was my turn to go ashore. I'd been counting on a few hours in Acapulco.

'How are you feeling?'

'Still a bit fragile. A little sailing boat is a lot different to a big cruise liner. It was awfully choppy. We got bounced around all over the place. Waves were coming at us, that high. I hated it.'

'Never mind. Dr Mallory brought you back safe and sound, and I'm sure he'll think of something a little calmer for your next date.'

Susan looked somewhat cheered. 'Yes, I expect so. He said we'd have a drink after tonight's show.'

'There you are. He's still interested.'

'Yes, he is, isn't he? And he's so nice. Listens to all my problems and seems to understand them. He said he'd work out a diet personally suited to my hectic lifestyle. It's all to do with metabolism. Isn't that kind of him?'

'Very kind.' I'd had enough of this conversation. I finished answering my emails and told Susan what needed looking into. One of the male dancers had volunteered to DJ late at night. He said he knew what he was doing. We'd already checked the ship's newspaper for tomorrow. There were no last minute changes, but Susan needed to review the spotlights in the Princess Lounge with the lighting man. Estelle had complained that they were all over the place. Maybe she had been all over the place.

'I don't want to talk to Estelle.'

'Then don't talk to her, write her a letter. Send a polite note to her cabin. Use your initiative, girl.'

I saw her hand close over a brass letter opener that was always on her desk. It was some market souvenir that she had picked up in Casablanca. The Arabic workmanship was rough but the knife was still sharp.

My photograph had been slashed with a knife. Could Susan have done it? But why? She had access to the key to the display cabinet. She was not exactly my number one fan, even if I had introduced her to Samuel.

I sent her a totally insincere smile. 'Don't worry. Estelle is a totally changed woman since romance came sweeping into her life. A little late perhaps, but still making her eyes sparkle.'

'Oh, really? I hadn't noticed. She's too old for sparkling eyes. It's disgusting at their age. They should know better.'

I couldn't get out of the office fast enough. I'd had enough of Susan Brook.

The quayside was busy with passengers getting on coaches, others trying to walk to town and being waylaid by taxi drivers. It was no distance. They didn't need a taxi. Passengers could walk anywhere in Acapulco, the old town or the new.

It was a fine, natural harbour and most of the passengers made for the famous Strip where the restaurants, luxury hotels and shops were, or to the Old Acapulco town which was centred round the shaded square in front of the cathedral. This downtown area was the hub for people-watch-

273

ing. The church wasn't that old but it was weirdly Byzantine with bulbous domes.

Most of our passengers were going to watch the cliff divers (the *clavadistas*) perform their spectacular leaps off the cliffs more than 130 feet above the sea. It was a nail-biting performance and the divers only got tips from their audience. The famous stars of the past, Errol Flynn, Lana Turner and John Wayne, as well as Frank Sinatra, had once owned homes in La Quebrada but they had long gone.

I managed to side-step the persistent taxi drivers.

'No, thank you. I want to walk,' I said. 'I'm getting fat.' I patted my stomach and they laughed, offering me an even cheaper fare. Maybe they thought I was pregnant and commiserated.

I wanted to walk along the Strip and go shopping. There were over 600 shops in Acapulco and I'd saved my shopping spree for here. There was everything from designer names to local handicrafts.

The big luxury hotels had the best views of the ocean, the city or the bay. It was a long walk round the bay. I stopped to look at the mermaid statue sitting on the rocks, not unlike the one in Copenhagen but smaller and not quite so sedate, and the pelicans standing guard close by on every outcrop.

Once Acapulco had been a target for pirate raids because of the silver being exported and exotic oriental items going the other way. They built a star-shaped fortress on the front and it was beside these tall walls that I was walking now. I reckoned there were still a lot of pirates around.

The taxi drivers would not leave me alone. 'No, thank you. No, *gracias*,' I said in English and Spanish. 'I want to walk.'

They clearly thought I was touched by the sun, and offered cheaper and cheaper fares to take me bargain shopping. I felt sorry for them. They only had a few hours in which to make some money.

There were so many bars and restaurants offering every kind of delicacy. Some of our passengers had already given up in the heat and were sitting at café tables shaded by big umbrellas.

I spotted Tamara Fitzgibbons strolling ahead, wearing a short strappy cotton dress which was far too revealing for the sanity of the taxi drivers. She was being accosted on all sides. I hurried to catch her up.

'Haven't you got a wrap or a shawl?' I said. 'Those acres of bare skin are sending the locals wild. You're going to be sorry.'

'I've got factor thirty-five on,' she said.

'I'm not talking about sunburn. I mean the hot-blooded Mexican men. They are not used to seeing this amount of flesh showing.'

'What about on the beach?'

'This is not the beach, this is walking about in the middle of town. If you look at the Mexican women out shopping, they are decently covered.'

Tamara was about to continue arguing with me, when the unexpected happened. A taxi drew up alongside and the driver leaned out of the window. He was dark and swarthy with the Aztec bone structure of his ancestors.

'You want a taxi, *señorita*?' he asked. 'Private taxi.'

'Oh yes, thank you,' she said, getting in the back. 'To the Strip, please.'

It was less than a ten-minute walk and Tamara was getting a taxi. It was a two-minute ride if the traffic was clear. Acapulco traffic was a nightmare. Road rules and speed restrictions were ignored. Pedestrians usually crossed streets massed in groups as that meant they were less likely to be run over by a manic driver.

'Tamara,' I called out. 'Come back.' But the taxi was speeding away. It was too late to stop her. Oh well, I supposed she could take care of herself. It was only a two-minute taxi ride.

The sun was blisteringly hot. The celebrity hotels sparkled like icing sugar. Enticing wavelets rolled along the shore but I didn't have time for a swim.

But I couldn't get it out of my head, the way the taxi had cruised alongside us. It was unusual. The drivers touted for passengers on the quayside, their vehicles parked a distance away.

It was a shop-till-you-drop day and I had my fill. I bought a local straw hat for Rosanna from a street trader, resisted the shell sculptures, glassware and jewellery. But I couldn't resist a pair of strappy blue sandals encrusted with gems. They looked gorgeous if somewhat dangerous. I'd probably cut my legs on the gems. I recognized the designer name, Fendi, but was unsure if it was genuine. I hadn't paid a

Fendi price.

It was five in the afternoon when I climbed the gangway to go on-board, showed my crew card, had my purchases scanned. I kept my eyes open for Tamara returning, but she wasn't around. I couldn't take Rosanna for a walk round the Promenade Deck until the *Countess* had let go her lines. It would be pleasant for her to see the sweep of the Bay of Acapulco as we steamed out into the Pacific Ocean.

'Is this another record?' said Samuel Mallory. He hadn't gone ashore. Too many patients. 'Back on time again?'

'I was hoping you'd notice,' I said. 'Have you seen Tamara? The girl from the art gallery.'

'No. Is it important?'

'I've got a horrible feeling...'

'Heartburn. Chew a Rennie. Drink a glass of water.'

'I think she may have been kidnapped. We've been warned, several times, about taxi drivers who take passengers up into the hills and then demand money before they'll bring them back to the ship. It has happened.'

'Kidnapped? Isn't that a bit extreme?'

'Believe me.'

Dr Mallory looked serious for once. 'That's true. And there was the couple who had everything stolen by a taxi driver, wallet, cards, currency. What makes you think that something has happened to Tamara?'

'It was the way the taxi appeared suddenly, like it was cruising. She was on her own. She was hardly wearing a dress, nothing decent, not the sort of thing to walk about in. And he said "private taxi" which was very odd. Before I could stop her, she had got into the taxi and it shot away.'

'Let's check whether she's back. I'll get on to the purser's office.'

But Tamara Fitzgibbons had not been checked back on-board. She would have a cruise card or a crew card like everyone else. Announcements began to come over the loudspeakers, asking certain named passengers to make their whereabouts known to Reception. The cruise card scanner at the top of the gangway was not a hundred per cent sure. There were occasional hiccups.

Tamara's name was on the list. Again. And again. I leaned over the rail, hoping to see a taxi screeching to a halt and Tamara flinging herself out and up the gangway. They would sail away without her. They never waited. If it was a passenger left behind, they had to make their own way to the next port of call to pick up the ship. Expensive.

'I think she's been kidnapped,' I told Richard Norton on the phone. 'Can we do anything?'

'I'll alert the police on shore, the British Consulate and our agents. They'll be able to enquire at the hospital, in case she's been in an accident. What does she look like?'

'She's about five foot three with light brown hair, around twenty-nine and wearing a very short white dress with shoulder straps.'

'It might be a red, white and blue dress by now.'

'That's not funny,' I snapped.

'Sorry, my wife is always telling me I have the weirdest sense of humour.'

His wife? I didn't even know there was a wife. First mention of wife's existence. Unknown factor. Had he let it slip by mistake? This does happen on cruises. Any on-shore relationships get conveniently forgotten. I wondered if Dr Mallory had commitments, kept out of sight.

'But I did manage to take some of the registration number of the taxi, despite the mud and dust on the plate,' I said, still reeling.

'Shoot.'

'There was a five, six and a nine. That's all I can remember.'

'Not exactly brilliant but better than nothing. I'll phone ashore.' Richard put the phone down.

That was me all over. Not exactly brilliant but better than nothing.

Twenty-Five

At Sea

Rosanna had been waiting for me all day. She knew she wouldn't be allowed out on deck until the ship was at sea. She had been moved to a secure inside crew cabin as Dr Mallory needed the isolation room. A male crew member had a chest rash and had to be kept in isolation till it was diagnosed as one hundred per cent not infectious.

'Thank you, thank you so much for coming,' she said. 'I'd like to see something of Acapulco. That great song and everything. My dad was always playing Sinatra. He was a number one fan.'

'Come along, on deck. It'll take a while for the *Countess* to sail through the bay and the Boca Grande. There's so much commercial shipping and other cruise liners. I've bought you a souvenir.'

She loved the cowboy straw hat and plonked it on her head. She looked so vivacious and happy, I almost felt like offering her a job on my team. She'd be a change from the sour-faced Susan.

When we got out on deck, she exclaimed with more joy over the sight of Acapulco Bay, all the gleaming white hotels and the mountains in the background, the incredible blue of the sea. At a distance from the litter and the traffic, it looked pure Hollywood and so glamorous.

'It's wonderful. I don't care if I do go to prison,' she said. 'This has been worth it. See Acapulco and die. Sorry, I didn't mean that. My poor dad.'

'I know you didn't,' I said. 'There have been enough deaths on this cruise. Two others, as well as your father. Did Dr Mallory tell you that?'

Her face sobered. 'No, he didn't say anything much, apart from my father being found in his magic box. Are you going to tell me? I might be able to make some sense of my father's death, if I knew what was going on.'

I saw no harm in telling her about George Foster, supposedly a heart attack, and Nigel Garten, supposedly a man overboard, possible suicide. 'Mr Garten had just bought a reproduction from the art gallery. They were both on table two, second sitting, which is also strange. And so was your father. He had been given a place on table two but no one remembers if he ever sat there for a meal.' I didn't say that maybe he was already dead.

'Who else sits there now?'

'Mrs Joan Foster, the widow, when she feels like coming down which is not often. Several new couples and some elderly ladies. The word has gone around that the table is jinxed and no one will sit on it. Too many accidents. I've eaten there a couple of times, so that it won't look so empty.'

281

'My father's death wasn't an accident, you know. He was always so careful. He knew his equipment, could work it blindfolded. I've seen him practising the procedure. He didn't just fall and get locked in. Or bang his head. No way.'

'Are you trying to tell me something that I don't know?' I asked. We were strolling the Promenade Deck in the evening sunshine. It was quite crowded with passengers hanging over the rails, catching a last glimpse of sunny Mexico, before we headed back to the Azores and Southampton. We had several days at sea now, another transit of the Panama Canal, and then the Atlantic and home.

'Casey. I can call you Casey, can't I? You are the one person who has been continually kind to me. Look, I'm not very bright. I haven't got a job or anything. I look after my dad between shows, that's all. But I watch a lot of television and it strikes me that all these deaths could be connected. And it must be something to do with the ultrasound scanning equipment my dad was being forced to bring on-board.'

'You may be right.' Rosanna might well be right.

'If we could find out who was making him bring it on to the ship, threatening him and everything, then I reckon you got the person who killed him and chucked that other passenger overboard. I don't know how the heart attack geyser fits in.'

We'd done one circuit. I could spare time for two more, making it nearly one mile. 'Oh, but he does fit in, Rosanna. George Foster was a director in a Bond Street art gallery called Fine Art. It's all to do with some famous painting, lost for years, that is actually hidden under a very ordinary reproduction. Though how anyone could paint over a masterpiece, I don't understand.'

'But it is done. I saw a programme about it. Television tells you a lot, you know. I don't just watch soaps.'

'And now the young woman in charge of the art gallery on board ship has gone missing. We had to leave Acapulco without her. I was the last person to see her, getting into a suspicious taxi. I should have stopped her.'

'What could you have done? Dragged her out by her hair? Hung on to the back of the taxi. Please, Casey, don't feel responsible. You couldn't have done anything.'

Rosanna was refreshing in her candour. She made me feel a whole lot better. What could I have done? That was true. I had been a witness.

We were on to circuit two. 'So, Rosanna, what do you think this is all about? Bearing in mind that you had this threatening phone call at home. And that you don't think your father's death was accidental.'

'OK, some greedy criminals have found out that this famous painting is hidden under a tatty reproduction on sale on this ship. George Foster is a proper legit art dealer, comes on cruise, hoping to spot it. But he dies. Heart attack or what. No chance of him finding it now. Nigel Garten spots it, buys it, then is toppled overboard. Goodbye Mr Garten.'

'And your dad?'

283

'I think he threatened to blow the gaffe. He was fed up with it. So they had to shut him up.'

'That's awful, but you could be right. Not all a coincidence.'

'No coincidence. All connected. Where is this painting now?'

'I believe Joan Foster has it. It's called *Sunset over Amalfi*. She bought a whole lot of paintings the other day, including the one that Nigel Garten had recently bought. They thought it would save all the hassle of probate and inheritance tax if they simply resold it. The painting had not left the ship, and was awaiting UK delivery.'

'Do we know what this famous painting is?' She seemed to know a whole lot more about it than I did. Television. Perhaps she watched the Open University.

'No.' I shook my head. 'But I looked up missing art work on the internet. There are quite a lot of missing paintings.'

'Well, I think I know,' she said with more confidence. 'That awful man who kept phoning me, who threatened my father. He said it was a Cézanne.'

'A Cézanne?'

'Oh yes, that's what he said. Something about the Orange Sea. I didn't understand what he meant. I don't know any French.'

'*La Mer d'Orange*? Or *L'Orange de Mer*? Is that what he said?'

'Yeah, something like that. I can't remember. I was too upset. I'm sorry, do you mind, can we talk about something else now?'

She'd had enough questioning. I tried to distract her as we walked the last circuit. A number of passengers were disappearing to change for dinner, first sitting. Second sitting had another hour or so on deck, more space, empty deck-chairs, the cool of the evening, receding coast-lines to watch in peace.

I had to change. Susan was no doubt exhausted by her day in the office, or was hurrying off for a drink with the charming Dr Mallory. If his surgery finished in time. He'd had a new crop of casualties.

I took Rosanna back to her crew quarters. It was a basic cabin. A female officer was waiting to take over. 'Would you like to come for another walk tomorrow?' I asked. 'We are at sea. All day. I should be able to find time.'

'Thanks. And thank you for the cowboy hat. I love it to bits.'

I was liking Rosanna more and more. A gutsy girl. She'd stowed away on-board to warn her father, but she hadn't known what she was warning him about. And she was taking his death well. As if she had known it would end in tears.

I took a quick bite in the officers' mess, a Caesar salad, looking totally out of place in a mid-calf coral silk dress and cropped white crochet jacket. I was dressed for Ascot or Good-wood without the horses. And I had to remember the two times table. Wear nothing too short, too tight, too revealing, too expensive. But the evening was cooling down and I felt the cold. Sometimes I even went to bed with a hot-water bottle. Dr Mallory would no doubt find that amusing. He'd ring up and say in his deepest voice, 'Shall

I come round and warm you up?'

The answer would always be, No, buster.

Someone on board had the answer to all those questions we had talked about, but who was it?

Word went round that Estelle was throwing a party that evening in the Galaxy Lounge when the last dancing had finished. She had invited almost all the crew, the entertainment staff and lots of passengers. I hoped she wasn't going to put the cost on her expenses. I wasn't signing for a party.

Joe Dornoch was leaning over a rail, up front, smoking a cigarette furiously. He looked hunted and ill at ease.

'Have you been invited to this party?' he asked, coughing on the smoke, waving it about in a fruitless way.

'Yes,' I said. 'Among a cast of hundreds. Is it a special occasion?'

'Yes,' he said morosely. 'Estelle is going to announce our engagement.'

'Congratulations,' I said. 'That's wonderful. As long as you don't want the captain to marry you. I don't think shipboard weddings are legal any more.'

He brightened slightly. 'Aren't they? Thank goodness. You see, I think Estelle is a stunning woman and she's wonderful, but I don't remember actually proposing to her. She says I did, but it's all a horrible empty blank to me.'

'Ah, then you have got a problem. You had better stop this party before it goes too far.'

'Estelle would be furious. And she's got some temper. You'd know that, only too well. She'd hate losing face in front of everyone.'

'Then you'd better let Estelle have her party and then break off the engagement, very quietly, later. But preferably not while we are at sea, please. She still has two more shows to do and I don't want her cancelling them. You'd better wait until we reach Southampton before you have your second thoughts.'

'Of course, I could just disappear. Do a vanishing act. I have another contract on a cruise ship which starts immediately. Just time to go home and get my shirts washed and ironed. Estelle doesn't know which line it is. I've never said.'

The way he mentioned it made it sound as if there might be someone waiting at home to wash and iron his shirts. But I said nothing. He looked unhappy enough.

'Go and enjoy the party. Play the loving fiancé. Blow a few kisses. You can do that. She's bound to want to sing some of her numbers.'

'She does. She's been rehearsing songs all afternoon. Can't you help me?'

'There's nothing I can do, Joe. At least she can sing and you can play the piano, quite brilliantly. It'll be fun. Just enjoy it. Let her have her engagement party. Look upon it as show business, another performance.'

'You won't say anything?'

'Of course not. It's between you and Estelle.'

'Thank you.' He looked relieved. I'd moved a weight from his shoulders.

I was treading on shredded glass between shows. Some of our lovely dancers were genuinely ill, others shell-shocked, allergic to nuts, had pulled ligaments, were sea-sick, hated their costumes, wanted to go home. I wished they were not so lissom and thin. Lunch was a lettuce leaf and a stick of celery. All their calories came from water. Daily intake: zero.

It was a procession of complaints. I dealt with each person with compassion and understanding. It was their lifestyle. They had to survive if they wanted another job dancing on shore or on ship. The shows were always choreographed and produced on shore, then contracted to ships. Tonight's show had to go on, however homesick they felt.

The only throwing up that was allowed was off stage.

'Think,' I said. 'This is a job. You have to do it. Sorry, but I can't control the sea. You knew it was a ship when you signed on. Did you think it was an airship? Or a hovercraft?'

I was racing between the shows. But all went well. No one fainted on stage. No one had a tantrum backstage. The dancers looked gorgeous, not a sequin out of place. They were great. They say the theatre is the best doctor.

'Well done,' I said as I went on stage to orchestrate the applause and the bows. My stomach was signalling a lack of food. Fortunately the band drowned the rumbles.

I knew I would have to make an appearance at the engagement party. Estelle would regard it as a slight if I was not there. But I slipped upstairs first to the Grill and ordered an omelette and chips. It wouldn't take seconds to make and I could eat it just as fast.

The waiter who served me seemed a little distant. I was used to lots of smiles and special consideration. A warm roll, butter pats, iced water, Miss Jones? Nothing. This one disappeared into the kitchen and didn't reappear. I had to ask if my omelette was ever coming or were they waiting for the eggs to be laid?

I hadn't seen this waiter before. He had short peroxide hair, gelled current spiky fashion. It was such an unattractive look. I couldn't understand why young men thought it made them look good. It was scarecrow mode.

The omelette was perfect. I wolfed it down and thanked everyone.

I only just made the party. Estelle was singing 'Some Enchanted Evening' to Joe's accompaniment. He looked gaunt and strained. Estelle looked radiant, in her favourite red dress. Her skin was taut and glowing. She'd been in the salon for hours, using her staff discount, allowing skilful hands to work wonders on her skin.

I took off the crochet jacket. It was warm in the crowded lounge.

'So shall we make this a double engagement party?' said Samuel, grinning as he slid to my side with a flute of something for me. It wasn't champagne. Some sort of sparkling white wine. I wished he didn't look so good, so dark and moody.

'You and Susan?' I said, with a perky smile of surprise. 'Oh, how lovely. Wonderful. I hope you'll be very happy together. I know she will be counting the days.'

'I really love your sense of humour,' he went on, sipping his drink. 'We have so much in common.'

'I didn't think we had anything in common. So, if you'll excuse me...'

I went over to Amanda Banesto. She was looking gorgeous in a flimsy cream dress, all legs and high-heeled sandals. 'How are you? How is your mother?'

'She went to the cinema this evening with Joan, you know, her long-lost sister. I don't know exactly what happened but they've got together and they are talking. They have been talking all day. So I can party and have fun.'

'That's great news. Miracles do happen. Forgive me for asking, but who is this handsome blond male who is often at your side? He looks very attentive.'

'That's Bruno. He seems to think he has to look after me, protect me.'

'He seems a nice young man.'

'Nice, yes, but sometimes a bit heavy going, boring. You can't have everything, can you? But he keeps the sharks away and I'm grateful for that.'

She laughed and moved on to join another group, networking with skill. Her model looks ought to get her on to television one day. She had the intelligence to be a presenter or news reader.

Richard Norton came over to me, pouring refills on the way from a big bottle of sparkling wine. Estelle was cutting corners by not having a lot of catering staff around. It was a do-it-yourself party. Pass the crisps.

'Casey, I'd like to run an idea past you,' he said.

'Shoot,' I said, using his expression.

'I want to set a trap, get this person out of hiding. Whoever it is must still be on the ship, waiting around for his chance.'

'Waiting for his chance for what?'

Richard looked baffled. 'There must be a motive and there must be a connection. I think this missing painting you mentioned is the key. Will you help me?'

'Am I to be the bait, the cheese in the trap? I'll only do feta.'

'I can't ask a member of the crew, against regulations, and I can't ask a passenger, much too dangerous.'

'But I'm crew.'

'Entertainments division, that's different. I couldn't ask an officer.'

I didn't see the difference. But at least Richard was thinking of doing something apart from sending emails ashore. And about time. Before the second sitting lost any more of its diners.

'What are you planning?' I was mellowing.

'The art gallery is closed at the moment because of Tamara Fitzgibbon's unfortunate disappearance at Acapulco. I thought you could open it for a special showing. Hold a competition perhaps? Spot the priceless painting or something? Have passengers come in and vote for which is the print with the Cézanne hidden behind it?'

'I don't even know for sure it's a Cézanne. It's all guesswork.'

'So will you do it?' he asked again, rapidly

291

changing the direction of the conversation. 'Will you be our feta cheese?'

'Shall I have to wear a silly costume?'

He was about to answer when Estelle switched on a music player and the Rolling Stones were thumping out 'Can't Get No Satisfaction' at maximum decibels. Conversation was out. He shrugged his shoulders and moved on with the bottle.

Estelle pulled Joe on to the dance floor and began gyrating her considerable curves in his direction. His face was a picture of acute embarrassment.

I shrank against a wall, wondering when I could decently leave. I was not necessary to the proceedings. I'd congratulated the happy couple and drunk two glasses of their bubbly. Conclusion: time to sleep.

Maria de Leger had the same thought. She appeared in the doorway of the Galaxy Lounge in a mauve satin dressing gown, her long white hair in a plait over her shoulder. She was very annoyed. She walked over to the music player and switched it off.

'*Mon Dieu*. I protest,' she said. 'It is far too late for this abominable noise. Passengers are entitled to sleep. It can be heard everywhere.'

Madame de Leger had a clear voice. It carried to all corners of the lounge and she looked a commanding figure despite her age. Estelle went redder than she had been before she started dancing.

'This is a private party,' spluttered Estelle, fuelled by several glasses of neat vodka drunk on the side. 'And you're not invited, grandma. Go back to your bed, you old crone.'

The French woman's eyes narrowed. 'I beg your pardon?'

'Put your teeth back in and clear off on your broomstick. We're enjoying ourselves. This is a party for young people.'

Maria de Leger walked over to the perspiring Estelle, and spoke quite calmly. 'You're enjoying yourselves because people like me risked our lives in war zones in France, killing Germans with our bare hands. Would you like me to demonstrate how I did it?'

Estelle wavered on her feet. Her befuddled mind wasn't taking in whether this was a hoax or serious. She then told Madame de Leger what to do to herself in unacceptable language.

In a second Estelle was in a half-nelson grip, one arm firmly pinioned behind her back. It was so fast I didn't see it happen. This was no frail, elderly lady. This was one still prime fighting machine.

But the hold was not tight enough to hurt and Estelle struggled out of it. She turned and picked up a pitcher of orange juice from a side table. It had hardly been touched. It went over Maria de Leger in a deluge of sticky orange liquid, drenching her, head to foot. The sound of shock stopped the party dead.

'*Alors*,' said Maria de Leger, after a pause. '*C'est domage.*'

'Go home, you old crone,' Estelle shouted.

'Turn off the lights,' I said, taking charge. 'The party's over.'

Twenty-Six

Panama Canal

No one took much notice of the Panama Canal on the return passage. Been there, seen that, done it. They wanted new experiences, new places. This was when the various lecturers worked their kit off, keeping the passengers diverted and amused.

But there was plenty to keep them diverted and amused this morning. The orange juice story went round the ship at a rate of knots.

I had last night's catastrophe to sort out. Captain Nicolas had summoned me to his office. He was not pleased. He had his stern face on, clicking and unclicking a ballpoint pen. There had been more than a few complaints about the noise and disruption. Passengers were known to sue if their quality of sleep was not one hundred per cent pleasant dreams.

As he often said, 'Ships have engines. What are we supposed to do? Tow them along behind?'

But this was even more nerve-racking. Captain Nicolas seemed to think I was responsible for the party. Estelle was in worse trouble. Her two final shows had been cancelled by Head Office and she was confined to her cabin for the rest of the cruise. Bad behaviour was not tolerated. Joe Dornoch was nowhere to be seen between his scheduled playing selections from shows. He was no doubt celebrating his narrow escape and rehearsing a moving farewell speech ... the shock, the embarrassment, the humiliation, but he would always love and respect her ... etc.

Captain Nicolas went straight to the point. 'Last night's fracas. I understand from other sources that you did not organize this party? Do you confirm this?'

'Yes, sir,' I said. 'I knew nothing about it until I was invited, late that evening. It was a private party.'

'But you were there. You should have kept it under control. Estelle Grayson is under contract to you.'

'Everything was under control until the music and the dancing started. It was the Rolling Stones, sir.'

'I'm surprised you recognized it. Why didn't you turn it off or turn the volume down? It was late at night. You should have known it would disturb sleeping passengers.'

There was no answer to that. I'd been distracted. I'd been talking to Richard Norton about this harebrained scheme of his, using me as bait. How could I tell Captain Nicolas that I'd been more involved in catching a murderer on board ship. Not an admission that would go down too well.

'And the unforgivable scene with Madame de Leger. Why didn't you stop it before it went too far?'

'It all happened so quickly,' I said. Dumb answer. This was not going to look good on any personnel report. 'In less than a minute, seconds in fact. And I was at the far side of the room, just about to go. I could hardly plough through like a Sherman tank. There were plenty of off-duty officers closer to the incident than me.'

Brilliant parting shot. Direct hit midships. All canons firing. Captain Nicolas looked slightly disconcerted. 'Unfortunately I don't know who they were,' he said. 'No one will admit to being at the party now. Sorry, Casey, you were scapegoat number one. You know how it is.'

I didn't know but there you are. 'I'm sorry it happened, of course. And if I could have prevented it, then I would have. I've lost a popular solo turn. Do you know anyone who can sing?'

'Madame de Leger was full of praise for the way you took her back to her cabin and saw to everything. It must have been very late indeed by the time you got to your own bed.'

'It was. Extremely late. And I had sticky orange juice all over me.'

'Have your dress dry-cleaned and send me the bill.'

'Thank you, sir. Very kind.'

I was dismissed. Captain Nicolas was a charming man but he could be terrifying at times. For a few moments it had been back to my schooldays and up before the headmistress when I was caught smoking in a bus shelter.

As I left the captain's office, Dr Mallory came out of his cabin. He'd showered and changed after his morning surgery and his dark hair was still wet like an otter.

'My word, you do lead an exciting life, don't you?' he teased. 'I wish I went to such lively parties. I only get invited to the dull ones.'

'That old lady knows how to throw a half nelson,' I said. 'I wonder what else she knows? Could she throw a man overboard? Or stuff a man into a magic box so that he suffocated?'

'Come off it, Casey. You like her. Everyone likes her. It's not Madame de Leger. Let's go and have a coffee. You need time to relax and talk.'

He steered me towards one of the lounges and within seconds a smiling stewardess had put a pot of coffee and some big cups and saucers on the table in front of us.

'How do you do it?' I asked, letting the arm-chair hold my limp body. I was drained. 'She knew what you wanted, without you saying a word.'

'It's a gift, Casey. Telepathic. If I sit down, it means I need coffee,' he said, pouring. 'I'll be mother. I prescribe ten minutes of caffeine and small talk. You look shattered.'

'I am shattered. I never got enough sleep. It was very late before Madame de Leger was hosed down and back in bed. We both needed a cup of tea. She is a remarkable woman. It isn't what she says, it's what she doesn't say.'

'Resistance worker?'

'More than likely. That's the impression although she doesn't ever say exactly. She's a mystery. But, I agree, I like her. I like her guts, her ability to survive. She is a tribute to all the women who did courageous things in the war.'

'So are we any closer to solving all our mysteries?' Samuel was pouring out seconds. He was obviously in need of caffeine as well. I didn't ask about his cases, the injuries, patient confidentiality and all that.

'Richard Norton is planning a trap with bait. Has he told you about it?'

Samuel looked at me sharply. 'No, he hasn't but don't do it, Casey. Forget it. If he wants bait then he can use one of his own people.'

'But I've almost promised...'

'Un-promise. I'm warning you, Casey. Have nothing to do with this plan. OK, I know I haven't exactly gone along with you in the cause of all these deaths, but listen to me now, stay clear. Don't get involved. Let the guys at South-ampton take over.'

'But it'll be too late then. The passengers will have disembarked and gone home. Every scrap of evidence wiped clean with disinfectant. No, it's got to be done while we are at sea, where nothing and no one can escape. And now, before we reach Ponta Delgada in the Azores.'

'For God's sake, Casey, you're mad.' He look-ed distraught. 'We've got a murderer aboard. Just wear your pretty dresses and keep out of his way.'

'It's not as easy as that,' I said. 'I have other responsibilities.'

'You're not responsible for sudden deaths.'

For once, he was serious. Samuel Mallory looking serious was disturbing. The sparkle had gone. Those eyes were peering into me, trying to reach my soul. My equilibrium rocked. Did he mean it? Was he really concerned? Men say one thing and mean another. It happens all the time.

'I can take care of myself.'

'I don't think you can. How many things have happened to you already? You got drugged, nearly pushed overboard, almost missed the ship, locked in the art gallery, a glass thrown at you? Are these all ridiculous coincidences? No, Casey, you are poking your nose into organized crime and that's not in your contract, is it? Stay out of trouble. Look, I'm warning you. Please take some notice.'

'You're exaggerating.'

'No way. These things happened. Think back.'

'Part of my contract is seeing to the welfare of passengers. And that's what I'm doing,' I said, dredging up what was left of my confidence. 'Welfare isn't only putting on shows and standing in for the bingo caller. I'm here to make sure that this cruise is the best holiday they have ever had.'

Samuel was looking at me with a strange expression. It could have been exasperation or admiration. Who could tell? He was an enigma.

He stood up. 'I have a couple of sick patients to go and see, cabin calls. Then I'm going to play quoits in some crew versus passenger tournament. I shall rid myself of any aggression in the time-honoured way of chucking quoits overboard.'

'We lose more quoits...' I said.

'Remember what I said. I don't want you as a patient after some horrendous stake-out in the art gallery.'

It was a sobering thought but I didn't want to think about it.

'Haven't you got a lifeboat drill this morning?' he added over his shoulder as an afterthought as he walked away. 'It's on the rota.'

I was down to my cabin in one minute, changed into full uniform and donned a lifejacket in the second minute, back to the Princess Lounge as the six bell alarm sounded. Those bells. The clocks were always moving, forwards or backwards. This one had caught me out.

'This is a practice drill,' said the loudspeakers. 'Passengers need not be alarmed. All crew to muster points.'

The Princess Lounge was muster point for a certain number of crew, stewards, and other personnel. They stood about in clusters, wearing lifejackets, grinning, not taking it very seriously. I had a walkie-talkie. I was being informed that there was a fire in one of the engine rooms and that an emergency fire-fighting crew were dealing with it. Not real, of course.

I went through the procedure of allocating lifeboats and they filed outside, crocodile style, one hand on the shoulder of the man in front, on their knees as if there was smoke. Fire on-board was the most feared disaster. It did not bear thinking about. But everyone had to know what to do in such an emergency.

A few passengers watched out of curiosity as we shuffled out on to the decks. If it ever really happened, then they would be an important part of what we were drilled to do. This time the lifeboats were not winched down, but sometimes when we were in port, the drill went further with mock 'casualties' and lifeboats launched into the water.

The loudspeakers continued to inform passengers that this was a practice drill and nothing to be alarmed about. Except that I had almost forgotten about it. Oh dear, Confused Casey. My concentration was being filtered down the drain.

The canal was choppy and churning with a wind force four or five. Not ideal for launching lifeboats. It was a darker blue than usual and the jungle trees were swaying on both banks. I saw an alligator slither down a bank and into the water with barely a splash. They gave me the creeps.

'My goodness, the things you have to do,' said Mrs Fairweather, accosting me outside the lounge as I took off my lifejacket and folded in the straps.

'Everyone has to know what to do,' I said. 'It could save lives.'

'It's so reassuring,' she went on. 'I can see you are in uniform, looking so official, but supposing it happened in the middle of a show or a bingo session?'

'No time for uniforms then. Grab a lifejacket and get to your muster station. Do you know your muster station, Mrs Fairweather?'

She smiled weakly. 'No, I'm afraid I don't.'

'It's on a notice behind the door of your cabin.'

'I never read notices.'

Thus spoke one of the ill-informed. I made her

301

promise to have a look and remember where her muster point was. She agreed but it was not something I could check on.

Richard Norton's scheme was scheduled for this afternoon. I was supposed to host an event in the art gallery. Guess which was the fake painting. Even I didn't know which one he had doctored. But I had a good idea of the real painting that the crooks were looking for. Joan Foster had it. *Sunset Over Amalfi*. And I knew why it was wrong. The painting had the sunset in the wrong place. Sun sets over the west. This painting was facing east. I'd been to Amalfi. Was it a mistake or a clue?

First I had to go and see Estelle Grayson. Her steward reported that she was having hysterics. It was not something that I wanted to witness but it was necessary.

I could hear the hysterics before I was halfway down the corridor. She was disturbing everyone within hearing distance. It had to be stopped. I knocked on the door and she opened it.

She launched herself on to me. A major shock. Several overweight stone of uncontrolled woman knocked me sideways. I hung on to the door.

'Casey, Casey, this is so unfair,' she shrieked.

'Hold on, Estelle,' I gasped. 'I can't help you if you don't let me breathe. Stand back. Take some deep breaths, slowly now.'

'I didn't do anything wrong. I'm innocent. Believe me. Singing is my life. I'm done for. This could ruin my career.'

'I'm well aware that this might give you the reputation of being volatile and a bit unstable and managements might be wary of booking you in the future.' I laid it on thick. 'It's too late now to undo how you behaved at your party but you can try to repair the damage.'

'Tell me how, please,' Estelle sobbed. 'I'll do anything.'

'First of all you must go and grovel before Madame de Leger. Take her a couple of your CDs and a bunch of flowers. She's not a vindictive woman. She'll take it all in good humour and maybe put in a good word for you.'

'I'll do that, I'll do that right away.' She was off to her mirror to repair the damage to her face first. I followed her to the bathroom door.

'And you need to email a genuine letter of remorse to Head Office. Say you were overcome by the emotion of the occasion. Say you didn't know you were drinking vodka, you thought it was orange juice. But you must sound sincere and penitent or they'll know you are just trying to save your job.'

'I will, I will,' said Estelle, painting on a remorseful face, very pale, no false eyelashes. 'Thank you, thank you, Casey. I feel so much better now. Maybe it'll work out all right after all.'

'As you are still technically confined to cabin, I'll arrange for your steward to escort you to Madame de Leger's cabin and then bring you back.'

Her face fell. She had scented freedom. 'Is that really necessary?'

'Yes, of course. Orders from Head Office, so don't argue. Don't argue about anything. Do as I say and it may all blow over.'

'Not like that blooming Hurricane Dora, I hope. I was so ill. I've never been so ill.' Her face brightened. 'I could say I was still suffering from the after-effects of the hurricane, couldn't I?'

She had a wardrobe full of CDs. She rummaged around and pulled out two. They would be top quality. Estelle could certainly sing, especially in a recording studio. All the faults erased.

'Compose your letter of apology and get a copy to me quickly,' I said. 'I'll see that it's emailed straight away. I shouldn't waste any time, Estelle. You've a few bridges to repair.'

I was also thinking of Joe Dornoch, who had clearly cooled but maybe not to past freezing point. He might like the new sincere, remorseful Estelle. She might suddenly look like a soulmate.

Twenty-Seven

At Sea

A crowd was gathering outside the art gallery. It had been closed since Tamara's unexplained disappearance in Acapulco. They were curious about this so-called competition. If I made a few sales, I'd have no idea how to process them. I'd take the money, sign a receipt and run.

Richard Norton had advertised a prize for the winner of the competition. The passengers lovèd prizes. Rumour had spread that it was a free cruise for two but I had my doubts. Conway were not that generous. More like a sweatshirt with logo.

No champagne this time around. No one had authorized it. The sun was a glowing orange globe high in the sky and the heat intense, blistering. The easterly wind was only force two. Hardly a breeze. People were glad to come inside to the air-conditioned cool of the gallery.

I wandered round, looking at the reproductions and prints on the walls and on easels, wondering which one Richard had doctored. There was a fourteen by twelve painting with huge daubs of acrylic paint, mostly white or bright blue, which looked suspect. It was a colourful scene. No one could argue with fishing boats drawn up on a golden shore, a sparkling sea in the background. A few well-behaved seagulls.

'Are you staying around?' I asked Richard. I didn't fancy being on my own. Anything could happen and it probably would.

He shook his head. 'Sorry, I can't. I don't want to be spotted,' he said. 'It might scare off the very person we are trying to entice into the gallery.'

'So who are we trying to entice?'

'I don't know really, Casey. Sorry, it could be anyone. There's a list as long as my arm.'

'How reassuring. What about my arm?' I glanced at the big man. 'You're not being fair to me. Is it a thirty-four inch arm, one an inch?'

'I'll leave you to it,' he said heavily, my attempt at humour not going down too well. Perhaps he was under a lot of pressure and it wasn't a good joke.

I unlocked the gallery doors and a crowd of passengers swarmed in. I hurriedly assembled my entry forms, designed that morning by Susan who prided herself on her presentational skills. She'd done a PowerPoint course. The entry forms were pretty snazzy, including the ship's logo and a background sketch of the cruise route. I liked it.

'Ladies and gentlemen. This is a competition to test your artistic scrutiny.' There was a faint titter. 'One of the paintings on show is a fake. See if you can spot it. Entry forms on my desk. Just put your cabin number and the number of the painting that doesn't stand up to its description in the catalogue. And there's a brilliant prize,' I promised recklessly.

I was asked a lot of questions along the lines of what have we got to do, which painting is it and where are the entry forms? Sometimes I don't think anyone listens to anything. Announcements are a complete waste of time.

'What if we all get the right answer?' someone asked.

'The winning name will be drawn out of a hat,' I ad libbed.

'Who'll do it?'

Neptune, a mermaid, a passing dolphin perhaps? I had no idea. 'The captain, of course. Captain Nicolas. On the bridge. A ceremony with every winning competitor present.'

That seemed to satisfy everyone and there was general milling around the gallery. It was not a competition which took very long. A ballot box, hastily borrowed from the bingo cupboard, was filling up with entry forms. The crowd was beginning to thin out.

'I simply can't make up my mind,' said Mrs Fairweather, hovering between two adjacent paintings. 'They both look fake to me. Can I put down both numbers?'

'Your entry might be disqualified.'

'Miss Jones, which one do you think it is? This Naples coastal picture or this Bengal tiger? Neither of them seem quite right.'

'The tiger looks a bit cross-eyed,' I said.

'Yes, it does or it could be all those facial stripes. They distort the face.'

The gallery was almost empty. I felt a shiver of

fear. This had not worked the way Richard Norton had planned. Soon it would be only Mrs Fairweather dithering about, and me. She had already filled in one entry form and then torn it up, the pieces scattering like confetti.

What had I let myself in for? Samuel had warned me, tried to prevent me going ahead. But I hadn't listened to him. I always knew best, carried away by an enthusiasm to get things done.

Mrs Fairweather was the last person in the gallery now. 'You've been such a help, dear. There, that's my entry.' She popped a multi-fold-ed form into the box. 'Changed my mind at the last moment. It wasn't either of those other two. I spotted a completely different painting. Obviously a fake.'

She left the gallery in a swirl of some pungent eau de cologne. I went down on my knees to pick up the confetti. A draught touched my face as the door swung back. Someone had come in.

'Allow me, miss.'

It was a white-coated steward. He began picking up the pieces of paper. I'd never seen him before. He was in his late twenties, spiky yellow peroxide hair, half-glasses. Then again, maybe I had seen him somewhere before.

'Thank you,' I said, getting up off my knees. He was wearing trainers with flashes, not the white lace-up uniform footwear. 'Have you come here for something?'

'I've come to clear the refreshments,' he said.

'We didn't have any.'

'Not the usual champagne and canapés?'

'No, nothing.'

'There must be some mistake. I was definitely told to come and clear up. Collect the empties.'

'I don't think I've seen you before. Where do you usually work?'

'The Terrace Café, miss.'

'I don't remember you and I eat there most days.'

'I've seen you, miss, many times, tucking into your bacon and eggs.'

He stood up with a handful of paper. He was of medium height yet he had a bulky strength. I looked at his hands. They were boxer's hands, fisty and knuckled, some of the skin was scraped. He wasn't wearing gloves. The catering manager was very particular that the stewards wore gloves, even when clearing.

'Really? How strange. I never eat bacon and eggs. Now, if you wouldn't mind leaving, I have the competition to sort out.'

'Really? But I've seen you eating bacon and eggs with the doctor,' he persisted. 'Your favourite meal, miss.'

I was getting fed up with this. 'He was eating bacon and eggs but I wasn't. Does it matter? Now if you'll excuse me.'

He stood there, crunching the paper in his hands. 'I'm not very happy about the way you are speaking to me,' he began. This was not nice. I did not like this turn of events.

My mouth nearly fell open, but didn't. 'Hold on, there. I'm not very happy about your attitude. I've only been pointing out that I don't need you here and asking you to leave.' I was still being polite.

'But I think you do need me, if you want to stay alive. If you'd like to enjoy another meal at table two, second sitting.'

I felt a scream rising up inside me but it didn't get out. He went over to the entrance doors and calmly shut them, turning the key and shooting the top bolt. 'Now you are going to tell me which is the faked painting, the one with the genuine article underneath. Or am I going to have to force it out of you?'

He turned the lights out. Richard Norton would think that the gallery was empty. That I had gone back to my cabin. That it was all over.

'I don't mind how long I wait,' he added.

I have been in a few tight situations. Passengers, entertainers, even crew, can be unpredictable, but this was without doubt the worst ever. I saw now beyond the yellow hair and the steward's uniform. This was Darin Jack, the absent DJ. He was after the priceless painting, the painting which I felt sure was safely in Joan Foster's stateroom.

'I haven't the slightest idea what you are talking about,' I said, smoothing out entry forms. Why do people have to fold everything into a miniscule wodge? 'This was merely a diversion, something to keep the passengers amused during yet another long day at sea.'

'You're no actress, Miss Jones. I'm not taken in for a moment. So tell me, which is the painting? I suggest you tell me. I have my own artistic skill. A very nice line in carving.' He took out a slim-bladed kitchen knife.

I was on my own. Everyone would think the gallery was closed and empty. I was stuck with a dangerous man. How dangerous, I was not sure. But dangerous enough to be waving a knife. I was not feeling too happy.

'I'm sorry, this competition is only for passengers,' I said, playing the naïve, useless, innocent fool. 'And even I don't have the answer. The only person who knows the true identity of the painting is the captain.'

'You really expect me to believe that?' DJ sat on the edge of the desk, totally at ease, enjoying himself. 'I doubt if the captain, in his busy day, keeping forty-five hundred tons of ship afloat and heading in the right direction, has time to bother himself about a piddling competition.'

I laughed. 'You're exactly right there. This piddling competition itself is hardly worth anything. The faked painting has no real value. It's just a con. A fun thing. We've made it all up actually.'

I saw a momentary flash of uncertainty cross his face. I had rattled him. He didn't know what to believe. Time now to be very careful. I didn't want to be carved up. It was a waiting game.

'Look,' I gabbled on. 'I'll give you an entry form and you can tell me which one you think it is. It's quite fun, guessing. Everyone enjoyed it.'

How was I going to get out of this? Where was Richard Norton? What was he doing? He ought to be checking up on me.

This man was not amused. Not a good sign. His sly eyes went blank and black. The dark face had no expression. He didn't have a soul. This

311

frightened me more than any words.

'Are you going to have a go?'

He said nothing but stroked the knife blade. I only caught a brief glimpse of it moving, a sort of tapered kitchen knife. He slashed at the nearest painting. It was a fast, vicious, vindictive movement. The knife tore through the canvas to the backing. In the half light, I couldn't see which picture it was.

I knew it would not be long before he started on me. My mobile was in my bag under the desk but he would stop me long before I got to it. This was not one of my better days.

My brain was barely working. It was not easy trying to plan an escape route when there was no way out. Samuel would soon be starting his evening surgery. Richard was otherwise engaged. I doubted if Madame de Leger would come to my rescue. It was up to me and my wits, however few of them were left.

'I hope you realize that you have just set off an alarm,' I said. 'Every picture is wired up to a central surveillance system. It won't be long before the Mounties arrive. And you don't really want them to catch you, do you? There are a lot of questions to be answered.'

I'd got him rattled again. I picked up a brass table lamp. There was still a lot of fight left in me. He began roaming like a caged beast. There was a fleck of foam on his mouth.

'What surveillance system?' he snarled. 'I can't see any.'

'You're not supposed to see it. Haven't you heard of ultra-violet sensitive microns?' I asked, hastily inventing. 'It's the very latest. It imparts the slightest movement to a main centre. Any minute now they'll be breaking down the door.'

'I don't believe you.'

'Can't you hear that vibration? It means the system has been alerted.'

There was no vibration apart from the normal thrumming of the engines. That low throbbing that was always there if you listened hard enough. Most of the time, it was a simple background noise, almost imperceptible, that one eventually took as normal. As normal as the sound of the sea and the wind.

DJ imagined that he could hear it. He was backing off.

'Don't think I won't be back,' he said. 'I haven't finished with you. I've some scores to settle up.'

I said nothing. I didn't want to break the spell. The harder he listened the more he would think he heard the vibration. It was the only weapon I had. His own fear.

He unlocked the door and slid back the bolt. He still wasn't sure. 'Just don't do anything that might make me angry,' he said. 'When I'm angry I can be really nasty.'

He was out of the door in a flash of yellow hair. I wanted to run outside but my legs wouldn't work. They were like lead. They had forgotten how to obey commands. After a few wobbles, I was across the gallery and hanging on to the door frame. The evening air and light was glorious. I wanted to float on deck and drink in the freedom. Drink in the sea, the endless sky, fresh air.

'Hi there, how did the competition go?' It was Ray Roeder. He was grinning, well understanding the necessity to fill in show time when we were at sea for a long stretch. 'Hey, are you all right? You look as if you have seen a ghost.'

I clung on to his arm. 'Please take me up on deck, Ray. I must have some air, see the waves, get out of this place.'

'Of course,' he said gallantly. 'Anything you say, Casey. Let's go walk.'

'I need to walk,' I whispered. 'Don't let anyone take me away from you. Hang on to me.'

He must have thought I was raving mad. A lunatic entertainments director. You get all sorts.

'Never, of course not,' he said, not understanding a word of what was going on. 'I am glued to your side, ma'am. Let's go look at the horizon.'

'Thank you, thank you,' I said. I was lost for any better words.

Twenty-Eight

At Sea

Ray was kindness itself. He bought a bottle of Macon Fuissé, a good white Burgundy, at the bar and steered me towards a secluded table on deck. Two glasses hung from his fingers. Perhaps he filled in resting time as a barman.

The sea had decided to calm me and was at its most blue and tranquil. It was like a silken quilt, rising and falling with a mermaid's breathing.

'Casey, you are safe now,' he said. 'Whatever it was that scared the daylights out of you, it's gone now.'

'He's gone – for the moment.'

'Oh dear, not a difficult passenger?'

'No, worse than that. More than difficult. I can't really tell you but I am warning you, never, never sit on table two, second sitting.'

He laughed, pouring out the wine. 'The table with the death jinx? No fear, you won't catch me within a hundred yards. I prefer the Grill upstairs anyway.'

'Have you ever seen a steward up there with very peroxide hair?'

'No, I can't say I have.' His face lost the laughter lines. He looked serious and older. 'Are you trying to tell me that something is going on, something that is not all luxury cruising to exotic places with high class entertainment thrown in at the end of the day?'

'I can't tell you,' I said, the alcohol numbing my nerves. It was a totally classy white wine. 'Passengers mustn't get a whiff of this.'

'I'm not a passenger.'

'Nor top entertainers.'

'Promise not to tell.'

It was hard not to confide in Ray when he was being so attentive. But I didn't know who I could trust not to spread the rumours. We didn't want a full-scale panic on board. I imagined passengers demanding that the captain make an unscheduled port of call and authorize planes to fly them all home. My contract would not be renewed. I needed my new career.

'Don't worry, Casey,' Ray went on. 'I know enough about cruising to understand when information is sensitive. But you were really scared back there and that shouldn't happen to a nice young woman like you. Surely you should report it to the security officer?'

'Yes, Richard Norton. Yes, I should and I will. But not quite yet. I'm enjoying these unexpected moments of fresh air, the lovely sea, and your company, of course.'

'Of course, the right company is essential.' But he wasn't taken in. He knew he was a stand-in. Any normal human being passing by the gallery would have done. He was twenty years older than me, but age didn't mean that much these days and he carried it well. He was younger than his years. And I was ageing by the minute. Put my name on a Zimmer frame. And can I have silver tassels on the handles, please?

'Did you ever meet Reg Hawkins, the magician, on the cruise carousel?' I asked, changing the subject. We knew very little about the man as a person.

'Sure, I've met him many times, known him for years. A brilliant magician, performs even in a gale force eight. How he did those tricks, so close to his audience, was a miracle. He deserved a better career. For some reason, he never quite made it. He should have been on television, a programme of his own.'

'You probably know that he was found dead on-board, inside his magic box?'

'Yes, of course. I was very upset when I heard that. A really nasty business. Yet strangely enough, I'm not surprised. He always seemed to have an air of doom around him. I don't know what it was but the last few times I've met him, he seemed very preoccupied and not himself.'

'Like he was being blackmailed or something,' I threw in.

'Maybe. But he was certainly not his normal cheerful self.'

'And Rosanna is also on-board.'

'Rosanna?' Ray was completely amazed. 'His daughter? But that's wonderful. I'm her godfather, not that I'm a good one. I simply send a decent cheque on her birthday and Christmas.'

'Your goddaughter? That's such good news. Would you like to see her?'

'I certainly would.'

Hallelujah. Brilliant thought, Casey. I'd arrange for them to meet. It would stop Rosanna from sliding into any sort of depression. She needed help too.

'We walk the Promenade Deck each day. She's under some sort of custody for being a stowaway. Perhaps you'd like to join us? I'm sure I can arrange it.'

He chuckled. 'I'd like that. I've known Rosanna since she was so high. I'll bring along some lollipops.'

'I think she's grown out of lollipops. I'll go fetch her.'

'When we've finished the wine,' said Ray.

But she hadn't grown out of lollipops. Ray brought iced lollipops and we attempted to walk the Promenade Deck three abreast, sucking the iced sticks, but it didn't work. I slipped behind and let them talk. Rosanna was over the moon, seeing Ray again. She hadn't known he was onboard. She had no way of knowing. No one gave her a ship's newspaper.

'Ray ... Ray, Uncle Ray, this is absolutely marvellous, seeing you here,' she said, hugging his arm. 'My dad's died, you know. It's so awful.'

'I know and I'm so sorry. Not so much of the uncle, please. I've got to think of my image.'

At some point along the walk Richard Norton joined us. He was full of apologies for not being around the gallery during the competition. He had some computer blip. I was not impressed.

'I was bait,' I said. 'You set me up and the bastard took a bite, with a kitchen knife. Why weren't you there? I needed you. I was nearly

318

victim number four.'

'I'm really sorry, truly I am, Casey, but I couldn't get away. I wouldn't want anything to happen to you. So he did turn up? I thought he would. Exactly what happened?'

Richard wasn't listening properly. He hadn't turned a whisker on the word knife. I could have said axe, tyre iron, battering ram.

'Yes, he turned up. Yes, he wanted to know which was the fake painting. Yes, he pulled a knife on me. Anything else you want to know before I sock you squarely on the jaw?'

It was the Burgundy talking courage. I couldn't sock anyone but Richard crimsoned and looked alarmed. He had let me down and I was not pleased. Maybe it showed on my face. I hoped it did.

'Perhaps you'd like to tell me what he looks like now. I expect he's changed his appearance.'

'He has bright spiky peroxide hair, is clean shaven and wearing a stolen steward's uniform but with his own trainers. But I should imagine that's all changed by now. He'll have shaved off the hair and tossed the uniform overboard.'

'Can you put a name to him?'

'I think it's Darin Jack, the DJ with a false passport who we thought had absconded in Barbados, but hadn't. I only met him briefly when he signed on at Southampton. He'd merely pretended to jump ship at Barbados. But whether he's the man we are looking for, I don't know. He certainly threatened me in no uncertain manner and it was really frightening.'

Richard put his hand under my elbow as if to

assure me of his protection. 'I'm really sorry, Casey. It won't happen again.'

'Too true it won't happen again. I'll make sure it doesn't and I won't go along with any more of your hare-brained schemes. You can be your own decoy. I'll get a duck suit for you from wardrobe.'

I felt better for saying it, but my heart was still fluttering at the thought of those moments locked in the gallery with Darin Jack. I'd been so scared that I hadn't thought to find out who he was. Now that was a big minus. Always get the name of the person about to knife you.

'I'm glad you haven't lost your sense of humour,' he said hopefully.

'I was about to lose a lot of other things,' I said. I was getting mad again now. The fear replaced by anger. 'He pulled a knife on me.'

Richard's face went white. It obviously hadn't registered the first time. He scanned my face and arms for nicks, counted my ears.

'Did you get h-hurt?' He was not only concerned for me but for himself. He would be in big trouble if he had knowingly put me in danger.

'Only my nerves, fragile and shredded. I really thought he was going for me. It was one of those very long and thin kitchen knives.'

Richard Norton was on his phone immediately. 'We'll pick him up right away for threatening behaviour. Yellow blonde hair, spiky, steward's uniform. What kind of trainers?'

'White trainers with red flashes and some sort of logo. I didn't spend much time looking at his feet. This is a waste of time. He won't be looking like that now.'

'People have been caught on worse descriptions. Lots of criminals forget to change their shoes. Feet are a comfort zone.'

I thought of my strappy evening shoes with skyscraper heels. 'Not for me, they're not.'

'I'm really sorry, Casey,' he went on. 'Thank you for coping. How did the competition go?'

Now he wanted to talk about the competition. Thank you, buster. 'Very popular but the entries need to be judged. I don't know the answer and I don't have the prize,' I said. 'Was it the white and blue fishing scene, all lumps of paint, put on with a knife?'

I flinched at the last word but he didn't seem to notice.

'No, that's authentic. I've met that artist. He lives in Benidorm and churns them out by the dozen. The fake one is *The Bengal Tiger*.'

'Oh dear, Mrs Fairweather thought it was that one and then changed her mind. She will be upset. By the way, what's the prize?'

Richard looked ill at ease. I'd never seen a man so discomforted. 'It's nothing special. A few vouchers.'

'Let me guess. Vouchers that have to be spent at the art gallery? Am I right?'

'Something like that. Let me know the name of the winner and we'll send a letter to their cabin.'

'Or winners. There might be several. No public award winning ceremony then, not like the writers' awards? No shaking hands with the captain and photos on the website?'

'I think we'd better play it down, just in case.'

'Just in case of what?'

But Richard wasn't saying. He sure was acting strangely.

'Very wise, Richard. Sorry, but I have to go. Another change coming up. One of my many during the day. I'd like to get back to the safety of my normal routine among non knife-throwing cabaret artists and staff.'

'Your photo got slashed.'

I'd forgotten that. So much had happened since then. Susan Brook was obviously the culprit. That's why I had left it in place, to show her that I didn't care what she thought.

My phone was ringing when I got back to my cabin. Rosanna had cheered up after her walk and talk with Ray Roeder. It must have helped immensely to know that she had an ally and old friend on board.

'Don't you ever answer your phone, Miss Jones?' asked a chilling voice. 'That's not very wise, is it?'

I slammed down the phone fast. He was still on-board.

Twenty-Nine

At Sea

'Miss Jones, may I speak with you?'

It was one of the young waiters from the Windsor Dining Room. I knew the face but not the name. He looked worried and apprehensive.

'Of course. What's the matter?'

He swallowed hard, his Adam's apple bobbing up and down. I had a feeling that this was going to be a long rigmarole and he was going to spill out a lifetime of personal problems. But he was young and far away from home.

'You remember Mr Foster? The gentleman who died of a heart attack on table two, early in the cruise?'

'Yes, Mr Foster. Very sad.'

'I was serving on the table that evening, as assistant waiter, vegetables and rolls, horse-radish sauce, you know, and clearing plates.'

All along I'd known there was something that I had missed that evening. I could still visualize the scene round the table and the spurt of cherry-red blood. This young man might be able to jog my memory. I nodded, not wanting to break his train of thought.

'I was part of the team that cleared the table

afterwards, double-quick. You understand? Everything has to be cleared away and re-laid. Cannot upset the other passengers. Very important.'

I nodded again. He was getting to the point of his story.

'It was all properly cleared, Miss Jones, I swear. But I forgot one thing. There was a jar of tablets beside Mr Foster's place, opened. I screwed the top on and put it in my pocket, without thinking. I forgot to hand it to the dining-room manager as I should have done. It is a rule. Anything found on a table must be handed in. I could lose my job. I cannot sleep because of the worry.'

I knew it was a strict rule. He could lose his job. Then his family would suffer. No money being sent home. But I was not going to report him.

'An easy mistake, really,' I reassured him. 'You were in shock. It was a dreadful thing to happen right in front of you, a death at your table, especially if you were serving Mr Foster. Where are the tablets now?'

'They are here. I kept them safe.' He handed over a small screw-top jar. They were multi-vitamin tablets. A well-known brand.

'Don't worry any more,' I said. 'I'll return them to Mrs Foster. There will be no need to explain how I got them. After all, I don't even know your name.'

His face broke out into a big smile, perfect teeth gleaming. 'I would be so grateful to you. Thank you, thank you, Miss Jones. Ahmed said

324

you would help me. He said you were a very kind lady.'

'Very kind,' I echoed.

There was time to take the tablets to Samuel. He ought to look at them, check them out. I remembered the scene quite clearly now. I had seen Mr Foster pop a couple of tablets into his mouth and down them with a drink of water. I looked at the directions on the label. Take with food. He'd taken them with food.

Samuel hurried out of his surgery, white jacket, immaculately pressed white trousers, stethoscope round his neck.

'Yes, Casey? Is this urgent? I'm busy.'

'These are Mr Foster's vitamin tablets. He took a couple almost immediately before he died. I saw him take them. Maybe they were doctored. Sorry, that's not meant to be a joke.'

'Multi-vitamins. So how do you think they could be doctored? Like injected with a syringe?'

It wasn't easy telling him. Part of me was wondering if I would ever know him better, if we would ever be closer and not simply friends who bantered and teased and argued. Those grey eyes often seemed to be saying something different to me, but I couldn't read them. I didn't know the code.

'They're gelatine shell capsules. You could carefully prise them apart and tip out the genuine contents. Replace with a different substance, then put the two halves of the capsule together again.'

'You do have one heck of an imagination.'

'But it is possible. I've tried it. The assassin's alibi would then be perfect. No one could have any idea when Mr Foster would take the doctored capsule. It could be any time, any day, anywhere.'

'I suppose you won't give me any peace till I've looked at this lot,' Dr Mallory groaned. 'I've enough to do.'

'Thanks.'

'You owe me a drink.'

'I'll buy you two.'

It was a busy morning and I was deep in speed-reading a rash of emails, when Dr Mallory phoned my mobile. I was trying to eat a shrimp and salad sandwich at the same time. Quite a feat.

'Who's a clever girl? I'll buy you three drinks, Casey,' said the good doctor. 'Spot on, Sherlock. There are slight traces of cyanide on the outer casing of the other capsules, obviously rubbed off from the doctored capsule. There'll have to be a PM now when we get back to Southampton. I'm going to inform the authorities but I doubt if they'll fly anyone out. No point.'

I sat back with a sense of relief but it was quickly replaced by fear. We had a murderer on-board. What if all the deaths were linked and I was still involved? It was not a pleasant thought.

'But are they linked?' I asked wearily. 'Reg Hawkins and Nigel Garten? Is it the same murderer?'

'How should I know? I'm only the doctor on board ship. I'm not a pathologist or detective. I only house the bodies till we reach Southampton. Ask your friend, Richard Norton.'

He put the phone down. I was rooted to the spot. Never before had I witnessed the slightest ill humour or temper in Dr Mallory. But there had certainly been a snap to those last remarks. The snap had almost bitten my nose.

'Thanks. I will.' The smile on my face only lasted till I reached the lift on my way to Richard Norton's office.

Later I wandered the Promenade Deck, barely recognizing anyone. I suddenly felt that I didn't have any friends on this ship. That was true. No one was exactly my friend. I knew dozens of people, several hundred by name, but none of them were actual friends. If I was murdered in my cabin tonight, Ahmed would be the chief mourner.

'Miss Jones? You are deep in thought. Care to join me for a few moments?' It was Madame de Leger, sitting in a deck lounger. She had a beautiful silvery-grey pashmina wrapped round her shoulders. There was occasionally a coolness in the air since we had left the Caribbean. She patted the empty chair beside her.

I sat down gratefully. She was always good company. She looked a little pale today as if the long cruise was a week too long and she wanted to go home. Many passengers found the same company, day after day, somewhat tedious.

'Are you ready to go home?' I asked.

'Oh yes,' she said. 'I should like to go home now. I've done what I came to achieve so for me the cruise is over. It has been very pleasant and

I'm glad that I came, but this is my last cruise.'

'Surely not? You'll come on lots more cruises.' It was the standard reply.

'No, my dear. I know when I have reached safe harbour point. It's not something I readily admit, but I am quite old. One should retire gracefully before the wheelchair phase sets in. I don't want to be wheeled round with people feeling sorry for me.'

'What will you do instead?'

'Stay at home and continue writing my memoirs. You never know, I may even get them published. People like reading about wartime exploits. But enough about me. Tell me why you are looking so worried.'

'It's all the sad deaths on table two. I can't get them out of my mind.'

'Natural causes, my dear, and accidents. Mr Foster died of a heart attack, what could be more natural? And poor Mr Garten, that was an accident. He fell overboard. Perhaps he'd had a little too much to drink and slipped. He did enjoy a drink or two.'

'It's quite hard to slip over a rail that high.' I indicated the height of the rail opposite us. Madame de Leger didn't know about Reg Hawkins. Perhaps that was an accident too. Maybe he had been rehearsing a new trick that went wrong.

She leaned towards me, a little frown adding to the fine lines on her skin. Her white hair was beautifully coiled round her head as usual, but a few strands had escaped in the breeze and they had a youthful look.

'May I ask a favour?'

'Yes, please do.'

'If I should die on the cruise, of natural causes of course,' she added with a faintly ironic smile, 'I want to be tipped overboard into the sea, like they do in films. Perhaps the jazz band could play something appropriate on deck, Cole Porter perhaps or Gershwin. I don't want to be taken back to England in a box and all those forms to fill in.'

'But you wouldn't have to fill in the forms,' I said ridiculously. Her favour had taken me by surprise.

She laughed. 'You always make me laugh. I don't want to be a trouble to anyone. Food for the fishes. Genuine recycling.'

'You are not going to die on the cruise,' I said firmly. 'You are going to go home and finish writing your life story and get it published. I shall be the first to buy a copy.'

'I shall send you one, complimentary, signed and all that. Now, I think it's time for a little sleep before dinner, or I shall have no appetite for that wonderful food. Nice talking to you.'

Madame de Leger got up and walked quite briskly inside. She didn't walk like an old person. I shivered. It had turned cooler or was it my imagination?

Then I saw a blue soft-covered notebook, tucked down the side of her chair. Her writing book. She'd left it behind. I got up to follow her but she had already disappeared and I didn't know her cabin number. I'd have to hand it in at Reception and get them to forward it to her cabin.

The pages flicked open in the breeze. It was full of small, neat handwriting. Some in English and some in French. Most of the entries were dated. I read a few lines. I didn't feel guilty about reading them. After all, she did say she was going to give me a copy.

June, 1940. Dunkirk. The shelling had been going on all night. We were hiding in an old farmhouse near the coast. They let us sleep in the barn but there was no sleep for us. The English officer wrapped me in his coat. It was covered in mud. Then later I slept in his arms. It was the only way we could find comfort in each other, trés domage.

In the morning, the shelling was worse. They said there were ships on the beaches of Dunkirk to take off the troops. Would they take me? After all, I was on their side. I worked for them. I risked my life too. But when I went outside, my bicycle had gone. I'd hidden it under some old sacking. The English officer had taken it. He was the only one I had told. Mon Dieu. *I would have to walk. My boots were wet and rotten.*

I put on his uniform coat and felt in the pockets in case there was any food. There was a letter addressed to him. I sat in a ditch and read it. His wife had given birth to a son. She was going to call him George. George Foster.

I sat back, unable to read on. George Foster. So

this was the proof of what I had begun to suspect from piecing together Maria de Leger's story. This war-time child would be about the same age as our George Foster, deceased. The writing blurred as I made myself read on.

The beaches were covered with the dead and dying. I did what I could to ease their deaths, held their hands, said prayers for their souls. The ships had all gone and so had the English officer. I found my bicycle, twisted and bent, thrown into a sand dune.

So much was abandoned, guns, ammunition, vehicles. I tried to start a small jeep which was not too damaged. That's when the Germans found me and dragged me out on to the road.

I spent the next years doing hard labour in a German prison camp. They could not prove that I was a spy. After all, I was French. I will not write about those years now. Maybe one day I will.

I closed the book. If the officer who stole the young Maria's bicycle was George Foster's father, then this gave weight to my previous suspicions that she had a motive. A motive which had stayed dormant in her heart for many years. It was an act of treachery to steal her bicycle after sleeping in each other's arms. And Madame de Leger would have access to cyanide.

Madame de Leger was returning on to the deck, looking a little anxious. She spotted me standing, holding her book. There was a sigh of relief.

'Ah, thank goodness. You found my writing book! I couldn't remember where I had left it. Such a nuisance, being forgetful.'

I handed it over to her. 'All that hard work, all your writing. You've been very busy.'

'Still it has kept me occupied,' she said, tucking it under her arm. 'This cruise has been very productive, one way or another.'

Then I remembered her other words. She had achieved what she had come on this cruise to do. Did that include making the innocent George Foster pay for his father's selfishness?

A crime of passion. After all, she was French.

Thirty

At Sea

I had deliberately put the unexpected phone call out of my mind. Nor did I tell anyone. There'd be an armed guard outside my door if Richard Norton got wind of it. But I left the phone off the hook. I didn't want any more calls.

This was becoming more confusing by the minute. There was Estelle to keep an eye on, also Rosanna, the Foster family group – including Joan and Helen and Amanda – the presence on board of a valuable painting under layers of thicker paint. And with Madame de Leger added to my list, I hardly had time to do my own work.

'I have made a decision,' said Susan, from her desk opposite me.

'Oh, yes?' This would be riveting. She was going to audition for the *X Factor*?

'I have decided to change my surname.'

Now I did look interested. 'Wow, Susan. Why?'

'Brook is so ordinary.'

'I think it's rather nice. All rural sounding, willow trees and kingfishers, etc.'

'I'm adding an *e* to the end of it. I'm Susan Brooke, with an *e* now.'

The anti-climax was too much for me. I tried not to laugh. 'You'd better tell Admin then,' I mumbled between suppressed giggles. 'So they get your pay cheque right. Don't want it going to the wrong Brook.'

I managed the weekly meeting of heads of departments without dropping any clangers. Most of the meeting was dealing with complaints. It always amazes me how many there are. People complain about the smallest thing. It did not seem necessary to inform them of Susan's new surname. She could do it herself.

Caution Casey. The beady Susan Brooke with an *e* might be making notes for all I knew. She still had both eyes on my job. My softening up had clearly not worked despite adding the delectable doctor as a bonus.

So many days at sea sometimes blur together, especially when it was the fathomless Atlantic

Ocean. In some areas, it's over 30,000 feet deep. I had to remind myself of the daily programme of events, the show productions, the guest entertainers, the different lecturers. Check everything, Casey. The daily temperature was steadily dropping. Our last port of call would be Ponta Delgada, in the Azores. The passengers were itching to set foot ashore, anywhere. Blackpool would do. I couldn't blame them. This was a long stretch at sea.

I scribbled out a list of suspects:

* Darin Jack – vicious DJ intent on finding the valuable painting.
* Joan Foster – perhaps she hated her husband, George.
* Helen Banesto – perhaps she hated George for jilting her.
* Maria de Leger – she had reason to hate George's father.
* Nigel Garten – also after the painting, now dead himself.
* Tamara Fitzgibbons – involved with the painting, now kidnapped?
* AOP – any other person?

This was now becoming absurd. I told myself to forget the whole thing. It was none of my business. There was enough going on on-board without my getting involved. I should be worrying about which dress to wear, not trying to solve suspicious murders. Not thinking was easier than thinking any day.

An email arrived from Richard Norton. It was

an official communication and began 'Dear Miss Jones'. It warned me to stay away from his investigations and not to talk to anyone at all about the various circumstances involved. Yours sincerely, etc. etc.

I was furious. I was the one who had acted as bait and nearly got knifed for her trouble. Now he was sending me some pompous letter telling me to keep my nose out of his business.

I sent off a reply immediately. 'Since when has my phone not worked? Since when have you forgotten where my office is? Since when have you stopped being a friend?' I didn't bother to sign it. He'd know who it was from.

He was round in minutes, sweating profusely. 'Look, Casey,' he said immediately. 'It's not safe for me to be seen talking to you.'

'Not safe for you or not safe for me?' I said.

He didn't answer. 'Look,' he said again. 'There's more to this than we ever suspected.'

'I've been telling you that since day one. No one ever listens to me.'

'Reg Hawkins' magic box has been broken into. It was being stored down in the stern hold. But someone took a crowbar to it.'

'They were after the mobile scanning system which Reg was being blackmailed into smuggling aboard. It's called an SEM – a scanning electron microscope. Ask Rosanna. She'll tell you how he was scared to death.'

'How do you know all this? So where is this SEM now, this microscope?'

'Perhaps it went overboard with Nigel Garten? Now that would be fool's justice, wouldn't it?'

'But someone has spotted the painting without the device.'

'They knew in which direction the sun sets. It was either an artistic mistake or a very clever clue left by the artist. I prefer to think it was a clever clue. Spot the deliberate mistake, and bingo, underneath is a valuable Cézanne.'

'How do you know it's a Cézanne?'

'I don't. But it came up on the Internet. One of his paintings disappeared from sight, some years ago, called *The Orange Sea* or something like that. Or it could be another painter and another painting. How are we ever to know?'

This little chat was clearing my brain. The other half was working out how Maria might have affected her revenge. It was cunning. The same brand of multi-vitamins was on sale in the small chemist's shop that sold medications, toiletries and photographic equipment. Maybe she had seen George downing his daily boost with food. She bought an identical jar, doctored a pill, and somehow switched jars. It could be done. A casual conversation at table two, a dropped scarf, a deft hand. Maria would have had a lot of practice at that in her days of hiding out in France.

Richard Norton left. We were both at sea.

Mrs Foster was walking the Promenade Deck, quite alone. It seemed she wasn't dressing for tonight's dinner. She'd lost interest in clothes. Maybe she wasn't going to eat.

'I'm sorry if I'm intruding but I wanted to ask if I could be of any help when we return to Southampton. Obviously, there are family members who will need to know the sad news.' My offer was genuine but it was not solely from my good nature.

'Thank you, Miss Jones, but Helen, my sister, is going to come back with me. She'll help me with all the arrangements.'

'That's good. I suppose Mr Foster's parents are no longer alive?'

'His mother died some years ago, but his father is still going strong at over ninety. He fought in the war, you know, was at Dunkirk. Medals and bars. Lots of decorations for bravery and a high rank. He didn't quite make a general, but he was a brigadier. He doted on George, who was a war baby, you know.'

So it was confirmed. The bicycle thief was still alive and living on a good army pension. No doubt Maria had checked that. Her revenge was even more devastating.

Joan Foster turned to me. 'I want to thank you for what you have done for Helen and me. I'm not sure how you engineered it, but I think you did and I'm really grateful. It was all very silly and such a long time ago. We need each other now.'

'I'm glad, too,' I said. 'Amanda and your sister will be a real support. Are you dining with us tonight?'

'In the Grill, I think. Some time later. Amanda is going to join me.'

'I'll leave you to your walk. This is the best time of the day.'

It had been a very long day. I could hardly remember when it had begun. Hours and hours ago and so much had changed since then. It was like the lovesick pirate, Frederick, who lived a year in an hour, a lifetime in a day, or something like that. My Gilbert and Sullivan is a bit shaky.

I changed into a cream silk tie blouse and matching trousers with an embroidered navy kimono jacket. It would be cool when the sun set and I was already feeling the cold. My flimsy long dresses could go back in store till the next Caribbean cruise. If I survived this one. I was beginning to have my doubts.

'So is my gorgeous cruise director ready for her evening stint?' It was Samuel Mallory, in full dress uniform, ready to preside at a party being thrown for some group. The POSH club perhaps.

'Of course,' I said, drinking in his quite dazzling appearance. George Clooney had better look to his laurels. And George Clooney was a dream. He was the sexiest man alive on the planet.

'Care to join me later and we can swop emails from the security officer.'

'Did you get one too?'

'Don't worry. I think everyone except the sauce chef got one. He's panicking. And the nearer we get to Southampton, the more he's panicking. The authorities will be down on him faster than a rifle shot.'

'Don't say that,' I shuddered. 'That's one thing we haven't had. Someone being shot. I'll see you later then. You'll find me somewhere.'

'I'll always be able to find you.' It was a throwaway line.

He flicked me a quick smile. I floated away,

superbly happy. No matter that Samuel didn't really mean it. Simply that he said it was enough.

It was a Ray Roeder special this evening. A tribute to Frank Sinatra, all the standards, the favourites. The show was an absolute knock-out and his CDs sold faster than strawberries and cream at Wimbledon. I think he winked at me as I swept on to the stage.

Those old Sinatra songs still had the power to move me. He was long before my teenage time but Roeder had somehow captured the man's voice. Close your eyes and Frankie was there.

I had decided between showering and washing my hair that I was not going to mention a word about reading Maria's memoirs and the contents. No one would ever suspect her. It could remain an unsolved mystery how George Foster's vitamin pills were laced with cyanide. It couldn't be proved. As long as no one else was accused of the crime. As far as I was concerned, I knew nothing.

What would be the point of arresting Maria and taking her to court? She was over eighty, easily. She was a war heroine in her own right. No sane judge would send her to prison. Perhaps an ankle tag while staying at the Ritz would be suitable custody.

Samuel was waiting for me outside the Princess Lounge. He was as immaculate as ever, even if his hair was a little ruffled. Some wandering female hands?

'I've been out on deck,' he explained. 'It got very hot.'

'These parties often are.'

'Have you had any supper?'

'There wasn't time.'

'Up to the Grill, then. They can rustle up an omelette in minutes. You can't exist all day without any food.'

'I had a shrimp sandwich.'

'So you think you can exist all day on a few shrimps? A seagull eats more than you do. This way.'

I followed Samuel to the lift up to the Lido Deck. The daytime Terrace Café had undergone its evening transformation with tablecloths, candles, place settings with cutlery and glasses. Not a tray or disinfectant wipe in sight. I could not see Mrs Foster and Amanda. Perhaps they had finished and left.

Samuel ordered two omelettes, one cheese and one mushroom, side salads and a bottle of Chardonnay. 'You can decide which one you want when they arrive. I can see you are too tired to make decisions at the moment.'

'Thank you,' I said. 'It's been one of those days, lasting about a hundred years. So much has happened.'

'Care to tell me about it?' he said, pouring the wine. 'Doctor confidentiality and all that.'

'I can't tell anyone.'

'So you know who slipped a capsule of cyanide into George Foster's jar of vitamins?' He was making a lucky guess.

'Yes, but I'm not sure and I'm never going to say.'

'Is that wise?'

'Funnily enough, it's very wise. Some pots are better never stirred.'

Samuel didn't laugh though I knew he wanted to. The laughter only got as far as his eyes. Our omelettes arrived and I took the less calorific mushroom one. I ate enough cheese to sink a ship.

There was little conversation as I was eating against the clock. The second show would be starting soon and I had to be there to do the introduction.

'Slow down. You'll get indigestion. You've twelve more minutes. I'll make sure you are there and get them to put the rest of the salad into a box to nibble in the wings.'

'Would you? I don't want to go on stage with omelette on my chin.'

'No chance of that.' Samuel leaned across the table and flicked a corner of his napkin across my chin. 'All gone now, baby.'

He could be quite bewitching. Maybe it was pity on his part. I was a stand-alone female who never seemed to have any leisure and was rarely surrounded by admiring male passengers. I could have pointed out that there were more than enough women on-board for the male contingent. They outnumbered the men four to one.

The second showing went spectacularly well. Ray Roeder came off, dripping with sweat. I handed him a towel. He nodded his thanks, mopping his forehead, no breath left. He went on again for a second round of applause.

I sailed on and described his performance in glowing terms. He took a third bow.

'That's enough,' he said as he came off. 'I need a drink.' He also needed a shower, fresh clothes and ten minutes with his feet up.

'We're selling your CDs in the foyer,' I reminded him. 'Sorry, you're still on duty.'

'Give me five minutes and I'll be there to sign them.'

Dr Mallory was also there, surrounded by his usual blonde harem, lashes fluttering and listening to his every word. He gave me a slight acknowledgement which I could not decipher. Then he tapped his watch which could mean anything. Then he smiled and the look in his eyes told me that he'd see me later.

That was all I wanted to know.

I was almost asleep when he joined me in a corner of the Galaxy Lounge where I was listening to the dance music. He handed me a plastic box of salad, watercress and radishes and a glass of orange juice with ice.

'I thought you might like to know that I have examined Reg Hawkins' magic box. It's quite likely that he could have shut himself in it and suffocated. It has a complicated set of locking devices and if he was crawling around inside, in the dark, he could easily have locked himself in.'

'What about the scratches and cuts?'

'They could have been caused as he tried to get out or attract attention. He had little space to move and there are traces of blood inside the box.'

'Are you trying to tell me that his death could have been accidental, self-inflicted?'

He nodded. 'Possibly.'

342

'Two out of three, one to go,' I said, munching through a mouthful of rocket. 'We might arrive at Southampton with a clean slate at this rate.'

'I doubt it,' said Samuel. 'Nigel Garten certainly didn't throw himself overboard. That blow on the head wasn't accidental.'

'Could he have hit his head on the way down? Or been caught by a propeller?'

'Totally different type of wounds. This was definitely a blow from behind with a heavy object, no grazing or slicing.'

I shuddered. It quite put me off the radishes. He took the box away from me. 'Had enough?'

'Yes, thank you. I think I've had enough of today too.'

'I prescribe a walk round the deck in the fresh air before going to bed. No arguing. Doctor's orders.'

So that's how I came to be walking round the deck at midnight, under a dark and starry sky, with the most attractive man on-board who was lightly holding my hand. I suppose he thought I might throw myself overboard. Overwork can do funny things to the mind.

Thirty-One

At Sea

'Susan! Good heavens! What on earth do you think you are doing?'

I had slept well for once, was up early for my morning mile, breakfasted in the Terrace Café and was surprised to find Susan in the office before me. She was not known for punctuality.

She was standing by the shredder feeding paperwork into it. I caught sight of a familiar maroon cover.

'Susan, that's a passport. Are you crazy? We never shred a passport. What are you doing?'

She looked flustered. 'I was just clearing out stuff. We accumulate such a lot of paper.'

'Whose passport is that? Show me.'

She handed it to me reluctantly. Several pages had already been torn out and shredded.

It was the forged passport of Darin Jack. I had put all his paperwork together in a file to return to Head Office once we got to Southampton. They would be looking into his references and bank details, etc. But no longer it seemed. Susan had successfully destroyed most of the evidence. And it was one of those hi-tech shredders that went crossways as well as lengthways, so no

344

glueing the bits back together.

'I can't believe this,' I said, trying to contain my anger. 'What do you think you were doing? We needed this evidence.' I managed to stop myself saying things like you stupid girl, damned fool, brainless idiot and other choice phrases. Mutiny in the office wouldn't help the situation. Susan's lower lip dropped.

'I thought I was being helpful,' she said, in an effort to retrieve the situation.

'What else have you destroyed?'

She looked terrified as well she might be. 'It's only a few bits and pieces.'

Her bits and pieces turned out to be the whole of the Reg Hawkins' file and most of her own personal file. She went a biological shade of white.

'Susan, have you gone totally out of your mind? This is gross incompetence. What did you think you were doing? There'd better be a damned good explanation.' An unexpected spurt of anger scalded me. I was red hot, rage soaked, almost incandescent.

Was it gross incompetence or a deliberate act to destroy evidence? It could be either. My mind went into overdrive. Had a vital clue been loitering in my own office all the time? Something that I hadn't noticed?

'I'm very sorry, Casey, but I am feeling very unwell,' Susan said, holding on to the edge of the desk. 'I'd like to go to the surgery and see the doctor.'

'Good idea, Susan,' I said, changing my voice carefully into neutral. 'You've obviously been overworking. Why not have the rest of the day off and take it easy? Sit on the deck and read a good book.'

'Thank you, I will,' she said, scrambling about and gathering her bag and escaping out of the office. She looked pretty awful. Drained and pasty.

As soon as I heard the outer door close, I was on the phone to Samuel. I didn't care if it was morning surgery and he was in the middle of a consultation.

'Sorry if I'm interrupting something,' I said, before he could complain. 'But Susan Brook is on her way down to you, feeling ill. I've just caught her shredding files. Important files belonging to Darin Jack, Reg Hawkins and her own.'

'So?' he said patiently. 'Is that infectious?'

'Can you give her an extra strong sedative or something? Something that will knock her out for the rest of the day while I make some enquiries?'

'Don't be ridiculous, Casey. Of course, I can't knock her out. Phone me back when you have got a more sensible suggestion.' I had interrupted something important.

He put the phone down. No help there. Richard Norton? Not after that email. The captain? Hardly the right person. Who could I turn to? There was no one. I was on my own for this one.

I began clearing up the documents Susan had removed from the filing cabinet. The name Tamara Fitzgibbons was typed on a cover. Where had Susan got that file from? Art gallery staff were not my responsibility. They were part of the marketing outlets. A totally different department on-shore and on-board.

I poured some black coffee to settle my nerves and settled back to read. They were starting to feel shredded. Ye Gods, I didn't mean that kind of shredded. All we needed now was a fire drill.

This was the worst feeling ever. Being entirely alone. The world was an empty place. There was no one there but me, spinning in a universe entirely on my own. I remembered the same feelings when I was a small child and something awful was about to happen, and again when I fell on stage and I lost not only my career but also most of my friends. They went on to dance in other shows.

It's always easier for men to join a new group of people. Their groups were always open to new members. Whereas it is different for a woman. Female groups tended to close ranks and they do not accept newcomers until they became acceptable. New friendships take time to nurture.

I was in that limbo time. I had made friends in my new job, but in truth I did not have a real friend.

Susan's body language had always been guarded, ill at ease. She did not like meeting my eyes. So what was all this about?

My curiosity made me leaf through some of the papers left on the desk and I made an interesting discovery. I could not believe my eyes. Tamara and Susan had both once worked at Fine Arts, the Bond Street gallery where George

Foster had been a director. They had kept that connection pretty quiet. It could be quite significant. There was a page of Susan's CV still intact. She had detailed her school and A-level results. Susan had also written that she had been in the school netball team.

Big deal. But did that mean she had an eye for shooting a netball and scoring? Or a glass?

I gathered all the remaining papers off the floor and locked them in my desk drawer. There was no duplicate key. So this must be the reason why Susan was destroying everything. There was a link and it could be the missing painting. DJ was after the painting at the competition. Reg Hawkins was smuggling in the SEM. Tamara worked in the gallery where the fake painting was on show and for sale, but only to the right person. And both women had both worked at Fine Arts.

It was like a spider's web. One fragile thread led to another and another, but they all hung together.

Mrs Foster had bought the painting and it was hanging on her stateroom wall or hidden under the bed. Her stateroom had earlier been ransacked and her husband's briefcase stolen. What had the thief been expecting to find in the briefcase? Some specific details about the painting? Some clue to follow?

And what was Susan up to? Had she been told to destroy everything or was she the mastermind, a sort of Miss Jekyll and Ms Hyde?

My mobile rang. 'Are you sure Susan said she was ill? She hasn't turned up.'

348

'I'll check her cabin. Perhaps she has gone to lie down.'

'Perhaps she's shredding the sheets,' said Samuel helpfully.

Her steward let me into her cabin, which was identical to mine only along the opposite corridor. I told him that I thought Miss Brook was ill and might be in need of a doctor.

'I haven't seen Miss Brook all morning,' he said. 'She was up very early.'

I bet.

Her cabin was in a shambles. She was in the middle of serious packing and half-filled suitcases and clothes were all over the place. It looked as if she was planning to disappear during our short stop at the Azores. That was tomorrow. There was a small airport on the main island, Sao Miguel. She could fly to anywhere. If she had the painting, she could be in New York, selling it to the highest bidder before we even knew she had left the ship.

It all seemed very clever if only I could work out what was going on. Tamara and Susan knew each other. One had disappeared in Acapulco, the other was about to disappear in Ponta Delgada. Darin Jack was still hiding aboard somewhere, wasn't he? Maybe Susan had been providing him with food and shelter and stolen clothes. Busy girl. No wonder she had been too tired to do her work properly.

But surely they wouldn't be planning to get off without the painting they had gone to so much trouble to smuggle on board? The one that was in Mrs Foster's stateroom at this very moment.

Why had I used the word smuggle? Because that was it. The painting had been smuggled on-board at some port, say Palma, and was about to be smuggled off again.

I hurried back to my office and turned on Susan's computer. I knew her email address but not the password. Somehow I had to get into her emails. I tried various words: cruise, liner, countess, anchor. All rejected. I tried colours, flowers, kings and queens. I tried careers, teacher, director, doctor...

I phoned Samuel.

'You again? This is called phone stalking. Is she in her cabin?'

'No, she's not there but she is packing. I'm trying to get into her emails.'

'That's a criminal offence.'

'I've got to but I don't know her password. Give me some ideas. Please, before it's too late.' I must have sounded desperate.

'She once had a dog called Sparky.'

I typed in Sparky. Bingo. 'Thanks, genius.'

It's funny how many people use pet cat or dog names for passwords. Sparky opened the door to Susan's secret life. There in front of me in the mailbox was an email letter from Tamara Fitz-gibbons, dated yesterday. She had read it but not deleted it. Tamara was apparently alive and well and with access to an Internet café. This was a reply to one Susan must have sent earlier.

The last sale of the painting was to Mrs Joan Foster. She bought it before I had wrapped it for delivery to Nigel Garten.

Due to his unfortunate accident, it seemed easier to let it go to Mrs Foster rather than let it get lost in some probate tangle. Safe keeping, as it were. We could remove it at a later date. No problem, eh?

There was too much risk keeping it in the gallery any longer. I was on tenterhooks all the time. It might be bought accidentally by someone without any knowledge, or worse still, stolen by someone who did know what they were looking for!!!

See you soon – roll on Florida and the good life together. We'll rent a villa near the beach. Tamara.'

I printed the letter and was then out of the office in a flash, folding the sheet of paper so that it went in a pocket. That one phrase stood out in neon. *We could remove it at a later date.* I knew what that meant. Mrs Foster was in danger.

Mrs Fairweather waved to me as I raced past but I didn't have time to stop and talk. I smiled and waved briefly. Maria de Leger was still writing her memoirs in a secluded corner. She nodded to me. There was an air of renewed gaiety round the ship. It was the thought of a port of call tomorrow, even if it was all fishing and whales and not a palm tree in sight.

There was no time to talk to anyone. I cursed the layout of the ship, all the corridors and stairs. It was such a long way to the upper deck state-rooms. I pressed on Mrs Foster's stateroom bell, and after a delay she answered. She was in casual trousers and a shirt, her face strained. I got the feeling I was unwelcome.

'Hello, Mrs Foster. I've called to see how you are,' I said, nearly breathless.

'You've been running.'

'Yes. Well, I thought I'd catch you before you went out on deck for a coffee.'

'I can make coffee here and sit on my own balcony.' She sounded distant and unfriendly. Had I upset her in any way?

'Of course, and very nice, too. I understand you bought some paintings at the art gallery and I was wondering what arrangements you had made for shipping them home.'

'I think it's none of your business,' she said sharply, trying to close the door. 'You'd better go. I have another visitor.'

Then I saw him, standing behind the door, reflected in a mirror on the far wall. It was Darin Jack, yellow hair shaved off, in jeans and T-shirt. He was holding a knife to Mrs Foster's back, the tip indenting the fabric of her shirt.

Our eyes met in the mirror.

'No, I've changed my mind. I think you had better come in, Miss Jones,' he said, stepping forward. 'How nice. After all, two's always company, isn't it?'

Thirty-Two

At Sea

Mrs Foster had been trying to save me, by getting rid of me at the door. It was very brave of her. I tried to give her some gesture of understanding as Darin Jack pulled me into the cabin. His threatening attitude at the art gallery came flooding back. We should have done more to find him, to restrain him. We had done nothing. Not exactly me, but what had Security been doing? Sending emails?

'So, Miss Jones. We meet again. How fortunate. I think you are going to be able to help me,' he said, herding us both into the sitting room area. He smelled strongly of stale sweat. Susan hadn't found him a shower. I sat down on the sofa, my legs unaccountably weak.

'I'm so sorry about the competition,' I said, pretending to misunderstand, playing for time. 'We had so many winners. We had to draw one out of a hat in the end.'

'No matter. In fact, I think I am the outright winner. The painting that so many people seem to be looking for is right here in this stateroom. But Mrs Foster seems to have forgotten where she put it.'

'Easily done,' I went on. 'Mrs Foster has not had a good cruise. It's been a traumatic time.'

'And it's about to get a lot worse. Of course, I sympathize with the untimely passing of her husband just when he was about to track down the Cézanne.'

'It's a Cézanne?' I exclaimed, open-mouthed. 'Good heavens, I didn't know that. And your husband was here on the cruise to find it?'

Mrs Foster nodded. She seemed relieved to talk about it at last. 'Yes, it wasn't only a lovely holiday although George needed a break. He heard through some contact that the painting was going to change hands on board the *Countess Georgina*. The genuine owner is a client of the gallery and the painting was in our hands, for some restoration work, when it was stolen and painted over. So George felt responsible.'

'Heavens,' I said faintly again. I could play gormless very well. No acting required. 'Stolen, you say?'

'Yes, he felt morally bound to make every effort to get it back. And I have done what he wanted. I've found the painting and it's going to be returned to the rightful owner.'

'But that's where you are mistaken,' said Darin Jack, helping himself to a whisky and ice. It was a generous tumbler full of the golden liquid. No bar measure. Had Susan been keeping him short?

'You are going to tell me where it is, Mrs Foster.'

'I've told you. It's not here any more. It's been removed. I decided it wasn't safe to keep it in this suite.'

'Then you are going to tell me where you have moved it to.' His sly eyes were hooded with menace.

'I don't exactly know where it is,' she said, shaking her head. 'And if I did, I'd never tell you. Never.'

He sat on the arm of the sofa, much too close to me for comfort. He took my hand and examined my nails. He was hardly admiring the silvery pink polish. 'Now Miss Jones wouldn't look so gorgeous without her nails, would she? And the pain, extracting them! Extremely painful, almost excrutiating. And think of all the blood on this nice carpet.'

He tilted my head up. 'Would Mrs Foster get a bill for the blood or would Conway foot the cost? Have they insurance or something?'

'Conway never charge for genuine accidents,' I said, sounding braver than I felt. He took a pair of pliers out of his pocket and looked at my nails closely. 'Eeny, meeny, miny, mo, which shall be the first to go? How about the little one?'

I got up quickly, wrenching my hand out of his grasp. 'I think Mrs Foster and I should have a private talk, alone. Perhaps we could come to some sort of compromise. After all, the rightful owner might be very relieved to get his Cézanne back. There might be a magnificent reward in the offing?'

I looked hopefully towards Mrs Foster. I wanted her to play along, to play for time. Someone was bound to come soon. Stewards were always changing towels.

'Naturally,' she said, catching on. 'I'm sure there's a magnificent reward. It could be arranged.'

'But the Cézanne is worth more than several million on the underground market. I think I'd rather have the going price, Florida and the good life.'

Ah, Tamara's phrase. Florida. So was that what they were planning? To disappear to Florida, buy a villa with pool, enjoy the good life in the sun. But how many of them? Who was going to dump who? They did not seem to me to be an ideal threesome. Someone was going to get the push. But which one? My betting was on the loathsome DJ.

'So shall we go into the bedroom, Mrs Foster?' I suggested. 'Just a quick talk. It won't take more than a few minutes.'

Somehow I was going to get Mrs Foster out of this. Wasn't there a communicating door somewhere for when these staterooms needed two separate bedrooms? I wished I knew the ship's layout more thoroughly. Or a telephone. Anything. It was worth trying. Or we could barricade ourselves in, though most of the furniture was fitted. I was beyond rational thinking. Send me on a course.

'I don't think so,' said Darin Jack, moving fast. He pushed Mrs Foster into a dining chair and in seconds was fastening her wrists to the arms and her ankles to the legs with twine. No doubt taken from our stores. Her face was white, her lips dry. She was very frightened.

'Now you'll get a good view, Mrs Foster. I

won't gag you because you'll be wanting to tell me where the Cézanne is.'

'Don't tell him,' I urged. 'We won't give in to these thugs.'

'Casey...' she said, weakly.

I ran out on to the balcony. The sun hit my eyes, blinding me. Quick girl, think. I could climb down a deck or climb sideways on to the next balcony. I looked about. Not many holds for either manoeuvre. The deeply blue rolling Atlantic was a long way down from this deck, full of dancing sparkles and white horses. I remembered the death-defying divers at La Quebrada, Acapulco, where they dived from the cliffs straight into the sea.

But I was hardly a death-defying diver. I could abseil if I had a rope. A sheet. Anything.

'Hold on a minute, Miss Jones. Not thinking of doing anything stupid, are you?' The knife was close to my ear. Another kitchen knife. Had Susan hidden him somewhere near the kitchens?

He was swilling a second glass of whisky. Good. The more the merrier. Let's get him under the sofa.

'Just taking in the view,' I said, returning inside, my brain running in circles. There must be something I could do. 'Tell me, exactly who runs this show? You, Tamara or Susan?'

He looked momentarily taken aback. He was foxed that I knew about the others. He was running through the possibilities, expecting the whisky to give him the answers.

'So who is the brains, the mover and shifter, the boss? Who says, do this, do that? And who is going to get dumped when the Cézanne is safely in some rich American's vault? I think it's going to be you, Mr Jack. You are not nearly classy enough for Tamara or rich enough for Susan. The ladies are just using you. A bit of macho meat in their game.'

This got to the raw. He snarled and flicked the knife close to my ear. I didn't like that. I've got such a lovely collection of earrings.

'Please, Casey,' said Mrs Foster. 'Don't say anything more. This is nothing to do with you. Let her go. Having Miss Jones here doesn't help. It's between you and me. Please let her go. She won't say anything. She's very sensible.'

'I'm very sensible,' I agreed. But I wasn't going to leave Mrs Foster.

He was pacing about, clearly out of his depth.

'No way,' said Darin Jack, going back to the drinks cabinet. He'd finished the whisky and was moving on to vodka. Excellent. 'Now let's get this straight.' He was already slurring his words. 'You have moved the painting? Right?'

'Right,' said Joan Foster. 'Into safe keeping.'

'And you are going to tell me where.'

'Yes, I'll tell you where if you let Miss Jones go.'

Thank you, Mrs Foster. Very clever. I liked it. I thought I'd muddled him up a bit more. He was already spilling drink on the desk as he poured a generous helping into a glass. He dabbed his fingers in the spillage and licked them.

'Nigel Garten, the man who bought the painting,' I threw in. 'Where does he come into all this?'

'An independent scout,' said Darin Jack. 'He follows up bargains for collectors and gets paid for his trouble. Don't know how he heard of it. We had to get rid of him.'

'Poor soul. He was only doing his job. Nice man.'

'He was in our way. The Cézanne had to stay in the gallery.'

'Of course, until you and Susan get off. Is that Ponta Delgada? Perhaps you have a private plane waiting for you. Though, of course, the painting is quite small. It could go in baggage if you fly commercial.'

Even Mrs Foster looked confused. Perhaps she had lost track of the days. It happens. Even I have trouble remembering the date.

'The Azores,' I added. 'It's our next port of call. Tomorrow.'

Wrong thing to say. It brought DJ back to the present. He only had until tomorrow. Time was running out.

'I don't care how long it takes. You two are staying here until the painting is in my hands. I suggest you tell me where it is, Mrs Foster. Who shall I ring? I will hold the phone to your mouth and you will tell them to return the painting to you, now.'

'No,' she said faintly.

'OK,' he said, grabbing my head. 'Which first, her nose or her ears?'

Now, I had always wanted a nose job but not this way. He nicked my nostril with the knife. Blood trickled down my chin. I licked at it with my tongue. I had a decent white shirt on. Blood is difficult to get out.

'I've an even better idea,' I said softly, sort of seductive and come-hither. I'm not good at seductive. 'Have you seen the bathroom attached to this suite? It's absolutely gorgeous.'

He looked puzzled. 'You want to go to the bathroom?'

'Yes, of course, and don't you?' I said, slightly moving my shoulder against him. It wasn't much of an encouragement but it seemed to work. 'There's a jacuzzi, you know, one of those big baths with lovely warm bubbles. Wouldn't you like a lovely bath with me in all those warm bubbles? We could take the vodka with us and have such a lot of fun.'

This didn't sound like me talking at all, yet it was me. I heard Mrs Foster gasp. Darin's alcohol-fuelled eyes clouded over with lust. He'd be hiding out on his own for a long time.

'Smashing idea, baby,' he said, slurring. 'Let's get your clothes off first.' His fingers went straight to the buttons on my shirt. I froze. I hadn't thought much further than pushing him under the bubbles, after a few more vodkas, or drowning him with the sponge.

There was a sudden, peremptory knock on the door. I jerked back.

'Room service,' came a voice.

DJ went straight over to Mrs Foster. 'Tell them no. Get rid of them.'

'I didn't order room service,' she said loudly. 'Go away.'

'Room service,' came the voice again. 'Please open the door. Your meal is here, Mrs Foster.'

DJ grabbed me and pulled me over behind the door, with the knife. He whispered into my ear, all hot and breathy. 'Tell them to go away. Say it's a mistake. If you say one word out of place, I'll stick this right into where it will hurt a lot.'

The blade was hard against my ribs. He unlocked the door and pushed me into the slight opening. Outside were Dr Samuel Mallory and Richard Norton, both in white steward outfits, a couple of burly sailors behind them and that blonde young man who was always with Amanda.

'Room service, ma'am,' they chimed together.

'Sorry, folks,' I said, keeping the tremble out of my voice. 'But Mrs Foster didn't order anything. It's a mistake. Would you please go away?'

'But we have Mrs Foster's order,' said Samuel, flourishing a trolley of covered food. 'Soup, grilled sole, side salad, apple charlotte and ice cream. May we come in and serve?'

Before I could answer, they swept in, pushing the trolley. It caught the unsteady DJ full in the knees. He went flying. The two sailors were on him in a flash and held him down to the floor. Richard Norton was doing something with restraints. The blond man went straight to Mrs Foster and began untying her. She wept into his shoulder, clinging to him.

'Thank goodness you came, all of you. This is Amanda's bodyguard, Bruno. He guards her,' she said. 'He has the painting. I gave it to him for safety.'

'And who are you?' I said to Samuel. I was

shaking and it was beyond me to stop a few tears. I was glad to see him. There was no laughter in his eyes but I wouldn't put it past him to offer me some ice cream.

'I could be your bodyguard,' he said. 'If I ever found the time.'

Thirty-Three

Ponta Delgada

I was given permission to go ashore at the Azores even though we were short of staff. Special dispensation by Captain Nicolas. Not exactly for valour, but mainly because Mrs Foster insisted that I deserved some time off to recuperate from my ordeal.

'She was going to sacrifice herself for me,' she told everyone, tearfully. 'Those beautiful nails. Wonderful girl.'

She was full of praise for the way I had coped though, truly, I'd done very little. Cracked a few jokes. Nearly made a Tarzan-like abseiling exit from the balcony without any ropes. Don't mention the jacuzzi.

Susan Brook was below decks, in custody. They'd found her in the Terrace Café stockpiling yogurts and biscuits into a beach bag. So was Darin Jack. He was probably in chains. There was a brig, or guardhouse, near the morgue. Very appropriate. They blamed each other for Nigel Garten's death. It was an accident. Like a blow on the head is accidental. They were being put ashore today into Portuguese police custody, waiting for Scotland Yard to collect them and fly them back to the UK for questioning and the judicial process.

I'd given Richard Norton a statement about being taken hostage with Mrs Foster, and the knife threat in the gallery. And I gave him the printout of Tamara's letter.

'You'll be asked to give further statements when we reach Southampton,' he said.

'I'm supposed to be doing a turn round,' I said. 'I'm working on the next cruise, you know.'

'I'll see if I can arrange for some officers to see you the morning of the turn round.'

We couldn't wait to be rid of both Susan Brook, with an *e*, and Darin Jack. My bullet list of suspects had been spot on. It was AOP. The wild cannon. We didn't know who had spiked my orange juice, but my bet was on Tamara.

Rosanna was released from custody as long as she was with Ray or myself or some responsible person. There had been several volunteers, including Amanda and Joan Foster. Being a stowaway was way down Rosanna's list of crimes. Stealing leftovers from passengers' lunch trays was hardly a capital offence. Captain Nicolas wanted to meet her. He'd been a great fan of Merlin the Magician.

'But how did you know where I was?' I'd asked a dozen times since.

'You had a whole network of friends who went into action. Quite an impressive back-up. Mrs Fairweather reported that you were in too much of a hurry to talk and looked quite distracted. Madame de Leger said you appeared very worried and immediately sensed that something was wrong. Your steward, Ahmed, was alerted by Susan Brook's steward about the state of the cabin and they reported back to the head steward, Karim, who is no fool.'

'Ahmed is so reliable.'

'And several passengers saw you running along decks, hurrying into the lift. One of the Lido deck stewardesses saw you ringing the bell of Mrs Foster's suite and a worried Mrs Foster answering. Someone is always watching, you should know that. Nothing is secret on board ship.'

'And they all did or said something?'

'A ragged chain of communication went into action but it worked. Purser's office, Security, me. It was Bruno who put us straight.'

'Bruno, young Bruno?'

'Not so young. Ex-Marines.'

'So?'

'Amanda's bodyguard, the blond guy. She's employed a bodyguard since her fiancé was killed in the road rage attack.'

I fingered my ear and my nose. They were still intact, still the same shape.

'Mrs Foster gave Bruno the painting to look after. She trusted him and no one would link him to her. It's now in the purser's office, locked in a safe. It's probably worth as much as the ship.'

'What an exaggeration, but maybe nearly as much. What about Tamara?'

'The Mexican police have been alerted. It won't be long before she's picked up unless she takes to the mountains. Not much fun living in the wild. No hairdressers or nail salons.'

Samuel had barely left my side since the hostage situation. Last night had been the Black and White ball, which meant that everyone wore black and white evening dress. It did look spectacular, very grand. I managed my usual duties on stage in a white chiffon dress with black gloves, though I was pretty shaky at first. I got a lot of applause as I went on stage, as it went round the ship that I was a heroine again. No dog involved this time.

Samuel was waiting in the wings to take me upstairs to the Grill for a quick bite between shows, but I couldn't touch anything. He force fed me a raspberry sorbet. Any appetite had fled.

Early this morning, the *Countess* made landfall with the Azores (the name is the plural of the word blue) and took on the pilot. The stern was swung to port for the approach to berthing, a tricky manoeuvre. But soon she was alongside and the mooring completed. The passengers could go ashore after all the formalities.

No one saw Susan Brook and DJ go ashore. But a security van arrived for them and the police came on-board to take them away. Richard Norton was the only person who saw them leave.

It was partly cloudy and fine with a light

breeze. The temperature was only sixty-one degrees Fahrenheit, or sixteen Celsius. Fleece time after the glorious Caribbean temperatures. The landscape looked rugged and green and beautiful with volcanic cones and craters. Not a whale in sight. It was a pleasant awakening for the passengers, who thought the Azores might be a disappointment. But the scenery was glorious, a cross between Switzerland and Hawaii.

'So where would you like to go?' Samuel asked, helping me off the last step of the gangway. Everyone kept helping me as if I was an invalid.

'You don't have to come with me,' I said. 'I can look around by myself.'

'You're not safe on your own,' he said, taking my arm. 'You'll end up involved in some ghastly situation and need rescuing again. One rescue per cruise is my limit.'

I did like having Samuel by my side. He was the perfect escort. He was wearing a V-necked cashmere sweater and a lightweight jacket with navy jeans. There was nothing remotely permanent about his company. It was purely a doctor/ patient relationship, I told myself. He'd dabbed some antiseptic on the cut under my nose.

'I wondered if you would like me a bit more if I did shorten my name to Sam,' he said casually again, for no reason at all.

'You could give it a try,' I said.

'How about going to see the twin lakes at Sete Cidades?' he suggested. 'We could take a taxi. No need to join one of the tours. They are apparently an astonishing sight.'

'They are two lakes joined together,' I said,

366

quoting the guide book. 'One an emerald green and the other a brilliant blue. Something to remember for a lifetime, it says.'

'Fancy something to remember for a lifetime?' His eyes were twinkling dangerously.

'I do, Sam,' I said, throwing caution to a light north-easterly.